RISING SUN
DESCENDING

WADE FOWLER

SUNBURY
PRESS

Mechanicsburg, Pennsylvania USA

Published by Sunbury Press, Inc.
50 West Main Street
Mechanicsburg, Pennsylvania 17055

www.sunburypress.com

NOTE: This is a work of fiction. Names, characters, places and incidents are the product of the author's imagination or are used fictitiously, and any resemblance to actual persons, living or dead, business establishments, events or locales is entirely coincidental.

Copyright © 2015 by Wade Fowler.
Cover copyright © 2015 by Sunbury Press.
Sunbury Press supports copyright. Copyright fuels creativity, encourages diverse voices, promotes free speech, and creates a vibrant culture. Thank you for buying an authorized edition of this book and for complying with copyright laws by not reproducing, scanning, or distributing any part of it in any form without permission. You are supporting writers and allowing Sunbury Press to continue to publish books for every reader. For information contact Sunbury Press, Inc., Subsidiary Rights Dept., 50-A W. Main St., Mechanicsburg, PA 17011 USA or legal@sunburypress.com.

For information about special discounts for bulk purchases, please contact Sunbury Press Orders Dept. at (855) 338-8359 or orders@sunburypress.com.

To request one of our authors for speaking engagements or book signings, please contact Sunbury Press Publicity Dept. at publicity@sunburypress.com.

ISBN: 978-1-62006-535-8 (Trade Paperback)
ISBN: 978-1-62006-536-5 (Mobipocket)
ISBN: 978-1-62006-537-2 (ePub)

Library of Congress Control Number: 2015933714

FIRST SUNBURY PRESS EDITION: March 2015

Product of the United States of America
0 1 1 2 3 5 8 13 21 34 55

Set in Bookman Old Style
Designed by Lawrence Knorr
Cover by Amber Rendon
Edited by Jennifer Melendrez

Continue the Enlightenment!

For Sharon

Chapter 1

8 a.m. Monday, August 15, 2011, Harrisburg, PA

"You're being downsized," Grayson Collingsworth said.

Revere Polk had just settled into the stuffed leather visitor's chair in Collingsworth's plush office on the second floor of the *Daily Telegraph*, three blocks off Market Square.

Rumors of layoffs were rampant in the newsroom. Revere—Rev to friend and foe alike—had rehearsed a dozen reactions and decided silence was the best strategy. He crossed one long leg over the other, cocked his head to the right, and considered Collingsworth as if he were sighting down the barrel of an assault rifle.

Down on the street, state workers scurried from the parking garages to their jobs in the halls of government. Harrisburg, the capital of Pennsylvania, cleaved to state government like a tick to a bloodhound.

The wood paneling of Collingsworth's office gleamed in the sunlight peeking through the curtains. Footprints would linger on the plush pile until the next vacuuming. The editor's big desk glowed with the patina of years of furniture polish.

Collingsworth lurked behind the desk, six-two, and 250 pounds—a collegiate linebacker going to seed in middle age. The trappings of power diminished him more than they built him up. Pockmarked and greasy-haired, he was a mutt misplaced at Westminster.

Younger by a decade and taller by a good two inches, Rev was a fit 210 pounds. He slouched in contemptuous nonchalance.

"Well, say something," Collingsworth barked.

Point for the home team, Rev thought. "So the profit margin's down to what, nine percent? Most businesses these days would kill for those numbers. Grocery stores get by on 2 percent ... or less."

Collingsworth's wince told Rev that his analysis was spot on.

"And your solution is to fire the experienced staff, and leave the news gathering to young pups who can't find their asses with both hands."

"It's the economy, Rev. You know that as well as I do."

The editor's gruff voice couldn't obscure the cheap whine he'd brought to this party.

"Christ, Gray, Jillian what's-her-name, your new city hall reporter, misspelled the mayor's name in the lead of today's A-1 story on the incinerator bond debacle and the dumb newbies on the copy desk didn't catch it until the suburban edition—and then only because I told them. Is that what this business is coming to?"

"Don't you want to hear the terms?" Collingsworth asked.

Rev's smile didn't reach his eyes. "Sure, Gray. Why don't you tell me how magnanimous you're going to be?"

"We're prepared to offer you a year's salary and medical benefits ... as long as you sign a one-year non-compete."

"I suppose you're offering Sophie the same deal?"

Collingsworth leaned back in his chair and made a tent of his fingertips. "Actually, we've asked Sophie to stay on. We can't empty the stable of all our investigative reporters."

Rev squinted, considered Collingsworth carefully. A nasty rumor of a fling between the editor and his favorite reporter had gained some traction in the newsroom.

"Yeah, and she'll be more inclined to skewer the democrats than the republicans."

Rev was being unfair to Sophie and he knew it, but his soul stung still from her abrupt dismissal of him two months ago from her heart and from her bed.

"I don't see a future for us, Rev," she had said. "You're obsessed by what happened to you in Iraq. I get that. But I need a man with a plan more long range than getting into my pants."

Rev's analyst was helping him cope with what Sophie called his "intimacy issues," but the roots of his despair were so deep that no amount of psychiatric Roundup seemed to suffice.

"It was the story on Sam Jenkins that tore it. Wasn't it?"

Collingsworth exhaled, long and loud, through his nose. "This isn't about politics. It's about economics."

"And the politics behind the economics are that the *Daily Telegraph* can do without an investigative reporter who impugned the war record of the speaker of the House of Representatives and the leading republican candidate for president of the United States."

"Who now is suing the pants off us, leaving us to pray that you 'ight," Collingsworth said.

"Of course I got it right. Just look at his Medal of Honor citation. The principal witness of his valor in Vietnam is his chief of staff. Andy Hawk isn't about to hop off the gravy train and tell the truth."

"Yeah, and your source who claims that Jenkins hid in a hole until the shooting was over is a mental patient. Wish we had known that before we published the story."

"A former mental patient," Polk said. "And besides, crazy people can tell the truth."

"The lawyers have been arguing about that for a month ... at $240 an hour."

"You sure you want me as a hostile witness at the libel trial?"

Collingsworth flashed a triumphant smile. "It's not going to trial."

Fury painted Rev's brow and cheekbones with blotches of red. "You bastards are settling, aren't you? You're selling out."

"The legal fees are eating us up with no guarantee of success. Jenkins is willing to accept our public apology and drop his lawsuit."

"And that makes me redundant."

Collingsworth slid a manila folder across his big desk. "This is our offer. You've got 14 days annual leave on the books. I want you to take them. Starting now. Unless I hear from you otherwise I'm going to assume you've accepted the buyout."

"And if I don't?"

"You'll be our permanent obit writer at minimum wage."

Chapter 2

4 p.m. Monday, August 15, 2011, Mechanicsburg, PA

"They're firing me, Nona. I'm 42 years old and I don't have a job. This economy sucks! And Grayson Collingsworth is an asshole."

Nona, a.k.a. Annie Mundy, crossed her legs at her ankles and straightened the creases of her slacks.

They were seated, uncomfortably, in Rev's opinion, in the sleek, sunlit living room of his grandmother's new duplex at Bethany Retirement Village. Rev couldn't put his finger on the source of his disquiet. It struck him that the house didn't smell like Nona. That her familiar furniture had been plopped down in a stranger's house.

Nona basked in her new surroundings. The soft sunlight, diffused through the Venetian blinds, illuminated crow's feet at the corners of her eyes and wattles on her jowls—homage to the passage of time—but her blue eyes were sharp and clear and her white hair was neatly coiffed about her heart-shaped face.

"Oh, boohoo. Get a grip on yourself. You're an officer in the National Guard. You've led men into battle, for Christ's sake. And here you are blubbering like a baby."

Rev laughed. "Thanks, Nona. I can always count on your wise counsel when the going gets tough."

Nona swallowed a smile. "Now rub some dirt on it and get back in the game."

"That's the problem. There are too many players and not enough roster spots. The news business is in transition. Advertisers are fleeing the traditional media for the Internet. Craigslist has all but wiped out revenue from classified ads and readers are flocking to Internet websites that offer free content and that tell them what they want to hear rather than what they need to hear."

"What do they need to hear?"

4

"That the emperor has no clothes; that the left is as wrong as the right. But the politicians in Harrisburg and Washington are more interested in scoring coup than addressing problems that threaten us all."

"They also needed to hear that Sam Jenkins is a charlatan," Nona said.

Rev winced. "A charlatan he may be but he's a powerful one. He persuaded the Collingsworths that they stand an even chance of losing at trial with dire consequences to the family fortune. Gray is determined to print a retraction."

"Do you think the Medal of Honor story had anything to do with your getting furloughed?" Nona asked.

"They leapfrogged over people with more seniority to cut me out of the herd," Rev replied. "It would have been far more cost effective to go after some of the 30-year dinosaurs in the newsroom—if the bottom line really was their bottom line."

"I suppose the blame is mine then. I put you onto the story in the first place."

"Tell me again how you knew Brett Faust had a story to tell."

Nona sighed. "We've been over this before. I can't tell you."

A career psychologist, Nona took her oath of confidentiality seriously. But, for the first time, Rev sensed some uncertainty in her voice. He pressed his advantage. "Come on, Nona, what will it hurt? I'd like to know why I'm losing my job."

Nona blinked and broke eye contact. "OK, I'll tell you because it's a moot point anyway. A colleague from the Mental Health Association called me in to consult on a Vietnam vet still struggling with post traumatic stress syndrome thirty years after the fact. Faust's account of the battle at Dak To was part of the case file. I read it and concluded that the world needed to know that the speaker of the House of Representatives is a fraud ... and a coward."

"So you sicced me on Sam Jenkins?"

"I take it that question is rhetorical?"

Rev realized that Nona was sitting on the edge of her chair. Something else was at play, but what?

"Come on, Nona. I can read your body language. There is more to it than that. Out with it."

Nona changed tack so quickly Rev didn't have time to duck the boom.

"Is your analyst helping you cope with what's really eating at you?" she asked.

The question whacked him in the head so hard that his eyes watered. "There's not enough dirt to rub on that."

5

"I wouldn't be so sure. I've lived a long time and I've never run out of dirt. I can help you, but you've got to let me in. It's cold here on the outside and your indifference makes my bones hurt."

"Now who's whining?"

"I'm not whining. I'm observing. What happened to you over there in Iraq that was so awful you can't forget it and get on with your life?"

"Innocent people died and it was my fault."

Rev hated himself for having relinquished even such a small portion of what he considered to be his personal pain ... and penitence.

"If innocent people died it was the politicians' fault and not yours. The Sunnis and Shiites have been fighting each other for centuries. Dubya didn't get that. He sent you into the middle of a Holy War."

"I know that, but my heart won't let me forget ..."

"Forget what?"

Rev shook his head. "Not yet, Nona. It's too soon. I need to wear the sackcloth for a while longer."

"You're a good man, Rev. The sooner you hop off your own back, the lighter the load will be on all of us who love you."

"I'll get through this," he said grimly. "Now I have to figure out what I'm going to do with the rest of my life."

"Is the newspaper offering you any type of severance?"

"A year's salary plus health benefits."

"Wow. What an opportunity."

"What do you mean by that?"

"Won't that give you the chance to write that book you've always been threatening to write?"

Rev was startled. "Uh. Sure. I guess so. Only problem is ... I don't have anything to write about. It was always, you know ... someday I'll write a book. It's every reporter's ambition."

"I think I might be able to help you out with a topic. I've been going through some old boxes trying to decide what I can throw away now that I've downsized from the old place on Apple Drive."

Nona rose from the sofa and walked across the room to a small built-in desk in her kitchen. "It should be right here on top." She shuffled through a stack of papers. "Oh, here it is."

She returned to the living room, inspecting the contents of a manila file folder. She handed Rev an eight-by-ten-inch photograph, yellowed about the edges and creased in one corner as if it had been stored in a book.

A tall man with high angular cheekbones and a shock of dark hair dominated the foreground. His hair was disheveled as if he'd just removed a hat. He was framed in the doorway of a hangar.

He wore a military uniform of some sort. The pants bagged at the thighs, tightened at the knees, and disappeared into calf-high boots. A vocabulary word tugged at Rev's memory. "Jodhpurs. This fellow is wearing jodhpurs."

"And a World War I naval aviator jacket," Nona added. "My Uncle Jake flew kite balloons and single engine float planes in World War I and torpedo bombers off the USS Enterprise in World War II. He was killed in 1968 in San Diego. Run over by a hit-and-run driver."

"That's too bad."

"Your tone tells me you don't care, and I get that. You have other things on your mind. But I think there's a story here and I'd like you to tell it. My father's older brother was mixed up in something toward the end of World War II. After all of these years, I'd like to know the truth about Operation Setting Sun."

Rev brought the picture closer. He studied his ancestor's face. Smelled the faint aroma of the chemicals that had developed and fixed the image he now held near. Jake stared back at him. There was a challenge in his eyes.

"What was Operation Setting Sun?"

"That's what I'd like you to find out."

Chapter 3

2 a.m. Tuesday, August 16, 2011, Middleburg, PA
The peepers calling from the creek just over the rise fell silent as if awaiting the outcome of an uncertain enterprise as Rog Richardson jimmied the front door of Middleburg Sporting Goods.

Richardson's companion, 18-year-old Johnston Bradley, wiped the sweat from his brow with the back of his left wrist and concentrated on holding the red-globed flashlight steady. His flight-or-fight instincts redlined when the door jamb splintered and the predawn silence shattered upon them like shards of a broken mirror.

"A little help here, Brad," Rog whispered.

Brad switched the flashlight to his left hand and pushed against the door with his right while Rog strained at the crowbar. The deadbolt surrendered and the door burst open with such force that both men tumbled into the shop in a tangle of arms and legs that would have been amusing under other circumstances.

As they regained their feet, Brad strained to hear any noise that might indicate that their presence had been detected.

"See, kid? I told you. No alarm."

Brad hated it when Rog called him "kid," although he gave Rog props for returning from Afghanistan as a newly-minted first lieutenant in the Pennsylvania National Guard.

Rog switched on his flashlight and collected the five-pound sledgehammer they had left on the front stoop. He knew what to expect, having visited the gun shop the afternoon before, feigning interest in a Winchester 30-06 deer rifle with an 8x scope.

The store room was situated directly behind the counter. "Step back, kid, and give me some elbow room," Rog said.

"Don't call me kid."

The sound of the sledge hitting the door lock echoed through the eerie silence of the dark gun shop where the angles of walls, displays, and door frames lurked ominously in the glow of their flashlights.

The lock gave way on the fourth blow and the door flew open.

Brad noticed it right away. A circuit box was situated on the back wall of the store room. An LED display flashed. He centered the circuit box in his flashlight beam. "Is that what I think it is?"

"Yep. It's a silent alarm. Must be connected to the storeroom door. I missed that when I cased the place. Let's get moving. I don't want to be here when the police arrive."

The object of their visit, a shipment of assault rifles and handguns, had arrived the day before, just like their source had said it would. Six boxes ready to be loaded into a 2003 Chevy Blazer, idling outside with the lights off and the license plate obscured by mud.

Brad's armpits were wet and his ears hurt from the strain of listening for sirens as they loaded the cases into the back of the Blazer.

Rog closed the rear hatch with a soft thump that Brad's imagination invested with far more decibels than it had, in fact, produced. Brad had barely settled in the passenger's seat when Rog put the Blazer into gear, turning from the gravel of the parking lot onto the blacktop before accelerating smoothly. He didn't turn on the headlights until they had rounded a bend about 100 yards down the road.

Rog winked at Brad. "Easy peasey. How 'bout it, kiddo? Now all we have to do is go to the motel and wait. The general said someone should be by to collect the crates by 0900 hours at the latest."

"Who's the general?"

"That's a need-to-know basis, kiddo."

The headlights of a vehicle overtaking them from behind illuminated the interior of the Blazer. Brad clenched his fists and tightened his sphincter.

They were on a straight stretch with a broken line down the center of the road. Rog was driving the speed limit, exactly, to avoid the attention of a police patrol.

The vehicle following them swung out into the opposing lane of the two-lane highway. The driver floored it and zipped around them. Both men relaxed as the car, a big nondescript Ford, opened up a comfortable lead.

Rog grinned. "Jumpy, aren't you, kid? Relax. The motel's just a few miles up ahead. We've made a clean getaway."

It wasn't long before they came upon a disreputable looking motel: 16 cookie-cutter rooms all in a row with an office at one end. A barroom, its roof line swaybacked like a racehorse gone to seed, squatted on the other side of the road directly across from the motel.

Rog activated his turn signal well in advance of the motel parking lot. He turned into the lot and backed the Blazer into the space in front of Room 16, which was the farthest unit from the motel office and was skirted by a dark woodlot.

Rog pulled a key from his pocket and opened the motel room door. "General said to leave the guns in the truck. We'll trade vehicles with the guys who come to pick them up."

Inside the room, Rog pulled a replica 1911 .45 automatic from the waistband at the small of his back and tossed it on one of the beds. "Damn thing's been digging into me for the last half hour. Now it's time for a drink. I have a fifth of Jack Daniels, but we need some ice and a mixer."

Rog grabbed an ice bucket from the counter top of the kitchenette. "There's an ice maker and a soda machine next to the office. Be back in a flash, kiddo, and we'll toast a successful mission, even if you are too young to drink."

Chapter 4

2:10 a.m. Tuesday, August 16, 2011, Middleburg, PA

State police Corporal Olivia Pearson faced a dilemma. She had been patrolling when the dispatcher alerted her to a crime in progress nearby. A late-model, maroon-colored Blazer idled in the gravel lot outside the gun shop. Exhaust billowed from its tailpipe. She was alone and reluctant to barge into an uncertain situation without backup. So she wheeled her unmarked Crown Vic around and backed into a private driveway 25 yards away.

She had just turned out her lights when first one figure and then another emerged from the front door of the gun shop, carrying cases of what she took to be guns or ammunition. They made two trips while Pearson quietly reported her situation to the dispatcher.

The Blazer exited the parking lot and turned right onto the blacktop, its headlights extinguished.

As Pearson followed, her radio squawked. "Unit 3 is four minutes away. What's your situation?"

"I'm in quiet pursuit of a maroon Chevrolet Blazer, model year 2003 or so, traveling west on TR 4232. The license plate is obscured."

Just then the driver of the Blazer switched on his lights.

"I'm going to pass this guy and keep tabs on him in my rearview mirror. There's not a turnoff for another four miles or so. Have Sam get close behind before he activates his siren. I'll set up a road block ahead and we'll have them."

"10-4, Liv," the dispatcher replied.

She drove carefully for three or four minutes, making sure to maintain her position about 100 yards ahead of the Blazer, whose headlights gleamed steadily in her rearview mirror. Pearson saw the Blazer turn right into the parking lot of a motel. She rounded a bend, executed a three-point turn, and crept into the barroom parking lot across from the motel.

Pearson keyed her mic. "I'm 10-84 at the Morning Star Motel. I've got two perps inside Room 16. Where the hell is Sam?"

A man holding an ice bucket emerged from Room 16. He was about 10 yards from the motel office when Trooper Sam Creswell's cruiser crested a rise on the road to the perp's left. His emergency lights slashed through the darkness. His siren wailed.

The perp dropped his ice bucket, reversed course, and fled into the woods behind Room 16. Pearson cursed. What to do? Chase the guy into the woods or close in on the second man still inside Room 16?

She punched her mic.

"We've got a perp fleeing into the woods to the west of the motel and another one in Room 16. I'm going after the man in the motel."

She jammed the Crown Vic into gear, activated her siren, and floored the car. Arriving just a few seconds before Creswell, she screeched to a halt, flung open the door of the cruiser, and drew her sidearm. Just then, a slender man brandishing a handgun burst through the doorway.

Pearson leaned forward, placing her elbows on the roof of the Crown Vic, and pointed her Glock 37 straight at the suspect's chest.

Sam Creswell's marked cruiser screamed into the parking lot spattering the side of the motel with gravel as he braked to a dead stop. He banged open his door.

"Police!" Pearson shouted. "Drop the gun and hands up, or I'll shoot!"

Her finger was tightening on the trigger when the man did as she ordered. His pistol clattered to the ground.

Trooper Creswell charged forward with his own weapon unholstered and ready. He kicked the perp's pistol out of reach. "Turn around! Hands on the wall!"

Pearson corralled the adrenaline rush as the first pulses of an inevitable headache squeezed at her temples. As her rational brain took over, she recognized that their suspect was young, acned, and scared shitless.

Without further instruction, the suspect turned toward the motel, placed his hands on the wall next to the door, and spread his legs wide apart.

"Easy, Sam, he's just a kid. I'm much more concerned about the one who got away."

Creswell cuffed the kid's wrists together.

"I'll call this in. Ask Troop H to dispatch their helicopter with thermal imaging," Pearson said. "I'm not about to go chasing what could be an armed man through the dark woods. Are you?"

Creswell thought about it for a moment and deferred to his superior.

"Good call."

Chapter 5

2 p.m. Tuesday, August 16, 2011, Middleburg, PA
"Colonel Simpson will see you now."

Sophie Anderson looked up from the August 2011 issue of *Hazardous Duty*—the Oliver Hazard Perry Military Academy's school newspaper.

She smiled at the young cadet in front of her. He was 17 or so. Ramrod straight, carefully pressed, and spit shined. There was a gold lanyard on his left arm.

"What's the lanyard mean?" she asked.

The cadet stood even taller. "I'm the brigade commander. Follow me, please."

Anderson was surprised that Simpson had agreed to see her. She didn't have an appointment. She'd driven to Middleburg on impulse, having just visited with her old college friend, Olivia Pearson, a corporal with the Pennsylvania State Police based in Selinsgrove.

Pearson had given her the skinny on the burglary arrest of Johnston Bradley, a cadet at the academy. Sophie wanted to gauge the reaction of the school's president, Colonel Randolph Simpson.

She suppressed a smile when she noticed the young brigade commander's discomfort as she uncrossed her legs. Rev Polk wasn't the only man to have told her that she had gorgeous legs. And she wasn't above using them to her advantage in her dealings with men.

"What's your name?" she asked.

"H-H-Harvey Coleman."

Sophie smiled and thought: By God he's blushing. I may be 36, but the equipment is still functioning.

"Where to, Harvey?" she asked.

The cadet made a parade ground right face. Sophie arose and followed him from the waiting room into a vestibule and then up a short flight of stairs to an office that occupied a mezzanine off the two-story entrance way of Founders Hall, which did double duty as the school's administrative office and auditorium.

Harvey knocked on the door.

"Come," said a voice from within.

The cadet opened the door and stepped back.

Sophie entered the dark-paneled office. The ballast of a fluorescent light buzzed like a bottle fly. The Pennsylvania and United States flags stood at attention on the back wall on either side of a big oak desk. Bookcases lined the walls to the left and right. A gun case containing three assault rifles, a Thompson submachine gun, and a holstered 1911 Colt .45 dominated the back wall between the flags.

A pretty, blonde-haired woman and two teenage boys stared at her from an eight-by-ten-inch framed portrait on the left of the colonel's desk. On the opposing corner was a picture of Simpson, in dress blues, shaking hands with President George Bush the first.

The pictures were trophies positioned for the admiration of visitors. They were portholes illuminating the character of the buttoned-up man behind the desk. Slender and bald, save for a two-inch-wide swatch of iron-gray hair above his ears, Simpson sported a pencil-thin mustache. He reminded her of David Niven.

Simpson waved her to a ladder-backed wooden chair positioned on the visitor's side of his desk. "Have a seat, Miss Anderson."

Sophie scrunched about trying to get comfortable on the chair, which had the ambiance of a block of concrete. Simpson obviously wanted to discourage visitors overstaying their welcome.

He studied the business card Sophie had given to the receptionist. "The *Daily Telegraph*, eh? Middleburg's a bit off your beaten path. Isn't it?"

"We consider ourselves to be the paper of record for Central Pennsylvania. And Middleburg's pretty much in the middle of Central Pennsylvania."

Simpson tossed Anderson's business card on the desktop. "Thus the name. So, what can I do for you?"

"I have a few questions about Cadet Johnston Bradley."

"Aha. I suppose my friends at the Pennsylvania State Police have issued a press release detailing Brad's brush with the law."

"Brad?"

"Sorry. A military habit. Poor kid has a general's name and a corporal's demeanor. The cadets, staff, too, call him Brad. Short for Bradley."

"Hitler was a corporal."

"Surely you're not going to compare Brad's transgressions with genocide."

"Kid's not as pure as the driven snow, either, Colonel. Christ, he burgled a gun shop and made off with 10 Sig Sauers, 10 AR-15s, and enough ammunition to start a small war. When the police caught up with him, he burst from a motel room waving a . 45 automatic. He's lucky he didn't get killed."

"You seem very well informed."

"It's all right there in the affidavit of probable cause."

Simpson stared at her without speaking.

To fill the dead air, Sophie added: "My friends in law enforcement tell me the Sig Sauer is the preferred handgun of America's Special Forces and the AR-15 is the civilian version of the M-16. With just a few modifications it will operate on full automatic."

"I don't need a lesson in firearms, Miss Anderson. They are the tools of my trade."

Anderson flipped through her notebook. "OK, Colonel, react to this. The gun shop owner said and I quote: 'It was almost as if the kid had a shopping list. He took the 20 most valuable weapons in my inventory and walked away from a drawer full of cash—the previous day's receipts.'"

The colonel sighed. "Off the record?"

Anderson clicked her pen. "OK."

"Off the record, I'll tell you that I don't have a clue what Brad's motivations were. He is a disturbed young man. His parents placed him with us in the hopes that we could straighten him out. Obviously, we failed."

His regret seemed so genuine that Anderson almost felt sorry for him.

He cleared his throat. "On the record, I will confirm that Johnston Bradley is a member of the senior class at Oliver Hazard Perry Military Academy and that he has been arrested and charged with the burglary of Middleburg Sporting Goods and with reckless endangerment and resisting arrest. He just turned 18, so his case is being handled in the court of common pleas rather than by juvenile authorities. We pride ourselves on transforming boys into responsible men. Brad's failure stains us all."

Simpson pointed a finger and cocked thumb at Anderson. "And that is all I'm going to say on the topic of Johnston Bradley."

"Cadet Bradley is telling police that he was operating under the orders of a member of the school staff, a Lieutenant Roger Richardson. What's your reaction to that?"

"No comment. And now, I must ask you to leave." He looked at his watch. "My board president is due to arrive in a few minutes. Don't want to keep him waiting."

Chapter 6

10 p.m. Wednesday, August 17, 2011, New Cumberland, PA

"Gray Collingsworth is an asshole, but I suppose I should thank him," Rev said.

"For what?" Sophie asked.

"For the pity fuck. That's what this is, isn't it?"

Sophie laughed and nuzzled her cheek into Rev's naked shoulder. They occupied his big bed in his narrow duplex on Fourth Street.

"Yes. Poor, poor Rev lost his job. Let me kiss it and make it better."

Just about every lovely square inch of the front of her pressed onto him. The familiar intimacy of their current positions—he on his back and she on top—set off a tuning fork deep within his soul.

"Are you purring?" Sophie asked.

"I prefer to think of it as growling."

"You're a big tough lion."

And then for a long while they didn't talk at all.

When he had regained his breath, he asked: "So why did you invite me to dinner, really?"

Sophie rose up on her left elbow and looked at him. "There you go again, talking to the ceiling and not to me."

Rev rolled over to face her. "Sorry." He blew a wisp of hair off her face.

"Actually, I wanted your help with the story I'm working on."

"The one you were talking about over dinner?"

Sophie nodded. "Johnston Bradley."

"The military academy cadet arrested for burglarizing a gun shop? See? I was paying attention."

"You were motivated by a desire to get into my pants."

"And you are motivated by a story. I know you, Sophie. You're on the trail of something more than a gun shop burglary."

She giggled. "At least I let you pump me ... before I pumped you."

"So, what can an unemployed journalist do to help out his more fortunate colleague?"

Sophie snuggled in closer. "This is pillow talk. Right? I'm not going to see my story on the AP wire?"

"They're not hiring. I asked."

"OK, here it is. Johnston Bradley is facing seven-to-ten in state prison and is eager to reduce his sentence. His court-appointed lawyer said the kid will give up the mastermind of the burglary if the district attorney agrees to two-to-five in county prison."

"And you know this because?"

"My college roommate, Olivia Pearson, a state police corporal, is the lead investigator. Liv is remorseful because she came within a hair trigger of splattering this kid's guts all over the side of the Morningstar Motel. Besides ... she thinks he's redeemable."

"For what? Valuable coupons?" Rev asked, mostly to reassure Sophie that he was still listening.

"Ha ha. Liv says that Brad—that's what they call him—has fallen in with some really scary companions ... paramilitary types who are preparing for the apocalypse. Brad told Liv that Roger Richardson, an instructor at Oliver Hazard Perry Military Academy, planned the burglary and escaped into the woods as state police closed in on the motel."

"Good stuff. Sounds like you've already got your story."

"Wait. There's more. Brad is telling the district attorney that if he'll soften the sentence he'll give up even more: the names of officers in a militia. They call themselves the Blue Mountain Boys. The gun shop burglary was aimed at arming the militia."

"The Blue Mountain Boys? That's rich. All this stuff is on the record?"

"I have it on the record that Brad implicated his teacher," Sophie said. "The rest ... is more speculative."

"Meaning Liv's job is on the line if you publish it without a secondary source."

"Right."

"So, what can I do to help?"

"What can you tell me about Colonel Randolph Simpson?"

Rev sat up suddenly and swung his legs over the bed.

Sophie gathered up the sheet as she maneuvered to sit beside him. She threw an arm over his naked shoulder.

"What's wrong, Rev?"

Rev took a deep breath and turned to face her. "Sorry. I just stepped on a psychic landmine."

"Care to explain that?"

"In a minute, perhaps. But first, to answer your question, Randolph Simpson was a career officer destined for flag rank. He'd been selected for brigadier general, but before his appointment could be confirmed some unsavory rumors escaped from the net the top brass tried to draw about Abu Ghraib."

"The torture case?"

Rev nodded. "That's right, the torture case. Some official memoranda bearing Simpson's signature survived the helter-skelter purge of documents that followed the disclosure that Iraqi prisoners had been humiliated and tortured at the prison. Simpson, more than merely being aware of the torture, had condoned it."

"And there went his appointment as brigadier."

"I lost track of him after that, but I understand he was allowed to retire with full benefits as a bird colonel," Rev said.

"Well this bird now is perched as president of the Oliver Hazard Perry Military Academy in Middleburg and I've got this gut feeling that he just may be one of the officers that Johnston Bradley is putting on the auction block."

"Interesting," Rev deadpanned.

"I'm more interested in that landmine."

"I was wondering when you'd get back to that."

"And ...?"

"I'll tell you, but not without my pants."

Chapter 7

10:30 p.m. Wednesday, August 17, 2011, New Cumberland, PA

Rev's big blue bathrobe swallowed her, but she didn't mind. She liked the intimacy of feeling something tight around her skin that had been tight around his. His smell, a faint peppery musk, permeated the fabric. And she felt more than a little bit guilty about her recent and somewhat sordid liaison with Grayson Collingsworth, even though it had saved her from the chopping block in the current round of layoffs.

Her first marriage had taught her that men are pigs. Rev had just about convinced her there were a few exceptions, but Iraq transformed him. Once fully engaged in relationship building, Rev now occupied a distant land in which emotional intimacy was not allowed. Lord knows she had tried to draw him out. To engage him in conversation more meaningful than 'Oh baby. Oh baby. That feels nice.' But he wouldn't let her in. He refused to tell her what had happened to him over there. And that reticence had festered at the center of their relationship, rotting it from the inside out. She needed the whole man. What was left was just not enough.

Rev had thrown on a pair of blue jeans, boat shoes, and a gray t-shirt. She was sitting at his kitchen table. He poured her a glass of chardonnay and busied himself building a Grey Goose martini.

The ice cubes rattling in the stainless steel shaker got on her nerves but she bit her tongue. She sensed that they were on the verge of an epiphany and she didn't want to spoil the mood.

He added a splash of juice from the olive jar, explaining: "I'm a journalist. I like dirt."

"A dirty martini; I get it. But you're stalling."

He poured the concoction into a large martini glass, dropped in three fat olives, and carried his martini carefully across the kitchen. He put the glass on the table and settled in behind it in a captain's chair.

He took a long sip. "Ah. Just right."

He took another sip. "You're right. I am stalling. Randolph Simpson commanded the court of inquiry that convened to determine whether I committed murder on April 15, 2004 in Fallujah. It was standard procedure ... anytime a civilian was killed."

Sophie sat up taller in her chair. She gulped her chardonnay.

Rev stuck his thumb and forefinger into his martini glass, pulled out an olive, and popped it into his mouth. His teeth ground the olive to pulp. Sophie resisted the impulse to pepper him with a thousand questions.

Rev took another sip of martini. "I was on patrol with my Stryker Company. I'd just been promoted to major. The lead vehicle in our patrol was an armored Humvee, but the metal plating had been jury-rigged in the field and the welds didn't hold when the driver, a young corporal from Minnesota, drove over the IED. The blast split the armor along a sloppy weld and the shrapnel blew off the left leg of the machine gunner and killed the driver outright.

"The gunner on the second vehicle saw a young Iraqi talking on a cell phone from an intersecting street just as the IED went off. I screamed at my men to stay in formation, but the blood lust overwhelmed them. IEDs were often triggered by cell phones. A half dozen of my men deserted their vehicles and went charging after the young Iraqi, who disappeared into an open doorway several houses down from the blast site.

"The medics were attending to the wounded. I shouted to my second in command to set up a perimeter and I went chasing after my men, who were chasing after the young Iraqi."

Rev took another long sip, got to his feet, crossed the kitchen, and poured the rest of the martini from the shaker into his glass. Settling back into his captain's chair, he studied Sophie over the top of his glass. "Sure you're ready for this?"

"If you can take it, so can I. But I have to ask. After all this time, why open up now?"

"I was afraid that I'd lose you, but I lost you anyway. You might decide to walk away ... again, once you hear what I did ... and what I didn't do."

"There are no guarantees, Rev. You're the most complex man I've ever known. But ever since Iraq I've felt that a part of you was ... missing."

"I misplaced it that day in Fallujah."

He downed the last of his martini. "I caught up with my men at the doorway." Despite the application of four ounces of vodka, his throat was thick with phlegm. He had to swallow a couple of times before he could continue.

"I told them that if we were going to do this we were going to do it right, one room at a time. Hug the walls; keep alert; be ready to shoot; and even more difficult, be ready ... not to shoot ... to hold fire even though every fiber of your being screamed at you to empty your weapon at whatever it was that had startled you ... just to be safe ... just to be sure. That's the challenge of dealing with civilians in a war zone. If the enemy doesn't kill you the rules of engagement will. It's the politics of the war on terror."

Rev was talking to himself more than to Sophie. He didn't look at her. He stared off into space. She hated it when he did that, but his engine was running on fumes. It would sputter and die if she forced him to shift from neutral.

"We searched the bottom floor first. The cups on the kitchen table were still full of hot tea, so we knew somebody was home ... that they probably had fled up the stairs because there wasn't a back door. Jimmy Rupp, a young Texan, and Alex Rodriguez, an even younger Hispanic kid, took the lead on the stairs. Tex and Mex we called them. They *were* inseparable."

His emphasis on the past tense made Sophie shudder.

"Sergeant Gary Casey followed them. Privates Thomas and Sharpe—I forget their first names—stayed at the foot of the stairs ready to discourage any hostiles who might arrive and attack us from below.

"There were three bedrooms on the second floor. The first two were empty. We heard whimpering from the third. We paused outside the door with Rupp, Rodriguez, and Casey, in that order to my right. They were locked and loaded with their M-16s pointed dead ahead. 'Don't get trigger happy, guys. Make sure of your target.'

"With my 9 millimeter unholstered in my right hand, I opened the door with my left and dove into the room. As I rolled to my knees, I was aware of my men following me. A man and a woman stood in the center of the room in front of a bed. She was holding a small child. The muzzle of an AK-47 appeared between them. The bomber we had chased from the street was behind them on the bed, using them as a human shield.

"'Gun!' I screamed. I should have pulled the trigger right then and there. I hesitated. The child couldn't have been more than two. The bomber began shooting. I emptied my 9, but it was too late. Tex and Mex were down. Shot dead. Casey was wounded. I killed them all, the bomber, the man, his wife, their child. Guilty or innocent; it didn't matter, but that wasn't my sin."

"Sin?" Sophie asked.

Rev's breath was coming in gasps as if he were running a race. He forced himself to slow his breathing. "Yes, sin. I can't get a hold of it in anything but religious terms. The man, his wife, their baby? They were dead as soon as we entered the room. There wasn't a scenario where they wouldn't have wound up dead. But Tex and Mex would still be alive if I had opened up as soon as I saw the gun."

"Where did the AK-47 come from?" Sophie wanted to know.

Rev shrugged. "Must have been hidden somewhere in the house."

"So the family probably was complicit?"

"The father, maybe. But not his wife and certainly not his child."

"What did the court of inquiry conclude?"

"Sergeant Casey's testimony was key. He told them that I had saved his life. That I put myself in the path of a bullet meant for him. That I was a hero. They gave me a Silver Star ... and a Purple Heart even though it was just a scratch."

He rubbed the scar on his left forearm. "But they couldn't give me what I need the most."

"What's that?"

"Absolution."

Chapter 8

11:30 a.m. Thursday, August 18, 2011, Mechanicsburg, PA

"Does the date April 12, 1945 mean anything to you?" Nona asked from her comfortable armchair in her brand new living room, where Rev continued to feel uncomfortable.

She had summoned him for lunch and the aroma of her famous chicken noodle soup, simmering on the stove not far away, had his salivary glands working overtime. But he knew there was something else on her agenda. She wasn't going to give up until he agreed to look into Operation Setting Sun. Rev knew this just as certainly as he knew the chicken noodle soup would be delicious.

Rev thought about it. "World War II ended in 1945. I think Berlin fell sometime in April. So my guess is that's the date Hitler committed suicide."

"You did a lot better on that test than most people of your generation. But you're off by a little bit. Hitler died on April 30, just 10 days after his 56th birthday. People of my generation remember stuff like that. Want to take another stab at it?"

Rev shrugged. "I've got nothing else."

"It's the day Uncle Jake visited us at our old homestead in Guilford County, North Carolina. He was on leave from the navy. He'd just been called east to confer with some big wigs in the War Department. He stopped by for dinner and spent the night with us before heading back to Hampton Roads, Virginia the next afternoon."

"Not fair. How would I know what one of my distant ancestors was doing on that day?"

"He's not a distant ancestor. He'd be your great granduncle. But you're right. It was a trick question. The only way I can remember it is that's the day President Roosevelt died."

Nona's eyes lost focus and Rev held his tongue, giving her time and space to ruminate.

After a while, she said: "That's why you're such a good reporter."

Rev cocked his head.

"See what I mean? You don't talk. You listen."

"I've gotten into far more trouble for things I've said than for things I haven't said."

"That's the mantra of a good reporter but it also explains why that pretty young woman, Sophie, doesn't come around anymore."

She had strayed at last into foul territory. Rev's face reddened. "Get on with your story," he growled.

Nona pretended not to notice the shift in his demeanor. "We were relaxing after dinner, listening to the radio, when the music program was interrupted by a news bulletin telling us that the president had died at Warm Springs. Dad pulled out a handkerchief and blew his nose, and Jake? Well Jake just sat a little taller in his chair and said, 'I wonder how that's going to affect my orders.'

"Dad said: 'What orders?' and Jake muttered: 'Loose lips sink ships. I love you, Bob, but I can't tell you where I'm headed next. It's top secret.'"

Rev leaned forward.

"Gotcha, don't I?" Nona asked.

"Don't look so self-satisfied."

"It's been sixty-some years, and I can't remember all that the two men talked about that night after they learned the president was dead. Dad loved FDR and was apprehensive about Harry Truman. He was an unknown quantity, although I think most people would agree that he turned out all right. Uncle Jake listened more than he talked. I could tell that he was preoccupied with something he couldn't discuss with the rest of us."

"What do you think that was?"

"It must have had something to do with the phone call we received the next morning. It came in at about 7:30. I picked up the phone on the wall next to the kitchen at the same time Uncle Jake picked up back in the living room. He was expecting the call and had asked us to stay off the line, but I was naturally nosy."

"Imagine that," Rev said.

"He said 'hello' and a woman's voice at the other end said 'Authorization code, please.' Uncle Jake spieled off a bunch of numbers. And the woman said, 'ID confirmed. Operation Setting Sun is still a go. Carry on as ordered.' Then she hung up."

"Wait a minute," Rev said. "You expect me to believe that you remember a conversation that occurred more than 60 years ago with that sort of clarity?"

"I wrote it down in my journal, which I've consulted and appended to my Uncle Jake file. I've always been a journal keeper. You know that."

"OK. I'll suspend disbelief for a while longer."

"Over breakfast, during a lull in the conversation among the adults, I blurted out 'What's Operation Setting Sun, Uncle Jake?' He inhaled his coffee and began coughing. When he caught his breath, he said, 'Eavesdropping is a bad habit, young lady. I think the two of us need to talk about that in private.'

"Uncle Jake pushed back his chair, stood, and looked at me sternly. I got to my feet and he said, 'I won't lay a hand on her, Bob, but she needs a stern lecture on minding her own business. Come with me, young lady.'

"Jake stalked out the back door from the kitchen with his ham-sized fists clenched at his sides and I followed, thinking to myself, 'Oh boy, I'm in for it now.' Uncle Jake was big, barrel-chested, and strong. Dad used to say if you hooked him up to the traces he could plow an acre quicker than our mule, Old Bessie.

"We walked outside and when he whirled around to face me, I was surprised to see a smile on his face. Uncle Jake laughed out loud. 'By God, Annie,' he drawled, 'you've got enough spunk for an entire division. You've heard something you shouldn't have heard, but I'm not fretting because I know I can trust you.'

"'You're not mad at me?' I asked.

"He replied: 'No more than I'd be mad at Old Bessie for turning a short corner on the way back to the barn. Don't make much sense to fault a critter that's doing nothing more than what comes natural. I can't tell you about Operation Setting Sun, but I can write, letting you know that I'm OK.'"

Nona ran out of steam and looked at Rev to assess his reaction.

"So did Jake write to you?" Rev asked.

"I got one letter from him after that. It had an FPO post mark bearing the seal of the USS *Portland*, dated August 14, 1945. The censors had a field day with the scissors. His letter was all chopped up; looked like a paper doll created by a drunkard. Jake told me that he had been wounded when his plane was shot down but was recovering in sick bay. But one peculiar thing did slip past the censors."

"What was that?"

Nona scrunched her eyes tightly shut and Rev imagined that she was willing a memory from her subconscious.

"He wrote something like this: 'The sun has set twenty or more times now on my special operation. In my darkest moments I realize that mankind learned nothing from the blessed Trinity."

"What does that mean?"

"I think that was Jake's way of telling me that Operation Setting Sun, whatever it was, failed."

"What about the blessed Trinity?"

"What about that indeed. Jake wasn't a religious man by any stretch of imagination. There's a hidden meaning in that remark. I'm sure of it, but I haven't been able to figure out what. That's why I'd like you to go to San Diego and backtrack Jake's life."

"No way, Nona. I'm way too busy. I've got to find a new job. I can't live forever on my severance and Guard pay."

"Pish tosh. You need to decompress, think about something other than yourself for a while." Nona patted his hand. "Humor an old lady. One of my biggest regrets is that I lost touch with Uncle Jake."

"I'm sorry, Nona. I'm not prepared to go chasing Uncle Jake's ghost across an entire continent just because you regret having lost touch with him."

"There's more to it than that. A month or so before he died, Jake sent me a letter ..."

"Aha!"

"He promised to tell me all about Operation Setting Sun. Called it the greatest adventure of his life. And sure enough a couple of weeks later I received a thick envelope containing the first installment of his life's story."

Nona's eyes pooled with tears. She pulled a handkerchief from her left sleeve and dabbed at her eyes.

Rev lost patience. "And? Come on, Nona. This is like pulling teeth. Rub some dirt on it and get back in the game."

Nona laughed through her tears. "I deserved that."

She took a deep breath. "I have a confession to make. In his memoir, Uncle Jake revealed that the commanding officer of Operation Setting Sun was responsible for the mission's failure."

"Is this the confession part?"

Nona nodded. "Care to guess the name of that officer?"

"Nope."

"I'll tell you anyway."

"Figured you would."

"Alan Jenkins."

The revelation didn't have the effect she'd hoped for so she repeated it. "ADMIRAL ALAN JENKINS. You know, the father of the speaker of the House of Representatives!"

"Son of a bitch," Rev said.

"Yes, he was, according to Jake's journal. And a racist and a bully to boot."

"Brett Faust had similar things to say about the admiral's son," Rev said.

"The apple didn't fall far from the tree," Nona agreed.

"So you aimed me at the son and now you're aiming me at the father. Jesus Christ, he must be long dead by now."

"What else do you have to do?"

"Find a job," Rev replied. "That's more important than solving a 66-year-old mystery and absolving you of guilt for having lost touch with your uncle. I'm sorry, Nona, but the answer is no."

"Not even for a bowl of my chicken noodle soup?"

"I won't sell out that cheap."

"Then I'll up the ante ..."

Nona arose from her chair and walked across her living room and into the kitchen. She collected something from the top of her kitchen desk and returned to the living room clutching three envelopes, two small and one large.

"What's that?" Rev wanted to know.

She handed him a fat, letter-sized envelope.

"And the winner of a free round trip ticket to San Diego is ... drum roll, please ... Revere Polk! You leave Monday morning. Your car rental and hotel reservations also are inside," she said.

Rev took the envelope. "I'm not making any promises."

She handed him a second small envelope, not nearly as fat.

"And this?"

"A copy of the San Diego newspaper's account of Uncle Jake's death. The reporter's name is Chad Tucci. He's still alive."

"How would you know that?"

"I may have been born in the ice age, but I know how to Google," Nona said. "His address and telephone number are inside."

"And the big envelope?" Rev asked.

"I've saved the best for last. Uncle Jake sent me this much of his journal. I'd like you to find out how his story ends."

Rev found himself reaching for the envelope, but Nona snatched it back. "You've got to promise me one thing. And this is really important."

"What's that?"

"You won't read this until you're on the plane to San Diego. If you decide not to go I want you to return this to me unopened."

"That's silly," Rev said.

"Silly it may be, but those are my rules."

Rev smiled in wonder at his grandmother.

"You're a tough old bird. I'll give you that," he said, at last. "I'll think about it over a bowl of your soup. But I'm not promising anything."

"I'll throw in a grilled ham and cheese."

"Swiss on rye, grilled in two tablespoons of real butter?" Rev said, hopefully.

"Only the best for my grandson."

Chapter 9

3:30 a.m. Friday, August 19, 2011, New Cumberland, PA

Rev could feel the familiar heft of his service pistol in his right hand. He could smell the gun powder. Tex and Mex collapsed in slow motion just as they had a hundred times before. Sergeant Casey screamed as the terrorist's bullet tore into his shoulder.

"Gun! Gun!"

His finger tensed on the trigger. His pistol roared again and again. Until it was empty and everyone was dead. Everyone except Sergeant Casey who said that Rev had saved his life, that Rev was a hero.

But Rev knew better. He was the coward who did not have the balls to kill an innocent man, his wife, and their child. Until it was too late. Until Tex and Mex were dead. Mex had a nine-month-old daughter who would never know her father.

The sodden sheets coiled about him like a sweaty anaconda. He kicked out with his feet. He was asleep, but he recognized he was doing these things. It was as if he was watching himself from the screening room of a movie studio, reliving his cowardice over and again. The director nudged him in the arm. "This is good stuff," he said. "The pathos is thick enough to cut with a knife. You really nailed this performance. You sold it and I'm buying it."

Part of him knew it was a performance and that only added to his guilt. Part of him was proud of what he had done. Part of him reveled in the bloodletting. Part of him was elated that he had survived while the others had died. Guilt is a jealous lover who demands that you think only of her. Rev was faithful to a fault.

The screening room walls flew away like leaves before a storm. This was new territory for his nightmare. In a breathtaking change of venue, he suddenly found himself on a pier at sunset.

The gray side of a mammoth ship rose above him, luminescent in the fading light of the sun, which hung on the horizon, a beach ball doused in lighter fluid and set aflame by a drunken sailor.

Heavy hawsers, taut with the task of holding the ship in place, disappeared into chocks far overhead. The hull vibrated with the power of the landlines that sent electricity coursing through the ship's circuitry. Rev imagined that the hull was pulsating, in and out, like the deep breaths of a great whale steeling itself for a perilous journey into the bounding main.

"She's a wonderful sight, ain't she?"

Rev turned. Without his noticing, a tall, solid-looking fellow in his late 40s, dressed in khakis, had approached him from behind. Rev didn't recognize the man's collar insignia, but it was clear that he was an officer of some sort. He was tall but stooped. Deep crow's feet were etched about his eyes and mouth. In his voice, Rev recognized the familiar North Carolina twang that underpinned Nona's speech even though she had lived for decades in the north.

"What ship is this?" Rev asked.

"Guess I can't expect a landlubber to recognize her, even though she will be the most decorated ship of the second Great War."

"The USS *Enterprise*?"

The man nodded. "That's right, son. The Big E. I rode her down the rails when she was launched. And I've served her ever since. I'm proud to be a plank owner. They put that in my obituary."

His face sagged. "The peculiarities of my current condition give me a window into her future. She'll be cut up for razor blades. What a tragedy for this elegant lady."

"Your present condition, what's that?"

"Why, I'm dead. Any fool can see that."

In his dream, Rev recoiled from the apparition that had snuck up on him from behind. He waited for the image to dissipate, to fade into the next scene. He longed for a scenario involving Sophie, a sarong, and a tropical island. But this particular specter was stubborn. He stayed put.

"Relax. You're alive and likely to stay that way for another 40 years or more if you lay off the sauce. You're visiting Hades on a special visa, one that's punched exclusively for warriors like you and me."

"Warriors?"

"That's right warriors called upon by our country to fight for what's right. In that service we can do no wrong ... as long as our hearts are pure. Your heart is pure; otherwise Charon would not have punched your ticket."

"Right. Greek mythology. I get it. Who are you?"

"I think you know the answer to that question, but what the hell."

The sailor came to attention and saluted.

"Master Chief Aviation Machinist Mate Jake Addison at your service, sir. You're due the 'sir' 'cause I understand you're a major in the Pennsylvania National Guard."

Rev returned the salute.

"Now that formality is behind us, I'll say my piece. Regret is eating you up, son. Put it behind you. Those souls you consigned to the underworld would have arrived here eventually anyway. Circumstances beyond your control condemned them to an early grave."

"That doesn't absolve me of responsibility. I'm still the one who pulled the trigger ... and the one who didn't pull the trigger soon enough."

"You're a decent human being. You wanted to save your men; you didn't want to kill an innocent family. There is no sin in that."

Jake Addison stepped forward and clapped Rev on the back. "Now, get on with the rest of your life."

"Aye, aye, Master Chief."

"That's more like it, boy," his great granduncle replied. "Now you can do something for me. I'm pissed and there's nothing worse than a pissed off E-9. Ask any swabbie. Master Chief ain't happy, ain't no one happy."

"What can I do for you, Master Chief?"

"Unmask the sumbitch who murdered me."

Rev groaned and rolled over in his sleep. He kicked at the bed clothes and resettled himself. REM kicked in anew. Sophie walked toward him across an expanse of white sand fringed by the gentle swells of a blue-green sea. She was smiling in a saffron sarong.

And a porpoise swam by whistling "Battle Hymn of the Republic" through its blowhole. Rev laughed out loud, waking himself up.

His head pounded like a wine and liquor hangover. He untangled himself from sweaty bedclothes and stumbled to the bathroom. He tried, unsuccessfully, to drown Master Chief Jake Addison in four Dixie cups of water.

"Shit! I've got to get this guy out of my head."

A voice in a slow southern twang mocked him from his subconscious:

"I'm not going anywhere, nephew, until you unmask the sumbitch who killed me. In that enterprise our self-interests collide."

33

Chapter 10

10 a.m. (CDT) Monday, August 22, 2011, Chicago, IL

Rev's ears popped as a flight attendant closed the main cabin door. He stretched his legs out in the empty space in front of the emergency exit and steeled himself for takeoff. He wasn't a white-knuckle flier, but he didn't relish the thought of the next five hours, locked up in a tiny capsule six miles above the ground. The fellow sitting next to him on the crowded flight from O'Hare to San Diego was of normal size and for the moment didn't seem inclined to chat, both of which were good things.

Rev coveted the solitude to stew on recent events that had him leaving town just as there seemed to be some hope that Sophie might take him back. There were a thousand good reasons to stay at home and little to profit in chasing a dream to San Diego, but he had to get Jake Addison out of his head.

Rev's reverie was shattered as the plane lurched from the jet way. He glanced furtively at the man in seat 19B, directly to his right. His row mate was staring straight ahead, studying the advertising posters affixed to the bulkhead behind the first-class toilet.

With nothing else to do, other than to try to avoid eye contact with his neighbor, Rev pulled an envelope from the pocket of his computer carrying case, which resided under his seat. He opened it and extracted a newspaper clipping.

By Chad Tucci
Staff Writer
City police are investigating a fatal hit-and-run accident that claimed the life of a decorated veteran of the U.S. Navy on Monday, June 3.

Police report that Jacob Addison, 75, of San Diego, was struck and killed by a blue late-model Chevrolet Impala sedan.

Witnesses said that the accident occurred as the victim was crossing Prospect Avenue in the crosswalks just north of the Grande Colonial Hotel in La Jolla.

"The old man was in the middle of the road, with no traffic coming from either direction, when this car suddenly turns off Jenner Street, with its engine revving and the tires squealing," said Henrietta Wilson of La Jolla.

"The old guy never stood a chance. The car hit him square on. Threw him up in the air and he came down hard on his neck and shoulder. By that time the car was accelerating north on Prospect Avenue. It never even slowed down," Wilson said.

"Thus far, all we know is that the driver was a young white male," said police spokesman Sam Elliott. "That's not enough information to put out an all points bulletin, but we'll continue to work on it."

Addison served for more than 30 years in the U.S. Navy. He was a certified enlisted Naval Aviation Pilot and a former flight instructor at the Pensacola Naval Air Station in Florida in the 1920s.

Addison was the leading chief petty officer for VT-6, the squadron of Douglas Devastators assigned to the USS Enterprise at the onset of World War II. The squadron lost 11 of its 15 planes during the Battle of Midway in 1942, but Addison survived and was mustered out of the navy as a Chief Aviation Machinist Mate in October of 1945. He earned a Bronze Star, Purple Heart, Presidential Unit Citation and the Navy Cross during combat in World War II.

Rev dropped the clipping onto his lap and stared out the window where a motorized baggage cart was making its way back to the terminal.

A male flight attendant brushed by so intent on closing the overhead luggage racks that he didn't see Rev's left foot, which had strayed a bit into the aisle. The attendant tripped, caught himself on the back of Rev's seat, and for a moment his professional calm fell away and Rev could read his mind.

Stupid fuck, pull in your feet.

The words arrived as if by telepathy at the same time a different set of words arrived in conventional fashion.

"Excuse me, sir. Please pull in your feet."

The plane took another turn on the taxi way. And the pilot's voice announced:

"We're next up for takeoff. Flight attendants, take your positions."

The engines roared and Rev grasped the armrests with fingers of steel as the pilot released the brakes and opened the throttles.

When the plane arrived at altitude and the fasten seat belts sign blinked off, Rev returned the clipping to his computer case and pulled out the fat manila envelope Nona had given him.

He opened the envelope and pulled out a sheaf of forty or so pages held together by a big black binder clip. The first page was a handwritten note:

If you are reading this you had better be on a plane to San Diego. Uncle Jake's letter and a copy of his journal follow. Enjoy! LOVE, NONA.

Rev looked over his shoulder, confirming that the seat behind him was unoccupied. He reclined his seat back two notches and began to read.

April 18, 1968
Dear Annie,
It will probably be a shock to you ... hearing from me after all of these years.

I've stayed in touch with my youngest sister, your Aunt Mary, but I'm afraid I've neglected my male siblings and their progeny.

Men are unlikely to reveal their weaknesses to other men. It's a survival instinct that has served our species well. Your father thinks of me as a naval aviator and war hero, but the truth is I am an old man, childless and lonely because the only woman I ever loved is long dead.

The last time we met, you were an inquisitive teenager. That phone call you intercepted all of those years ago set me off on my life's last and greatest adventure—Operation Setting Sun, Vice Admiral Alan Jenkins commanding.

Jenkins is retired now, of course, but like most turds he bobs to the surface of whatever cesspool he inhabits. This time it's politics. He's an adviser to former Governor Ronald Reagan, who aspires to be president of these United States.

Your Aunt Mary tells me that you have an interest in our family's history. So I am sending you the first installments of a memoir that culminates with my account of Operation Setting Sun and explains why Admiral Jenkins engineered its failure.

I'll leave it to you to decide whether it should be shared outside the confines of family.

With all my love,
Uncle Jake

Chapter 11

Jake's Journal

As I write these words in the spring of 1968, I am a 75-year-old man who has reflected long and hard on whether history would be better served by honesty or discretion.

Once a sailor. Always a sailor.

So, fuck discretion!

And forgive my French.

My name is Jacob Wissler Addison. I was born on Jan. 20, 1893 in Moncure, Chatham County, North Carolina, the second son of Burwell and Elvira Addison.

Burwell, a sharecropper, married well. Elvira was of the local gentry. Her father, Hamilton Thompson, a fire brand of a Methodist preacher, sported a curly red beard, wore linen suits, and possessed a magnificent voice that could reach the back row of tent meetings without the artifice of modern amplification.

Mama ended up with a sharecropper because she caught the measles in her teens and was all but deaf. She was past prime marrying age with no particular prospects when Papa rode to her rescue. He was an amorous old goat. My older brother, Bill (1892), and I (1893) were followed in quick succession by Maude (1896), Edwin (1896), Daisy (1898), Robert (1900), and Mary (1902).

Papa ingratiated himself with a carpetbagger named William Wissler, a native of Pennsylvania who acquired 500 acres of Haw River bottom land and built a spacious brick house in town that his uppity wife refused to live in. She favored the log cabin summer home Wissler soon built for her hard on the banks of Haw River.

Papa was more than happy to move his family into the large rambling house and to fill it with his children. He demonstrated his appreciation by naming his second son after his patron, which explains my middle name.

Papa hoped Bill and I would perpetuate the family tradition of squatting on another man's land and toiling in his fields. Bill escaped his fate because a cloud of gas that drifted over the trenches at Argonne in 1918 made him unfit for the rigors of farm work.

I was luckier. By the time the Great War rolled around, I was a seasoned aviator and soared above my poor brethren slogging it out in the trenches below. Alas, I fell victim to a more insidious torment. I have squandered a large portion of my life in the service of Bacchus, who promised me solace from wartime torments but never really delivered. I was a drunk and whore monger until my second wife, dear sweet Emika, rescued me.

It was not an overnight transformation. I often backslid and didn't completely escape the perdition of whiskey until I was well into middle age, and then with the considerable support of Alcoholics Anonymous. I was discharged from the naval service in October of 1945 and, using the GI bill, matriculated at San Diego State University where I majored in English. So these are the ruminations of a reformed and educated drunk, delivered with all the benefits of hindsight, tempered with regret and redeemed by the love of a good woman.

My naval career began in 1909, shortly after my 16th birthday, when I made my way to Raleigh, lied about my age, and swore an oath of allegiance to the United States of America. I hopped a train to Norfolk, Virginia, where I was welcomed with open arms by the navy.

At the end of basic training, I was branded as a seaman apprentice and dispatched to be part of the commissioning crew of the battleship USS Utah, Captain William Benson commanding. I was a country boy and excelled at small arms training, but aboard the Utah, my blacksmithing skills attracted the attention of the chief machinist mate. Shaping metal, as it turned out, was almost as important aboard a battleship as it was on the farm.

On Jan. 5, 1914 the Utah was ordered south to Cuba on a training mission only to be diverted to Mexico in support of the occupation of Veracruz. I mention this for two reasons. First, the attack on Veracruz marked the beginning of my association with naval aviation, and second it was the first time I was fired upon by hostile forces.

By that time I was a machinist's mate third class. I was 21 years old, as strong as I would ever be, and certain that I would always be young, healthy, and confident enough to spit in the devil's face. I soon was to learn that the devil cannot be bearded with impunity.

The navy had established a relationship with Glenn Hammond Curtiss, who had developed a float plane that commanders hoped would be useful in aerial reconnaissance in support of fleet operations. I didn't know much about airplanes, but I was familiar with fabricating parts for the small engines the navy employed on motor launches and such.

I was loaned to a young ensign named Jeremiah Martin, a graduate of the nascent naval aviation training center at Pensacola, Florida. Captain Benson ordered me to assist Ensign Martin in the maintenance of his Curtiss seaplane, which he used to reconnoiter Veracruz in the days before our invasion.

I helped Jackson repair a wing strut and was rewarded by an invitation to join him on a reconnaissance flight. The seaplane was underpowered and it took us almost twenty minutes to attain enough speed to become airborne, but once we were ... what a thrill!

The buffeting of cross winds and caprice of down drafts were exhilarating. As we swooped low over the rooftops, we startled the hoards of buzzards feeding upon the carrion that accumulated in the streets of that dreadful city due to the laziness and neglect of the indigenous population.

We overflew an old harbor-side fort, which was being used as a prison to hold the wretched souls with the temerity to oppose Victoriano Huerta, Mexico's oppressive president vilified by his nickname—the Jackal. The stench from the prison rose up to greet us and the guards shook their fists and aimed their rifles at us, although no bullets passed our way that I could discern.

That airplane ride gave my aspirations a 180-degree change of course, which led to my being certified as an enlisted naval aviation pilot, NAP for short, six years later at Pensacola, Florida. I knew how to fly long before that, but the navy often marches to a slow cadence in affording official certification of fait accompli.

My part in the invasion of Veracruz can be attributed to a farm boy's familiarity with firearms. I had keen vision and the serenity of spirit and steadiness of hand necessary to spot, sight, and fire a rifle, placing my shots where I wanted them to go.

That skill landed me with the invasion force of nearly 400 blue jackets and Marines who stormed ashore to initially welcoming crowds of Mexican civilians on the morning of April 22, 1914.

For the first several blocks of our invasion we were unopposed, but gradually forces loyal to the Jackal realized our intent: to prevent the off-loading of Remington machine guns and ammunition dispatched by Kaiser Wilhelm for the support of President Huerta in his ongoing fray with Pancho Villa.

We accomplished our mission. We seized the Custom House and prevented the German flagged-but American-owned ship, the

Ypiranga, *from delivering its deadly cargo. But, we also enraged the civilian population, which soon was taking pot shots at us from doors and windows as we passed by.*

We blue jackets were thrust into the role of ground troops but we were unaccustomed to the tactics of street fighting. We bunched together in groups like soldiers on a parade grounds and thereby took more casualties than we would have had we adopted the tactics of our enemies, who sniped at us from bell towers and windows and from behind walls, always on the move, elusive as the hot winds that scoured our faces with dirt and offered us no solace from the oppressive heat.

By the second day, I had become adept at darting from doorway to doorway, running in a zigzag pattern like a merchant ship trying to avoid a submarine's torpedo, and firing my rifle and pistol from the hip because the difference between life and death often occupied the milliseconds it would take to bring the rifle to my shoulder or my pistol to full extension.

On April 23, I was dispatched to deliver supplies of food, water, and ammunition to Ensign and later Captain Edward McDonnell on the roof of the Custom House. For his bravery in manning that post while blue jackets died at his side, McDonnell was awarded the Medal of Honor.

A Mexican darted directly in front of me from a side street to my left. I was running with my Springfield at port arms and with a heavy backpack bumping up and down on my shoulders. In retrospect, I realize he probably was running to escape our snipers, who had taken up positions in buildings surrounding the Custom House. He was armed with a pistol. His voice was a scream.

He fired first, emptying his pistol at me with an abandon fueled by adrenalin and fear. The bullets skittered off the cobblestones and chipped mortar from a house behind me. They were well off their mark, but they loosened my bowels.

I dove, rolled, and came to one knee directly in front of him. I pulled the trigger, worked the bolt, and fired a second time. Only then did I recognize that my assailant was no more than a boy. Thirteen years old at best. And then he was lying dead in front of me. My bullets had shattered his heart as well as my own.

There is nothing more gut wrenching than taking a life at point-blank range. That is what drove me to drink: the vision of that boy, his eyes devoid of the spark that illuminates the soul. Alas, there is no absolution in Bacchus. That dead boy has stared at me from the bottom of many a whiskey glass.

Chapter 12

Jake's Journal

On January 20, 1930, my 37th birthday, I met an angel. I had just made warrant officer for the third time having climbed up and down the ranks as alcoholism marched steadily across the landscape of my psyche and commanding officers lamented the decline and predicted the ultimate demise of this salty old seadog.

I don't know why the navy put up with me as long as it did. Back then, drunkenness was the norm for career sailors like me. Drunkenness and tattoos. I had a beauty, the prow of the USS Utah, my first ship, emblazoned across my right shoulder, the handiwork of an inebriated Norfolk tattooist. The fleshly Utah lists to port to this day as she steams across a sea of saggy old man skin gathered about her like the folds of a fan.

That image comes courtesy of my creative writing teacher back at the U who encouraged me to come up with pretty ways to express ugly things. Said that made my writing almost as colorful as me. I think she had a daddy complex and liked the dangerous miasma that percolated around me on days when I really needed a drink and stared at her with the naked sexual desire of one starved for the tender touch of a woman.

Where was I? Oh yes. My 37th birthday. The day I met an angel. I was rubbing elbows with the elite that night. A certain lieutenant commander, a graduate of the U.S. Naval Academy with a social register upbringing from hoity-toity Boston, threw a bash at his rented digs in San Diego. He invited me to make an appearance, to celebrate my birthday and my return to the good graces of the navy, and, perhaps, to form a liaison with one of the many young nurses he promised would be in attendance. Nudge. Wink. Nudge.

I pre-partied with the chief's mess at the Naval Air Station, San Diego, and by the time I showed up at Lieutenant Commander

Conrad's place I was, in old navy parlance, three sheets to the wind.

Conrad had a sheet or two a flapping his own self. He greeted me at the front door and thrust a gin and tonic into my hand.

"Jake! It's great to have you aboard. Make yourself at home. The bar is that-a-way."

He waggled his thumb over his right shoulder and staggered off to talk to a leggy blonde situated at the apex of a group of young women lingering in Conrad's foyer as if too much danger lurked in the dark recesses of this lion's den. On the exposed right flank of the blonde bombshell's entourage perched a beautiful flower.

Even in my drunken state, I could tell that this woman was special, possessed of an absolute sense of calm despite an atmosphere permeated with booze and testosterone. She saw me staring at her and a smile lit her face. She was oriental, but of what precise origin I couldn't say, befuddled as I was with drink and to an even greater extent by the epiphany that struck me the moment I laid eyes on her.

"Jake, my boy," I said to myself. "There is a woman to make you give up your evil ways and howl at the moon in gratitude."

A poet would tell you that in that moment I recognized my own counterpoint in the human continuum. That there resided the yin to my yang. That I had finally encountered my soul mate among the teeming masses of souls clamoring for their own soul mates over the vast oceans of time and place.

Or some such shit. Simply put, I was smitten.

And then she was swept deeper into the lion's den by the arrival of another group of young men and women, laughing and talking and smelling of the dry desert air that swept across San Diego that January eve.

I was desolate and took solace in a second gin and tonic, and then a third, and probably a fourth and a fifth as well, which explains why I woke up on the ground next to my car to the voice of an angel.

Her voice floated to me from above. "Are you all right, sir?"

I opened one eye and she stared down at me solemnly.

As I struggled to rise, she knelt beside me. Gentle fingers fluttered across my forehead. Her palm cupped my jaw. Her eyes stared into my soul. "Could you get to your feet if I helped you?"

"Stand back. I'd hate to fall on you."

I grabbed the handle of the rear door of my old Ford and tugged, gaining my feet inch by inch. Leaning back on the car for support, I observed that I was a good foot taller than the beautiful young woman who stood before me. A China doll came to mind.

As I smiled down at her, I was visited by the certainty that if I didn't move fast I would bespatter her with vomit. I staggered to the hood of the car, bent over, and threw up in the gutter beside the right wheel. As I retched, this wretched man felt a gentle arm of support and condolence cast across my shoulder.

"Shh. Shh. You poor, poor man. You have a gentle soul. What pain in your life has reduced you to this?"

I straightened, tugged my handkerchief out of my pocket, and wiped the vomit from my chin. I focused on the one of her in the middle, which I assumed was the real one. "My name is Jake Addison. I'm a pilot and a drunk and I'm glad to meet you."

I offered her my hand.

She demurred. "Perhaps when you've cleaned yourself up a bit."

Sensing my disappointment, she quickly added: "My name is Emika. I am Japanese and a Christian. You have welcomed the devil into your soul. I can help you cast him out."

Her voice carried just a bit of the stereotypical sing song that movies were destined to thrust upon the Japanese in the dark years to come, but it was imbued with such kindness that it didn't matter much then or later.

"Well, Emika, thanks for the offer, but I don't think you want to associate with the likes of me. Besides, the devil and me, we're best buddies. Why would I want to cast him out? Now, I'd best be getting back to the base. They have to let me in there."

"I'm not going to let you drive in this condition."

I reached in my pocket and offered her my keys. "Well then why don't you drive?"

I woke up the next morning with a raging hangover to the piercing scream of a tea kettle's whistle.

"Please make it stop."

I opened my eyes.

I was on her couch.

She floated into the room with a hot cup of peppermint tea.

I drank it. I was restored.

Chapter 13

Jake's Journal

Emika and I were married on April 15, 1930. I had a 24-hour pass. We drove to Yuma, Arizona and woke up a justice of the peace.

On our first wedding anniversary, I got new orders. I was among 12 enlisted naval aviation pilots tapped to crew a squadron of P2Y-1 seaplanes from North Island, San Diego, to the Naval Air Station at Coco Solo in the Panama Canal Zone. Once there, we were to staff a new permanent patrol squadron protecting the United States' interests in the Caribbean.

The P2Y-1 had long legs. It was a biplane and the engine and prop were affixed to the top wing right behind the pilot. We flew through nonstop. I can still remember the multi-storied thunder head that chased us into Coco Solo.

We landed on choppy waters, taxied to the ramps. The ground crews were tying our planes down when the first drops of what became a torrential rain began to fall. We huddled in a hangar with the rain pounding on the tin roof like Gene Krupa on a bender.

Coco Solo had housing for enlisted men and their wives. Emika joined me four weeks later, just in time for a get-to-know-you tea with Commander Alan Jenkins, the brand new station chief at Coco Solo.

I'm a drunk and if there's one thing a drunk can do it's recognize another drunk, which I did, immediately, in Alan Jenkins, the son of a bitch. Emika had me on the straight and narrow by then, although I sometimes backslid. The tea was at 2 o'clock in the afternoon on a Sunday at the officers' club, and Commander Jenkins was already in the bag. I could tell it by the careful way he walked and by the deliberation with which he answered questions and greeted his subordinates.

Emika, having been with me for some time, recognized it, too, but the rest of the gathering seemed oblivious. To the uninitiated,

Commander Jenkins came across as a thoughtful, deliberate, and imminently pleasant man.

To that list several sharper characteristics beg to be added, such as functional alcoholic and insufferable bigot. These were to have a profound effect on the history of the second Great War in a fashion I will soon describe, but for now, suffice it to say that Commander (and later Admiral) Alan Jenkins was a tough son of a bitch who prospered because the command structure is predisposed to confuse toughness with competence.

Jenkins was consistently tough and inconsistently competent. His competence ebbed when it collided with his prejudices and that, I think, is the reason he failed to report intelligence that could have saved hundreds of thousands of lives, both Japanese and American, at the end of World War II. But, in relating that, I am jumping ahead of my story.

Getting back to that introductory tea at Coco Solo ... a receiving line soon formed and Emika and I joined it. I was invited because, under her calming influence, I had been promoted a pay grade and my request for a commission awaited the attention of the new commanding officer of Coco Solo Naval Air Station, whom I was about to meet.

Emika was so proud of me. She was the first to greet Commander Jenkins as we inched forward in the receiving line. When she offered him her hand he ignored the gesture, but he addressed her pleasantly. "What a gorgeous young woman. What is your name, dear?"

"Emika Addison, and this is my husband, Chief Warrant Officer First Class Jacob Addison."

"I am acquainted with your husband. His request for a commission, with the glowing endorsement of his commanding officer, is on my desk, awaiting my signature. But for the moment, I am more interested in you. I am told that every Japanese name has a meaning."

"Yes. That is so."

"What does Emika mean?"

My wife blushed. "Blessed beautiful child," she whispered.

"Well if you are blessed, God has a funny way of demonstrating that, hooking you up with a man like Jacob Addison. He's got grit, I'll give him that, but his service record reads like a dime store novel."

At this point I stepped forward and saluted.

"I'm the blessed one, Commander. I'm steering a straight course these days, thanks to Emika."

Commander Jenkins saluted and shook my hand. "Good for you, sailor. I plan to act on your commission ... expeditiously."

Which, in fact, he did. Two days later I was summoned to his office. He eyed me up and down and said:

"Despite your colorful record I would be disposed to commission you as a lieutenant junior grade were it not for the fact that you are married to a fish-eating Jap. She reeks, Warrant Officer. I won't countenance an officer under my command being married to a stinking Nipponese. Get rid of her, Jake, and we'll talk about your commission. That's all. Dismissed!"

I went out that night and got rip-roaring drunk, broke the jaw of a petty officer second class on the shore patrol, and ended up in the brig.

I told Emika that's what derailed my commission; she didn't need to know the truth.

Chapter 14

11 a.m. Monday, August 22, 2011, Selinsgrove, PA

Sophie Anderson studied Johnston Bradley through three inches of bulletproof glass. He looked back with sunken eyes, underscored by fiery blotches of acne high up on his cheekbones. His knuckles whitened as he strangled the handset of the phone he held tight to his ear.

The visitors' room at Snyder County Prison exuded an institutional ambiance: painfully spartan, puke green walls with threadbare indoor-outdoor carpet underfoot.

Fear deposited a shiny desperation in Brad's eyes.

His words arrived in Sophie's handset with tin-can-and-string fidelity.

"I've got to get out of here. They put me in the same cell as a child molester for God's sake."

"Your bail's only $20,000," Anderson noted. "A bail bondsman would charge ten percent to spring you. That's two grand. Can't your parents come up with the money?"

"Dad wants to teach me a lesson. He's a real asshole. What's bunking with a faggot going to teach me, other than how to take one in the ass?" Brad blushed fiercely. The pustules on his face took on an almost iridescent hue. "How about it, Ms. Anderson? If you bail me out of jail, I'll make it worth your while. I know some stuff that will sell a lot of newspapers."

"Call me Sophie. I might be willing to stand for your bail, if you can tell me what you're peddling."

"Peddling?"

"What you can tell me about who was behind the robbery of Middleburg Sporting Goods?"

"They catch Rog yet?"

"Roger Richardson?"

Brad nodded. "That's right. I'd feel a lot better spilling my guts if that crazy fuck was off the streets."

"Lieutenant Roger Richardson is back on the job as a math teacher at the academy," she said. "There is no physical evidence to support your contention that he participated in the burglary."

"What? His fingerprints must have been all over the gun shop ... the Blazer, too."

"They were, but the gun shop owner remembers him from the day before. Said he was interested in buying a deer rifle for his nephew. As for the Blazer, Richardson reported it as stolen two days before the burglary. That explains his fingerprints ... in both places. The state police know there was another person involved in the burglary, but neither trooper got a good enough look at your accomplice to identify him."

"That puts me in deep shit, doesn't it?"

"Even deeper than you may think."

"What do you mean by that?"

"Richardson claims you stole his Blazer and that you implicated him because he gave you five demerits for a uniform violation that landed you on KP."

"So I'm facing car theft charges, too?"

The incredulous look on his pimply face made Sophie want to cry.

"Jesus Christ! What kind of rat bastard do they make me out for? Do you think I'd steal a truck and falsely accuse someone of a crime just because I had to wash a few pots and pans? Mom and Dad must. They've left me here to rot."

Brad knuckled snot from his upper lip with his free hand.

"I don't know what to think," Sophie replied. "I don't know you well enough to reach those sorts of conclusions. I do know this, though."

"What?"

"Richardson has an alibi. He's got a reputable witness who swears that they were on a fishing trip along the Juniata River. He says that he and Richardson camped out overnight on an island and didn't get back until the day after the robbery."

"Who's the witness?"

"Bill Kambic."

"Major Kambic, the vice president of the academy?"

"That's right."

"He always seemed like a straight shooter to me. Why would he lie for Rog?"

"I have no way of telling whether he's lying or you are," Sophie said.

"I thought you were on my side."

"I'm not on anybody's side ... other than my own. You want a get-out-of-jail card? I need some quid pro quo before that happens."

"What's that mean?"

"It means that you have to tell me something verifiable to whet my interest before I agree to help you out."

Sophie hated herself for playing hardball with this kid, but she'd been a journalist long enough to put up a wall between what was right and what was in the best interest of the newspaper and its readers. And her personal feelings couldn't be part of that equation. What she thought didn't matter. What she could prove was the essence of the thing.

"OK. The gun shop was phase one of a two-part operation to equip a squad of the Blue Mountain Militia for a special mission," Brad said.

"What special mission?"

"That info was above my pay grade, although I could make a pretty good guess, if you gave me the proper incentive," Brad said. "But I can tell you about phase two for ... what did you call it? Quid pro quo?"

"Shoot."

"Phase two is the robbery of the First National Bank of Liverpool," Brad said. "Rog and I cased the place, together, two Saturdays ago."

"Interesting, but hardly verifiable."

"I rented a safe deposit box there," Brad said.

"So?"

"Would you like to know what I put in the box?"

"Sure."

"A loaded Colt 1911 .45. Rog stole it from the armory at the military academy."

Sophie's pulse quickened. "Why?"

"Wells Fargo delivers a fresh batch of cash the beginning of each month. I was going to use the gun to rob the bank ... from the inside out. And Rog was going to drive the getaway car."

"Sounds like Rog was prepared to leave you holding the bag, just like the gun shop gig."

Brad shook his head vigorously. "Don't think so. He said it was special ops training for the big job coming up."

"The one above your pay grade?"

Brad smiled. "Maybe it was and maybe it wasn't. Bail me out a jail and I'll prove what I'm saying is true. I've got a video."

Sophie leaned forward in her chair. "A video of what?"

"Of me and Rog and a few of the officers of the Blue Mountain Militia planning the gun shop and bank jobs ... I uploaded the video to YouTube."

Brad read the panic on Sophie's face.

"Relax. It's password protected. You'll need my YouTube user name and password, which I'll give you as soon as you post my bail and get me out of here!"

Chapter 15

3:30 p.m. Monday, August 22, La Jolla, CA
Rev uncrossed his legs and tugged straight the creases on his khaki Dockers for the hundredth time. He was seated on a loveseat next to a fireplace in the lobby of the Grande Colonial Hotel in La Jolla. He could hear glasses clinking and a woman's laughter coming from the bar, which was just a few steps away.

He licked his lips and imagined what a cold beer would feel like sliding down his throat right now. His wristwatch, which he had reset to PDT, read 3:30 in the afternoon, but his biological clock operated on EDT and told him cocktail hour was nigh.

Chad Tucci was 15 minutes late for their appointment. Rev wondered if there had been some misunderstanding about the time or if Tucci had decided that he had better things to do than talk to a colleague from Harrisburg, Pennsylvania. He'd sounded friendly enough over the phone.

It was Tucci, in fact, who had suggested that they meet at the Grande Colonial.

"Sure I remember that hit-and-run," Tucci said when Rev called him on Sunday afternoon. "There was something fishy about that accident, as I recall, but I'll have to take a run through my notebook morgue."

"You still have a notebook you used forty years ago? I thought I was a pack rat, you must be—"

Tucci finished the sentence for him. "Obsessive compulsive? Not quite. Or at least only with topics that were really important to me."

"Such as my great granduncle Jake?"

"Such as Ronald Reagan. I was the political reporter for the *Union Tribune* in those days. Reagan had won the California republican primary for president the day before and some of his key advisers were meeting at the Grande Colonial to see if they could map out a strategy to wrest the republican nomination from Richard Nixon."

"So you just happened upon Uncle Jake's accident?"

"That's right. Let me see if I can dig up that notebook and we'll meet in the lobby of the Grande Colonial. Sometimes it helps me to return to the scene of the crime. Jogs my memory. That sort of thing."

"How will I know you?"

"What do you look like?"

Rev told him.

"It shouldn't be too hard to find a skinny, six-foot-five guy with black hair, but you could make it easier on me by sitting on the sofa next to the fireplace in the lobby."

Which was why Rev Polk didn't stray into the bar. Even though it was by his reckoning 6:30 and a beer would have tasted divine. His patience soon was rewarded. A short, slender man with thin, neatly parted white hair, wearing a polo shirt, tartan golf shorts, and boat shoes with no socks, strode into the lobby and walked toward him. The old man had a dark surfer's complexion that looked as if it had been applied chemically at a tanning parlor.

Rev stood and found himself staring at the top of the old man's head.

Tucci stuck out his hand. "You must be Rev Polk. Sorry I'm late. We ran into a slow foursome on the back nine."

Tucci studied Polk up and down. "They sure grow them tall in Harrisburg, Pennsylvania."

A response flew to Polk's lips before his internal editor could slash it with a red pen. "And they sure grow them small in San Diego, California."

By that time, the two men had clasped hands. Tucci reacted by pumping Polk's hand with even more enthusiasm. "Well-spoken, sir. I deserved that."

His smile was genuine. "Follow me. Let's visit the scene of the crime."

They walked out onto Prospect Avenue. The afternoon sun, filtered by a high haze, cast the buildings and cars in subtle pastels. Rev pulled a pair of Ray-Bans from his shirt pocket and put them on. In so doing, he lost a step or two on Tucci, who walked with such vigor that Rev had to hurry to catch up.

Tucci stopped abruptly. "I was standing right about here when the accident occurred in the crosswalks right there." He pointed to parallel lines drawn on Prospect Avenue, about 25 yards ahead.

"So you witnessed the accident?"

"I had just left a meeting with one of Ronald Reagan's principal political advisers. He called me at the newspaper and requested an audience at the Grande Colonial ... wanted to critique Nixon's plan to end the war in Vietnam."

"What was the adviser's name?"

"I'm not sure I remember," Tucci said.

For the first time Rev's reporter radar kicked in. Tucci was hiding something. But what?

Tucci patted his shirt pocket and pulled out his own sunglasses, which he settled on his nose. "Ah, that's better. Now what was the guy's name? Finklestein? Finkenbinder? Damn! I just can't remember."

Tucci's words were machine gun quick, nervous, almost manic.

"Fink. That's right his name was Fink. Bill Fink, funny name that. Fink said that Nixon's campaign strategy on the Vietnam War was an insult to the intelligence of good men. To tell you the truth, I agreed with him. Nixon was telling everyone that he knew how to end the war but he wouldn't reveal his plan until he was elected. It was a silly strategy and Fink and I had a good laugh about it. He told me that the smart money was fleeing to Reagan, who, if he played his cards right, would win the republican nomination on the third or fourth ballot. You paying attention, son?" Tucci asked.

"Huh?"

"You're giving me that thousand-yard stare. What's on your mind?"

Rev lied. "I was thinking that I would have liked to work with you."

Tucci lifted his sunglasses from the bridge of his nose and stared at Rev intently for a moment before dropping them back into place. "I'll take that as a compliment."

"I meant it as one."

"Where was I? Oh yes. My head was spinning with ideas as I walked along this sidewalk. I was writing the lead of my story in my head. Once I get the lead right the rest of the story just flows."

Rev nodded. "Me too."

"I saw your uncle step off the curb on the other side of the street there."

"Actually, he's my great granduncle, or something like that."

"Right. Your grandmother's uncle. I'll call him Jake, that's easier. Jake made it about a third of the way across when I heard tires squealing as a car rounded the corner there at Jenner and Prospect. The car accelerated as it completed the turn and must have been going 50 mph or so when it struck Jake, who by then had made it to the middle of the street."

"Did you get the license number?"

"Nope. It happened in a flash. I'm sorry if this is painful, but the impact tossed Jake up in the air a good ten feet and he came down on his head. The car never even slowed down. Just kept on accelerating as if nothing had happened."

"You said on the phone that there was something fishy about the accident ..."

"I reviewed my files. All I could find was a note I wrote to myself forty years ago. It said 'young man at Jake's house?'"

"What's that mean?"

"Don't know."

"Doesn't sound fishy to me," Rev said.

Tucci tapped his temple. "Sorry about that. Old brain."

Brakes screeched. A horn blared in the street. A young woman in the crosswalks where Jake had died turned to confront the driver of a red Jeep Cherokee who had stopped just inches from a collision. The young woman glared at the driver, gave him the finger, and moved, grudgingly, out of the way. The driver blew his horn and burned rubber as he accelerated on down Prospect Avenue.

Tucci tugged a handkerchief from his back pocket and mopped his brow with it. "Whew. That was close. Thought history was about to repeat itself."

Rev ignored the interruption. "Where did you get the details about Jake's service record?"

"What?"

"Your story talked about his service in the navy ... at the Battle of Midway. Where did you get that information?"

"I don't know. Probably cribbed it from his obituary."

"It wasn't in his obituary, at least not in the death notice Nona gave me," Rev said.

"Who's Nona?"

"My grandmother."

"Of course."

"You positive you can't remember anything else?"

Tucci bristled. "Listen, son, it was forty years ago. You're lucky I retrieved that much from this old data bank."

Rev relaxed. Exhaled. "You're right. I was being pushy. I was expecting far too much from such a cold case. It's just that I hate to disappoint Nona. She raised me ... after my mother died ..."

Avuncular now, Tucci stepped forward and patted Rev on the back.

"That's all right. No offense taken. I'm grasping at straws here, but I think that note I wrote myself all those years ago was a reminder to interview a young man I encountered at Jake's house after the accident. I went there to see if his next of kin could give me any reason he might have been murdered."

"Murdered?" Rev said.

Tucci was nonplussed. "Well, it could have been murder. Sure looked to me like the driver of that car was aiming to run Jake down."

"So it comes down to my investigating a forty-some-year-old accident that might have been a murder, without any real leads. Talk about your cold case," Rev said. He hated himself for sounding so whiny and he glanced at Tucci to gauge his reaction.

Tucci looked ... sympathetic. He pulled an old notebook from his back pocket and flipped through it.

"Ah. Here it is: 4606 Altadena Avenue, San Diego. That's where your uncle used to live. I'd go there if I were you. Talk to the current property owner. Ring some doorbells nearby. You're a reporter. You know the routine."

"That's all you've got?" Rev asked.

Tucci stroked his chin. Something surfaced for a moment in his expression. Was it resolve, regret, or indecision? Or some combination thereof? Rev's receiver wasn't tuned to the right channel and the moment passed.

"Yeah. That's all I got. Go visit Jake's old house. That's the best I can do for you."

Chapter 16

11 a.m. Tuesday, August 23, 2011, Selinsgrove, PA

Sophie wished she had worn slacks rather than her distract-the-enemy skirt, which she had tugged down as far as possible after settling into the driver's seat of her 2010 Ford Fusion. Johnston Bradley occupied the passenger's seat next to her.

Had she done the right thing, bailing him out of jail? She'd revealed some cleavage during her meeting with the bail bondsman and he'd slashed his fee. Cost her $1,500. Money she had set aside for a vacation to Nevis. But, what the hell. If this panned out, Gray Collingsworth, with the proper motivation, would let her recoup the loss on her expense account.

She had plugged her destination into the on-board navigation system of her new Ford. The computer voice guided her along Old Colony Road from the prison and told her to make a left turn onto Salem Road.

Sophie noticed that a black Ford F-150 pickup with deeply tinted windows and oversized tires had filled up her rearview mirror.

"That guy must be in a real hurry," she said.

"What?"

Sophie waggled a thumb over her shoulder. "That pickup is right on my tail. Hope we come to a straight stretch so he can pass."

She glanced in the rearview mirror again. No change. The pickup was a car length or less from her back bumper. She tapped her brakes and the pickup slowed behind her, maintaining its relative position. Still way too close for comfort.

Brad pulled a folded piece of paper from his shirt pocket. "I've got something for you."

"What's that?"

"Quid pro quo. The username and password for the YouTube account so you can watch the video."

"I was planning to watch it with you, so you can commentate."

"Commentate?"

"Yeah, you know, give me the story behind the story like football analysts on TV."

"Oh, yeah, right."

"I was planning to buy you lunch at BJ's Steak and Rib House in Selinsgrove. I'm told it's the best eating in town, and they have a hotspot so we can watch the video while we eat."

Up ahead, a white panel van with black lettering on the side backed onto Salem Road from a driveway. The van began to move slowly to the east. Sophie slowed, but she still closed quickly on the van. She checked the pickup in her rearview mirror. If anything it had edged even closer. With her attention on the pickup behind her, Sophie didn't see the van in front of her lurch to a stop, almost until it was too late.

"Shit!"

She slammed on the brakes, hoping the pickup driver would react in time to avoid rear-ending her.

She had been traveling at about 40 mph and the abrupt deceleration had both Sophie and Brad straining forward against their safety belts. The brakes of the pickup screamed behind her. The pickup fishtailed, filling her rearview mirror again. It screeched to a halt with a soft bump that told her it had nudged her back bumper.

In her mirror, she saw the front driver's side door of the pickup fly open. A short, squat man wearing jeans, work boots, and a t-shirt emerged from the pickup and started toward her car.

Her car doors automatically locked when she hit 15 mph, so she felt insulated from the road rage that apparently was building behind her.

She wasn't prepared for the tall man with shoulder-length hair who emerged from the panel van in front of her. He was wearing cutoff jeans, sneakers, and a sleeveless t-shirt that exposed elaborate tattooed curlicues decorating both arms from shoulder to elbow.

More troubling was the huge handgun he grasped in his right hand.

The men split up. The one with the gun came to her side of the car and the short man who had emerged from the pickup went behind her Ford and leaned on the front-door panel next to Brad, who turned and gave him the finger.

The tall guy tapped on her side window with the barrel of his pistol and said, "Hey, Brad! Tell her to roll down the window so I don't have to break it out."

"You know these guys?" Sophie asked.

Brad nodded. He slipped the piece of paper with the YouTube information between his seat and the console, winked at her, and mouthed the words "quid pro quo."

"I'd do as he says if I were you," Brad said out loud.

Sophie activated the auto-down feature of her window.

The tall guy tucked the gun in the waistband of his cutoffs. "That's better than a broken window isn't it?"

"Who are you and what do you want?" Sophie asked.

"I've come to collect Brad and to offer you some advice."

Sophie looked at Brad. He seemed surprised, but not frightened.

"It's OK, Sophie. I'll go with them. They won't hurt me. I know them."

"So, what's the advice?" Sophie asked.

The tall guy fingered the butt of his pistol. "You and your boyfriend need to back off the story you're working on. If you keep after it, bad things will happen ... to the both of you."

"I don't have a boyfriend."

"Sure you do. Rev Polk. Works for the *Telegraph* just like you do."

"He's not my boyfriend," Sophie said, just to buy time. She was confused. What did Rev have to do with the Johnston Bradley story? Sure, he'd provided background on Colonel Simpson, but that was pillow talk. How would anybody know that unless they had bugged Rev's bedroom? That thought creeped her out and she shivered. "What story?"

"You're a smart chippie; you'll figure it out. Just back off! Coming, Brad?"

Brad punched the button unlocking his door. The short man opened the door from the outside and stepped back. "Come with me. My ride is much better than that piece of shit Jerry drives."

Brad stepped out of Sophie's car.

"Make sure you make all your court appearances!" Sophie yelled.

Brad turned and leaned back into the car. "I'll be there, Sophie. I really appreciate what you've done for me. Maybe I'll see you out there in cyberspace."

The short guy grabbed Brad's arm and escorted him back to the pickup truck.

Meanwhile, the tall guy ran back to his van. He made a three-point turn and took off heading west on Salem Road. As he passed by, Sophie read the lettering on the side of the van: "Jerry's

Plumbing Service, Selinsgrove, PA." Behind her the pickup reversed, turned, and followed the van.

Sophie jotted down both license plate numbers in her notebook. She took a deep breath, shifted her Ford into drive, and quickly abandoned any thoughts of trying to follow the two vehicles.

Her assailants obviously were unconcerned about her calling the police. And why shouldn't they be? Brad had left with them willingly, and if she told police that she had been threatened with a gun, well, it would be her word against theirs.

She continued east on Salem Road toward Selinsgrove, wondering what to do next.

Her phone was synced with the on-board computer in her car. She pushed a button on her steering wheel. The computer chimed and its electronic voice said: "Please say a command."

"Phone."

"Phone," the computer repeated. "Please say a command."

"Call Liv."

She answered on the second ring.

"Hey, Liv. Can you meet me at BJ's in Selinsgrove in about 15 minutes?"

"Hey. You're in town? That's great. I'd love to see you, but can you give me 30? It's my day off. I just got out of the shower. I need some time to pull myself together."

"Sure, 30 minutes works. It will give me time to shake hands with a Bloody Mary. I need to steady my nerves."

"Yeah, you sound a little off, girl. What's up?"

"I'll tell you over lunch. I've got some information about the gun shop burglary that I think you'll find interesting."

Chapter 17

12:30 p.m. Tuesday, August 23, 2011, Selinsgrove, PA

Liv Pearson looked nothing like a state police trooper as she slid into a high-backed wooden booth next to her good friend Sophie Anderson at BJ's Steak and Ribs in Selinsgrove. Without her uniform and gun, she looked more like an underclassman at Susquehanna University, whose students and faculty, come 8:00 p.m., would jam the joint with demands for ribs, wings, and beer.

Pearson was five-six-ish, honey blonde, and slight. Her tough-guy demeanor was the final piece of her state police uniform. She put it on after squaring up her gun belt and clinching tight her hat. Today, she was dressed in civvies—designer jeans, a sleeveless blouse, and sandals. Her toenails were painted blue.

"How's your love life now that you've shed Rev Polk?" Liv asked without preamble.

Sophie laughed. "That's my girl. Always cut to the chase. Shedding Rev is a work in progress."

Liv studied her friend like a scientist considering a lab specimen. "Ugh, I can tell by the look on your face. You've slept with him again."

"Just once. It was OK, but ..."

"But what?"

"Too much baggage. He asked me for absolution for Christ's sake."

Liv raised an eyebrow. "Absolution from what?"

Sophie cut her eyes back and forth, looking for eavesdroppers. "For killing some civilians-in Iraq." Sophie sighed. "Dammit, Liv. I can't absolve him. I'm not even sure I have it in me to forgive him myself. Anyway ... I have a couple of days to figure out how to tell him that it's over. For real this time. He's chasing a story in San Diego."

"I thought you said that the newspaper had laid him off."

"It did. Actually, he's doing a favor for his grandmother. She wants him to get to the bottom of a hit-and-run accident that killed her uncle more than 40 years ago."

Liv pretended to shiver. "Talk about a cold case."

"Frozen, but I did help him file a Freedom of Information request for a special military operation the old guy was involved in way back in 1945. I've got a friend, a GS-13, who is expediting the paperwork."

"Interesting."

Sensing a lack of conviction in her friend's voice, Sophie veered sharply to the matter at hand. "The case the two of us are working on has heated up, though."

The perfumed debutante sitting next to Sophie abruptly became a state police trooper. "I'm working a case. You're working a story. You've got to keep that distinction straight!"

"Me-ow!"

Liv giggled from behind her tough-cop mask. "OK, whadaya got?"

They were interrupted by a waitress wearing a name tag that read "Millie."

"Hi, I'm Millie. I'll be your server," she said, unnecessarily.

"I'll have a Yuengling draft and a steak salad with Ranch dressing," Liv said.

Sophie hadn't even bothered to look at the menu. "Wow that was quick."

"I eat here often, don't I, Millie?" Liv asked.

The question took Millie by surprise. "What? Oh. Hi, Trooper Pearson. I didn't recognize you with your clothes off."

Liv hid a smile behind her hand.

Millie blushed. "I meant without your uniform."

"I know what you meant, Millie."

"And I'll have the same thing," Sophie said. "But could you substitute grilled chicken for the steak?"

Millie departed for the kitchen and Sophie wrested her laptop from the bag at her feet.

While her Toshiba warmed up, Sophie described how she had bailed Johnston Bradley out of jail only to have him kidnapped.

"You should have called 9-1-1 right away," Liv said. "Goddamn it, Sophie, it's a sure case of terroristic threats at the least. Hell, I'd probably tack on simple assault to give the DA some wiggle room on a plea bargain. You sure Brad was OK with leaving with them?"

"He seemed to be. Told me he'd be sure to make his court dates and that maybe he'd see me out there in cyberspace."

"Did you get the license plate numbers?" Liv asked.

Sophie nodded.

"Gimmie."

Sophie dug her notebook out of her bag and flipped it open to the page on which she had written the license plate numbers.

Liv pulled her cell phone from her purse. She punched in a number and drummed her fingers on the tabletop while she was waiting to be connected.

"Who's this? Hey, Bill. Pearson here. Could you run a couple of tags for me?" She read off the numbers. "Yeah, that's right. Call me at 444-3129 when you've got something. Thanks."

Liv put her cell phone on the tabletop. "He'll get back to us in a few minutes. So, what else you got?"

Sophie paused with her hands poised over the keyboard of her laptop. She waved a finger. "Give me a minute."

Millie showed up at that moment with their beers, one of which spewed frothy foam on the tabletop next to Sophie's laptop.

Sophie dabbed at the beer with her napkin while the laptop booted. "Good. Computer's recognized an unsecure wireless network," she said, more to herself than to her companion.

"What are you doing?" Liv asked.

"Accessing a video that Brad uploaded on YouTube. He says that it will prove that the gun shop burglary was a conspiracy of the Blue Mountain Boys."

"Those quacks?"

"You know about them?"

"Most local police officers do. They practice at shooting ranges. We practice at shooting ranges. We've met."

"Who's in charge?" Sophie asked.

"Depends on who you talk to. The guy I know best is named Colin Butdorf. Says he's a captain in the militia. He's an ex-Green Beret. Served in the Gulf War. We went out a couple of times. A nice enough guy, but his politics are to the right of Attila the Hun. But, then, my sergeant, the guy in charge at Selinsgrove, is almost as reactionary. These are weird times, Sophie."

"You got that right. The whole world's going nutty at the same time journalism is going into the toilet. It won't be long before there's no one left to record the craziness, except for the special interest bloggers and who the hell is vetting them?"

Millie showed up with their salads. Liv sent her back to the waitress station for a clean fork because the one rolled up in her napkin was caked with gunk.

Sophie, meanwhile, entered Brad's username and password into the appropriate fields. "I'm in!"

Liv arose and slid onto the bench seat beside Sophie, forgetting for the moment about her dirty silverware.

The YouTube viewing window went from black to gray and a spinning circle announced that the video was loading. Johnston Bradley's pimply face filled the screen.

Sophie noticed that the audio was turned down on her computer. She adjusted the volume.

"There that should do it," Brad said.

He stepped back from the camera.

"He must have been using the webcam on his laptop," Liv said.

The webcam captured the retreating form of Johnston Bradley, who walked across the room and took a seat at a chair with his back to the camera. The angle of the shot suggested that his laptop was positioned on a high shelf in a paneled office.

Centered in the viewfinder was a large oak desk. Pennsylvania's state flag and the Stars and Stripes were positioned along the back wall on either side of the desk. Directly behind the desk was a gun cabinet.

"That's Colonel Simpson's office at the military academy," Sophie said.

The audio captured the sound of a door opening and a man's voice.

"Why hello, Brad. I like a man who shows up early for a meeting."

The newcomer passed in front of the camera and sat down in Colonel Simpson's chair. His hair was cut in a military buzz cut. A prominent nose, lazy right eye, and thick black horned-rim glasses dominated his features. He was wearing army camos.

"You know him?" Liv asked.

Sophie shook her head. "What are those pins on his collar?"

"They're oak leaves: the collar insignia of a major in the army," Liv said.

"How do you know that?"

"Cops know a lot of things."

"Well, if he's a major, my guess is that it's Bill Kambic, vice president of the academy, the guy who alibied Roger Richardson," Sophie said.

"How do you know that?" Liv asked around a mouthful of salad.

"You told me. On the phone."

"Remind me to be more reticent around reporters," Liv said.

Sophie punched pause on the video and opened a new window in Internet Explorer. She navigated to the Oliver Hazard Perry Military Academy's website and clicked on the tab marked administration. She scrolled past Colonel Simpson's picture and bio and arrived at Kambic's.

"Yep that's Bill Kambic all right. Lazy eye and all," Liv said.

Sophie closed the window and resumed the video.

Another man came into the room and sat down in a chair next to Johnston Bradley. His features were visible in profile.

"That's Roger Richardson," Liv said. "I interviewed him in person the day after the robbery. He denies it, but I'm pretty sure he's the bastard that escaped into the woods and left Brad holding the bag on the gun shop burglary. Just couldn't see him well enough in the dark."

"Well, men, now that we have a quorum, let's get this meeting started," Kambic said on the video.

"Can you turn that up a little? I'm having trouble hearing it," Liv said.

Sophie bumped the volume to maximum.

"Brief me on where we stand on the arms deal," Kambic said.

"I've scouted the gun shop and didn't see an alarm system. Should be pretty easy to break in," Richardson said.

"Gotcha," Liv exulted.

Sophie paused the video. "Yeah, but is it admissible? I get the feeling that this might fall in the category of an illegal wire tap."

"You let me worry about that. Play the video."

Sophie did and the spinning circle resumed on a black screen. "Damn. Must have lost the signal. She checked her connection status. "Nope. Four bars. What the fuck?"

A dialogue box opened and the gremlins that abided in Sophie's laptop informed them: "The video you requested is no longer available."

Liv's cell phone chirped. She looked at the screen. "It's Bill at DMV." She answered the phone. "Whadaya got?"

Liv moved her thumb up and down as if she were clicking a pen. Sophie nodded and slid her notebook and a pen down the tabletop to her friend.

Liv jotted the information on a blank page in Sophie's notebook. "Got it. Thanks, Bill." She stowed her cell phone in her purse and sighed. "Got to go home and change into my uniform— on my day off. I think Jerry Slike and Furnley Franklin will take me more seriously if I'm official."

"Furnley? How will you be able to take someone named Furnley seriously?"

"Oh, I'll take him seriously, all right. Jerry Slike, too. He's the owner of the van and probably the son of a bitch who threatened you with a gun. These bastards are armed and dangerous, Sophie.

You're going to have to sit this one out, although I may call you in to identify them once they've been ... neutralized."

Her evil grin demonstrated that no matter how Liv dressed, underneath there was always a doberman with sharp teeth ... and claws.

Chapter 18

9:30 a.m. (PDT) Tuesday, August 23, 2011, San Diego, CA

Rev Polk glanced at his wristwatch and seethed at the traffic piled up in front of him like segments of a huge caterpillar. His flight didn't leave until 1:30, but Nona had rented the car on priceline.com and to ensure the cheap rate he had to have it back by 11:30 a.m.

That gave him two hours to negotiate his way along unfamiliar roads and through heavy traffic to the airport, including the stop he planned to make at Jake's old address. He'd brought his portable GPS along, but he hadn't updated the software in ages. Who knew how reliable the disembodied female who resided therein would be in these unfamiliar climes.

The temperature already had topped 70 degrees. Earlier that morning, over his complimentary continental breakfast at the Hampton Inn, television weatherman Kearney Mesa had predicted a high of 84.

His GPS told him to expect the trip of eight and a half miles to take 15 minutes. He had been on the road for 30 minutes already, but the clock had only counted down four minutes thanks to the goddamn traffic jam on I-805. He finally edged around a jackknifed tractor trailer and the road cleared before him.

"In 2.2 miles, turn right onto El Cajon Boulevard, Exit 16," intoned the woman resident in his GPS.

Rev didn't know what to expect as he followed the GPS's final instructions, "Just past 50th Street, turn left on Altadena Avenue. Your destination is two tenths of a mile ahead on the right."

Rev parked his car along the curb in front of a one-story Spanish-style house with a red tile roof. A low wall fronted the house, which, like the wall, was cream-colored and stucco. A flagstone walkway led from the sidewalk through a gate to a turret-shaped entryway, which divided the house neatly into two wings.

He climbed out of the car, stretched, and glanced to his left and right along the quiet street to see if there were any witnesses to his lunacy. Chad Tucci had been annoyingly circumspect in his suggestion that Rev might find some answers to his questions by visiting Jake's former house on Altadena Avenue. Using the Hampton Inn's free internet service, Rev accessed a reverse directory, hoping to find a phone number associated with that address. To no avail. Whoever lived there was keeping a low profile ... number unlisted.

And then there was that goddamn dream. Uncle Jake talking to him in the shadow of the USS *Enterprise*. Rev knuckled his eyes and stared at the house. Fallujah had knocked his psychic balance on its ear. His whole life seemed fuzzy now. It was as if he were watching himself go through the motions of living. Mundane tasks had assumed a weight not commiserate with their import. At times he was so paralyzed that it took an effort of will just to follow the imperative of a bursting bladder to the closest rest room.

"Get a grip on yourself, man. You can do this. Just walk up to the front door and knock."

As he neared the front door, which was painted the same red as the colorful roof tiles, he noticed a cardboard box on the stoop far enough back to be out of the door's path. Something furry was sticking out of the top of the box. He realized that it was the head of a cat. As he got closer, a horrible truth pounced: the cat was dead. Blood matted the fur around its nose and oozed from beneath a piece of duct tape that encircled the poor beast's snout, giving it a bizarre sort of tin-man grin. The flaps of the box top were folded about the head, supporting it and ensuring a grisly display for the homeowner when he opened the door.

Rev nudged the box with the toe of his shoe, hoping that it was a prank. That it was a stuffed animal smeared with lipstick. Some idiot's idea of a sick joke. But there was no doubt about it. PussPuss was dead. He knew the cat's name because it was written on the box top:

"Silence is golden. Just ask PussPuss."

What the hell did that mean? What had he stumbled into? He didn't need this in his life right at this moment. He was turning to leave when the door creaked open.

A tall, fit, Asian-looking man who appeared to be in his mid-60s stood at the door. He was wearing khaki slacks, a red polo shirt, and boat shoes without socks. He peered at Rev through thick, wire-rimmed bifocals.

"May I help you?" he asked.

"I'm hoping you might know someone who used to live at this address. What's your name?" Rev asked.

"Daniel Sh—" The man glanced to Rev's left. Saw the box. Saw the cat. "Oh my God! What am I going to tell the grandkids? They loved PussPuss."

He took off his glasses and wiped his eyes with his knuckles.

"I hope you don't think I had anything to do with this," Rev said.

The man settled his glasses back on his nose. "Why would I think that? This is a neighborhood fight and now it's escalated to the point that I'll have to call the police." He shook his head as if awakening from a bad dream. "Now, who are you and what can I do for you?"

Rev took a deep breath and rattled off his prepared spiel: "My name is Rev Polk. An ancestor of mine, Jacob Addison, used to live at this address. I'm in town on business and I promised his niece, my grandmother, Annie Mundy, that I'd stop by and see if anyone remembers him."

The man eyed him curiously. Rev felt uncomfortable because he had lied. Annie Mundy hadn't asked him to stop by. Chad Tucci had. But that was the sort of thing you just couldn't try to explain to a stranger.

"I'm afraid that I don't know very much about the former owners of this place, although the name Jake Addison is familiar."

"Why is that?"

"It's on a journal I found three months ago hidden away in a box in a crawl space above the entryway here." He motioned above his head with his right hand. "I've lived here for years, finally got around to some renovations."

"Do you still have the journal? Mister ... ?"

"Just call me Dan."

Dan stepped out on the porch, carefully avoiding the box containing his dead cat. He took several steps forward out onto the front walk and looked carefully to his left and right. Turning, he asked: "Do you have a briefcase or something in your car?"

"I have a computer case."

"That should work. Why don't you go get it? The journal is in pretty rough shape. You're welcome to it, but it would be better if you carried it away ... carefully, inside a briefcase."

Rev thought Dan was one weird duck, but if he was willing to part with Jake's journal, he'd play along.

"Sure. I'll go get it."

"OK. I'll leave the front door unlocked. Just come inside."

Rev collected his computer case. He stepped around PussPuss's remains and opened the front door. The foyer floor was hardwood. An oriental carpet runner stretched forward down a long hallway. Dan called from the back of the house.

"Come on back. I'm in the kitchen."

Rev walked past a dining room on the right and a living room on the left. He imagined that the kitchen and bedrooms were along the back of the house. And he was right.

Dan sat on a tall stool pulled up to an extended kitchen counter that obviously did double duty as a breakfast nook. A three-ring binder, the kind of notebook high school kids carry to class, sat on the counter top in front of him.

"It's a good thing you showed up. I was about to throw this away. My wife can't abide clutter. She's been bugging me to get rid of it."

"You're sure you don't mind?"

Dan smiled. "Mind? You'll be doing me a favor. I'm a pack rat married to a neat nick."

He motioned to the binder. "Go ahead. Take it."

The binder was heavy. Jake must have had a lot on his mind. Rev resisted the impulse to open it. He slid the binder into the front compartment of his computer bag and Velcroed it shut.

"Thank you."

Dan stood and glanced at his watch. "You're welcome. I don't mean to be rude, but my wife is due home in a few minutes, and I'd like to have poor PussPuss out of sight before she arrives."

"Of course."

Dan followed Rev down the front hall. Rev opened the door; they said their goodbyes on the front walk.

"I hope your grandmother finds some solace in her uncle's journal," Dan said.

"What do you mean by that? Have you read it?"

"Just a page or two. Jake seems to be a colorful character."

Rev cast his eyes back to the front porch. Back to poor PussPuss. "Well, OK. And sorry about your cat."

As he started down the walk, he heard Dan say, "You know I never really liked you, PussPuss. I put up with you because Lois loves you, the grandkids, too ..."

Rev settled in behind the wheel of his rental and sat for a few minutes, taking it all in. Dan's neat house; the flower beds sharply edged; the grass a healthy, well-watered green even in this arid clime. There was a subtext to his encounter with Dan, but the meaning of it escaped him. He studied the mailbox, noting the careful way Dan had emblazoned his last name in big black capital letters on its side. Rev smiled, put the key in the ignition, cranked the engine, and drove away.

Chapter 19

3 p.m. Tuesday, August 23, 2011, Middleburg, PA
Colonel Randolph Simpson lined up the disassembly notch on his 1911 Colt .45 and pressed the barrel pin. He removed the bushing and popped out the barrel. He had fired the gun that morning on the academy's pistol range. It reeked of gun powder. The rote of disassembling and cleaning his weapon served an ancillary purpose. It lubricated his mental mechanism, which needed a greasing because he was up to his ass in alligators. The press was all over the gun shop burglary and his senior staff was closing ranks around Lieutenant Roger Richardson, whom he longed to fire and be done with it.

The Ballistol left a Teflon silkiness on Simpson's fingertips as he massaged the cleaning lubricant into the recoil spring.

His phone rang. The private line. The one that circumvented the switchboard.

Simpson sighed, dropped the spring onto the hand towel he'd spread out on his desktop, and wiped his hands on a rag.

He picked up the handset and punched the blinking button on his desk phone.

"This is Colonel Simpson."

The voice on the other end was gravelly and abrupt. "Have you found my kid yet?"

"No. I'm afraid not, Mr. Bradley. He's kept a low profile since his release from prison."

"Who the hell bailed him out? I wanted him to stew in jail for a couple more days."

"Sophie Anderson, a reporter for the daily newspaper in Harrisburg, paid the bail bondsmen. I understand she is just as upset as you are. She was expecting more of a return on her money."

"What's her interest in Brad?"

"She seemed to think that he could tell her something about a wider conspiracy in the gun shop burglary."

"Brad is a true believer who has been deceived by the devil among you there at the academy. Pray you can root him out before he destroys all of you. And pray you find my son before I do."

There was an eerie quality to Bill Bradley's words. Randolph Simpson had grown up Methodist and had rubbed elbows with Pentecostals and Southern Baptists at church camp. The type of God men like Bill Bradley worshiped—cruel, vindictive, and more inclined to teach with the fist than the kind word—was nothing like what Randolph Simpson imagined God to be.

"Brad is 18 years old and an adult in the eyes of the law. As long as he makes his next court appearance the police are disinclined to intervene, although they are monitoring the situation."

Simpson realized he was talking to dead air. Cell phones were so anticlimactic. You couldn't slam down the receiver. Where was the catharsis in punching a button?

Simpson had little empathy for Bill Bradley, but he did feel guilty for what had happened to the man's son, who was serving as his spy among the ranks of the Blue Mountain Boys. The crazy politics of the militia had infested the middle management of the military academy and Simpson was determined to root it out. Bradley's disappearance made it difficult to close the net on Lieutenant Richardson. And Major Kambic's insistence that he and Richardson had been on a camping trip when the burglary occurred complicated the situation even further. Simpson knew that Brad was telling the truth and that Richardson and Kambic were lying. But why? And even more importantly, how could he prove it?

Typical of the sort of teacher willing to work for the puny salary offered by the academy, Richardson inched his way through East Stroudsburg University. He graduated, barely, with a 2.2 GPA, which explained why he ended up in the Pennsylvania National Guard rather than following the more prestigious path from West Point to the regular army. During his recent deployment in Afghanistan, Richardson hadn't shit his pants or shot a civilian, so the Guard, in its infinite wisdom, had promoted him to first lieutenant. Simpson had reviewed Richardson's personnel file and he knew that his predecessor had hired him because he was the only candidate for a position that had been open for three months.

Simpson's intercom buzzed. The voice of his secretary, Julie Dunby, floated toward him. "Lieutenant Richardson is here to see you."

"Send him in."

Roger Richardson slouched into his office with a fuck-you demeanor.

He grabbed the back of the colonel's visitor's chair and was about to sit down.

"Stay on your feet, Lieutenant. This won't take long. Major Kambic has vouched for you, so I'm not going to fire you ... even though Cadet Bradley has implicated you in the burglary of Middleburg Sporting Goods."

"Cadet Bradley is a vindictive reprobate," Richardson asserted with the conviction of a man who had just looked up the words "vindictive" and "reprobate" on dictionary.com. "I put him on KP and he saw this as a way to get even. It's as simple as that, Colonel."

"I've got this gut feeling that it's far more complicated than that. If this was the real army I'd have you posted to the motor pool in the Aleutians. You're the sort of officer who would have gotten fragged in Nam. It pisses me off that I'm forced to tolerate your kind, but my tolerance has its limits. You're on notice, Lieutenant. If I hear even one more whisper of impropriety on your part the door won't be able to hit you in the ass on the way out because my foot will get there first."

The tongue lashing straightened Richardson's spine and put color on his cheeks. But to his credit, he offered not a word in his defense, recognizing that would make things even worse. "Is that all, sir? I've got a class convening in 15 minutes."

"That's all. Get to your class."

Richardson made a parade ground about face and stalked from the office.

Simpson picked up a brush and sprayed Ballistol on the end of it. He inserted the brush into the barrel of his 1911. He pushed until the tip appeared at the other end then, turning the brush back and forth, slowly pulled it out. He sighted through the barrel to see if any powder residue remained.

His intercom buzzed. Julie said: "Colonel Simpson, I have a woman on the line who claims to represent Speaker of the House Samuel Jenkins. Says her boss wants to talk to you."

Simpson spent more time than was necessary wiping his hands on a rag. He owed Jenkins some allegiance because the speaker had gone to bat for him when the Abu Ghraib shit hit the fan, reducing him to this. He swept his eyes across his mean office, noting the fraying carpet; the cracks and nail pops in the drywall; the peeling paint on the door frame; the scratches on his desktop.

He picked up the phone and stabbed the blinking button. "This is Colonel Simpson."

The secretary's voice broadcast the arrogance of reflected power. "Hold for Speaker Jenkins."

Simpson bit his lip and endured the silence. His lower status ordained that he wait on hold while the speaker picked his undershorts out of his ass crack and sniffed his fingers.

"Colonel Simpson. How are you, sir?"

Simpson glanced at his watch. He'd been on hold for two minutes and thirty-three seconds, about par for the course.

"I'm doing fine. What can I do for you, Mr. Speaker?"

"It's more a matter of what I can do for you."

"What do you mean by that?"

"Well a little matter has come up here that I think you can help me with. If the result of our—" he paused to clear his throat— "collaboration is what I expect, well maybe, just maybe, your appointment to brigadier goes through after all and you can climb out of that shit hole in Pennsylvania."

Simpson wondered how to play this. His banishment to the military academy was a subterfuge. He was on a special assignment that required the appearance that he had been disgraced. He was collecting a brigadier's pay package from the U.S. government, even though, by all appearances, he was a disgraced army officer serving a bread-and-water sentence in purgatory.

"You still there, Colonel?"

"I'm listening."

"Good. Now, as you may know, our Democratic president has an imperial hair up his ass on the topic of domestic terrorism. He's impaneled a bipartisan committee to assess the threat of homegrown terrorism, which he'd love to link to the ultra-conservative wing of the Republican Party. I am trying to rein in this witch hunt and I want you to help me."

Simpson decided to be non-committal. "You're on the committee?" he asked

"That's right. My clipping service has flagged some stories from the daily newspaper in Harrisburg that suggest that a group calling itself the Blue Mountain Boys has organized in your neck of the woods."

Simpson buttoned down his response. "I've read the stories, too, Mr. Speaker."

"Good. Then I won't have to get you up to speed. Anyway, I've dispatched Andy Hawk of my staff to assess the situation there on the ground in Harrisburg."

"Actually, it's Middleburg."

"Right. I'd like you to brief Andy on the lay of the land. Make some introductions for him among people familiar with the militia. You know, state police, the sheriff, local politicians. That sort of thing. Hell, you may even know some of the militia men themselves."

"And for that, you're willing to revisit my appointment to brigadier?"

"Well, there's obviously more to it than that. But this is an open phone line. It would be better if you and Andy discuss this in person. He'll be in touch. I'd like you to clear your calendar and give him as much time as he needs."

"I will, of course, make myself available to Mr. Hawk."

"Carry on then, soldier."

"Yes, sir," Simpson replied.

Chapter 20

12:30 p.m (PDT) Tuesday, August 23, 2011, San Diego, CA

Rev Polk's cell phone chirped incessantly in its little plastic bin on the conveyor belt as he stepped through the metal detector at San Diego International Airport. But the infernal machine beeped and he had to endure a wanding and a pat down. He snatched his cell phone from the bin, which also contained his keys and pocket change. He glanced at the display and saw that he had a missed call from Sophie.

That she had called pleased him more than was reasonable. He had taken their relationship for granted for far too long. He didn't realize how much being in a relationship had meant to him. Without that anchor he had drifted off into a sea of regret. Now that there was a glimmer of hope, he was determined not to mess things up.

He grabbed the handle of his carry-on and lifted it from the conveyor belt. He settled into a seat as far away from other passengers as possible in the lounge next to the departure gate and pressed the button to return her call.

Sophie answered on the third ring. "Hey, stranger."

"Hey yourself. Sorry I couldn't take your call earlier. I was going through airport security."

"You find out anything interesting about Nona's uncle?"

"Maybe. I got lucky. I went to his old house. The homeowner gave me a journal of Jake's that he found recently in his attic."

"I'd call that more than lucky. Miraculous would be a better word."

"You've got that right," Rev agreed.

The silence became awkward.

Sophie took a deep breath. "Actually, I called to deliver a warning from a man carrying a really big gun."

She had his attention now. "What do you mean by that?"

She told him about her encounter with the two men who had driven off with Johnston Bradley.

Rev's reaction was similar to Liv Pearson's. "Goddamn it, Sophie! How can you be so nonchalant? The man waved a gun at you for God's sake."

"Nonchalant doesn't describe it. I've had a day and a half to cool down. Right afterward it took a large lager to soothe my nerves."

She was lying, but it was a necessary deceit. The truth would have prolonged his agitation. Another tactic well learned in the war between the sexes—or should she say the exes? That was a dilemma for another day.

"So, the kid who burgled the gun shop is on the lam and you're on the hook for his bail?"

"Actually, the bail bondsman is."

"Wait a minute. You said something about a warning."

"That's right. From the tall guy with the long hair and the tats."

Rev interrupted. "The one with the gun?"

"Yep."

"What's the message?"

"That me and my boyfriend, and by that I assume he meant you, should lay off the story we're working on."

"Is that a direct quote, or are you paraphrasing?"

"I wasn't taking notes. Not with that big pistol sticking out of the waistband of his cutoff jeans. But I'm fairly certain that he did say this: 'If you keep after it, bad things will happen ... to the both of you.'"

"That's it?"

"Yep."

"What story are we working on?" Rev asked.

"That's what I've been asking myself ever since. We discussed the gun burglary after dinner at your place and later ..."

"In bed. Yeah. I remember."

"You sure you didn't discuss our conversation with anyone?" Sophie asked.

"Yes!"

"That's what I figured. And if that's the case, the only thing I can think of is that he was referring to our Freedom of Information filing for Operation Setting Sun. Both of our names are on the application."

"Shit," Rev said. "How could a World War II special op and a forty-year-old hit-and-run case in San Diego have anything to do with a gun shop burglary in Snyder County, Pennsylvania?"

"Beats me."

After she'd hung up with Rev, Sophie stared out her kitchen window and drummed her fingers on the counter top. For some reason, Johnston Bradley's final words to her as he climbed out of her car came back to her in a rush.

What was it he said?

"Maybe I'll see you out there in cyberspace."

Sophie wasn't due at work until 5 p.m. to prep for a city council meeting at 7:00. Grayson Collingsworth was on a rampage: "No more overtime!"

Luxuriating in the intimacy of being alone in her own house with only her thoughts to keep her company, Sophie ran some water into her electric tea kettle and plugged it in. She put two tea bags in a mug and collected her laptop from its case in her bedroom. She sat down on a stool at her kitchen counter and booted up her laptop while she waited for the kettle to do its thing. She found the gurgling hiss of the kettle comforting.

She launched Internet Explorer and navigated to YouTube. She clicked on the blue highlighted "sign in" link and entered the username and password Johnston Bradley had given her.

Her pulse raced when she saw that there was a new link for a video. She clicked on it and Brad's image flickered onto her screen.

He was in a dark room, sitting at a desk illuminated in the faint light of a goose-neck study lamp. The right side of his face glowed in the lamplight. Shadows consumed the left side of his face.

"Hey, Sophie," Brad whispered. "Sorry I had to take down the other video. I did it to prove to them I am still on the team. These dudes are way scarier than Rog. They're talking some really wild shit. They're probably just blowing smoke, but Furn tells me there's going to be this big meeting tomorrow afternoon to plan an assassination. Says I'm invited, too. That this will be my chance to meet the general. I volunteered to videotape the meeting for distribution among militia members. Jerry seems to think that's a good idea. They want me to copy it to DVD, but my plan is to stream the video live to my website. Check your work e-mail. The one they publish below your byline in the newspaper. I've sent you the web address and a password. You should be able to record the meeting on your laptop. Then you'll be able to prove what these dudes are up to. How's that for quid pro quo?"

Sophie heard the sound of muffled voices off camera.

Brad turned his head and looked over his shoulder away from the webcam. "Don't these guys ever sleep? Got to go. Check your e-mail."

The video ended abruptly.

Sophie exited YouTube and pulled up her e-mail account. Sure enough, she had a message from Brad.

It read: "Hey Sophie. Here's the address for my website— http://www.JohnBrad615.com. The password is all lowercase 'radiohead521.' Tune in about 6:00 p.m. and watch the show. These assholes are talking about killing the president."

Sophie snatched her cell from the tabletop and selected a number from her electronic address book.

"Hey, Gray," she said when the editor picked up. "The gun shop case is really heating up. I need to borrow Chuck Wennington this afternoon for some computer geek stuff, and I won't be able to cover city council tonight. Get Fulkroad to fill in. He's just as familiar with the incinerator bond controversy as I am and he would welcome the extra hours."

"I don't know about that," Gray said. "The publisher is all over my ass about overtime. We're in a situation here, financially. You know that."

"And we're in a situation here, romantically," she reminded him.

She could hear him sweat.

"I hate it when you do that," he said, his voice hoarse.

"Do what?" she asked, feigning innocence.

"Take all the time you need," he said, finally. "Just keep me up to speed with developments."

"That's my boy," Sophie said. "Always willing to catch up."

Chapter 21

2 p.m. (MDT) Tuesday, August 23, 2011, somewhere over Nevada

Rev didn't get to read Jake's journal until about forty minutes into the crowded flight to Chicago. His seat mate was fat and talkative.

"I'm Bill Buffington," he announced. "Pleased to meet ya. I work in IT. Just finished a big job in San Diego. I'll sure be glad to land at O'Hare. These crowded flights are a real bitch for someone my size." He patted his belly. "I'll swear the airlines shrink the seats a little more each time I fly."

Rev had no interest in the relative merits of Mac and IBM servers and their attendant software, but he listened politely as Big Bill prattled on and on. It was obvious that the guy was a white-knuckle flier, and to ignore him would risk a messy meltdown.

When Bill finally excused himself to go to the bathroom, Rev wasted a few moments of his life wondering how Big Bill would navigate in the tiny lavatory. Pushing that image aside, Rev stood and wrestled his carry-on from the overhead compartment. He pulled out Jake's journal, dropped it on his seat, and re-stowed the carry-on in the overhead.

Bill emerged from the lavatory, ran his hand down the front of his trousers to make sure his zipper was up, and lumbered down the aisle. Rev stepped back so Bill could climb into his center seat.

Rev picked up Jake's journal and sat down, grimacing as he struggled to reestablish his personal space with as little contact with Big Bill as possible.

"Whatcha got there?" Bill asked.

Rev lied. "I've got a big meeting coming up as soon as I land in Harrisburg. I need to be up to speed with this by then. So you're going to have to excuse me."

Big Bill wasn't going to give up that easily. "What do you do for a living, Rev?"

"I'm an evangelist. I'm doing some church seeding in Harrisburg. Tell me, Bill, have you accepted Jesus Christ as your lord and savior?"

"Uh. Actually, I'm Jewish." Bill grabbed his newspaper from the seat pocket in front of him, and Rev was free, at long last, to peek inside the binder.

There had to be 200 typewritten pages or more. The first forty or so pages were familiar, the same as the chapters Nona had shared with him. But Rev was excited to see how much new material there was. Flipping through the pages, he noticed only a couple of strike throughs. The deep impressions on the paper indicated that Jake had a heavy hand on the keys. He imagined Jake was a two-finger typist. He could see him pecking away at the keys of an old Royal or Underwood more than forty years ago in that neat little Spanish style one-story house on Altadena Avenue.

As Rev held the journal in his hands, he felt a connection with Jake Addison he could not explain. He imagined that Jake had usurped fat Bill's seat on the airplane. Jake put a hand on Rev's arm, squeezed it and said:

"We're warriors, Major. The two of us. Never forget that. What we did, we did for our country."

Chapter 22

5:30 p.m. Tuesday, August 23, 2011, Enola, PA

Chuck Wennington arrived at Sophie Anderson's house at 5:30 p.m. Chuck didn't mind being called the *Telegraph*'s resident geek, although he bristled at the newsroom's other moniker for him—Horny Chuck.

Recognizing Chuck's native raunchiness, Sophie had dressed in shape-hiding clothes: baggy jeans, a loose long-sleeved t-shirt, and a sports bra to minimize the allure of her breasts. No reason to give him false hope.

Her feet were bare and her toenails were painted red when she answered the door and stepped back to let him enter her house.

Chuck was about six feet tall, desperately skinny with a big nose and prominent Adam's apple. He wore wire-rim glasses, designer jeans, sandals, and a retro Grateful Dead t-shirt reminiscent of the American Beauty tour. He carried a black canvas computer bag on his right shoulder.

He ran his eyes up and down her body and frowned in disappointment.

"Nice toenails, Sophie."

"I should have worn combat boots and a chastity belt."

Out loud, she said: "Hi, Chuck. Thanks for coming over. My laptop's on the kitchen table. Follow me."

Chuck leaned his computer satchel up against a table leg and sat down in front of Sophie's laptop, which already on. Moving his fingers across the keys and touch pad, he tutt-tutted over the sorry state of her Toshiba Satellite. He took a CD from his computer bag and installed a program to capture whatever video Johnston Bradley streamed to his website.

All the while, he kept up a nonstop monologue that Sophie was ill-disposed to interrupt because he was operating on the proper side of sexual propriety.

"God. This machine is a pile of shit. When was the last time you defragged it? You've got about nine software updates waiting to be installed. We don't have time for that now, but you really should keep it updated. If you'd like, I'll check out your computer once a week, just to make sure it's up to snuff. How about an anti-spyware program? I've got one in my bag that I'll be glad to install for you later. How about those Philadelphia Phillies? You still go to their games? I think they're grossly overpaying Ryan Howard. How can you stand there and take strike three in the deciding game of the NLS? And he's making $25 million a year. Did I tell you how pretty your toes look? I like that shade of red."

All the while, his fingers were flying over the keys of her laptop. He launched Internet Explorer, noting: "You know FireFox is a much better browser. Moreover, it's free; all you have to do is download it from their website. Now what's that URL?"

Sophie slid across the table a piece of paper with the web address and password. He typed in the address, hit return, and sat back in his chair.

"Boy, this is taking a long time to load," he said. "I wonder who is hosting his website. You got DSL or cable modem?"

"Comcast cable," she replied.

"Verizon just installed fiber optics in this neighborhood. Think your service would be much faster if you switched."

"Yeah. The guy next door switched. Says he saved a few bucks, but his service is not that much faster. I called Comcast about my bill. They matched what he's paying. I'm satisfied."

The website loaded and Chuck clicked on the video link. He launched the recording software, stood, and allowed Sophie to take his place in the chair in front of the computer. Chuck stood behind her and leaned forward with his hands on the back of her chair so he could watch, too.

When the video stream loaded, Johnston Bradley was standing in front of a webcam, which she guessed was situated on a high pedestal of some sort and aimed across a wooden stage floor. The limited range of the webcam suggested that Brad was in a large, well-lit room. She could see two rows of folding chairs on a polished green tile floor below the stage in front of the podium.

Brad whispered, "Hey, Sophie." He hunched low in the frame and she could hear his fingers clicking over the keys of his computer. "I hope you've tuned in early because this shit is really getting weird. Slike and Franklin are real assholes. Nothing like Rog, who is just playing soldier. These guys are the real deal; card-carrying whackos. I'm still not sure who the general is, but they say he's going to be at the meeting tonight. That he's going to tell us who the target is. Franklin says it's our nigger president."

The tinny microphone of Brad's laptop picked up the voice of a man off camera. "Who are you talking to, Brad?"

"Hello, sir. Didn't know you were part of this. I'm just talking to myself. I do that when I'm trying to solve a technological problem.

"Sophie wouldn't be that newspaper reporter, would she?"

"I've got a bad feeling about this," Sophie said.

She heard footsteps, as if a large man was ascending steps to Brad's right, out of the camera's range.

The sound of movement stopped. Sophie guessed that whoever the newcomer was, he was standing directly behind the webcam facing Brad.

"I think you're lying to me, Brad. You've been the weak link in our chain from day one. I told Lieutenant Richardson that you were too young. He vouched for you. Now it looks like someone's going to have to vouch for him."

There was a metallic sound. Two clicks.

"Jesus Christ. Quit playing around! Goddamn it, Sophie. He's got a gun!"

Johnston Bradley was backing away from the webcam when a loud explosion assaulted their ears. The video captured the moment Brad's soul fled his ruined body. The look of surprise in his eyes would haunt Sophie Anderson for the rest of her life.

His forehead exploded in a red froth as he fell away from the camera. His murderer must have bumped the podium as he stepped forward to examine the body. The camera angle changed. The flickering image showed the edge of a stage and polished tile on the floor at the audience's level.

The video feed ended abruptly.

Sophie pushed her chair back, stood, and threw herself at Chuck Wennington.

Chapter 23

Jake's Journal

December 7, 1941, the day that lives in infamy, to paraphrase our late great president, began at sea ... at least for me, which is probably why I am still alive to write these words.

We were steaming back to Pearl Harbor having delivered Marine Fighting Squadron 211, Major Paul Putman commanding, to Wake Island. We were supposed to have returned on December 6, but one of the destroyer escorts in our group was running low on fuel and we had to slow and turn to put her on our lee while refueling her in rough weather.

This put us behind schedule, so we were still about 200 miles out to sea on the morning of December 7 when word began filtering through the ship that the Japanese were attacking at Pearl Harbor. A lot of us thought it was a drill.

A master chief hull technician, a big fat Texan whose name is obscured in my memory by the mild dementia that afflicts all men my age, rushed by me on the hangar deck shouting: "I've got a hundred dollar bill that says that this is the mock attack the wardroom has been whispering about."

The military commanders at Pearl Harbor were rumored to be plotting a war game—with the collusion of local radio stations, which were going to broadcast a false report that the Japanese had attacked—to test our readiness in the event of the real thing.

Nobody covered that chief's bet because Admiral Halsey had made us all jittery.

We had no sooner cleared the harbor on the trip to Wake, when Halsey made an announcement over the ship's loud speaker system.

He ordered us to remove practice rounds from all guns and replace them with live ammunition; he threatened to court martial anyone who broke radio silence and he concluded with the following blunt declaration:

"We will stand by to sink any (enemy) aircraft, surface craft, or undersea vessel we meet on the way out or the way back. This is war."

That's my best recollection of his words, as I write this twenty-five years after the fact. Halsey was ballsy, there's no doubt about that.

Although the dander of my shipmates was well-raised, I was ambivalent about the prospects of war. It was difficult for me to demonize the race that had developed and nurtured dear sweet Emika before sending her off to America where she fell in love with this reprobate for reasons that to this day escape me.

Without knowing of the attack, 18 Dauntless dive bombers from Scouting and Bombing Squadron 6 had flown off on the morning of December 7 to take up their stations on Ford Island while the Big E was in port. They flew into the Japanese attack and the jittery guns of our own forces. We lost seven of those planes. Scuttlebutt had it that at least one of them, as well as two of six Wildcat fighters we launched later that day, were shot down by friendly fire.

I was the leading chief petty officer for VT-6 the Enterprise's squadron of torpedo bombers. We flew a metal monoplane known as the Douglas Devastator, TBD for short. The Devastator, at that point more than six years old, was due to be replaced by the faster and more agile Avenger. But you go to war with the assets you have at the time, not the ones you are likely to have in the future.

After the Japanese attack on Pearl Harbor had been confirmed, we stayed at flight stations launching planes to search, fruitlessly as it turned out, for the Japanese who had accomplished their purpose—the crippling of the U.S. Pacific Fleet—and were hurrying home to savor their great victory.

We pulled into Pearl Harbor in the early evening of Monday, December 8, past the smoldering ruins of the once proud Pacific fleet with Halsey's promise ringing in our ears: "When we're done with them the only place Japanese will be spoken is hell."

As we neared our berth, we had to maneuver around the ruins of the ancient battle ship USS Utah, which I had served aboard as an able-bodied seaman during the Veracruz campaign. She was being used as a target ship and had wooden platforms fitted over her turrets to protect them from the impact of the practice bombs. She must have resembled an aircraft carrier from above and her presence near the Enterprise's berth probably contributed to Japan's certainty that the Big E had been sunk on December 7.

Ballsy Halsey kept his flag aboard the Enterprise *in the early stages of the war as we sortied in the Marshall Islands and accompanied the Hornet on the Doolittle raid on Tokyo in April of 1942. My role in these missions was minimal, although I kept busy haranguing my subordinates to stay on top of the maintenance schedule for our decrepit Devastators even though we were expecting delivery of the new Avengers any day.*

The Devastator was an accident waiting to happen. It was slow, 200 mph at top speed—half that when laden with a full load of fuel and a torpedo—and it took forever to climb to rendezvous altitude. It also was prone to stall on landing, which was what happened to Lieutenant Commander Gene Lindsey, commander of VT-6, on the eve of the greatest naval battle of World War II: Midway.

In May of 1942, shortly after our mad dash to the Coral Sea where we arrived too late to save the Yorktown from a battering, Ballsy Halsey's frantic pace finally caught up with him and he was forced ashore to deal with a case of the shingles. He was replaced by Admiral Spruance, who gets the credit, deserved or not, for our victory at Midway.

My ambivalence about the war was a card arrayed close to my chest, but as we departed Pearl Harbor in late May to confront the Japanese at Midway, I tipped my hand. I was re-reading a letter from Emika that had arrived in the last mail when Chief Aviation Machinist Mate Mitch Conley poked his head into my tiny stateroom to see if he could borrow the services of one of my petty officers who had a nice hand on the metal lathe.

Emika had posted her letter from the Manzanar Internment Camp. Authorized by Roosevelt's Executive Order 9066, the camp had opened in March of 1942, and Emika was relatively new to it having arrived there the end of April.

I suppose that if I hadn't been married to Emika, I would have thought of the internment camps the way most Americas did at the time, as a necessary evil to protect Japanese Americans from the wrath of the rest of us and the rest of us from the possibility that some Japanese Americans might act on sympathies that lay with their homeland.

Emika had included a picture that showed her sitting on a rough looking cot holding a chubby cheeked infant that apparently belonged to one of her fellow inmates. In the picture, her circumstances appeared to be so primitive that it made my blood boil. Her quarters were a far cry from our house on Altadena Avenue.

"Whatcha reading, Jake?"Conley asked.

"A letter from my wife," I replied, absentmindedly.

At that point, the picture Emika had included eluded my grasp and fluttered to the deck.

Conley stooped, picked up the picture, and looked at it.

"By God, Jake, why are you toting around a picture of a fucking Nip and her little fucking nipper? Is it a target for your dartboard?"

I hopped off my rack and glowered at Conley, who retreated a step or two and assumed a defensive posture. Conley was a heavyweight boxer, fleet runner up, but the rational part of me that knew he could kick my ass was shouted down by the rash Jake who in a perverse sort of way relished a beating at that point.

"Give me the picture, Mitch, and shut the fuck up."

My face was flushed with rage ... not so much at Mitch but at the whole God damn situation. There I was sailing into harm's way bent on killing my wife's people and they on killing me.

"Whoa. Jake. Take it easy. Who's the fucking Nip? That's all I want to know."

"She's not a fucking Nip, God damn it. She's my wife."

With those words my secret was out. Mitch Conley was an inveterate blabbermouth. It wouldn't be long before the whole damn ship knew that Jake Addison was married to a Japanese woman, although they would not refer to her that kindly.

"Your wife," Conley sputtered. "How could you be married to one of the yellow bastards who murdered all those men on December 7?"

"I married her eight years ago, long before we went to war. She's a naturalized citizen. More American than you or me, and how are we treating her? We have locked her up in prison for Christ's sake."

"Prison's too good for the likes of her. We should line 'em up and shoot 'em every one for what they did, the sneaky yellow bastards!"

I tried to snatch the picture from Conley, which was a big mistake. He mistook my darting hand for an attack. He dropped the picture, and as my eyes followed its fluttering path to the deck, Conley struck me with a quick right cross to the jaw the sent me crashing back onto my rack.

Conley picked up my picture, spit on it, and tore it in half. He tossed the ripped snapshot onto my chest and stalked out of my stateroom, which is why I spent the entire night of June 3 cannibalizing parts from one of two disabled Devastators and installing them in the other so that Lieutenant Commander Gene

Lindsey, the skipper of VT-6, could send 15 torpedo bombers at the Japs rather than 14 the next day at Midway.

When I ran down Gene Lindsey in the pilots' wardroom at 0300 hours on the morning of June 4, 1942, he was chatting over a cup of coffee and sandwiches with Lt. Jim Gray, commander of VF-6, who would be flying fighter support for our old Devastators.

Lindsey's ribs were taped and his eyes were black and blue, testimony to a bad landing eight days earlier as VT-6 arrived aboard the Big E while we were steaming toward our rendezvous with destiny at Midway. He'd cut his throttle prematurely and the big Devastator bounced across the flight deck, hurtled over the port side catwalk, and slid into the ocean. Lindsey, his bombardier, and radio man had to be rescued by the Monaghan, the plane guard destroyer.

"When we begin our torpedo run, I'll alert you on the radio," Lindsey was saying as I approached.

"How will I be able to tell that it's you? There's bound to be a lot of radio chatter," Gray asked.

Lindsey rubbed his brow with the back of his right hand and winced. "I'll say come on down, Jim."

At that moment he saw me out of the corner of his eye. "What's on your mind, Chief?"

"I want to come, too."

"On the sortie?"

"That's right."

"You lost your wings three months ago. The medical officer wouldn't sign off on your flight status. Something about high blood pressure as I recall."

"Your blood pressure is probably high, too. There's a war on, damn it."

"This wouldn't have anything to do with the scuttlebutt I heard recently. Something about your being married to a Japanese woman? You don't have anything to prove to me, Chief. I know your heart is in the right place."

I looked at Lindsey and frowned. He was 20 years my junior, but my sense of him was that he would not take kindly to familiarity on the part of a chief petty officer, even one of my seniority.

"My wife's got nothing to do with it. I fought the Germans 25 years ago from a Sopwith Camel. I'm fully qualified to fly the Devastator. Damn it, I want my shot at the Japanese, too. They've been shooting at me for the better part of six months now. It's high time I start shooting back."

Lindsey stared at me. His eyes almost crossed with the effort and I remembered hearing that he was having trouble with his vision. He was too damn proud to take himself off flying status on the eve of the big show, the stuff of medals ... and promotions. I thought about mentioning his infirmities—the cracked ribs, black eyes, sore muscles, poor vision—but I bit my tongue.

"I appreciate your offer, Chief, but I don't have a ride to offer you. We've only got 14 planes fit for duty and they are all fully crewed. Hell, I had to tell my own plane captain, John Eberle, that he couldn't have a ride. He wasn't too happy with me, I'll tell you."

"Actually we have a 15th Devastator ready. I stayed up all night cannibalizing parts from T-15 and installing them in T-7. She's ready to fly and so am I."

"You got anybody to ride second seat?"

"How about Ron Graetz? I heard him say he was off rotation and itching to get a chance at the Japs," I said.

The word Japs tasted foul on my lips and I offered a silent apology to Emika.

"What do you think, Jim?" Lindsey asked the fighter pilot.

"I think that if the chief has provided you with another plane, then maybe you should give him a shot, although I'm not sure why anyone in their right mind would want any part of this turkey shoot."

Lindsey laughed and winced at the pain it cost him. "You're right about that, Jim, but I'd say our old Devastators will be the turkeys and it's the Japs that will be doing most of the shooting. Command says we'll be launching nearly 60 torpedo planes, carrier and land-based. By the law of averages, at least a couple of us are bound to get lucky and score some hits ... as long as your Wildcats keep the Zekes occupied."

"You call and I'll come on down," Gray said, "but give me plenty of warning. I'll be up around 20,000 feet. I'll need all the altitude I can get to drop in on a Zeke. Those bastards can fly circles around the Wildcat."

"I'm sure you you'll do fine, Jim. In fact, I'm counting on it," Lindsey said. "OK, Chief Addison. Square away your second seat and I'll let you come along, but remember we'll have to drop low and slow to give the Mark 13 a chance at a true and hot run. Things could get real interesting."

"I'll find a second-seater. Thanks, Skipper. I won't let you down."

It was Jim Gray who let us down. He never did come on down even after things got interesting, to borrow the late Gene Lindsey's euphemism. Gray and his comrades burned all their fuel at high altitude and went home without engaging the Japanese.

Chapter 24

Jake's Journal

There's something unnatural about being catapulted off the undulating deck of an aircraft carrier at sea, particularly when you're almost 50 years old and the breadth of your naval aviation experience involves long leisurely takeoffs aboard more sedate float planes.

As of June 4, 1942, I had a grand total of 40 takeoffs and 39 landings from the deck of the USS Enterprise *noted in my logbook. The numbers don't match up because of a mechanical problem that diverted one of my landings to the Naval Air Station at Hampton Roads.*

There was nothing elegant about flying the Devastator. It crawled into the air. After an initial kick in the ass from the catapult, takeoffs were a heart attack in slow motion.

Your chest heaves, you can't get enough air. The deck falls away behind you. You flirt with the waves. Altitude is a coy mistress. She teases you, tempts you. Come hither, sailor boy. You gain 200 feet and lose 100 to a sudden down draft. And finally, a jerky climb smooths out as you claw, inch by inch, into the air and join your squadron in the billowy azure above the Pacific amid cottony cirrus clouds.

I piloted the last of Gene Lindsey's Devastators to leave the Enterprise *on the morning of June 4, 1942. My wheels cleared the deck at 0755 hours, and I joined the entourage of torpedo planes circling above the* Enterprise. *Wade McCluskey's dive bombers had taken off at 0706 and burned precious fuel for nearly 40 minutes while we struggled to clear a foul deck below.*

McCluskey left without us at 0745 hours to intercept the Japanese fleet some 140 miles distant. And there went our plan for a coordinated simultaneous attack, Wade McCluskey from above, Gene Lindsey from the wave tops, with Jim Gray keeping the Zekes off our tails. Zeke was the more prevalent Navalese for the

Japanese Mitsubishi fighter back in the day. Most people would recognize them by the name Zero.

I couldn't round up Ron Graetz, so I settled on an RM 2 named George Abbernathy to ride in the back seat. He was in charge of the radio and the 30 mm machine gun protecting us from the rear. In addition to the Mark 13 torpedo snugged up under our belly, we also had a 30 mm machine gun synchronized with the propeller, which I could fire at targets to our fore.

Since this was a torpedo run, we had no need of a bombardier, who would have ridden in the middle seat and would have flopped on his belly to use the Norden bomb sight had we been dropping bombs from altitude rather than making a torpedo run from the wave tops.

As I joined the VT-6 above the Enterprise, Gene Lindsey's voice crackled over the radio. "Now that Chief Addison has joined this group grope, let's go find the Japanese."

It wasn't quite as simple as that.

We had to wait for Jim Gray's Wildcats to launch and take up their station above before we could set our course for destiny.

I have read various accounts of the Battle of Midway, most of which conclude that the attack of the Devastators was foolhardy; that the plane was moribund; outclassed by the enemy and that the pilots had precious little practice in dropping their torpedoes because torpedoes were too precious to be wasted on practice.

The Mark 13 torpedo was a piece of shit. No doubt about that. The magnetic exploder was unreliable. And the conventional wisdom about how to drop it was dead wrong. Subsequent tests demonstrated that the torpedo was more likely to work if dropped at a higher altitude with a steeper descent. But on June 4, 1942, our pilots were instructed to drop their torpedoes from the wave tops at a distance of slightly less than 1,000 yards from the target while traveling at a speed of 80 knots.

Those drop tactics made the Devastators sitting ducks for the swarms of Zeroes in the air over the Japanese carriers on June 4.

The American carriers at Midway—the Yorktown, Hornet, and Enterprise—while under the tactical command of Rear Admiral Fletcher aboard the Yorktown, were positioned far apart from one another and operated independently. As it developed, there was both virtue and danger in this positioning. More about that later.

The Japanese, on the other hand, fought as a unit, with the air groups of their carriers—the Akagi, Kaga, Soryu, and Hiryu—cooperating on the task ahead: a concentrated strike on the airfield at Midway Island. Simultaneous launches of squadrons of fighters, dive bombers, and torpedo planes from the decks of the Japanese aircraft carriers allowed them to concentrate forces quickly and converge on their targets, but they also left their decks cluttered with aircraft ready for follow-up action. The tactical advantage of attacking in unison and in force was lost in the Battle of Midway, where the better strategy, from the Japanese standpoint anyway, would have been to have all of their aircraft aloft rather than sitting like bombs on the hanger deck when the American dive bombers struck.

That's not to say mistakes weren't made on the American side of the battle, too.

We had the advantage of surprise, but our attacks were not coordinated and at the end of the day the outcome rested on luck enabled by the valiant sacrifice of the pilots and crews of the venerable Douglas Devastators.

Before I recount my own small contributions in the Battle of Midway, I'll offer you this background.

On June 4, 1942, we hurled a total of 51 torpedo bombers at the Japanese aircraft carriers at Midway. Only seven of them returned. That's a loss rate of 86 percent and ranks right up there with the charge of the Light Brigade in terms of wartime futility, particularly since not one of our torpedoes exploded on target.

The first to attack was a contingent of six of the new Avenger torpedo bombers dispatched along with four Army B-26s from Midway atoll shortly after 0600.

They attacked the enemy carriers at a few minutes after 0700. Only one of the Avengers limped back to Midway. Two of the four B-26s were destroyed. I read later that one of the dying B-26s narrowly missed the bridge of the Japanese aircraft carrier Akagi. Scared the shit out of Admiral Nagumo, the bastard in command of the sneak attack on Pearl Harbor.

VT-8 from the Hornet began its attack on the Akagi at 0925 hours. All 15 of its planes were shot down and all but one of their pilots perished.

Of course we didn't know any of this as we arrived on the scene about an hour later. And neither did the 15 Devastators of VT-3 from the Yorktown, which followed us in what turned out to be a suicide attack on the Hiryu.

We'd been in the air for better than two uneventful hours and the object of our mission, at least in my mind, had been consumed by the routine of flying a steady course and keeping my old Devastator on station. If I had allowed myself to think too far ahead, I would have crashed my plane into the sea right then and there and saved the Japanese the trouble.

The tedium dispersed in an instant as the Japanese fleet materialized on the horizon in front of us. Following Gene Lindsey's lead, we began to slow and descend as the Japanese carriers turned away from us striving to put more sea between us and them as we strove to put less in our classic hammer-and-anvil approach.

The AA fire from the support ships thickened, black smoke filled the sky, and shell concussions buffeted us. We had been instructed to maintain radio silence, but there was nothing approaching silence now as the pilots screamed out warnings to each other.

Somewhere in that cacophony I heard Gene Lindsey holler:

"Come on down, Jim!"

"Come on down, Jim!"

"Come on ..."

I lost the rest of it as George Abbernathy opened up with his machine gun from the rear seat. I juked left and right as George screamed out headings to avoid the Zekes, which were among us like lions in a herd of wildebeests.

Somewhere in the middle of all this the smell of shit permeated the cockpit. I thought for a minute that George had lost control of his sphincter, but then I realized it was me.

A Zero with its guns blazing flashed in front of me on the trail of one of our Devastators. I opened up with my machine gun and was gratified to see a puff of smoke as the Zero jigged among the tracers and then it was gone. Don't know if I got the bastard or not. I like to think I did.

George screamed from the back seat and that was the last I heard from him.

Looking over my shoulder, I noticed that his head was missing.

I was skimming the wave tops now with the Kaga in my sights. I punched the torpedo release button. Nothing happened.

Gene Lindsey's Devastator cart wheeled into the ocean to starboard.

My cockpit was covered in oil. I'd sprung a leak. I couldn't pull up. The ocean beckoned. I cut my engine, feathered my prop, and waited for the inevitable.

The ocean is a hard thing, even at 80 knots. I managed to keep the nose up. I bounced, once, twice, a third time, and a fourth. I was a skipping stone, slowly losing momentum on the flat surface of a placid lake.

The water rose up about me as the Devastator skidded to a stop.

There was blood in my eyes. I must have hit my head on the instrument panel. My teeth hurt. I realized I was missing a tooth, bottom left, next to the canine.

I sucked at the empty socket and spat blood. I released my seat belt and struggled from the cockpit. The Devastator groaned and complained like a footsore basset on its way home from a rabbit hunt.

The Devastator fell away below me; the suction of its departure tugged me downward, inviting me to succumb to the inevitable, to sink into the welcoming arms of a remorseless sea like millions of sailors had done before me.

Mae West saved me.

I was plucked from the sea three days later, bleeding and delirious, by the heavy cruiser USS Portland, *Captain Alan Jenkins commanding.*

The great man himself came to visit me in sick bay.

I don't know what I was expecting, but I shouldn't have been surprised.

He pulled a chair up to my bedside, stared into my face with what I mistook to be compassion and said, "Tell me, Chief, what do you think of your Nip wife now?"

"Fuck you, asshole," I replied.

And there went my Navy Cross.

I settled instead for a Purple Heart, a Bronze Star, and orders stateside, where I was put to work inspecting aircraft as they came off the lines at Consolidated Aircraft Corp., San Diego, California.

My war was over.
Or so I thought at the time.

Chapter 25

8:30 a.m. Wednesday, August 24, 2011, Selinsgrove, PA

Liv Pearson watched Johnston Bradley's murder with the dispassion of one inured by training and experience with the horror humans inflict upon one another.

"Jesus Christ," she said. "Is this real? It can't be real. No one would commit a murder in front of a camera."

"If it's a fake, our technology geek at the newspaper says it's a good one. But Gray Collingsworth is not going to touch a story until we determine that the video is genuine, 100 percent genuine," Sophie said.

"Gray Collingsworth?"

"My editor."

"You showed this to your editor?"

Sophie nodded. "Late last night."

"He saw it before you bothered to call law enforcement? I always thought you were a person first and a journalist second. That's why I've cultivated your friendship over the years, even though we're antagonists by occupation. Sophie, I feel like you've stabbed me in the back."

"And now you're acting like a police officer first and a person second."

Liv shrugged, conceding the point. "Touché."

"So you're bringing me in because you need my help substantiating a story?" Her voice was under control now, but her eyes lacked their usual friendly sparkle.

All Sophie could do was nod.

Liv's face was more composed now and Sophie thought she detected the reawakening of her old friend behind the cop eyes that now stared at her.

"OK, let's get this straight. You found a message from Johnston Bradley on YouTube in which he advised you to check your e-mail."

Sophie nodded.

"And that e-mail contained the address of his website and a password to allow you to access a video he intended to stream there?"

"That's right," Sophie said.

"Do you still have the e-mail and is his YouTube message still active?"

"Yes and yes. I've saved both of them to my hard drive."

"And in one of the messages, Johnston Bradley said that the Blue Mountain Boys were planning an attack on the president of the United States?" Liv asked.

"Yep."

"OK. I need to bounce this off Sergeant Collins, my station chief. He'll probably want to get the FBI involved, the Secret Service, too, because of the implied threat to our president. The feds are pit bulls. If there are any skeletons in your closet, they're going to find them. I'd hate to be you over the next several days. I'd keep my doors locked and my windows shuttered, if I were you."

"Thanks for the warning."

Liv changed gears. "What do you hear from Rev Polk?"

"I talked to him a yesterday, just before he got on a plane for home. We're supposed to get together this afternoon to compare notes. Why do you ask?"

"Did you tell him about Furnley Franklin's warning?"

"Yeah. He didn't understand it either. We aren't working on a story together, unless you count the Freedom of Information filing about his uncle's military career."

"He's not helping you on the gun shop burglary story?"

"No. I told you that," Sophie said.

"You sure?"

"Yes, I'm sure. Why do you doubt me?"

"Your recent behavior warrants doubt."

"I suppose it does. Sorry."

"So we've got to conclude that there's some sort of connection between a forty-year-old hit and run in San Diego and a burglary slash homicide in Snyder County. I wonder what it is," Liv said.

"Rev and I have been asking ourselves the same thing, although he doesn't know about the murder. Not yet anyway. But he has stumbled on a journal written by Jacob Addison."

"The vic in the old hit and run?" Liv asked.

"That's right. He said that he would be reading the journal on his way home. I haven't heard from him in a couple of hours. Maybe he's mined some nuggets," Sophie said.

"Why don't you call him and find out?"

Sophie dug her cell phone out of her purse and punched the speed dial for Rev's phone.

Liv smiled. "You broke up with him, but you kept his number in your contacts?" she asked, arching an eyebrow.

Sophie was gratified to see something of her old friend emerge from the barrier she had built up between them. "I was just ..."

Liv finished the sentence for her. "Keeping your options open?"

Sophie held a finger to her lips as she listened to Rev's voicemail pick up. "No answer."

"Be sure to keep me apprised of developments on Rev's end," Liv said.

"Let's keep Rev's ass out of this, although it is one of his best features."

Liv laughed. Sophie's old friend was back.

"Cute. Now, I've got some cop stuff to do."

"Such as?"

"Such as calling Johnston Bradley's parents to let them know their son may be dead."

Chapter 26

1 p.m. Wednesday, August 24, 2011, Selinsgrove, PA

Bill and Alice Bradley sat stiffly on folding chairs pulled up to a long table in the break room of the Pennsylvania State Police Station at Selinsgrove. Liv Pearson's tiny cubicle was too small to accommodate visitors, so she had commandeered the break room, where she could, at least, offer the bereaved family a cup of crummy coffee to wash down their despair. She closed the break room door, the equivalent of a tie on the doorknob in the testosterone-infused state police station.

Liv sat across from them. She stared at the Bradleys over the top of her laptop computer.

Bill Bradley, six-two and 220 pounds, had the craggy demeanor of a whiskey-drinking, cigarette-smoking truck driver, but his clothes—jeans and a t-shirt—were gathered about him like a freshly made bed. His cowboy boots were newly polished. His wife, slight and demure, wore designer jeans, a sleeveless blouse, and bejeweled sandals that sparkled with glitter.

It was clear to Liv that Alice brought class to the relationship. Bill supplied the brawn.

The Bradleys lived in Rochester, N.Y. He worked for Roadway; she was a high school art teacher. Liv knew these things because she had learned to let people ramble.

The decision to show the Bradleys the video resided at the station chief's level. Sergeant Collins insisted it was the right thing to do.

"There's something about this video that doesn't seem right," he had told her.

"What's that, Sergeant?"

"Can't put my finger on it. My gut tells me the alleged victim's parents will be able to sort it out."

Liv shook her head, returning to real time.

"You sure you're ready for this?" she asked the Bradleys.

Bill engulfed Alice's small hand in his large one. They looked at each other, exchanging the unseen signals of a long-married couple. It was as if they were alone in the room; Liv Pearson, for the moment, was a mere afterthought.

Alice turned from her husband and stared Liv straight in the eyes. "Our faith in God will see us through. We're ready."

Liv pointed and clicked, launching the video that Sophie Anderson had captured from the Internet.

She stood and turned the computer around so it faced the Bradleys. "I'll let you watch this alone. Back in a few minutes."

Liv left the break room on wooden legs. She wasn't sure if she had done the right thing, leaving the Bradleys alone with their grief. But the tuning fork that vibrated in the center of her soul told her they needed to say goodbye to their son without the intrusion of strangers. Besides, maybe Sergeant Collins was right. Maybe the video had been faked. But to what purpose?

She gave them five minutes and then headed back to the break room full of dread about the emotional maelstrom that awaited her there. The Bradleys had turned their folding chairs so that they now sat knee-to-knee, facing each other. They were holding hands and smiling.

Alice looked up as Liv came into the room. "It's a fake. The video is a fake."

Liv sat down across from them. "What makes you say that?"

Bill Bradley cleared his throat. "Our son is a weirdo. That's why I sent him off to the army ... to military school. I hoped he'd grow out of it ... learn the path the Lord has chosen for him. Billy Kambic is a good man, a preacher. I thought he'd show Johnston the way."

"What my husband is trying to say is that our son is an artist—a performing artist. He likes to shock people, and one of the ways he does that is to produce ... disturbing videos with the intent to set the norm on its ear."

"You're saying that your son has made videos like this before?" Liv asked.

"Not precisely like this, but similar," Alice said. "He persuaded a 15-year-old girl who lives next door to participate in a video that made it appear as if she had hanged herself. He called it a snuff film. The girl's parents were not amused."

"I thought maybe the army would straighten him out. I was wrong," Bill Bradley said.

"The army?" Liv asked. "That's the second time you've said he joined the army. I thought he was a schoolboy."

The Bradleys looked at each other.

"Army ... military school. It's all the same thing," Bill Bradley said.

Alice squeezed her husband's hand. "Johnston is a non-conformist. That's what makes his alleged association with a right-wing militia so ridiculous. I'm thinking maybe he did it just to punish his father. He probably was amused by the irony."

"Irony?" Liv repeated.

Alice nodded. "Johnston is rebelling from the path the Lord has chosen for him. For him, this is nothing more than a lark. He made that video to make us think he was dead ... to punish us for forcing him to walk the straight and narrow."

"And for refusing to bail him out of jail," Bill Bradley added.

Liv cataloged her impressions of Johnston Bradley. When he emerged from that motel room, waving a pistol in the air, he didn't look like a kid on a lark. He struck her as sincere and scared, but sincere and ready for action.

"I hope you're right, Mrs. Bradley. Our experts are poring over the video. If they reach a similar conclusion, I'll be sure to let you know. But I think you have to at least prepare yourself for the possibility that your son has been murdered."

"Show me the body, and I'll believe it," Bill Bradley said.

His wife nodded. "You can't have a murder without a body."

At that moment, Trooper Sam Creswell burst into the break room. "I've just been watching the video and I think I can identify the room where the murder occurred," he blurted out.

"Whoa, slow down there, Sam. We've got civilians present," Liv said.

Creswell blushed. "Sorry. I should have waited until you were through here."

Bill Bradley pushed his chair back and stood. "I'm glad you didn't. What can you tell us about the alleged murder scene?"

Creswell looked at Liv for guidance.

She shook her head. "This is Bill Bradley, father of the ... alleged victim."

"Oh, Christ. I'm sorry, Liv. Got to learn to put a muzzle on."

Creswell extended his hand to Bill Bradley. "Nice to meet you, sir. Sorry for being so indiscreet."

Bill shook the trooper's hand.

"The murder scene?" he asked.

"Oh, yeah. Right. I'm afraid I can't reveal that information until we've confirmed it," Creswell said.

Liv added, "That's right, Mr. Bradley. We don't want to share anything that might not be true."

Bill stood taller and edged closer to the state police officers.

Liv braced herself for a scene.

Alice rescued them. She laid a hand on her husband's forearm. "Now, Bill. You know how impetuous you can be. I'd hate for you to go off half-cocked and do something we'll both regret."

He glared at the officers. Glared at his wife.

She smiled at him. He exhaled and smiled back. His anger escaped like air from an open tire valve.

Sensing the tide had turned, Liv said: "OK, folks, why don't I show you out and Trooper Creswell and I can get busy chasing down his new lead. We'll call you as soon as we know anything definitive. I promise."

"We can find our own way," Bill Bradley said, shouldering past the troopers.

Alice followed him, observing: "Bill has mellowed considerably. We thank God for that. Ten years ago, he would have knocked you both on your butts and I would have been visiting him in prison."

"Yes. Thank God for that," Liv said under her breath as Alice cleared the doorway. She balled up her fists and turned to face Creswell, who retreated a couple of steps and held out a hand as if he were trying to stop traffic.

"I know. I know. I fucked up," he said. "It won't happen again."

"It had better not," Liv said through clenched teeth. "Now, out with it."

"What?"

"Are you really that dense? The murder scene?"

"Oh, yeah. Right. The meeting room of the Trevorton Rod and Gun Club. It's about twenty miles outside Middleburg heading toward McClure. I took my nephew there for a hunting class when he was 12 years old so he could get his license."

Without another word, Liv turned and headed for her cubicle, a bloodhound on a fresh trail. The rush got her out of bed every day. She loved it and hated it at the same time.

Chapter 27

2 p.m. Wednesday, August 24, 2011, Middleburg, PA

Andy Hawk cleared the door frame by a fraction. Randolph Simpson guessed him at 6' 7", give or take.

Simpson extended his hand across his desk. "Nice to meet you, Mr. Hawk. Have a seat."

The two men shook hands.

"Call me Andy," the giant said, wincing as he lowered himself into Simpson's visitors' chair, which creaked in protest. "Bad knees. Too much basketball for too many years."

Simpson smiled in sympathy. "I feel your pain. I had to give up tennis two years ago." He flexed his right elbow. "Tendonitis."

Hawk was a solid 250 pounds or so with just a slight bulge at the middle, but he was florid of face, suggesting the heavy consumption of alcohol. A high and tight military haircut did not enhance his features.

Hawk wore his years, more than 60 of them, in his jowls. The tight haircut and his puffy cheeks and neck made his head look all the broader. A giant chipmunk came to mind.

His most conspicuous feature, apart from his overall size and chipmunk jowls, were piercing light blue eyes, which at the moment were steadfastly locked upon Randolph Simpson.

As the seconds piled up on each other, Simpson shifted in his chair and made the first feint in an unfolding game of cat and mouse. "So you were with the speaker at Dak To?"

Hawk blinked and smiled, pleasantly. "That's right. I was platoon sergeant, just finishing up my third tour with the 503rd Airborne. The speaker was platoon leader, a brand new second lieutenant, and green as they come, but he had fire in his belly. I'll tell you that."

"I understand you were ambushed on Hill 875," Simpson said.

"You must have read Sam's Medal of Honor citation. We were pinned down pretty good. Took a lot of friendly fire, too. It was a real cluster fuck. Sam Jenkins spit in the devil's eye that day."

Simpson baited the bear. "What do you think of the story the AP picked up recently regarding the speaker's Medal of Honor?"

Hawk sat up straight in his chair and slammed his fist down on Simpson's desktop. "It was unadulterated bullshit! Goddamn Rev Polk for kicking over that anthill. He must have a real hard on for Sam cause he's sniffing around another story that could hurt us. But Brett Faust? He's a liar and coward and a whack job to boot."

"I've read that Corporal Faust has a history of mental illness," Simpson said.

Hawk seemed mollified. "I'm sorry about my outburst. It's all moot anyway. The *Daily Telegraph* is going to issue an apology and expose the troubled background of Faust and his accomplices. The democrats were swift-boating to smear a potential republican candidate for president."

"Swift-boating? Wasn't that a republican ploy against John Kerry?"

"Whatever," Hawk said. "It's all politics."

"If the *Telegraph* is going to apologize, you couldn't have handpicked a more fortuitous time. The primary season is upon us," Simpson said.

"Which brings me to the reason for my visit."

The two men stared at each other.

Simpson studied Hawk, willing him to flinch first, but to no avail. Giving up, he said: "I understand Speaker Jenkins would like me to arrange an introduction to people who might be involved in a militia called the Blue Mountain Boys."

"That's right. This new task force investigating domestic terrorism is a real witch hunt. We think this militia is benign, that it's being smeared in service of the political agenda of the extreme left. The militia had nothing to do with that gun shop burglary and I'd like to expose the press's liberal bias in its pursuit of this and other similar stories."

"That would fit in nicely with the speaker's own political agenda," Simpson said. "But this seems like it could be handled by a more junior member of his staff. This is legwork, not policy."

Hawk puffed up his chest, apparently taking Simpson's observation as a compliment. "Well on the surface, this might seem to be a minor interlude. Something else is brewing that may pose a more significant danger."

"What's that?"

Hawk shifted in his chair. "Before I tell you, I've got to be sure we're playing for the same team. The speaker is a powerful man who can help rectify your—" Hawk cleared his throat— "public relations problem, but we need your assurance that ..."

"I'll play ball?"

Hawk cleared his throat again. "Yes. That's right. Will you?"

"You can tell Sam Jenkins that I have his back."

Hawk relaxed and slumped back in his chair. "OK. Here it is. Years ago, at the end of World War II, the speaker's father, Admiral Alan Jenkins, was involved in a special navy operation, the details of which could easily be misconstrued by the press in a negative light that would smear the Jenkins family at the precise moment he is ascending on the national stage."

Simpson was intrigued. He was expecting something more current. But he was a student of the Second World War and this interested him.

"What sort of naval operation?"

"I don't want to get into that right now," Hawk said. "Suffice it to say that Rev Polk and his girlfriend, another reporter for the *Daily Telegraph*, have filed a Freedom of Information request regarding this special op."

"What does that have to do with me?" Simpson asked.

"Well, it occurred to the speaker, well, actually to me, that it would be nice to have some assets on the ground here in Harrisburg to contain the situation."

"I won't be breaking into the Watergate?" Simpson asked.

Hawk threw up his hands. "Oh no, Colonel. Sam doesn't expect anything of that nature. We just need an introduction to someone who might be willing ... to use your analogy ... to break into the Watergate. Someone so far removed from the speaker that there can't be any question that he wasn't involved."

Simpson was visited by an epiphany.

"You think that maybe someone in the Blue Mountain Militia might be willing to contain the situation."

Hawk nodded.

"Well, if I was trying to establish contact with the militia, I'd start with Major Bill Kambic. He's vice president of the academy and I don't trust him one little bit. In fact, as soon as I can prove he's involved with the burglary I intend to fire him, even though his father, George, is the state senator from Bellefonte and a major general in the Pennsylvania National Guard."

"I was afraid that might be your reaction. You asked what you can do for Sam. Well, it's a simple as this. Leave Bill Kambic in place. He is positioned to do a great service for our country. The type of service you were trying to do when you signed off on the harsh interrogation of prisoners at Abu Ghraib."

"So let me get this straight: you don't really need information about the militia. You already know who they are," Simpson said.

Hawk raised his hands as if in benediction.

"And all you want me to do is ... nothing."

Andy Hawk smiled. "Yep. Simple isn't it?"

"I've been retired to the Army Reserve. I've become an expert at doing nothing," Simpson said.

Hawk rose to his feet, towering above Simpson.

"That's right, General. And I'm not using the honorific sarcastically. You do nothing, sit tight and wait, and poof, you're an active duty brigadier. It's as simple as that."

"Would you like me to give Major Kambic a call? He's probably downstairs in his office right now."

"That won't be necessary. We already have met. Bill knows what we want him to do."

Hawk arose, nodded, and left Simpson's office without another word, ducking slightly as he walked through the door even though he didn't have to ... an artifice the tall often impose on the less tall, just to rub it in.

Simpson drummed his fingers on his desktop for a few seconds after Hawk left him.

He pulled his cell phone from the top drawer of his desk and accessed the address book. Punching the proper speed dial shortcut, he pushed back in his chair and waited. The phone rang five times before it was answered, just like always.

"Speak," said a gruff voice on the other end.

"Good afternoon, Mr. Director," Simpson said. "Sam Jenkins has risen to the bait. Asked me to give Billy Kambic a pass."

"Jenkins himself? Or one of his minions?"

"Andy Hawk just paid me a call."

"Excellent. That means we've got Jenkins' attention."

"Goddamn it, Ted, I'm not cut out for this spy vs. spy stuff. I'm a soldier, not James Bond," Simpson said.

The voice on the other end of the line chuckled. "Carry on 007. We'll bring you in from the cold soon. I promise."

And then he was gone.

Chapter 28

3:30 p.m. Wednesday, August 24, 2011, McClure, PA

Liv Pearson straightened the creases on her trousers and squatted next to Mervin Jablonski, the state police's crime scene technician, who was busy scraping residue from the hardwood floor of the meeting room stage at Trevorton Rod and Gun Club.

Luke Walls, president of the Rod and Gun Club, sat glumly in a folding aluminum chair in the front of ten rows of similar chairs lined up like a formation of soldiers at parade rest. He had been reluctant to give Liv Pearson access to the facility, but the threat of a warrant more far-reaching than the physical evidence the meeting room might contain won him over.

Liv suspected that a thorough forensic inspection of the facility and its bookkeeping would turn up information that the club would prefer to keep from the prying eyes of the Liquor Control Board and of investigators looking into the propriety of small games of chance.

"Whatcha got, Merve?"

"Don't know yet, Liv. Might be blood."

Merve collected the substance on the blade of a scalpel and smeared it onto two microscope slides, one of which he placed in a plastic envelope and the other of which he subjected to an on-the-spot Teichman test. Applying a drop of fluid from a small squeeze bottle, he grunted in satisfaction as the sample crystallized.

"Yep. The Teichman shows it's blood all right."

He scraped up some more, smeared it onto a second tile and then a third, sealing them in the same envelope with the first.

"I got plenty for more tests," he said. "We've got the alleged vic's blood type, don't we?"

Liv nodded. "His parents have supplied that information. It's O negative."

"You positive?"

"Actually, I'm negative. But I'm also certain."

The repartee was practiced, part of their shtick.

"Good. Looks like a pretty good splatter here. Must be at least two or three cc's."

"I lose that much when I cut my legs shaving. Is that all you can find? The video suggested a pretty catastrophic blood loss. I don't care how carefully they cleaned, there should be residue everywhere," Liv said.

Merve shook his head. "This is all I could find."

"What's this?" Liv asked, pointing to a discoloration in a deep groove between two boards on the stage.

"I saw that," Merve said. "It doesn't bloom under the ultraviolet. It's reddish, but I don't think it's blood. Want me to do a Teichman?"

"Nope. But I would like you to take samples. There seems to be more of it over here, closer to the edge of the stage," she said.

Merve shined his ultraviolet light on the boards where Liv was pointing. "Not blood, but I'll collect the samples."

Liv stood and stretched her back.

She walked to the edge of the stage and jumped to the floor two feet below right in front of Luke Walls, startling him. She sat down beside him, crowding his personal space, which was her intent.

Up on the stage, light flashed as Merve took close-ups of the alleged crime scene with his digital camera.

"So, tell me again. Who rented the room last night?" Liv asked.

Luke sighed. "It's like I said. There is no record of a rental last night, but that doesn't mean one of the board members couldn't have had something going on. They all have keys."

"How many board members are there?"

"Seven."

"Can you give me a list of their names and telephone numbers?"

Luke reached into his shirt pocket. "I thought you might ask for that." He handed her a folded up piece of paper. "Call them. But you'll be wasting your time. They'll all say they weren't here last night."

"You've warned them that I'd be in touch so they can firm up their alibis?"

"Just trying to help, Officer."

Liv unfolded the piece of paper and scanned it.

She wasn't surprised to see Bill Kambic's name on the list, but he wasn't the only Kambic.

"George Kambic is the treasurer?"

"That's right. Senator Kambic is a founding member. So what?"

"Isn't he a big wig in the Pennsylvania National Guard?"

"He's a major general. But, I repeat. So what?"

"And he's Major Bill Kambic's father."

"Again. So what?" Luke said.

Liv tapped the paper with her right index finger. "Just collecting information, Mr. Walls. Any of the men on this list belong to the Blue Mountain Boys?"

Luke stood suddenly and stepped away from her. "That's none of your business. Membership in a militia is protected by the Second Amendment to the Constitution."

"I'm not disputing that, Mr. Walls. I'm just—"

"Yeah, I know, collecting information. I don't think I'll be answering any more of your questions, Officer Pearson.

Liv tapped her shoulder insignia. "It's Corporal Pearson, actually. I can't make you talk to me, but I will warn you, all sorts of federal agencies are sniffing around this case, the FBI; the Bureau of Alcohol, Tobacco, Firearms, and Explosives; the Secret Service. I'm liaising with all of them."

Alarm was written across Luke's face. "The Secret Service? What would the Secret Service's interest in this, uh, alleged murder be?"

"In the course of our investigation we've stumbled on some information suggesting that there might be a threat to the president involved in this case. You're sweating, Mr. Walls. Why are you sweating?"

Walls ran a finger under the edge of his collar. "Because it's hot in here."

"The choice is yours, Mr. Walls, but if you stonewall me, you'll end up testifying before a grand jury, which has the legal authority to compel you to speak. Having said that, I will acknowledge a citizen's right to bear arms and join a militia."

Luke said, "Well, I don't know ..."

Liv pressed her advantage. "Heck, I know some of you guys anyway."

"Who?"

"Colin Butdorf, for one. I've run into him a couple of times at the pistol range. He says that he's a captain in the Blue Mountain Boys. And then of course there are his friends, what are their names? Jerry Slike and Furnley Franklin?"

She was guessing now, but Luke Walls' face suggested that she had guessed right.

"If you know so much, then you tell me who on our board belongs to the Blue Mountain Boys."

Liv laughed. "Boys? You call yourselves boys? How apropos. A bunch of men playing with guns ... a bunch of boys playing soldier."

"We do more than play. We train. We'll be ready when the time comes."

"The time comes for what?"

"To protect our country from the Muslims, the socialists, the liberals, and the minorities who want to take all of our rights away from us and redistribute what we have among people who haven't worked for it."

Liv laughed. "I'm going to make a wild guess here. I'm betting that every one of the men on this list is a member of the Blue Mountain Boys."

"Prove it."

"I will. Proving it is what I do."

Chapter 29

3:30 p.m. Wednesday, August 24, 2011, Enola, PA
Sophie Anderson heard the familiar growl of the small gas engine that powered the mailman's right-hand drive truck as she logged onto her computer whilst seated at her kitchen table.

Her cell phone rang.

Chuck Wennington was on the line. "Hey, Sophie. I've been going over the video we downloaded off Johnston Bradley's website and I think I've stumbled on something you'll find interesting."

"What's that, Chuck?"

"Well, you know at the end of the video where the angle of the camera changes and we can see the victim's legs above the shiny tile floor?"

"Yeah. I remember that, although I've been trying to forget."

"I took a real close look at one of the tiles and I saw a reflection."

Chuck paused and Sophie realized she wasn't making the appropriate listening noises. "A reflection of what?"

Chuck didn't reply. Sophie figured she'd done her part, so she waited him out.

"I'm betting that it's a reflection of the man who killed him."

Outside, Sophie heard the mailman stop at her box. The engine grumble diminished as he shifted into park.

"You still there, Sophie?"

"Yeah. I'm still here, Chuck. I'm not supposed to know this, but a source in the state police tells me there is some doubt that Brad was killed. His parents say it's a snuff film, a hoax. Apparently he has a propensity for hoaxes."

"A propensity for hoaxes?" Chuck repeated. "You're doing that writer's stuff again, aren't you? Trying out a phrase and seeing how it sounds."

Sophie laughed. "Guilty. I was just warming up my computer to write a story ... that Gray probably won't have the balls to publish. He won't truck with unnamed sources and I've got to protect my source on this one. Her job's on the line."

"Her?"

"Oops."

Chuck said, "Gray won't hear it from me."

"Thanks. But you know what? Even if Brad's 'murder' was faked, it still would be nice to see who was with him at the time that video was made. How clear is your image?"

"The guy is wearing an army uniform. No hat, but clearly a uniform. The image is clear enough to identify him ... if I knew who he was."

"Why don't you shoot the picture to my personal e-mail account? Maybe I'll be able to tell who it is."

"It's already there. I sent it ten minutes ago. Take a look and call me back."

The engine growl of the mailman's truck increased as he pulled away from her box outside.

"I'll do that, Chuck. Thanks. Listen. I've got to go. The mail just arrived and I'm expecting a package for Rev."

"Rev? I thought the two of you were ... history."

The jealousy in his voice was palpable.

"We are ... we're just working on a story together. Period. Thanks again, Chuck. Bye."

Sophie punched the end button and climbed to her feet.

By the time she made it to her mailbox the boxy mail truck had pulled out of sight, but the smell of its exhaust lingered.

Sophie rifled through her mail. Among it was a large manila envelope from the department of the U.S. Navy. Rev's Freedom of Information package had arrived. She shoved her mail under her arm and returned to her kitchen table. Other than the manila envelope from the navy, the rest of the mail appeared to be junk. She flipped through it and tossed it on the table.

She tapped her finger on the envelope. She was dying to open it. She glanced at her wrist watch. She was expecting Rev within the hour. Better wait for him, she decided. She picked up her cell phone, then thought better of calling him. He wanted to talk to her about what he had learned in San Diego ... about what his great granduncle Jake's reminiscence had revealed. He said it was hot and he didn't want to spoil the surprise by teasing it on the phone. She'd be patient.

To discipline herself, she put the package from the navy out of sight on the top of her tall kitchen hutch.

Just then, her doorbell rang. She wasn't expecting visitors—besides Rev, who never rang the bell—so she approached her front door with some trepidation. She glanced through the sidelight flanking the door on the right. There was a box on her front stoop. She opened the door.

Jerry Slike jumped from behind a big holly bush next to the door.

His long hair hung in greasy tendrils to his shoulders; there was a wild look in his eyes, and his big gun was pointed squarely at the center of her chest.

"Boo!"

She stepped back from the door as he pushed his way inside.

"Box was a great idea wasn't it?" he asked. "Figured you'd think I was UPS. I wouldn't scream if I were you. Screaming makes my trigger finger itchy. And you don't want me to scratch."

Sophie was too startled to scream. Too startled and too scared. She retreated farther into her house as Slike closed the door behind him.

"You just picked up your mail. I want to see it."

"Why this sudden interest in my mail?" she asked.

"It isn't sudden. This is just the first time in a couple of days you've gotten to it before me."

"What are you looking for?"

"A certain package, which could be dangerous if it fell into the wrong hands ... namely yours and your asshole of a boyfriend. Give it to me and this never happened."

"And if I don't?" Sophie asked.

She was trying to be tough, but there was a tremor in her voice.

Slike heard it and laughed. He brushed a tendril of greasy hair out of his face.

"You don't want to know the answer to that question. Show me your mail. Or I'll show you mine."

He grabbed his crotch with his left hand and motioned with his gun in his right. He followed her down the short hall to her kitchen, which occupied the back of the house.

She stepped to one side and pointed at her kitchen table. "It's right there. And as you can see there are no packages. Only bills and junk."

Slike rifled though the pile of mail.

"Goddamn it, woman, if you're holding out on me it's going to be bad for you."

"I'm not holding out."

Sophie was pleased with herself. No tremor in her voice this time.

Slike noted the difference. "I'm not the sort of guy who gets his rocks off knocking a woman around. I told the general right from the start. I don't hit women."

"Does that mean you won't shoot them, either?"

There was a worried look on his face. Sophie guessed that he had overplayed his hand. That he had gone off script and wasn't sure what to do next.

"You got a sweater or something?"

Sophie was startled by the non sequitur. "Why would I need a sweater? It's warm outside."

"To hide the fact that your hands are tied up."

Slike pulled a zip tie from the back pocket of his jeans. "Cross your hands in front of you. That will be less conspicuous."

"Why would you want to handcuff me?"

"So you don't go slapping at me when I put you in the truck."

"You don't want to do that, Jerry. Kidnapping is a felony. Right now, the worst my friend, Liv Pearson, could hang on you is terroristic threats, a misdemeanor of the second class, or so she says."

"Yeah. I've met your bitch of a friend. Tiny little cop with a great big gun. Pulled me over on Front Street. Said I'd better leave you alone, or else. You can tell she scared me. Now cross your wrists in front of you." He punctuated the command by poking her in the stomach with the barrel of his pistol.

Sophie didn't think Slike would kill her on purpose, but she didn't want to give him the chance to kill her by accident. She crossed her wrists and he secured them with the plastic tie.

Slike closed the lid on her laptop, unplugged the power cord, and wrapped it around the outside of the case. He put the computer under his arm. "There may be something interesting on here. Let's take it with us ... just in case. Now, move!"

He waved the pistol toward her front door.

As she left the kitchen, Sophie tripped over one of the high stools arrayed at her kitchen counter. The stool toppled to the floor, which was her intent.

With his one arm full of computer and the other handling the gun, Slike made no move to right the toppled stool. They paused at the front door.

"I might have a sweater in the hall closet," she said, figuring that one of her neighbors might see her climb into a pickup truck wearing a sweater in 80-degree weather and maybe tell the police.

"Never mind that. The sweater's probably a bad idea. Let's get out of here. I'm going to let the general sort this mess out."

As they were leaving, her cell phone began to ring from atop her kitchen hutch. She must have left it there when she hid Rev's package out of temptation's way.

"Forget the phone. You won't be needing it."

Chapter 30

4:15 p.m. Wednesday, August 24, 2011, Enola, PA
Rev Polk knocked on Sophie Anderson's door for a third time.

He felt the familiar anger that welled from within when things didn't go his way.

Rev didn't blame Sophie for the anger he felt when she didn't answer the door. His short fuse was nobody's fault and everybody's fault. He did what his analyst suggested: forgive everyone. That thought lowered his blood pressure.

He tried the front door. It wasn't locked. That was a bad thing. Sophie always locked her door. He stepped into her foyer.

"Sophie? "Hey home, I'm honey."

Silence.

He walked down the hall to her kitchen. He saw the overturned stool. His blood pressure redlined. Sophie was a neat nick; she'd never walk away from an overturned stool. He bounded through her house, opening doors, looking in closets (he wasn't sure why), calling her name.

Nothing.

He returned to her kitchen, in a panic now. Where the hell was Sophie? They had a date for 4:00 p.m. It was 4:15. He had a lot to tell her and she had told him over the phone that she had a lot to report, too. Wouldn't tell him what though, playing the lady-of-mystery card. He hated it when she did that.

Where the hell was Sophie?

He thought of Sophie's friend, Liv Pearson, the state police trooper. He should call Liv. That's what he should do. No, wait. Why not call Sophie's cell first? Just to make sure there wasn't a completely logical explanation as to why she had left her front door unlocked and hadn't righted a toppled stool. He unclipped his cell phone from his belt and scrolled down to her name in his contacts list. He was about to punch send when he heard her phone ringing.

It was close by, but where?

He cocked his head and located the source. He was tall enough that he didn't have to stand on a chair to reach the top of her hutch. Her phone sat on a manila envelope. He noted that the return address was the Navy Records Center. The Freedom of Information request must have come through. But he had more pressing things to attend to.

He answered Sophie's phone. "Hello?"

"Who's this?" the caller demanded.

It was a man's voice. He sounded familiar, but Rev couldn't place him.

"Who's this yourself?"

"Where's Sophie?"

"I'd like to know the same thing. I'm Sophie's ..." Rev hesitated. He wasn't sure why. "Friend."

"I heard you two broke up."

Rev placed him. "Chuck?"

"That's right. So, you don't know where Sophie is?"

"I'm standing in her kitchen and she's not home. Her door was unlocked. A kitchen stool has been knocked to the floor."

"That doesn't sound like Sophie," Wennington said.

"Why are you calling her?"

"To see if she got an image I e-mailed her."

"An image of what?"

"You don't know?"

There was a pleased tone to Chuck's voice. Knowledge is power.

"Know what?"

"About Johnston Bradley. He's dead. Or may be. Police are investigating whether a video showing his murder is real or a fake. The image I sent her may be of Bradley's murderer!"

"Shit! When did all this happen?"

"Yesterday. I sent her the picture today."

"Sophie told me that there had been some developments in the gun shop burglary case," Rev said. "She said we'd talk about them this afternoon. I had some things to tell her, too, but she's not here ..." Rev was rambling. He was usually reticent around Chuck Wennington, whom he considered to be an ass. Everyone knew that Chuck had a thing for Sophie. It was a newsroom joke, one that Rev had never laughed at. He stopped himself. Took a deep breath. "Why don't you send the image to my e-mail account, too? Maybe it holds a clue about what happened to Sophie."

"No way, hombre," Chuck said. "You're not on staff anymore and the image is a resource in an ongoing investigation. I don't want you selling it to the enemy."

"Oh come on, Chuck. I've signed a non-compete. Besides this isn't about the news; it's about helping out a friend who's missing and may be in danger."

"I'll have to think about that," Chuck said.

"Fuck you!" Rev replied.

He punched the end button, cutting Chuck off.

He paced around Sophie's kitchen table three times. He sat down, launched the browser on his iPhone and Googled the Selinsgrove State Police Station. He punched the link to dial the number. He caught Liv just as she was coming off her shift.

"Shit," Liv said. "I was afraid something like this would happen. If she's missing then my prime suspects are Furnley Franklin and Jerry Slike. They're old hands at kidnapping. You at Sophie's now?"

Rev was slow to realize that a response was warranted. "Huh? Oh, yeah. I'm in her kitchen."

"OK. Here's what I want you to do. First of all, don't touch anything. I want to get a crime scene technician out there to take some fingerprints. See if anything suspicious pops up."

"Oops."

Liv sighed. "OK. We'll have to fingerprint you, too, to eliminate your prints from the suspect pool. Stay put. I can be at Sophie's place in 50 minutes or so. I'll try to borrow a lab tech from Troop H in Harrisburg. He or she might get there first. If they do, let them in. Got it?"

"I love a forceful woman."

"What's that?"

"I said, I'm not stupid. I don't need to be spoon fed."

"Yeah, right. Stay put!"

"OK. OK."

Rev was talking to himself. Liv had already hung up. He stared at the manila envelope from the U.S. Navy. It clearly was addressed to Sophie and he was pretty certain what it contained. Would it reveal a motive for her apparent kidnapping? Would it confirm what Uncle Jake had told him ... from the grave? There was no way of telling unless he opened it.

Rev pulled his pocket knife from his pants pocket and made a neat slit under the envelope flap just the way Sophie would have done it. He pulled out a sheaf of two dozen or so pages stapled together in the upper right hand corner.

Rev read the document. It didn't take long; just 21 pages. The report confirmed Jake's assertion that Alan Jenkins had commanded Operation Setting Sun. His journalistic juices flowed, diluting his worry about Sophie and feeding his guilt for being so unconcerned about the woman he had loved.

"It sucks being me," he announced to the empty room.

Using his iPhone's built in camera, Rev took a picture of each of the pages and slid them back into the manila envelope. He returned the envelope to the top of Sophie's hutch.

He retrieved his briefcase from the back seat of his car and returned to Sophie's kitchen table to review Jake's journal ... to admire how it dovetailed with what he had just learned about Operation Setting Sun. If what he suspected was true, he could understand why a presidential candidate would be eager to suppress evidence that his father had committed a war crime ... no, more than that: a crime against humanity.

Chapter 31

Jake's Journal

By April of 1945, my life had settled into a dreary routine. Warrior to desk jockey is a precipitous fall. I landed as a nine-to-five guy, punching a clock at Consolidated Aircraft Company in San Diego. I was still in the navy, collecting the grandiose pay of $200 a month and living, alone, in my house on Altadena Avenue.

I visited Emika every other weekend at Manzanar Internment Camp, as my work schedule allowed. I missed her terribly. I was lonely. I missed the camaraderie of my friends and associates in VT-6. A lot of them were dead; killed at Midway. Some of those who survived were reassigned to the USS Hornet, sunk not long after Midway at the battle of Santa Cruz. Talk about jumping from the frying pan into the fire.

I followed the war in the Pacific grimly as we struggled to capitalize on the advantages we garnered at the expense of so many good men from the torpedo plane squadrons of the Enterprise, Hornet, and Yorktown.

I was the old warhorse turned out to pasture and it would have been easy for me to cry in my beer, to disappear into a bottle. To say, fuck it, I've done my share; the world won't end if I don't get up today and drag my ass to work and sign off on another float plane destined for delivery to some backwater of the war in the Pacific.

But every time I sat down with a bottle to drown my sorrows, the thought of how disappointed Emika would be kept me sober.

Sobriety was tolerable with Emika's love and kindness close at hand. Absent her calming influence and I became as ornery as a footsore mule, to borrow a saying from Burwell Addison, who knew a lot about mules but not much about his second oldest son. He could never understand why I'd rather swab a deck than plow a field.

The trip from San Diego to Manzanar Internment Camp was no picnic. Three hundred and fifty some miles in my old Studebaker on rationed gas. So you can imagine how angry I was when I showed up the third week in April to find Emika gone. No forwarding address. I spent a night in the local hoosegow when I objected too vociferously to her absence and to a lack of information about her presence. A lieutenant commander was dispatched from San Diego to spring me from jail.

He told me not to worry. My wife was fine. Just a paperwork snafu. She'd been transferred to another internment camp due to overcrowding at Manzanar. I'd hear from her soon. And he handed me a fresh set of orders. The ink on them still wet. I was to report forthwith to the U.S. Naval Air Station at Hampton Roads, Virginia.

Son of a bitch! The order had such immediacy that they gave me my own plane. I piloted a long-range Curtiss PBY seaplane, fully armed with a crew of eight because it was wartime and it was conceivable, although unlikely, that we might encounter the enemy along the way. I took a southerly route from North Island, San Diego and stopped off at my old stomping grounds, the Naval Air Station at Pensacola, Fla., to refuel and grab a couple of hours of sleep. I made it to Hampton Roads in a little better than two days, fretting all the while about my wife. Where the hell was she?

There was a car waiting for me at the seaplane dock. A big Packard painted olive green with a general's star on the front fender. I bid the crew goodbye, old friends of two days and a sweaty night at Pensacola.

My driver, a taciturn black army sergeant, usually drove for Brigadier General Colton Smith. That much he told me and little else. I could tell that the good sergeant thought it beneath him to chauffeur a mere enlisted man just three pay grades above his own.

He opened the back door for me, grudgingly, and I climbed in while he stowed my kit in the trunk. I would have insisted on riding up front, had he not been a Negro. I am a product of my upbringing. The social difference between a black sharecropper and a white one in the pecking order of turn-of-the-century North Carolina was miniscule, but it was important to my family and to those like us. Being poor and white beat being poor and Negro hands down. We cleaved to that advantage with the desperation of drowning men.

I have often reflected on how a man with my social prejudices could have become so enamored of an Asian woman. It would be glib to conclude that love is blind. But the vision of true love is microscopic; it sees beyond surface attributes to the soul beyond. In my later years, I have contemplated on the theology of reincarnation. I believe that I have lived before and that in those lifetimes I have encountered and loved the soul resident in Emika not once but many times over. And I pray that I will encounter her again somewhere ... sometime.

"Where are we headed?" I asked my Negro driver.

"I've been told you don't need to know that, Chief Addison," he replied as he settled in behind the wheel and eased the big Packard into reverse to back away from the hangar. With that, we retreated into a mutual silence that remained unbroken over the entire trip of forty or so minutes.

As a pilot, I have an impeccable sense of direction. Our course took us south from the Naval Air Station, then west across the Nanesmond River Bridge on Highway 17, which veered north at Raggy Island and crossed the James River drawbridge. I knew from having been stationed at Norfolk with VT-6 before the Enterprise was ordered west to San Diego that we were passing Langley Airfield.

We crossed land the Union and Confederate armies had fought over during the Peninsular Campaign of 1862 and ended up at a nondescript, two-story brick building with a marble columned entryway, situated several miles to the north of the airfield in the midst of an industrial park.

The building consisted of an original central portion offset by two wings that obviously had been added after the initial construction because the brick was of a different color. A railroad spur ran behind the building, beyond which was a grouping of four warehouses.

The black sergeant pulled the Packard to the curb and announced: "Building 587. This is where you get out, Chief Addison."

He said nothing more, returning to the sullen silence that had defined our association.

I realized that this was a strategy in the ongoing and never-ending class war between poor whites and blacks. He perceived me by my accent and the hash marks on my uniform sleeve to be white trash unsuited for anything other than a career as an enlisted man. He would offer none of the courtesy black people of his generation were inclined to offer those they perceived to be of the white gentry.

"Where should I go, Sergeant?" I asked.

He turned his head and smiled, his white teeth gleaming with the thrill of having recorded a small victory. He had made me ask.

"You do what you want to do, Chief, but if I were you, I'd saunter up that walkway yonder to the front door and see if they'll let you in. If they don't, I'd go around back where they receive the colored folks and po' white trash."

I am usually slow to anger, but the sergeant's truculence had my dander up.

"Aren't you going to open the door for me?" I asked. "And what about my kit?"

"Open it your own damn self, Chief," he replied.

The barb popped the balloon of my self-importance.

I laughed.

"I guess we know each other pretty well, don't we, Sergeant?" I asked, as I alighted from the back seat of the general's Packard.

"Don't worry about your kit," he replied. "I'll be waiting here for you when you're done. Them's my orders."

The sergeant tipped his hat insolently over his eyes and leaned back behind the wheel to take a nap.

I slammed the door and stretched the kinks out of my back. The spring air on my cheek put a bounce in my step. I was overcome with the sensation that a great opportunity awaited me inside Building 587.

As I approached the front door, I noticed the letters NACA embossed in the concrete near the apex of the portico. Below it were the words Research Laboratory.

I took the two steps to the door in one leap.

Chapter 32

Jake's Journal

"May I see your ID card?"

The young Marine stationed at the door of Building 587 didn't bother with a salute.

He was a lance corporal and wore a 1911 Colt .45 on his right hip with the arrogance of a teenager suddenly vested with authority over life and death.

I dug my ID card out of my wallet and handed it to him.

He studied it with the intensity of a schoolboy translating a passage in Latin. "Welcome aboard, Chief Addison. They're waiting for you in the second floor conference room. Follow me."

He led me to a set of stairs to the left of the entrance and we huffed and puffed up 24 steps. Well, he strode purposefully and I huffed and puffed, counting the steps to divert my attention from the tightness developing in my chest.

We walked a short distance down a hall and the Marine opened a door and stepped back, motioning me to enter the room beyond.

I stepped inside and he closed the door behind me.

The room was rectangular with two rows of windows on the wall directly opposite the door. The top row was pushed open because the spring day was warm and promised to become warmer as the sun climbed higher in the sky. The overhead lamp was lit unnecessarily.

Sunlight streaming through the open windows illuminated a long cherry wood conference table flanked by an array of straight-backed chairs. Two men sat at one end of the conference table.

One of them occupied a captain's chair at the head of the table. He was facing me as I entered the room. Bald-headed and mustached, he wore a suit and sported a U.S. Naval Academy tie Windsored tightly beneath the collar of a starched white shirt. Another man, wearing the uniform of a U.S. Navy rear admiral, according to the thick bar of gold at his cuffs, sat with his back to me.

The admiral turned as I entered the room. There sat Alan Jenkins, my old nemesis from Coco Solo; the man who had insulted Emika and derailed my commissioning as a U.S. Naval officer.

The civilian at the head of the table arose and walked toward me.

"Good afternoon, Chief Addison," he said, extending a hand in greeting.

"I think you know Admiral Jenkins. My name is Gerome Hunsaker. I'm U.S. Navy, too—a commander, retired. These days I teach aeronautics at MIT and chair the National Advisory Committee for Aeronautics. NACA for short. That's the acronym you probably noticed over the front door."

As I shook his hand, I took measure of the man.

He was as neat as the father of the bride. Bald on top, with a fringe of hair cut short rising above his ears for three inches or so. His mustache was peppery, thick, and clipped neatly above the lip and below the nose.

I recognized the name. Gerome Hunsaker, the Einstein of the U.S. Navy, a co-designer of our much-maligned torpedo planes. I offer his curriculum vitae from the vantage point of hindsight, this having been written in 1968. Hunsaker is a pioneer of naval aviation and winner of the prestigious Guggenheim medal. As I write these words, he is still ensconced as the chairman of the aeronautics department at MIT and continues his association with NACA, although by act of Congress it now is known as NASA and has been charged by the late great Jack Kennedy with putting a man on the moon before the decade ends. Lord, I hope I live to see that.

Hunsaker was a vocal and ardent opponent of our deployment of the atom bomb, although at the time I had no idea of what that was. Nobody, outside a tight-knit group of government scientists, flag rank military, and bigwigs in the state department, was aware of the so-called Manhattan Project.

"Have a seat, Chief," Hunsaker said, motioning to a chair to his port side across the table from Admiral Jenkins, who didn't bother to rise but nodded at me sullenly as I sat down.

"We have a special mission that, we think, is perfect for a man of your experience, training, and proclivities," Admiral Jenkins said, without preamble.

"Proclivities?" I asked.

"Sorry to use vocabulary beyond your pay grade," he responded. "You know, your abiding love of the Japanese people."

Hunsaker caught the barb. He sensed my anger and laid a gentle hand of restraint on my arm. "Gentlemen. Play nice." He glanced at Jenkins, who scowled and leaned back comfortably in his chair, having once again placed a burr under my saddle.

"What Admiral Jenkins is trying to say is that we would like you to embark on a diplomatic mission that requires an experienced pilot to navigate a float plane through dangerous airspace," Hunsaker said.

"The navy has a thousand men who fit that description, almost all of them younger than me," I noted, cutting my eyes toward Admiral Jenkins.

"That may be so, but you have a special qualification that makes you practically one of a kind," Hunsaker said.

"What's that?" I asked.

Instead of answering, Hunsaker veered off course.

"Are you familiar with the Aichi 13?"

"The Jake?" I asked.

Hunsaker looked confused.

Jenkins came to his rescue. "The boys in the fleet call the Aichi 13 the Jake. It's a nickname. What Mr. Hunsaker is getting at is this. We have captured, restored, and modified an Aichi 13 and we'd like you to fly it in on a diplomatic mission to the mainland of Japan."

"Jesus Christ," I said. "That's a fool's errand if I ever heard one. I'd more likely be blown out of the skies by our own boys than by the Japanese. Besides, didn't we throw diplomacy out the window after December 7, 1941? Roosevelt won't settle for anything less than Japan's unconditional surrender."

"That is precisely what this mission is all about," Hunsaker said.

"What?"

"We want you to fly a senior diplomat and an interpreter to Tokyo to help negotiate Japanese surrender with a senior Japanese official who has begun to see the futility of his country's position and may be willing to end hostilities before we commit another million men on both sides to early graves," Hunsaker said.

"Sounds like you're offering a carrot without a stick, Mr. Hunsaker," I observed.

"Oh, we have a stick," Admiral Jenkins interjected. "A really big stick, and I think we should just go ahead and use it."

"Our new weapon is a Pandora's box," Hunsaker said. "I am a member of the scientific community that is developing it, and I can tell you this: none of us are certain it will work. If it does, it will unleash forces that could annihilate all of mankind. It is far better to threaten its use than to use it."

"What are you talking about?" I asked. "What weapon?"

Admiral Jenkins leaned across the table and stared at me with an unsettling intensity.

"None of this leaves this room," the admiral said. "Do you understand?"

I nodded, almost dreading what he would say next.

"We have developed an experimental weapon ... a bomb capable of destroying an entire city and killing all of the people who live there," Jenkins said. "We want you to fly a senior diplomat to Japan so he can warn them that we are prepared to deploy this weapon unless they surrender immediately."

I could tell that he wasn't kidding. I pulled a handkerchief from my back pocket and mopped my brow. It had become uncomfortably hot in the conference room.

"What makes you think I'm the man for this job?" I asked.

Admiral Jenkins arose, crossed the room, and opened the door.

The young Marine was still standing outside.

He snapped to attention and saluted.

Jenkins returned the salute.

"It's time, Lance Corporal," he said.

The Marine nodded and left on a mission I couldn't begin to fathom.

Instead of returning to his seat, the admiral waited impatiently by the door and jingled the change in his right pocket.

"We can't send you off to Japan without a proper interpreter," he said without turning to me. "Ah, here she is now."

And Emika stepped into the room.

Chapter 33

Jake's Journal

"Emika? Is it really you?"

I stood, pushing myself away from the table, oblivious to the disdain of Admiral Jenkins and to the amiable presence of Gerome Hunsaker, whom I could see in my peripheral vision rubbing his hands in delight like a small boy on Christmas morn.

"Yes, it is really me," Emika said.

And she threw herself into my arms.

I couldn't tell whether the sobs were coming from me or from her.

I drew her to me so vigorously that she struggled for air around our kiss.

"By God I missed you, woman," I said after breaking contact to give her room to breathe.

"And I you," she gasped.

"How long have you been here?" I asked.

"Here as in Virginia? Or here as in Building 587?"

That was my Emika, always a literalist.

"Both."

"In Virginia, for the past week. In Building 587, off and on, but most recently since 10:30 this morning, waiting for you."

"Why are you here?"

"You mean you don't know?" she asked. She looked over my shoulder at Admiral Jenkins and Gerome Hunsaker for clues as to how to respond.

"I'll take that one," Admiral Jenkins said. "Emika is here because she is related by marriage to Baron Kijuro Shidehara."

I stared at my wife in wonder.

"And who is Kijuro Shidehara?" I asked.

"A distinguished diplomat and a man of peace, who just might be willing to broker Japan's surrender, once we prove to him that

we have a weapon capable of destroying his homeland," Hunsaker replied.

"You are related to a Japanese baron?" I asked Emika.

"Actually, she is the granddaughter of Iwasaki Yataro, and the niece of his daughter, Masako, who happens to be Kijuro's wife," Jenkins replied. "You don't know much about your Nipponese wife, do you, Chief Addison?"

Thirty years in the enlisted ranks surfaced. "Who the fuck is Iwasaki Yataro?" I snarled. "And what does this have to do with me?"

Emika laid a hand on my arm.

"I am sorry, husband, for having not told you of my past. I left my homeland in dishonor."

She hung her head for a moment and drew a deep breath.

"My grandfather, Iwasaki Yataro, was a founder of the Mitsubishi Company. Kijuro Shidehara married his fourth daughter, my aunt."

"Mitsubishi? That's the company that builds the Zeke, isn't it?"

"The Zeke?" Hunsaker asked, tripping over the newer slang.

"Also known as the Zero—Japan's front line fighter plane," Admiral Jenkins interjected.

"You are related to the company that's killed so many of us?" I asked before my brain had a chance to edit what was coming out of my mouth.

My words landed like a company of Marines. I could see the light flicker behind Emika's eyes as a little bit of her love for me died. Luckily, there was plenty of love left. It wasn't long before the softness returned to her demeanor and she was mine again, although subtly different, her love diminished for the moment by the betrayal of my words.

She stated the obvious. "I am not responsible for the actions of my countrymen. It was they who cast me out."

"Cast you out?" I asked, humiliated that I was forced to have such an intimate conversation with my wife in the presence of a man I hated, a man who had ruined my naval career or at least deprived me of a commission that was rightfully mine.

Emika didn't shy from the subject now that it had been broached.

She looked at me directly and said:

"I was raped by a third cousin, a bastard of the Samurai tradition to whom I was betrothed. I refused to marry him even when it became apparent that I bore his child. When my son was born, he was adopted by Kijuro and my aunt and I was sent away to America to reflect on the consequences of defiance."

Her words overwhelmed me. My sorrow pushed aside all hatred of the smirking Alan Jenkins. My wife had suffered much in silence. She had refused to avail herself of the sympathy and support I would have offered her gladly. Instead of resenting her lack of candor I was overcome with admiration of her strength. And of her forgiveness. She now was poised to help the very sons of bitches who had locked her away in jail.

"Your father must be a proper bastard," I said, finally.

"No. Just a product of our culture," Emika replied, demonstrating her forgiveness anew.

"And what of your son?" I asked.

"I have not seen him since, although Masako sends me snapshots from time to time. His name is Kobayashi. He is a navy lieutenant and a fighter pilot. Masako tells me that he has brought great honor to our family."

"And how would you know that?" I asked.

I was angry, petulant, and humiliated that the two other men in the room already seemed to know the secrets Emika was sharing with me for the first time.

Emika nodded at Admiral Jenkins and Gerome Hunsaker.

"With their help, I have been able to establish contact with my aunt and her husband. I have received a letter from them and have sent them one in return."

"Actually, the overture was from Shidehara. He intimated through Swiss diplomatic channels that he represented a growing coalition of Japanese statesmen eager for peace. He suggested that your wife would be an appropriate liaison should we be willing to come to the table," Hunsaker said. "And we replied that a quick surrender would be in their best interests, before we loose a plague upon Japan ... and upon all of mankind, too, for that matter."

Jenkins harrumphed. "Your assessment of the dangers is pure hyperbole, Commander Hunsaker," Jenkins said, overtly drawing attention to his colleague's lesser rank.

"President Roosevelt shares a similar assessment, otherwise he would never have ordered this ... overture," Hunsaker replied.

Jenkins shrugged, acknowledging defeat.

"That's right. And I'm following orders, facilitating the transport of Chief Addison, his wife, and Claude Forsythe into the maw of the enemy, God help their souls."

"Who is Claude Forsythe?" I asked.

Hunsaker replied: "The man Roosevelt has selected to carry the carrot and the stick to Tokyo. Emika and Claude have been conferring for the past week. He speaks Japanese, and she has been helping him polish his skills."

"Then why send Emika along at all?" I asked.

"Because her uncle requested it. Shidehara is more likely to trust her than an ivy-league diplomat," Hunsaker said.

"So Forsythe is a puppet?"

"I wouldn't call him that," Hunsaker replied. "He is Roosevelt's surrogate. He is the American demanding peace. Your wife will have to persuade her countrymen of what will happen if he is spurned."

"And how will she do that?"

"We are arranging a test of our new weapon," Hunsaker said. "And we'd like you to be there to witness it. I think a first-hand account of the capabilities of our gadget might convince the Japanese to pack it up."

"So, what do you think, Chief Addison? This is an all-volunteer mission. If you decide not to take it on, there will be no recriminations," Jenkins said.

"If it truly is all-volunteer, then neither I nor Emika, will have anything to do with it," I replied. "I won't risk my wife's life on a pipe dream. I say drop the bomb and have done with it."

Jenkins smiled broadly. "That's what I told President Roosevelt," he said. "And I think most of America's fighting men would say the same thing."

"That's why civilians have to command the military in a democracy. It can't be the other way around. You don't have to look any farther than Japan for proof of that," Hunsaker said.

"I agree with Mr. Hunsaker," Emika interjected.

She took a deep breath and cut off my balls. Figuratively speaking. "Husband, I would not be the woman you love if I ignored a chance to save millions of lives. I am going regardless of your decision."

Her words were a slap in the face, but I had them coming.

I knew my wife. She was kind, courageous and, when she made up her mind, resolute. I took both of her hands in mine and surrendered to the inevitable.

"And I would not be the man you love if I allowed you to do this on your own."

Jenkins and Hunsaker exchanged looks.

"Don't you have something you'd like to tell Chief Addison?" Hunsaker asked.

Jenkins reached into his pocket and displayed two pins on the palm of his hand—two silver bars each, the collar insignia of a lieutenant in the United States Navy.

"The president has instructed me to confer upon you this commission," Jenkins said.

I could tell that the words cost him plenty. He was red-faced, breathing like a marathoner on the final hill.

He handed me the collar pieces and stepped back.

"So, now what?" I asked.

"Emika and Claude need a few more weeks of preparation," Jenkins said. "It will take time because everything has to be filtered through the Swiss. And I need to finalize plans for your transport. I'm leaving for Seattle this evening to brief the skipper of the USS Gardiners Bay on what we expect of his ship."

"The Gardiners Bay?" I asked.

"She's a brand new seaplane tender. You'll rendezvous with the Gardiners Bay near Midway. The Jake will be on board. The tender will take you within seaplane range of Tokyo. The captain will think I'm crazy, but he'll follow orders and so will you."

"And what are my orders?"

"It will take a couple of days to install the landing gear on your Cat. I'm told your family lives near here ..." Jenkins said.

"That's right. Chatham County, North Carolina."

"You have three days' leave. Visit your family. Say your goodbyes and then report to Seattle no later than 0800 hours April 22. We want you to familiarize yourself with the captured Jake, take it up for a couple of test flights. Get a feel for how she handles," Jenkins said.

"What are my travel arrangements?"

"The Cat will be at your disposal. We're retrofitting her with wheels so she can take off and land from tarmac as well as the sea. She will be waiting for you at the airfield, fueled, crewed, and ready to go" Jenkins said.

"And what of the test?"

"You will receive instructions at the appropriate time," Jenkins said.

He saluted me and held the salute until I returned it.

"Aye aye, sir," I said.

Chapter 34

Jake's Journal

And then there was light ... before the dawn.

It seared our retinas, painting a high New Mexican mesa with an unhealthy cacophony of brilliant whites, yellows, and oranges selected from Dante's palette. The concussion that followed would have knocked us from our feet had we not been cowering on the ground near an observation post about six miles from ground zero.

We were deafened by the roar of the chain reaction that consumed matter more voraciously than a fat man set down before a feast. It felt as if someone had opened the doors of a gigantic blast furnace. And a mushroom cloud some 40,000 feet at its highest point bloomed like an obscene fungus fertilized by the offal of a million wars from the dawn of time to the present.

I stared into the face of God that rainy July morning on the day the sun rose twice over the Alamogordo Bombing Range in New Mexico, and I wondered at the hubris of the men who had unleashed this horror upon His creation. Alas, Lucifer had much to celebrate in the swirling radioactive shroud that mankind had so suddenly pulled tight about the world.

Emika, Claude Forsythe, and I witnessed America's first test of the atomic bomb because President Harry S. Truman, or someone who spoke for him, had decided that if we were to persuade the Japanese that they faced Armageddon, we needed to speak with the authority of the damned.

And damned we were forevermore by the certainty that we had at last and irrevocably cast ourselves from Eden. Encased in the atom was the power to reduce the world to the chaos that had preceded Genesis.

When I left the National Advisory Committee for Aeronautics in April of 1945, I had been told that America possessed a new weapon capable of ending the war at a single blow. But I had no concept of its dimensions.

Even its creators didn't know what to expect when they flipped the switch on what will forevermore be known as "The Gadget." Would the yield be the equivalent of five hundred tons of TNT or fifty thousand tons? Or would it ignite the atmosphere, killing all life on earth?

The eggheads assembled for the atom bomb test, called Trinity, had no idea.

The answer, as I later learned, was twenty thousand tons, but the difference between five hundred and twenty thousand tons didn't mean much to the four hundred or so observers gathered on July 16, 1945 in a tiny corner of what is now the White Sands Missile Range.

At the end of the day there is not one whit of difference between a bicycle and a steamroller for the bug crushed beneath its wheels.

Lying there with the heat of the sun on my cheeks, even though the sun had yet to rise, I realized that we had signed up for a fool's errand. Nobody would ever believe us if we told them what we had witnessed.

The next day, when we climbed into the sleek Buick usually reserved for General Groves or Robert Oppenheimer, the project's military and civilian managers, respectively, our driver, a quiet American Indian named Joe Chee eyed the package Forsythe held gingerly at arm's length with some suspicion.

"You're not supposed to leave here with anything 'cept your skin," he observed.

Forsythe handed him a chit signed by General Groves himself authorizing us to transport from Trinity one eight-ounce lump of radioactive trinitite, a grayish green glass into which the sand for a half mile radius around ground zero had been transformed in a layer an inch or two thick by the explosion of The Gadget. Or was it an implosion? The scientists had argued about that at the observation post while awaiting the test.

The radioactive trinitite would set a Geiger counter ticking. It was the final piece of evidence we hauled to Tokyo as a warning to the emperor of the price of Japan's continued resistance. We carried the sample in a lead- and felt-lined metal box, wrapped in silk and tied up with a silken bow.

We also were given a short, five-minute film strip prepared by Julian Mack and Berlyn Bixler, the official photographers of the apocalypse. But film strips can be faked. So much rode on Claude Fortsythe's silver tongue and even more on my dear wife's power of persuasion. The Japanese, I reckoned, were much more likely to believe one of their own. Although in disfavor, Emika was of *patrician lineage, and what would it profit her if Japan's inevitable defeat occurred now or four months from now?*

As a guard tugged aside a barbed wire barrier at Stallion Gate, the southernmost portal to the Trinity site, Chee glanced at me appraisingly.

"Where are you bound for next, sailor?" he asked.

"I'm headed west," I said.

"How far west?"

"To where the rising sun is descending."

"What's that mean?"

"I'm courier ... a bearer of ill tidings."

Chee grinned. "Be careful of that," he said.

"Why?"

"I hear they always kill the messenger."

His words rang in my ears as the big Cat the navy had entrusted to my care cleared the runway at the Alamogordo airfield, some 60 miles as the crow flies from the spot they still call Trinity.

And we set off to the land where the rising sun was descending.

Chapter 35

5:30 p.m. Wednesday, August 24, 2011, Enola, PA

Sophie's doorbell chimed, breaking Rev's concentration on Jake's journal. Liv Pearson stood on the doorstep wearing her state police uniform, the strap of the silly Smokey Bear headgear cinched up tight under her chin. Rev opened the door and Liv burst into the foyer, all starch, leather, and attitude. The handgun, strapped in its holster below a broad black leather belt on her right hip, gave the attitude some teeth. Rev thought she looked like a French poodle wearing a Doberman pinscher suit. She didn't bite, but she barked: "What are you smiling at, asshole?"

There was something ridiculous in the macho accoutrement that adorned the tiny angry woman confronting him. Rev swallowed his smile and took aim at contrition.

"I'm sorry, Liv. It's just that your hat ..." He shook his head and focused. The hilarity that seized him was maniacal and arose from the crossroads where grief and desperation collide.

"Sophie is missing, and I'm worried sick," Rev added.

Liv took off her hat and slapped it on her thigh.

"There might be a completely benign reason for Sophie not to be at home. We will find her. Finding people is what I do. And, Rev?"

"Yes."

"It's part of the uniform. I have to wear it. So lay off the hat, OK?"

Rev touched his right forefinger to his right brow, saluting her candor. "I know you don't like me, but we're on the same team now. What can I do to help you find Sophie?"

"It's not that I don't like you. I just like Sophie better." She pointed a finger at him like a gun. "You put her through hell. You don't know how many bottles of wine we killed talking about YOU, trying to figure YOU out. She thought YOU were deep, the tortured warrior; that sort of shit. I told her YOU were just an asshole. That she didn't need an emotional cripple fucking up her life. I told her to forget about you and buy a dog."

"If she had followed your advice, she might have been better off. A dog might have protected her."

"Nah. She was talking about a shih tzu. Just as much love, less shit."

"I understand that the young man Sophie bailed out of jail has been murdered," Rev said. "Do you think that could have anything to do with her kidnapping?"

"It's a place to start. Hopefully we'll know more when my crime scene team gets here. Loo said they still had to clear a murder scene in Dauphin."

"You wouldn't happen to know Sophie's e-mail password, would you?" Rev asked.

Liv was surprised by the non sequitur. "Why?"

"She left her cell phone behind. I found it on top of the hutch in the kitchen when Chuck Wennington called."

"Who's Chuck Wennington?"

"The *Telegraph*'s resident geek. Said he'd just e-mailed Sophie an image that might be of Johnston Bradley's murderer. But he wouldn't send it to me because I don't work for the paper anymore."

"You got your computer with you?" Liv asked.

Rev nodded. "In the kitchen."

"Show me."

She followed him back the hall to Sophie's kitchen.

Liv sat down on the edge of one of Sophie's two kitchen chairs and straightened the creases of her black uniform pants. The satin stripes down the legs of the pants shimmered in the late afternoon sunlight streaming through the kitchen window.

Rev sat down on the other chair. He whisked Jake's journal off the table and secured it beneath the front flap of his computer case.

He unzipped the case, pulled out his computer, turned it on, and drummed his fingers impatiently on the tabletop while it warmed up.

"What's that you just put in your briefcase?"

Rev considered. What the hell. "It's a journal written by Jacob Addison, my grandmother's uncle," he said.

"Is that the guy who was killed by a hit-and-run driver all those years ago in San Diego?"

Rev nodded, surprised that she knew about what he considered to be his personal business. "Sophie told you about that?"

"Yep. That's what best friends do. Share things. Think there are connections among Jacob Addison's death, the gun shop burglary, and Johnston Bradley's murder?" Liv asked. She could tell the question startled him. "We speculated about that. Like I said, we're best friends, and we were trying to figure out what happened to Johnston Bradley. His ... apparent ... murder really shook Sophie up."

"Apparent?" Rev asked.

Liv bent forward with her elbow on the tabletop. She rested her chin in her palm and studied Rev for a few seconds before replying. "Guess it won't hurt to tell you this. We were able to pin down the alleged crime scene—the Trevorton Rod and Gun Club. I was up there this morning with the forensic guys. We found some blood, but not nearly enough to suggest the sort of gore we witnessed on the video."

"So, what does that mean?"

"I don't know. There were traces of bleach, which could have been used to clean up the crime scene, but there was something else that the forensic guys are worrying over."

"What's that?"

"Corn syrup, food coloring, and corn starch; I scraped the residue off the floor myself."

"What does that mean?"

"Those are ingredients of fake blood."

"So you found fake blood and real blood at the crime scene?"

Liv nodded. "That's right."

"What do you conclude from that?"

"That maybe Johnston Bradley was really shot, or maybe somebody wanted us to think that he was shot, but he wasn't."

"If you were involved in some sort of right wing conspiracy, why would you want to attract the attention of law enforcement by staging a fake murder?" Rev asked.

"You know about the connection with the Blue Mountain Boys?" Liv asked.

"Sophie told me. We were lovers, remember?"

Liv pretended to shudder. "No accounting for taste."

Rev grinned. He was beginning to warm to Liv Pearson. "So, why would Johnston Bradley want to fake his own murder?"

"That is the six million dollar question."

"My laptop is loaded. Sophie has a wireless router and it's asking me for a password. Any ideas?"

"Why don't you try her e-mail password?"

"And that is?"

She spelled it out for him.

"Try r-e-v-s-a-n-a-s-s-h-o-l-e."

Rev laughed. "Any punctuation?"

"Nope."

"I'm in."

Rev launched Internet Explorer, navigated to the *Telegraph's* webmail site, and typed in her username: s.anderson@telegraph.com. He typed in the password and Sophie's e-mail queue loaded on his screen.

He opened the message from Chuck Wennington, which read:

"Captured this image reflected in the tile floor from the video of the alleged murder. See if you can make out who this is." Rev double clicked the attached JPEG file.

Liv stood and leaned over his shoulder.

The image was blurry. It was like looking at a picture of a man taken on the far side of a dirty aquarium. The features were bloated and blurry but recognizable.

"I think I know that man," she said. "I'm pretty sure it's Colonel Randolph Simpson."

"You're right."

"How would you know that?"

"I served with him in Iraq."

"I'd say that Colonel Simpson has some explaining to do," Liv said.

Chapter 36

10 a.m. Thursday, August 25, 2011, Juniata County, PA
Sophie Anderson awoke in a panic. She was lying on her back in the dark on something cold and hard and dusty. The air smelled of dirt and mildew.

The darkness threw her. Last thing she remembered it was mid-afternoon and sunny. She concluded that the absence of light was artificial. But even that realization didn't help the claustrophobia. Panic constricted her throat making it difficult for her to breathe.

Was she in a room or a cave? How far away were the walls? Were they six inches from her nose or 30 yards away? Not knowing drove her crazy.

She forced herself to slow down, to take deep measured breaths, just like her yoga teacher taught her. Inhale for twenty seconds, exhale for fifteen. Count it out. Her pulse slowed. The steady thudding of her heart was reassuring.

Last thing she remembered it was Wednesday afternoon. How long had she been unconscious and why? She had to concentrate. Stumbling about in the dark could wait. She needed to evaluate, discriminate. Think.

She rubbed her palm across the floor. Raised her hand to her nose and sniffed.

Dirt. She thought: *"What kind of structure has a dirt floor these days? A cabin? An outhouse? A barn?"*

None of those options made any sense. She should have been able to see light between the cracks in the boards. There was no light to be seen.

What type of structure would be designed with no windows and apparently no doors? There was a conundrum. She thought about that for a while but couldn't come up with any answers.

Jerry Slike and Furnley Franklin.

Their names came to her abruptly.

Slike had kidnapped her from her house. Why had that been so hard to recall?

He shoved her into the truck, a black Ford F-150 with oversized tires. The truck Furnley Franklin was driving the day she bailed Brad out of jail and encountered her nemeses along the roadway. Brad had gone with them, willingly, or so it seemed at the time.

Then the image of Brad's face as the bullet took his life leapt into her consciousness. The splatter of gore—all captured on the goddamn video and streamed out over the Internet where the obscenity of his murder was loosed on an unsuspecting public.

She forced herself to slow down, to breathe in and breathe out. As long as she was breathing everything was OK.

Slike hadn't blindfolded her at the beginning of their trip. That was ominous. If he didn't care if she knew where they were going did that mean she wouldn't be coming back? She remembered worrying about that as they drove along Route 11-15 through Wormleysburg, Enola, and Perdix, with the railroad tracks to their right and the Susquehanna River, broad and brown, playing peek-a-boo through the trees that skirted the tracks.

They chased a Norfolk Southern freight train, chuffing along to their right. The clatter of the cars made it through the closed windows and the quiet whir of the truck's air-conditioning. She glanced at the speedometer. They were going 45 mph and were gaining on the train. She counted forty cars before the tracks and the roadway diverged and the train was lost behind a screen of trees.

At Duncannon they diverted onto Route 274 and followed it north and west to New Bloomfield. They turned left around a monument in the town square and headed west through a broad valley, passing grazing dairy cattle, rich earth planted with alfalfa and corn, and a sprawling high school.

Slike drove carefully. He had stayed within the speed limit, never more than 55 mph, even on the rare straight stretches. And he refused to tell her anything. That was the maddening thing about it.

"Where are we going?"

She had asked him that twenty times or more.

"You'll know . . . when it suits me."

His cell phone chirped. He answered it, listening for a while without saying hello.

"Yeah. She's sitting right here beside me. We'll be at the rendezvous in about ten minutes."

So this was planned. Slike wasn't working without a net after all. She was in deep shit.

He hung up the phone.

"Who was that?" she asked. "And where are we going?"

"You'll find out soon enough," Slike sneered.

They turned north onto Route 74 and drove past the little crossroad village of Erly. A sign indicated there were seven more miles to Ickesburg. They'd been on the road 50 minutes, maybe more.

She had watched the scenery and memorized the names of crossroads and villages, businesses and churches they had passed so she could remember their route and tell Liv where they had gone, directing her to the bad guys' lair. Assuming she escaped. She had to assume that or she would have started to cry and she couldn't abide crying in front of the greasy-haired asshole driving the pickup.

Slike slowed as they passed white clapboard houses along Route 74 on the fringes of Ickesburg. According to the signage, Route 74 was also known as Veterans Way. They passed an imposing red brick building, St. Paul's Lutheran Church, as advertised by the marquee.

Just beyond the church, Slike turned left into the parking lot of the post office next to a white panel van with the words Jerry's Plumbing Service emblazoned on the side.

The driver's side door of the van opened and Furnley Franklin emerged. He had something in his right hand. The chunky assed, weight-lifting asshole carried a syringe.

At that moment, Slike turned and flopped over her, pinning her body to the seat as Franklin opened the passenger side door.

"Don't struggle," Slike said. "If you do it will hurt a lot more."

Franklin shot a thin stream from the hypodermic.

"Making sure there's no air bubble," he explained. "Don't worry, lady. I was a navy corpsman ... served with the Marines in Iraq. I've shot many a Gyrene up with morphine."

Franklin's fingers bit into her forearm.

"Morphine!" Sophie screamed. She looked frantically around the parking lot, hoping to see somebody, anybody positioned to come to her rescue, but the post office was closed. She felt the needle jab into her arm followed by a warm sensation as the fluid rushed in.

Franklin dropped the syringe onto the macadam and ground it underfoot.

"She'll be in la la land in about five minutes. I gave her enough juice that she should sleep for at least 12 hours."

Sophie snapped back to the present. Twelve hours? Had she been out that long?

The smell of dirt and mildew and the darkness of the crypt were claustrophobic.

"Help," she screamed. "I've been buried alive!"

Her voice echoed eerily, offering some clues as to the dimensions of her crypt.

"No, you haven't."

A man's voice floated to her across the darkness.

He sounded familiar—but it couldn't be. Johnston Bradley was dead.

"Brad," she shouted just to be sure. "Is that really you? You aren't dead?"

"Yes. It's really me. And, no, I'm not dead, although I'm the next thing to it. It's Sophie, right?"

"That's right."

"I was sleeping when you arrived. Your scream scared the shit out of me."

His voice sounded weary. Like he'd aged 20 years. Like he was toting a 50-pound pack filled with pain.

"So you staged the video ... but why?"

"To attract the attention of authorities. It was Colonel Simpson's idea ... to get the police sniffing around the Blue Mountain Boys. Maybe force them into a mistake."

"Simpson's involved? How so?"

"We're both regular army on detached duty ... to ferret out a conspiracy. You know. Spy stuff."

"Wouldn't a simple phone call to the police have sufficed?"

Brad didn't answer.

Instead, she heard a scuffling, shuffling sort of noise.

"Say something, Sophie," Brad said. "I need to hear a human voice. I've been alone here in the dark for at least 24 hours. They train you for isolation in Special Forces, but they can't simulate this."

"Special Forces?"

"This would be a lot easier if you'd move toward me. My hands are tied behind my back. I'm tired of crawling. And I can't get to my feet because a couple of my ribs are broken. Every time I try to stand it feels like I'm getting stabbed in the side."

"Stay still and keep talking," Sophie said. She wiggled her arms, nonplussed because they moved freely. She remembered being handcuffed. "My hands aren't tied. I'll come to you."

She pushed herself up onto all fours and stood, rising up slowly because she didn't have a sense of how far above the ceiling lurked.

"Do you have any idea where we are?" she asked, having gained her feet without bumping her head.

"Yeah. I was conscious when they brought me here. And beat me up."

Sophie took a few steps toward the sound of Brad's voice. "So, where is here?"

"Here is the indoor shooting range of the Trevorton Rod and Gun Club. It's in the boonies. More than 50 miles from the clubhouse, the middle of Juniata County," Brad said. "I've been here before. It's where the Blue Mountain Boys train their new recruits in how to fire the M-16."

"So you faked your own death to get the police involved, streamed a video to the Internet ... and then what happened?"

"The Blue Mountain Boys must be more technologically savvy than I thought. Somebody must have hacked into my e-mail, found the message I sent you, and intercepted the video that I streamed to my web site."

Sophie shuffled forward, scuffling her feet until she thought she was pretty close to Brad.

He confirmed this by bumping her ankles with his feet.

She couldn't help herself. She screamed.

"Easy, woman, it's all right. Pull up some dirt and have a seat. There's a lot we need to discuss."

"Such as Special Forces?" Sophie asked.

"That's as good a place to start as any. My name really is Johnston Bradley. I never lied about that, but I'm a little older than 18. I was picked for this mission because I look young, but I'm really 24. I've been in the Green Berets for four years now. I'm a staff sergeant, an E-6."

"So, why were you pretending to be a student at the military academy?"

"I'm not sure I should tell you this, but it's unlikely either one of us will survive, so I might as well come clean."

"Jesus Christ, Brad, you're scaring me. A lot of people will be looking for me before too long. So we should be all right. Tell me we're going to be all right!"

"I wish I could," Staff Sergeant Johnston Bradley replied.

Clad in foul-weather gear, Chief Machinist Mate Jake Utley stands beside his seaplane. This photo probably was taken sometime between 1930 and 1935 when Utley was stationed with the patrol plane squadron, VP-7, based in San Diego. In the early 1930s, VP-7 was dispatched to make a photographic survey of the territory of Alaska, which wouldn't become a state until 1959. VP-7's logo, reminiscent of the Keystone Cops, is visible on the fuselage to Jake's right..

Chief Machinist Mate Jake Utley (circa 1930-35), sits atop a foot locker, probably in his quarters with VP-7, then assigned to make a photographic survey of the territory of Alaska. To Jake's right is a large camera he used to take aerial photos of Alaska long before it became a state.

Chapter 37

Jake's Journal

Above the Pacific Ocean, I played tag with an angry thunderhead glowering like a jealous husband. Roiling cumulonimbus, dark and foreboding, buffeted the PBY Catalina and threatened to engulf us. I diverted course, glancing at my wristwatch and cursing. I would be at least an hour late for the rendezvous with the Gardiners Bay.

The Catalina, Cat for short, was a sturdy, long-range flying boat capable of taking off and landing in just about any ocean of the world. But, having my wife on board made me a cautious pilot. There were enough dangers on our horizon without courting another one. I'd flown through thunderheads before and lived to tell the tale, but I wasn't about to risk Emika.

A young lieutenant junior grade named Jed Campbell occupied the second seat. He was short on height and short on patience. Thought he was bulletproof. I didn't want to be around him when he found out he wasn't.

He tapped the dial of his wristwatch with a forefinger. "We're going to be late, Jake."

"I know that, but we won't do anybody any good if we crash this bird in a thunderhead at sea thousands of miles from the nearest land. Discretion is a virtue, boy, and the sooner you learn that, the longer you'll live."

Jed Campbell bristled at the word "boy." He was a paper tiger poised for immolation in combat, a lot like the young, college-educated naval officers who piloted most of our torpedo planes at Midway. Their courage made promises their skills as pilots could not keep. And they died—almost to the man because they were indiscreet.

I was among a half-dozen enlisted Naval Aviation Pilots (NAP, for short) who flew in the torpedo plane squadrons at Midway. We were experienced pilots. We flew courageously, but carefully, and all but one of us survived a battle in which 85 percent of the torpedo planes were shot down. We did our duty and we lived because we were discreet.

I thought about trying to explain that to Lieutenant Junior Grade Jed Campbell. It was a story that could save his life if he cared to listen. I glanced at him and the words died on my lips. Campbell was sitting straight up in his seat; his jaw set. He was ready to spit in the eye of the thunderhead. He thought I was a coward.

My words would have been wasted. I swallowed them and banked the big Cat, smiling as our heading came back to within two degrees of our plotted course.

I slapped Campbell on the back. "Make haste slowly, young man."

"What does that mean?"

"It means that the best time to recognize a cliff is before you step off it."

"You're speaking in riddles."

"Life is a riddle. The trick is to live long enough to solve it."

"And you think you have?"

I wagged a thumb at the compartment behind the cockpit where Emika was wedged. "I have, with the help of a good woman."

We flew on for a few more minutes in silence, leaving the thunderhead behind. I put us back on course and turned to Campbell. "How long do you figure it will take us to reach point Bravo?"

I knew the answer, but Campbell needed to invest some intellectual capital in our safe arrival. He studied our bearing, glanced at his watch, and looked at the chart on his lap on which he had recorded our various course changes as I skirted the thunderheads.

"I'd say we'll be on station at 1500 hours, nearly 50 minutes late and with just enough fuel to make a careful approach," he replied.

"Think you've got that figured bang on," I said. "But I'm going to throttle back and arrive a little later with more fuel onboard. I want the wiggle room for at least one wave off."

My investment in human relations paid off. Campbell actually smiled. "You remind me of my old man. He's a carpenter and careful just like you. Know what he'd say in a situation like this?"

"Nope."

"Measure twice, cut once," he replied.

"I'd probably get along well with your dad. Now give me a fresh ETA given our reduction in speed."

Campbell wet the end of his pencil and scribbled on a note pad. "I make it 1535 hours."

We picked up a ship's wake at 1520. Campbell pointed it out to me almost dead ahead. I nodded and altered course slightly to follow the wake. I eased back on the throttle and engaged the flaps to begin our descent. The hunch was a good one. We came up on the ship from behind. I keyed a switch querying the ship's remote identification beacon and received a positive response. We were an hour late, but we had found the Gardiners Bay.

"Why don't you set us down, Mr. Campbell? I know how boring it is to ride second seat. A little activity will do you good."

The Gardiners Bay changed course below us and I realized that the ship was coming around so that we could land into the wind and taxi into the protection of her lee side.

"You have the plane, Mr. Campbell," I said.

"I have the plane," he responded.

I took my hands off the yoke and stretched out my triceps behind my head.

Campbell steered past the ship, brought us around in a gentle banking turn, and nosed us down. Soon we were skimming the ocean surface, which was gentle enough, wave height of less than a foot and nary a whitecap to be seen.

The landing was gentler than most and I gave Campbell an appreciative thumbs up. The Gardiners Bay had slowed to a crawl, giving Campbell the license to taxi alongside, which he did smartly.

I unstrapped, rose to a crouch, and shook Campbell's hand. "Good landing. I guess this is where we part company. I'll leave you to the refueling. It's time for me to collect our passengers and their gear."

Gardiners Bay dispatched its recovery boat. To accommodate the civilians, the skipper dropped a platform over the side and hoisted us aboard with a crane. I was grateful because the alternative would have been to clamber up a cargo net hung over the side. There was no reception committee to speak of. A tall, desperately thin young sailor came bounding down the starboard side ladder from the superstructure and snapped me a salute. "Lieutenant Addison?"

I returned the salute. "None other."

The stripes and insignia on the sailor's right sleeve identified him as a quartermaster striker.

"My name's Fowler, Robert H. I'm the duty quartermaster. The captain relieved me of the helm and asked me to show you and your guests to your quarters. We'll be getting underway as soon as the Cat is refueled and takes off. Captain would like to see you on the bridge in 15 minutes."

Fowler bent and picked up Emika's sea bag. "Follow me."

We climbed the exterior ladders to the second level of the superstructure. Fowler opened a watertight door and led us into officer's country. Emika and I were given a tiny stateroom all to ourselves. I wondered who among the wardroom had been displaced from their quarters to accommodate the visitors.

I left Emika to move us in and followed Fowler and Forsythe down a passageway to the small stateroom Forsythe was to share with the ship's navigator, a lieutenant named Richardson.

Forsythe had a nervous bladder and asked to use the head. Fowler pointed to the facilities and escorted me to the bridge.

"You realize that just about every man on board is envious of you," Fowler said as we climbed the stairs toward the bridge.

"Why's that?"

"Because you get to bunk with a lady, and a very pretty one at that."

Fowler obviously lacked the xenophobia endemic in the fleet. But his face went scarlet, afraid that he had overstepped his bounds.

To ease his discomfort, I replied:

"That's no lady; she's my wife."

"Well, I hope one day to find a wife as pretty as yours."

"Handsome young man like you should have no problems in that regard," I said as we stepped onto the bridge. "I think you'll do just fine in the wife department."

A familiar man occupied the captain's chair bolted to the deck on the port side of the bridge. He swiveled as I stepped onto the bridge.

"There you are, Addison, and it's about goddamn time," said Admiral Alan Jenkins. "You've got millions of lives to save."

Chapter 38

3:30 p.m. Thursday, August 25, 2011, Middleburg, PA

Colonel Randolph Simpson secured a web belt about his midsection and checked to make sure the holster hung comfortably at three-quarters thigh below his left hip.

He wasn't left-handed, but he could draw quicker, line up a target more efficiently, and shoot more accurately if he drew across his body.

The pistol instructors at the academy refused to believe it, but the stopwatch didn't lie; he was a hair faster drawing across his body. Case closed.

Simpson eschewed the stainless steel Sig Sauer favored by Special Forces. He carried a 1911 Colt .45 because he liked the heft of it and because, with it, he hit what he aimed at, never mind the recoil that other sharpshooters complained of.

He was wearing his Army Combat Uniform, his boots laced tight, his patrol cap squared on his head. He was ready for action, prompted to do something, anything, by the unexplained absence of Staff Sergeant Johnston Bradley.

Brad was AWOL at a critical juncture, just as they were poised to close the net around the masterminds of the Blue Mountain Boys. Simpson was locked and loaded, ready for action but unsure of his next move.

He unsnapped the holster flap and did a couple of quick draws, aiming the 1911 at various targets in his office at the military academy. The movement was practiced, efficient ... but utterly pointless. It was late afternoon on a workday, with the cadets hurrying back to their dorms to get ready for the evening meal.

A red button lit up on the phone on his desk at Oliver Hazard Perry Military Academy indicating that Major Bill Kambic was talking to someone on his line. The phone system at the academy was antiquated, and the listening gear Simpson had attached to it allowed him to eavesdrop on Kambic's conversations with impunity. His orders were to unsnarl the rat's nest Kambic and his father, state senator George Kambic, had assembled around the academy.

His eavesdropping to date had borne little fruit; circumspection was the order of the day in conversations among Major Kambic and his co-conspirators. And Kambic's father, who also was a major general in the Pennsylvania National Guard, had never deigned to talk to his son—at least not on the office phone at the military academy when Simpson was listening in.

Simpson knew that state police Corporal Liv Pearson and a forensic team had paid a call on the Trevorton Rod and Gun Club. He hoped that the police investigation into the feigned murder of Johnston Bradley would turn up the heat on the organizers of the Blue Mountain Boys and crowd them into a mistake.

Simpson holstered his pistol and opened his desk drawer. He took out a headset and punched a button on the wireless device that allowed him to eavesdrop. With the headset in place, Simpson found himself in the midst of a conversation between two men, one of them obviously his subordinate, Major Bill Kambic.

"You're sure our friend is locked down tight?" he heard an unfamiliar voice ask.

"Yes. He is quite at home ... on the range ... and in no position to utter a discouraging word," Kambic said.

His braying laugh ground on Simpson's ears and pissed off the man he was talking to.

"Cork it, Billy," the other man said. "I've told you a hundred times that your laugh gets on my last nerve."

The rebuke made Simpson guess that he had stumbled into a conversation at long last between George Kambic and his idiot son.

Major Kambic's response confirmed it. "Sorry, Dad."

The father's voice softened. "It's OK, Billy; we're all under a lot of pressure right now. Has our guest told us anything useful?"

"Thus far he has resisted considerable motivation to share pertinent information," Bill Kambic replied. "But we are about to become more persuasive. It seems he has a younger brother. We plan to—"

"This would be a good time to shut up, Billy," his father interrupted.

"Oh. Right. Too much information. You need deniability, so my ass is hanging out there ... again."

"Yeah, and I'm about to kick you in it. Now what about that woman reporter?"

"We have that situation contained as well," Bill Kambic said.

Simpson sensed indecisiveness in the tone of the response. So did Billy's father.

"You sure?"

"Yeah. She's buttoned down tight. No worries."

Senator Kambic sighed. "We've got to hold things together for two more weeks. I'm counting on you to do that, Billy."

The phone line went dead.

Simpson took off his headset and stowed it in a desk drawer. He was pretty sure the two men had been talking about Sergeant Bradley and Sophie Anderson. He was pretty sure the home on the range comment referred to the gun club's shooting range in Juniata County. Kambic had asked permission to transport the more promising marksmen among the cadets there for advanced training.

With one phone call, he could summon the assets to effect a rescue, but there are few things in life less subtle than a Special Forces platoon, which would save Sergeant Bradley and, perhaps Sophie Anderson as well, but blow the mission to uncover precisely what the Blue Mountain Boys were up to. He wondered if Johnston Bradley had figured that out.

It was possible, but highly unlikely, that Bradley had told Anderson and that's why she had been snatched as well. Simpson thought about that for a while. Brad wouldn't have breathed a word, not without his OK. Something else was happening. Something Simpson didn't understand, at least not yet. Maybe Sam Jenkins was pulling the strings. Could Sophie have uncovered the World War II skeleton rattling around in the speaker's family closet?

The important thing was that Staff Sergeant Bradley, his family, and now a newspaper reporter who probably knew too much were in the wind. What was he going to do about it?

He made for his office door and stopped several feet in front of it.

The warrior in him dictated that he needed to pinpoint the location of the shooting range, drive there, and either rescue Johnston Bradley or die trying. But his reaction was tempered by responsibility to the mission. He wouldn't shy from risking his life if it accomplished the mission, but a precipitous rescue attempt, while strategically attractive, was not warranted tactically.

He returned to his desk, sat down, and pulled his cell phone from a buttoned-down pocket on his right thigh. He'd programmed State Police Corporal Liv Pearson's cell phone number into his electronic address book. She had given it to him with instructions to call if anything pertinent to the case occurred to him. Which it had.

Chapter 39

4:30 p.m. Thursday, August 25, 2011, Selinsgrove, PA
"So far, we've got nada," Liv said. "No witnesses, no leads. No nothing."

"Not even fingerprints?"

"Plenty of fingerprints. Yours. Mine. Sophie's. And a half dozen others. But no hits in any database."

"There's got to be something," Rev said.

"I'm sure there is. But I'm dealing with a bit of a jurisdictional problem. Sophie lives in Enola. That's East Penn Police turf. The chief, Frank Conrad, is a retired state police trooper. He's keeping me in the loop, but I can't press him too hard."

"Why hasn't he hauled Colonel Simpson in for an interview?"

"There's nothing to link Simpson to Sophie's disappearance. They are two separate investigations."

"Then why haven't you interviewed Colonel Simpson yourself, regarding Bradley Johnston's alleged murder? That's your case, isn't it?"

Liv flushed. Had he pushed her too hard? He didn't care. "At the very least, Chuck Wennington's enhancement of the video puts Simpson at the murder scene. Chuck e-mails Simpson's picture to Sophie, who disappears. You can't write that off as mere coincidence."

Liv clenched her fists. Then relaxed them. "You love Sophie. Or think you do. I get that. So I'll cut you some slack. Our techs haven't been able to reproduce Wennington's work. At least not at the same fidelity. The best they can pull from the video is a blurred image that could be anybody in a uniform. I've called Colonel Simpson, of course. Left my cell phone number with his secretary ... on three occasions. But without any hard forensic evidence putting him at the alleged scene, the station chief is reluctant to sweat him."

"Alleged?"

"No body. No murder," Liv said.

"What about Sophie's body?"

"I haven't thought about anything but that since she disappeared."

"It's hard to believe horny Chuck is better than the state police pros."

"Horny Chuck?" Liv asked.

"It's what he's called on the newsroom ... for obvious reasons."

Liv sighed and drummed her fingers on her kitchen tabletop. She had invited Rev to her house to give him an update on the state police's inquiry into Sophie's disappearance. Fraternization with a witness was a procedural faux pas, but for some reason it had seemed right to her. Given his aggressive demeanor, she was beginning to regret that decision.

"I put out an APB on the license plates of the two guys who plucked Johnston Bradley from Sophie's vehicle," she said.

"Slike and Franklin?"

She cocked her head at him.

"I read the police incident report. I'm a journalist, remember?"

"Yeah. You're the enemy. I keep forgetting. Forgot it with Sophie, too ... a lot. To my subsequent regret. So far there have been no sightings of either vehicle."

Her cell phone chirped. She tugged it out of her trouser pocket, glanced at the display, and frowned. Apparently she didn't recognize the incoming number. She answered the phone on the third ring. "Corporal Pearson."

Rev watched her while she listened. Her eyes widened.

"You call at an opportune time. I think you can help with my investigation into the apparent murder of Johnston Bradley. Maybe even the disappearance of Sophie Anderson."

Liv listened while Rev fidgeted.

"Yes. That's right, the reporter. She may have been kidnapped from her home. Sometime yesterday afternoon."

Rev shrugged his shoulders and raised his hands, palms up, impatient to know who Liv was talking to.

Liv made a slashing motion across her throat with her free hand and listened some more. "Yes. I know the Red Rabbit." She glanced at her wristwatch. "An hour from now? Yes, I can be there."

Liv smiled at Rev and swirled an index finger in the air.

"Actually, Major Polk is with me right now. He's helping me look for Sophie Anderson. They were colleagues at the *Daily Telegraph*."

Liv listened some more.

"Yeah, we think the two might be related, too. Yes, I can give Major Polk the message. Goodbye."

She ended the call with a stab of her finger. "Colonel Randolph Simpson says hi. He came clean on the Johnston Bradley murder. There wasn't one ... a murder that is. Now Brad is missing, too. And he thinks the two of them may have been snatched by the same perps."

"What about the videotape?" Rev asked.

"It was a hoax. Part of a plan to smoke out a plot ... against the president."

"Of the United States?"

"No. Of McDonald's. They're calling it the Big Mac conspiracy."

"Smart ass. An assassination plot?"

"Colonel Simpson's not sure, but he wants our help freeing Johnston Bradley and, probably, Sophie as well. He thinks he knows where they are. But he wants us to do this quietly, under the radar. Doesn't want to spook the alleged conspirators."

"Why doesn't he just call the police?"

"I am the police, remember?"

"Oh yeah, right. And you're willing to play ball?"

Liv's eyes narrowed, but then her features relaxed. "Yeah. For now ... as much out of consideration for Sophie as anything else. Colonel Simpson wouldn't give me the whole story over the phone, but he's right. Smaller is better. If we go blundering in with a SWAT team, guns blazing, we'll get Sophie killed. Johnston Bradley, too, for that matter."

"It's that serious?"

Liv nodded. "We're supposed to meet Colonel Simpson at a drive-in burger joint near Duncannon at 1800 hours."

"The Red Rabbit?"

"That's right. You know the place?"

"Yep. Let's get there early so we can eat a Bunny Burger and fries."

Liv ignored the interruption.

"Colonel Simpson will take us to where he thinks Brad and Sophie are being held and we'll decide whether it's safer to try to rescue them ourselves or call in the Marines."

"We?" Rev asked.

"That's right, we. Colonel Simpson remembers you well. Said if we get into a fire fight, he can't think of many men he'd rather have with him than you. You'll be drawing major's pay this mission."

"Simpson must have some clout to accomplish that. I'm on inactive status ... for medical reasons."

"Do you have a sidearm?"

"I've got a Glock 9 in my trunk. Put it there right after Sophie disappeared, just in case."

"You got a carry permit?"

"No. You going to bust me?"

"Not under the circumstances. But the more important question is do you think you'll be able to use it if it comes to that?"

"Sophie told you about ... my problem."

Rev looked so miserable that Liv stepped forward and patted his arm.

"Sophie and I are best friends, and best friends tell each other everything."

He rallied bravely. "So you know about the mole right on the end of my ..."

Liv laughed.

"Big toe," Rev said.

"Asshole," Liv said.

"Yep. That's my password. And, yes, if it means saving Sophie, I'll be able to pull the trigger."

Chapter 40

4:30 p.m. Thursday, August 25, 2011, Juniata County, PA
"Major General George Kambic is a Looney Tune," said Johnston Bradley, his voice low and hoarse in the darkness. Sophie wasn't sure why he was whispering. There wasn't anything either of them could say that could worsen their present circumstances.

She concentrated on his words, but a growing imperative distracted her.

She needed to pee. She had attended to nature several hours ago while Brad slept, but he was awake now and the thoughts of crawling off somewhere in the dark to pee on the dirt floor creeped her out on a couple of levels.

This reminded her of camping—and she abhorred camping. She had reached détente with the space beyond whatever four walls occupied her at any particular time. Peaceful coexistence; that was the ticket. She wouldn't pee in the bear's den if the bear afforded her the same courtesy.

Moreover, attending to bodily functions in the near presence of a man she still considered to be a pimply faced teenager was fundamentally disquieting. The thoughts of pulling down her pants and squatting a few feet from him, even in the dark, made her shudder.

Brad noticed she wasn't making listening noises. "Where are you?"

"What? I'm right here."

"No. I mean, where are you, mentally? Here I am laying out the story of your newspaper career and you seem ... distracted."

"Oh. Sorry. It's just that I need to pee."

She imagined Brad was grinning. But when he spoke she heard no laughter in his voice, merely regret.

"Well go pee. I've peed twice since I've been here ... in my pants ... because the bastards tied my hands behind my back and I'm not limber enough to unzip my pants with my teeth."

Sophie wrinkled her nose. "Yeah. I noticed."

She stood, ducking, because no matter what Brad said about the distance from the floor to the ceiling she wasn't sure of her prison's dimensions and she didn't want to add a bump on the head to the growing list of indignities that assailed her.

She counted off 15 paces and turned 180 degrees so she was facing Brad. She pulled down her pants, squatted, and pulled her panties as far forward around her ankles as possible to keep them out of the splatter. When she was finished, she tugged up her pants and, counting her steps, returned to Brad.

She sat down beside him.

"Feel better?"

"Much."

"Good. And I didn't see a thing, other than that beauty mark on your left thigh."

"Lucky guess. Now get back to your story."

Brad laughed and then gasped at the cost of laughter on broken ribs. "OK. Like I said. George Kambic is a nut job with a pretty simple belief system."

"What's that?"

"If you aren't white and a Christian, just like the founding fathers, then you are the enemy."

"George Kambic sure has a lot of enemies."

"That's right, and he's bound and determined to defeat what his son calls the forces of darkness."

"And our black president is commander and chief of those forces, right?"

"That's right."

"So what's his grand plan?"

"I had just closed in on the fact that George Kambic pulls the strings of the Blue Mountain Boys when the bruise brothers closed in on me," Brad said. "They intercepted my e-mail to you and they brought me here for a little conversation."

"Do they know about the snuff video?"

"Don't know. I had just cleaned that up when the boys showed up for a big powwow. They pretended like everything was copacetic. Like I was part of the inner circle. Lured me into a false sense of security. Then slapped the cuffs on and carted me here for some enhanced interrogation."

Sophie winced, catching the implication of the euphemism. "What do they want to know?"

"Who I'm working for."

"And who is that?"

"The United States government, which has afforded us this opportunity to die for our country."

Sophie fought to keep the panic out of her voice and failed. "Die! Nobody said anything about dying!"

"Well, I just did. These guys are fundamentalist nut jobs. And whatever their secret is, they're determined to keep it to themselves. I've got the bruises and broken bones to prove it."

"I was supposed to meet with my boyfriend, this afternoon. Well, actually, he's my ex-boyfriend. But when he finds out I'm missing, he'll come looking for me." The words made Sophie feel better. They started off shaky but ended up sounding brave—at least in her ears.

"How do you expect him to find you? Do you come equipped with GPS?"

Sophie thought for a couple of moments before she answered. "Rev is ... resourceful and resolute."

Brad laughed. "It sounds like you're describing a Boy Scout. No wonder you left him. Or did he leave you?"

"None of your damn business." Sophie's ears burned. Rev was a Boy Scout. In the Gary Cooper mold. Strong and silent. It was among the reasons she had broken things off. Rev wasn't investing any emotional equity in the process of relationship building. He was a good Scout to be sure, but she had been unable to crack the hard veneer of reticence that protected him like a turtle's shell. Since Iraq, that is.

She changed the subject. "Thoughts of a home-grown terrorist in command of a regiment of National Guardsmen make my blood run cold."

"For all his faults, my sense is that George Kambic is subtler than that. He won't attack with a regiment. A guerrilla action is more likely," Brad said.

"What do you mean?"

"I mean, the guy's a graduate of Harvard Law School, for Christ sake. He's smart. I get the idea that his intent is to stage some sort of display that will galvanize what he thinks is a large and silent opposition among white Christian males to being governed by a black man who kowtows to the minorities and the Muslims."

"So you don't think he poses a direct threat to the president's life?"

Brad veered off course. "Do you believe in Our Lord Jesus Christ?"

"What does that have to do with the going rate for a blow job in Bangkok?"

Brad laughed and gasped. "Where did you come up with that gem?"

"Rev says that a lot when I wander off point."

"That has a military ring. He in the service?"

"Yep. A major in the National Guard; he's done one tour in Afghanistan and two in Iraq."

"That would make him resourceful," Brad said.

"And resolute," Sophie added.

Brad repeated the question. "Do you believe in Jesus Christ?"

"I was brought up a Catholic, but I've deteriorated into Unitarianism. I practice birth control and I don't genuflect."

"So you'd call yourself what? An atheist? An agnostic?"

"I'd call myself a humanist."

"What's that mean?"

"I think that we shouldn't fob responsibility for evil off on the devil and give God all the credit for the good."

"I'll bet you vote democratic, too."

"I vote for the best candidate, who often happens to be a democrat," Sophie replied.

"What's your definition of good and evil?" he asked.

"What?"

"Humor me."

"OK. I think the good can be defined as putting the community ahead of the self."

"So you think that if you act in your own self interest, you are guilty of a sin?" Brad asked.

"No. I think that self interest more often than not coincides with the interests of community. What's good for me is often good for you."

"You aren't a democrat. You're a fucking socialist."

Even though he couldn't see her, Sophie stuck out her tongue.

"And what of evil? Or sin, if you prefer?" Brad asked.

"Sin is acting in your own self interest even if it harms other people. I've been doing all the soul searching here. What about you? Do you believe in Jesus Christ and what's your definition of good and evil?"

"I grew up Pentecostal. I believe that Jesus died to absolve us from sin and then arose from the dead to show us there is nothing to fear in death for we will be resurrected in the body," Brad said. "And I think Christ sometimes leads us to do things that others would consider to be a sin."

His reverent tone snuffed Sophie's snort. But she did observe: "The greatest sacrifice one can make for another is to sacrifice their life. For me, the resurrection cheapens Jesus' sacrifice."

"That is an opinion our constitution empowers you to hold," Brad said.

There was a hostile undertone to his voice and Sophie shivered. "What of good and evil? How would *you* define them?"

"Good is doing what my superior officers tell me to do and evil is the opposite."

There was a playful tone to his voice now and Sophie was relieved.

"I do know this," Brad continued. "Good and evil are at the crux of the conspiracy that George Kambic and his son, Bill, have gathered around Oliver Hazard Perry Military Academy."

"How so?"

"Bill is the pastor of Faith United Christian Church, which meets Sunday evenings in the Chapel of the Military Academy. He preaches a lot about good and evil."

"So?"

"Want to know who his congregants are?"

"Almost as much as you want to tell me."

"Most of 'em are members of the Blue Mountain Boys. Their core group, which he calls the Christian Soldiers, numbers precisely 12 men. All of them are graduates of the Military Academy with at least one tour in Army Special Forces under their belts. Your friends, Slike and Franklin, are Christian Soldiers. One weekend a month, they camp out, conduct military drills, and then get together for worship right here on the rifle range. It's a sort of military revival meeting."

"God and guns," Sophie said.

"More like guns for God. Does the number 12 mean anything to you?"

"It's a dozen."

"And the number of Jesus' disciples. Our boy Billy has a Messianic delusion and he plans to lead the Christian soldiers on a big mission of some sort next month ... I just haven't figured out what it is. They suspect that I am Judas and they are reviewing their association with me to determine what I might have shared with the Romans. Confining me here is a test."

"How so?"

"If someone comes to rescue me ... well, I am the enemy and they'll kill me without compunction. In their system of ethics, my murder would be both just and moral."

"What about me?" Sophie hated the whine in her voice.

"I haven't figured that out, either. Do you have any idea of what you might know that threatens them?"

"Just that I've been sniffing around the subject of the Blue Mountain Boys ... and I'm a newspaper reporter."

"That wouldn't seem to be enough to warrant the risk of kidnapping you. There's got to be something else, Sophie. Think!"

"Well, Furnley Franklin did demand that I hand over a package I had just received from the U.S. Navy."

"What's in the package?"

"Whatever the U.S. Navy feels it can release under the Freedom of Information Act about a World War II era special project called Operation Setting Sun," Sophie said.

"Did you give it to him?"

What was that? Eagerness in his voice?

"Nope. It arrived in the mail this morning right before Slike burst into my house, but I had hidden it away intending to give it to Rev this afternoon."

"What's Operation Setting Sun?" Brad asked.

"I don't know. I didn't open the package. It's still on top of my hutch in the kitchen as far as I know."

"Good. Now see if you can loosen the plastic ties they used to bind my hands."

"How?"

"Use your teeth."

"Ew, no!"

"Sophie, c'mon. I'd do it to help you."

"Why would I want to put my face that close to your ass? You smell like piss."

"What else do you have to do?"

"Uggggh . . ."

Sophie inhaled one more gulp of fresh air before she held her breath and chewed.

Chapter 41

4:30 p.m. Thursday, August 25, 2011, Middleburg, PA

Bill Kambic lived in one of those old homes that grace small-town Pennsylvania, in which none of the 90 degree junctures of floor, walls, or ceiling are quite square. Over the years the foundation had settled on the west side. A marble dropped on the hardwood in the living room would roll across the hall into the dining room and settle along the four-inch baseboard that Kambic had stripped of paint and restored to its original natural hardwood finish. Refinishing the woodwork was a pain in the ash, but it gleamed now in the light streaming through the old-fashioned double-hung windows, which were counterbalanced by lead weights.

The narrow, three-story brick row house had teal-colored shutters and a slate roof. It faced south on a narrow lot on Main Street in Middleburg. Kambic had lived there for five years with his wife, Sharon, who had escaped to Harrisburg, telling him she could no longer abide his radical politics, the weird sex and, most of all, "this one-horse town."

Kambic didn't miss her. He enjoyed his own company and was relieved that, although they had not practiced birth control, their marriage had been childless. The last thing in this world he needed was a rugrat. He didn't care much which one of them was sterile. He had no intentions of remarrying, even though his father from time to time hinted that he'd like a male heir to carry the Kambic name forward to the next generation.

The name might be a loss, but not the genes. Kambic was short, portly, balding, and myopic. The lenses of his Buddy Holly style horn-rims were Coke-bottle thick. The cadets called him Mole, sometimes to his face. It was an affront to machismo that he accepted with equanimity because it suited his purpose to seem ineffectual.

He dropped that pretense when he ascended the pulpit of Faith United Christian Church. The power of the Lord made him an eloquent speaker, and in those moments, in his own mind, anyway, he was six feet four inches of chiseled muscle with flowing blond hair and perfect vision, just like his savior Jesus Christ. Delusional or not, that was how he imagined his listeners perceived him as well. His congregation, almost exclusively ex-soldiers nursing grudges of various sorts against their civilian masters, met on Wednesday evenings for Bible study and on Sundays for worship—when the Christian Soldiers weren't bivouacked on the mountain land Trevorton Rod and Gun Club owned near Licking Creek in Juniata County. It was there that the cinder block rifle range was hidden, dug into a hillside far from the prying eyes of law enforcement who would object to the variety and style of the weapons fired and brim-stoned there.

Kambic sat in his living room in his favorite leather Barcalounger, working on next Sunday's sermon on his laptop computer while he awaited the arrival of his father. He glanced at his watch and wondered what was keeping the old man.

Senator Kambic's principal legislative office was situated in Bellefonte, Centre County, but he maintained a store front office in Middleburg to serve his Snyder County constituency. The elder Kambic was due to visit Middleburg to hand out $30,000 in legislative initiative funding to enable the reroofing of the municipal building. The press called the funds allocated to state legislators to fund pork projects Walking Around Money. The judicious expenditure of WAM funds empowered Kambic's re-election every four years.

His real purpose in coming to Middleburg was to visit his son and iron out the final details of their grand master plan, which was nearing fruition after years of careful nurturing.

The doorbell rang. Bill Kambic closed his laptop and climbed to his feet.

He greeted his dad at the door.

"You got the recording studio set up?" the father asked the son.

"Yep. We're ready to roll."

Bill Kambic led his father to the dining room, where he had established work stations for the two of them on either side of Sharon Kambic's cherry table, which he had acquired along with the house and all it contained by giving her an obscenely large cash settlement. His lawyers told him he could have done much better, but the money bought her silence on the bizarre acts he demanded of her to enable their sexual congress. He now adopted a pay-as-you-go attitude toward sexual relief. The prostitutes, however, quickly wearied of dressing as men and donning plastic penises. They seldom returned for a rematch, even though he tipped them lavishly.

A high-end digital tape recorder sat in the middle of the table and was attached by a curlicued cord to a microphone propped up on a tripod. A sheaf of ten or so pages, neatly stapled on the top left hand corner, was positioned on the table in front of their chairs.

Senator Kambic pulled out his chair and sat down. "Are these the scripts?"

His son nodded, glancing around to make sure they had everything they needed to record a couple of messages for their enemies to intercept to nudge them in the direction they wanted them to go.

"You're sure that Major Simpson bit on our little phone charade?"

"It's Colonel Simpson, Dad."

"I know that. I just enjoy demoting him."

"He bit."

"How can you be sure?"

"It pays to appear incompetent," Bill Kambic replied. "We've got our own listening devices in place and Colonel Simpson was not as circumspect in his conversation with State Police Corporal Liv Pearson as we were in ours."

"What do you mean by that?"

"After he intercepted our phone call, he placed a call of his own ... to Pearson, who apparently was consulting with Rev Polk at the time over what they should do about the missing Sophie Anderson."

"That was fortuitous timing," Senator Kambic observed. "Seems we caught two fish on the same hook."

"And now it's time to fillet them. My guess is that Colonel Simpson himself will lead an assault on our shooting gallery to rescue Johnston Bradley and Sophie Anderson."

"And we're not going to warn Frick and Frack that an attack is imminent?"

"There's no need to talk in riddles here, Dad. This place is free of bugs; I swept it myself not a half an hour before you arrived. Slike and Furnley Franklin have their instructions."

"Just so we're clear on that point, what are their instructions?"

"Just like you ordered. If they are attacked, they'll wound our friend Brad in whatever way circumstances permit and kill the girl. Tell me again, why are we killing the girl?"

"Because it serves the purpose of our friend, Samuel Jenkins."

"What purpose is that?"

"I have no idea, but when the shit hits the fan, Jenkins will have our backs as long as we scratch his now."

"Murder is some pretty hard scratching."

"This is an omelet worth cooking and we've got to crack some eggs," Senator Kambic said. "You OK with sacrificing Frick and Frack?"

Bill Kambic nodded. "We'll be sacrificing far more than them if we see this thing through to the end. It is the lot of Christian soldiers to countenance sacrifice in the service of the greater good. That's the message of this Sunday's sermon," he said.

"We are, then, resolute?"

"Yes. America has reached the tipping point. The mud people outnumber us. And we'll never win another presidential election ... unless we act precipitously."

"Easy, Reverend. You're preaching to the choir, here." Senator Kambic settled his reading glasses on the end of his nose, picked up his script, and paged through it.

"You sure Colonel Simpson will intercept this recorded message as well and react appropriately?"

"He's a smart man. We'll have to be subtle."

"And you think this is subtle?" his father asked, waving the sheaf of papers in the air.

Bill Kambic's response carried the certainty of an evangelist set out on God's course. "It has a razor's edge."

Chapter 42

5:45 p.m. Thursday, August 25, 2011, Juniata County, PA

Liv Pearson peered at Rev over the seat back. "You OK?" She was swallowed by the cockpit of Randolph Simpson's big Land Rover. The expensive vehicle strode with the authority of a well-bred horse, nimble and sure-footed, as Simpson maneuvered around and over rocks and potholes.

Rev always got carsick when he rode in the back seat. He should have insisted on riding up front, but he would have had to explain why and didn't want to suffer that affront to his manhood.

He could almost hear the disdain in Liv Pearson's voice as he imagined what she would say if he threw up. "So the big tough soldier has a nervous tummy?"

His admiration for her and the importance he attached to her opinion of him were surprising. She was strong-willed and assertive, but her small size made him want to protect her. He was feeling things for her better unfelt because she was, after all, the best friend of his ex-girlfriend. There were few more powerful taboos.

He hoped that she was fighting similar impulses, but it would be presumptuous to ask. What he was feeling was just plain wrong because Sophie was in danger and he loved Sophie. Or was he just grateful to her because she was pretty and had been willing to share her time and body with him, at least for a while?

He forced his mind down another road. How could they be sure that Sophie and Johnston Bradley occupied the same cell? Randolph Simpson thought that they did, but neither thinking nor hoping would make it so. Either it was true or false, and he didn't have the answer key to the test his life now imposed upon him.

He burped, swallowed bitter bile, and realized that Liv was still waiting for an answer. What had she asked him?

"You OK?" she repeated.

Her face, sun-kissed and freckled, was so compelling in profile that he almost lost context again.

Focus, Rev!

"I'm fine. Just wondering whether the Bunny Burger was a good idea."

"Mine tasted fine," Liv said. Her eyes twinkled.

The Land Rover clunked into a pothole so deep that even its well-pedigreed suspension jolted their spines. They climbed over a ledge of limestone that protruded from the rough shale of the primitive road they were following toward the mountain land owned by Trevorton Rod and Gun Club. Simpson muttered to himself at the controls of the Land Rover; he shifted into low four and slowed to a crawl.

Rev forced himself into recon mode, thinking of the task ahead. He tried to imagine the forces that would oppose them and he inventoried their assets. He carried his personal sidearm: a 9 mm Glock with a 20-round clip—the anathema of gun-control advocates, who pointed out, and rightly so, that such a large capacity enhanced a madman's ability to commit mayhem. But the extra ammo had saved his life on at least one occasion in Iraq and it felt comforting now to know that whatever challenges lay ahead, he was unlikely to run out of ammunition.

The last time he had pulled the trigger in anger he had killed four people, three of them innocent bystanders. The faces of the man, his wife, and their child watched him now as he prepared to embark on another mission without a clearly defined target or a well-thought exit strategy.

Simpson was a reassuring asset to take into a fire fight. He'd seen the elephant and was armed to drop him. The 1911 Colt strapped around the colonel's waist didn't possess the capacity of Rev's Glock, but the big .45 slugs would stop whatever they hit, dead in its tracks. There was no such thing as a flesh wound when a .45 slug was involved.

The good colonel had raided the armory at the military academy for an M-14 carbine, which would come in handy if they encountered an entrenched and determined opponent. Rev hoped they wouldn't need it.

Liv Pearson's arsenal included her service weapon, a Glock 37, chambered for .45 GAP ammunition. She also carried a snub-nosed .38 in a holster Velcroed to her right ankle. Rev had served with women in Iraq and found them to be reliable comrades in arms. They were the equal of men in terms of courage under fire, but their lack of size and strength made them of less certain worth in hand-to-hand fighting, despite the efficacy of a kick to the balls as a playing-field leveler.

"How much farther?" Liv asked, breaking Rev's reverie. "It will be dark in a couple of hours."

The Land Rover crawled over a large rock in the road. "We've got to be close," Simpson muttered.

His words were prophetic.

As the SUV rounded a sharp curve to the right, they encountered an aluminum-slatted fence blocking the roadway at the bottleneck of a small clearing with enough room to park two cars. The fence was chained to a large oak, and a heavy padlock secured the chain.

Without comment, Simpson made a three-point turn in the clearing, poising the Land Rover for a quick getaway if it came to that.

"Looks like it's shank's mare from here on out," Rev observed.

"What the hell does that mean?" Liv asked.

Simpson grinned, clearly glad for the chance to be lighthearted.

"You probably should arrest him for an anachronism of the third degree. What Rev is trying to say is ... we walk. I could cut the padlock, of course, but GoogleEarth shows it's less than a half a mile from this point to that small grouping of buildings on the mountaintop. I'd rather arrive more inconspicuously than in a Land Rover."

Simpson turned off the engine and opened his door.

Rev climbed gratefully from the back seat and stretched. Liv alighted from the front and stood beside him. She was wearing jeans, hiking boots, and a t-shirt with the words Harrisburg Mile emblazoned across her ample chest.

Rev towered a foot above her. He and Simpson wore ACUs. Rev glowered down at Liv without meaning to. "You sure you're up for this? Your ass is really hanging out there. We're acting on information from an illegal wire tap and we don't have a warrant. You've wandered real far off the reservation. You OK with finding a new career if we end up screwing the pooch on this one?"

"I don't screw pooches."

Rev laughed.

"OK. Let's gear up, soldiers," Simpson said.

He stepped to the rear of his Land Rover and opened the hatch.

Inside, in addition to the M-14 carbine, were three sets of Interceptor Body Armor, IBAs being the standard bulletproof vest of U.S. Army troops afield.

Liv noted that they afforded more complete protection than the standard issue vest of the state police and she no longer regretted having left hers at home.

The camo-colored vests fastened about the neck and in the crotch and would protect their torsos from small arms fire. Simpson had done the best he could on sizes. Rev's was a bit small and Liv's was a tad large.

After they had donned them, Simpson looked at Liv, critically. "Be careful not to present a profile to the enemy," he said. "Your armor gaps at the chest. You'd be vulnerable to a well-placed shot from the side."

Rev's armor was tight at the crotch and neck, but he welcomed its protection and he offered no complaints.

Simpson wore his custom fitted vest with the authority of one used to command.

"Follow me," he ordered.

Liv fell in behind Simpson and Rev brought up the rear as they proceeded single file along a rocky mountain road, their sidearms unlimbered and ready for action.

Chapter 43

5:45 p.m. Thursday, August 25, 2011, Juniata County, PA
"I'm almost through," Sophie said. "Give me a minute and I'll take one last chomp on it."

Her teeth and tongue were sore and she tasted blood. She must have abraded one of her gums on the plastic tie that secured Brad's hands behind his back.

Brad's skin was salty, with just a hint of vinegar. The inadvertent taste of it on her lips and tongue reminded her of her favorite Herr's potato chips. And that thought made her stomach rumble.

"It's OK. I think I can break through now." Brad strained and gasped at the effort's cost on broken ribs.

The plastic gave way and he screamed as his hands flew apart. "Jesus, that hurt."

Sophie found him in the dark and hugged him, but not too tightly.

"Now I'm going to take a proper piss," Brad said.

He fumbled for a moment in the dark before announcing:

"I can't feel my fingers. I don't suppose you'd be willing to help me with my zipper?"

Sophie laughed. "I think we know each other well enough now."

She ran her hands down the front of him, found the waistband of his trousers, pinched the top button between the fingers of her left hand and probed about with her right until her fingertips encountered the zipper pull. She tugged it down against the upward pressure of her other hand.

"You've done this before."

"You can fumble it out all by yourself. I don't know you quite that well," she replied.

She heard him moving away from her in the dark and without thinking turned from the noise.

She tried not to listen but she discerned a distant splatter. Deprived of her vision by the absence of light, her hearing had become more acute. She heard Brad fumble with his pants and curse.

"Goddamn it! I can't manage this fucking zipper. At least the horse is back in the barn."

"You mean the pony?"

"You peeked!"

"Well, so did you."

She realized that they were flirting, sort of, and then that Brad was standing next to her again.

"You sure you don't know what was in that package that Slike tried to steal from you?" he asked.

She didn't wonder at the non sequitur. Prison time, she realized, was ... disjointed.

"I didn't have time to open it. I had just tossed it on the top of the hutch in the kitchen when Slike arrived."

"Well, whatever it contains, it must be pretty damn important for the Blue Mountain Boys to break cover in such a spectacular way," Brad observed.

Before Sophie had the chance to reply, a door banged open at the front of their prison and light streamed in from beyond.

The result was devastating. The door was of western exposure and the sun, even dampened by the trees that surrounded the shooting range, shot daggers into their eyeballs.

Sophie heard a man yell.

"We've got to secure the prisoners!"

The sudden light blinded Sophie. She heard running footsteps and discerned movement. Her pupils were so dilated from the strain of trying to see in the dark that seeing in the light was almost as impossible.

She swung her fists at the blurry shapes that assaulted her. Rough hands grabbed her.

A punch to the stomach forced the air from her lungs. She collapsed, but someone caught her. She was aware, but vaguely so, of cursing and of the sounds of a struggle.

Brad, apparently, also was fighting back.

She heard a scream and realized it was her own. She was being dragged from the darkness toward the light, but by whom?

Jerry Slike was her guess. Whoever held her was too tall to be Furnley Franklin.

"Sophie! Sophie!" she heard someone call.

She gasped as she recognized Rev's voice.

Chapter 44

6 p.m. Thursday, August 25, 2011, Juniata County, PA
They trudged up the steep dirt road with a dying sun at their backs. Rev sweated silently in his body armor and wondered what awaited them at the top of the hill. His companions were silent. He could only speculate on what they might be thinking.

Simpson was a soldier and, by his account, a spy eager to come in from the cold. Like all spies, you had to consider his true motivations. It was unsettling to go into battle with someone who might change sides in the midst of a fire fight. Simpson had baggage, no doubt about that. He insisted that the whole Abu Ghraib controversy was a subterfuge to burnish his credentials for the inspection of the right-wing malcontents he was seeking to infiltrate. But was he telling the truth?

It didn't matter. Rev had his orders. General Malcolm Meredith, commanding officer of his guard unit, had phoned him not an hour after Simpson's call. Rev was activated and at Simpson's beck and call. Talk about clout.

Rev's opportunity to rescue Sophie rested on trusting Simpson, at least at this juncture. But he was prepared to react on a hair trigger to any evidence that Simpson had brought another agenda to this dangerous dance. He couldn't be frozen by indecision as he had been in that tenement in Fallujah. Shoot first, ask questions later. That would be his mantra.

Liv's motives were clearer, but her value in a fire fight was less certain. She had assured him that she consistently scored at the head of the class in the state police's mandatory small arms tests, but shooting at silhouettes and at a man who was shooting back were two different things.

Rev was no chauvinist. His experiences in Iraq had taught him that a woman was just as quick to the trigger as a man, oftentimes quicker. And he had no doubt that Liv was on his side. She wanted to save her friend. More than that, she wanted to save

Johnston Bradley, a young man who had so recently occupied the sights of her service weapon.

Sophie had laid the story out for him. Liv would have been found faultless had she dropped Johnston Bradley in his tracks when he had emerged from that motel room brandishing a handgun. Brad owed her his life. Rev was pretty certain that Liv felt indebted to the young man as well. In the perverse logic of the battlefield, Liv held Brad up as living proof of her own humanity.

The Trevorton Rod and Gun Club's redoubt occupied a mountainside in what the American Indians had called the Kittatinny Mountains. GoogleEarth showed a cluster of three buildings, one of them in the style of a log cabin. Simpson had speculated that this was the bunkhouse.

The other two were one-story cinder block buildings. The smaller of them was within 30 feet of the log cabin. It was small, 100 square feet at the most, probably a storage shed, Simpson had surmised.

The larger cinder block building was dug into the hillside about 50 yards away with its only apparent door facing west. Its dimensions spoke well for it being a shooting range. The target wall had the hillside directly behind it to stop any errant rounds and to dampen their sound. Trees and underbrush were cleared in front of the building and on its flanks, giving any occupants a 180-degree kill zone to the front and sides.

The steep hillside to the rear of the building precluded an attack from behind, at least by a force of their size, armament, and intentions. They could have lobbed RFGs at it from the trees on the hillside above, but that would not have been conducive to the health and well-being of the hostages.

Their only option was a frontal attack across the open kill zone. In that enterprise, the elements were, for the moment, favorable. The sun was low on the horizon and would be to their backs, blinding the opposing force. It was a slight advantage, but Rev was grateful for it.

While he was contemplating these things, Liv tripped and cursed. Looking down, Rev saw a taut wire strung along the ground at ankle height hidden in the underbrush.

"Shit! Our arrival isn't a secret anymore."

"What do you mean?" Simpson asked.

"Liv just tripped a wire. It didn't go boom! So it's probably an alarm. We'd better get going!"

Rev charged ahead at a dead run. Liv and Simpson had no choice but to follow.

They bolted through the tree line and into the clearing just as two men burst from the front door of the cabin. One of the men was tall with shoulder-length hair, the other short and muscular. Both carried handguns, but no assault rifles were evident. That was good news.

Rev could hear the men calling to each other as they ran across the clearing toward the low-slung cinder block building dug into the hillside. It would have been a simple matter to drop them with a few well-placed rounds from the M-14.

That thought must have occurred to Simpson. Looking over his shoulder Rev saw the colonel snap the rifle to his shoulder trying to get a bead on the running men.

As they drew closer, Rev could see that the taller of the two was fumbling with a large padlock securing the front door of the building.

"Stand down, soldiers," Simpson roared. He fired a shot that gouged a splinter from the door frame.

Rev, Liv, and Colonel Simpson were barely fifty feet away when the front door sprang open and the two men darted inside. This would be a pistol fight after all.

Rev charged ahead. Simpson and Liv trailed him on his left and right, respectively. He unholstered his Glock and dove through the door, rolling off his right shoulder to a crouch.

"Sophie! Sophie!" he screamed.

Rev was confronted with an open room. He could barely make out the back wall, 50 feet or so away. Four people struggled toward him. A short man grappled with a rangy young man, who couldn't seem to raise his hands. The short man swung a vicious right and the young man collapsed to the ground.

Sophie was in the grasp of the tall, long-haired man, who was using her as a shield. Her eyes wild, she moved like a puppet controlled by the man behind her, who was shoving her toward the door.

Liv and Simpson arrived too late to make the fatal assessment.

The man holding Sophie had a gun and he was tall enough that Rev had a clear shot.

Rev leveled his Glock and squeezed the trigger.

His gunshot loosed a fusillade.

The tall man went down. The short man returned fire. Sophie fell. Rev couldn't tell if her assailant had dragged her down or if she had been hit. The short man staggered and fell face first under the withering fire laid down by Liv and Simpson. Rev rushed to Sophie's side.

Then all was silent. Save for Rev's sobs.

A tentative tendril of blood bloomed from Sophie's mouth and laid a trail of crimson across the porcelain skin of her chin and neck.

"Not again. Not again. Dear Jesus, not again," Rev keened.

Chapter 45

8:30 a.m. Friday, August 26, 2011, Washington, DC
Andrew Hawk settled into the visitor's chair in Samuel Jenkins' office. Polished wood paneling and a thick carpet gave the office the reverent trappings of a choir loft.

"Back at last are you, Andy?" Jenkins said. "Give me a report on your activities for the past two weeks. I've read your e-mails, of course, but you know I grasp things better when I can talk man to man."

"Where do you want me to start?"

"With Colonel Randolph Simpson. What do you make of him?"

"At the moment, he's a mushroom."

"A mushroom?"

"He's in the dark and I've shoveled a lot of shit on him."

Jenkins' laugh was brittle. He didn't have a sense of humor and often looked to his wife and to his staff for cues on when it was time to laugh. "You're certain that Simpson is playing for the other side?"

"He showed up on cue after the Kambics staged their little telephone subterfuge. Makes me think he was part of the fake murder that has law enforcement breathing down the Kambics' necks at this critical juncture."

"And the outcome of the colonel's raid?"

"Was exactly what we'd hoped for. We sacrificed two pawns, but our knight is positioned for checkmate."

"What's Kambic's next move?"

"Which Kambic?"

"The senior; he's the one that counts."

"I'm not so sure of that."

"What do you mean?" Jenkins asked.

"I sense that maybe there is more to junior than meets the eye."

"I thought junior was a religious nut job," Jenkins said. "The world is coming to an end, Amen. That sort of thing."

"He is religious. So is his old man. But in junior's case ..."

"Spit it out, man."

"Billy boy is jobbing all of us. I think his religious beliefs are more smoke than fire. Religion is a means to an end rather than an end in and of itself. I think Billy is a mercenary angling for a life of ease on a tropical island where the natives tolerate androgyny."

"Huh?"

"Billy is a woman trapped in a man's body."

The look on Jenkins' face was priceless. His naiveté defied his life experience as a soldier and legislator. "You're saying Billy wants to be a woman?"

"A really ugly woman," Hawk said.

This time he didn't have to laugh alone at his own joke.

Jenkins brayed, reminding Hawk of why it was better not to amuse the speaker of the House of Representatives. The speaker pulled a handkerchief from his back pocket and blew his nose. "So, you think he has an agenda that supersedes our own?"

Hawk stroked his chin. "He recognizes an opportunity for himself within our plan."

"Is there any danger in that?"

"I don't think so. I'm just saying that he bears watching. That's all."

"That's interesting," Jenkins said. "His father sees him as a buffoon and is setting his son up for a fall in the event that the plan goes off the rails, which by the way is exactly what we want to happen."

"It wouldn't surprise me if it turns out the other way around. Billy is cunning," Hawk said. "He may even have divined our purpose, but it doesn't matter to us which Kambic remains standing at the end game."

"So you're asking for the flexibility to make an alliance with Billy boy rather than his dear old dad, if that makes more sense as events unfold?"

Hawk nodded.

"You've got it. What will the Kambics do next?"

"They are poised to give the Christian Soldiers their marching orders in a way that Simpson is sure to intercept."

"So, we're sending ten good men on what amounts to a suicide mission."

Hawk didn't hear any remorse in Jenkins voice. He was stating a fact. Nothing more.

"We did the same thing in Vietnam, and look what it earned us," Hawk said.

"A Medal of Honor and the best seat in the United States Congress," Jenkins said.

"There's a bigger prize at stake this time."

"This isn't about personal rewards, Andy. You know that. We've got to reclaim this country and put it back on the path envisioned by the founding fathers. Those ten men are a down payment on a new order. Let's not forget that."

Hawk wasn't chastened. It was what he expected to hear, and he was glad that he had heard it.

"Now, how about Rev Polk?" Jenkins asked.

"Gray Collingsworth tells me that the *Daily Telegraph* will print a retraction on Polk's story impugning your Vietnam War record as soon as we sign off on the settlement."

"That'll emasculate the motherfucker!" Jenkins exulted.

"And Polk's girlfriend?"

"You mean ex-girlfriend? She didn't survive Colonel Simpson's ill-conceived rescue."

"More collateral damage?"

Hawk nodded. "But it's collateral damage with a purpose. Polk is going to be so busy dealing with funerals and filling out police paperwork that it will be a long time before he gets around to wondering what became of the Freedom of Information paperwork on Operation Setting Sun."

"You've retrieved the package?"

"Yep."

"How?"

"Let's just say that we had an intelligence officer in place who told me where to look. The bad thing is ..."

"What?"

"By the time I got to the package, it already had been opened."

"So, the cat's out of the bag. Who do you think may have read it?"

"I don't know. The girl, or maybe Polk," Hawk said.

"Damn. Kambic sent in a barber when we needed a surgeon. Best case scenario is that it was the girl and that the knowledge of what it contained died with her."

"And the worst case is that Rev Polk read all about Operation Setting Sun and has connected the dots. At the end of the day, it doesn't matter. I've been assured that any subsequent requests for information on that topic will be lost in an endless paper loop."

"I'm not sure why that didn't happen in the first place," Jenkins said. "I thought we had that door locked down tight."

"A GS-13 in the records department lost his job over it. His successor will be more careful," Hawk said.

"So we're safe. Polk won't be able to persuade any reputable publisher to take a chance on a story about me or my family after the *Telegraph* prints its retraction, but I'm still worried about the California connection."

"Chad Tucci? I scared him off talking to Rev Polk, I think. But maybe it's time for another road trip?"

"Make it quick," Jenkins said. "I want your boots back on the ground here when the Kambics make their play."

"I'm already on my way," Hawk said.

Chapter 46

11:30 a.m. Friday, August 26, 2011, Dulles International Airport, VA

Andy Hawk flew first class because there wasn't enough room for his long legs back in coach. He waved off the flight attendant, a middle-aged woman who materialized at his elbow with a glass of champagne as soon as he settled into his seat.

"No thank you. But you could bring me a beer."

"Heineken or Budweiser?"

"Bud will do," Hawk said, shaking his head derisively as the attendant waddled away.

He mused that flight attendants used to be young and pretty and no one winced when you called them stewardesses. Now the friendly skies were served by old broads, fat broads, and skinny homosexuals. Hawk missed the good old days.

Sam Jenkins was resolved to set things right. And Andy Hawk was resolved to help him. He had killed for Jenkins before and now he was about to do it again. These were crimes that did not stain his soul because they were in the service of the greater good. Hawk avowed this to be true because it was the only way he could sleep at night without enduring the jeering of the souls he had consigned to hell. He contemplated these things as he kicked off his loafers, pushed back his seat, and fell asleep. The attendants were still loading the plane.

Neither the middle-aged flight attendant nor her assistant, who happened to be a pretty young woman, had the courage to awaken him. His Budweiser was returned to the galley without comment. The plane took off without Hawk's seat back being in the upright position—the first of many infractions he would commit on his mission to San Diego in the service of the next president of the United States.

Turbulence over Kansas woke him. He flipped through a *New Yorker* magazine the passenger before him had left in the seat pocket, listened in on the movie for a few minutes, and then tugged a novel titled *Rainbow Six* from his carry-on. Tom Clancy's book involved a plot by radical environmentalists to purify the earth by killing off a significant portion of the dirty human population.

Hawk liked the author's politics. The book disdained environmentalists, which was in keeping with Hawk's own proclivities. God had given mankind dominion over the earth. Fuck the tree huggers. He turned pages and plotted what he'd do after he landed in San Diego.

They had his car waiting at the Avis desk. The Camaro had a built-in GPS, just like he'd ordered. He punched in the address and followed the turn-by-turn directions of the disembodied voice that floated toward him from the dashboard.

When the GPS system suggested that he was nearing his destination, he stopped at a convenience store/gas station and asked for the key to the bathroom. He knew never to start a stakeout with a full bladder.

He bought a Coke and a package of cheese and peanut butter crackers, climbed back into the car, and resumed his trip.

"Your destination is ahead on the left," the GPS voice intoned a few minutes later.

He pulled the car over to the curb and watched the house. He really didn't have a plan other than to watch and wait. His patience was rewarded forty-five minutes later. The front door of the neat ranch house swung open and a small, dapper man in his eighties emerged, blinking in the sunlight of a brilliant early afternoon.

The house had a garage, but a car was parked in the driveway, a late-model Cadillac. The man carried a thick manila envelope. He shoved it under his arm as he fumbled the keys from his pocket. Chad Tucci opened the driver's side door of the Cadillac and climbed in. He was so short that he practically disappeared behind the wheel.

Tucci turned to look over his shoulder as he backed from the driveway. They had met years ago and Hawk didn't want to take a chance that Tucci might recognize him. He bent and pretended he was searching for something on the floorboard as the Cadillac drove by.

Hawk had already decided that he wasn't going to follow his prey. This was a job that demanded privacy, and the privacy he sought lay in the old man's house.

With the old man out of sight, Hawk pulled away from the curb and drove around for five minutes, canvassing the area. He turned off the air conditioning and rolled down the windows—even though the day was hot—to get a better sense of the rhythms of the neighborhood. He was pretty certain that there would be no witnesses to his malfeasance.

He parked the Camaro at the curb, strode purposefully up the old man's front walk, and rang the doorbell even though he knew no one was at home. The lock yielded quickly to Hawk's pick, and as the door swung open he spoke in a loud voice:

"Uncle, it is so good to see you."

He paused in the doorway and hugged the air, pantomiming the act of greeting a loved one, and then he stepped inside and closed the front door.

Hawk slipped a pair of latex gloves out of his pocket and put them on.

He made his way around the house quickly and found what he was looking for in the old guy's study, in a filing cabinet arranged alphabetically, in a folder bearing Sam Jenkins' name.

Returning to the kitchen, he put the folder on the table and rummaged about in the old man's refrigerator, where he found a six-pack of Negra Modelo. The geezer had good taste.

Hawk opened kitchen drawers until he found a church key. He popped the top of a Modelo, sat down at the table, and savored the feel and aroma of the ice cold beer on the back of his throat as he made his way through the file, which appeared to contain all of the materials Chad Tucci had employed in blackmailing the speaker of the House of Representatives.

"Should have gone after him years ago," Hawk thought.

He worried a bit about the brand new copier that occupied the corner of the desk in Tucci's study. "I wonder..."

He was on his third beer when he heard the garage door begin its assent. Tucci was pulling into the garage this time.

The door from the garage opened into the kitchen. Hawk pulled a blackjack from his back pocket and positioned himself so he would be hidden by the door as it opened.

The old man didn't suspect a thing.

Thwack. The blackjack smacked into the mastoid bone behind Tucci's right ear and the old man went down without a whimper. Hawk used one of the old geezer's own kitchen knives to slit Tucci's throat. He had swung the blackjack hard enough to kill, but he wanted to be certain.

He rinsed the knife off in the kitchen sink and re-stowed it in the proper slot in its wooden block. He used a paper towel to wipe out the sink and threw it away in the trash can under the sink.

He walked into the living room and adjusted the thermostat on the air-conditioning to its coolest level. That way it would be awhile before the old guy began to stink.

He used his handkerchief to wipe off the front door handle, waved over his shoulder as if he was bidding someone adieu, and walked slowly to his car, pausing to study the sky as if reflecting on a beautiful day.

He returned his car at the Avis rental desk, explaining to the clerk that he had been called suddenly back to the home office and wouldn't need the car after all.

He sat in the airport lounge and browsed departing flights on his smart phone. He booked a flight back to Dulles with a changeover in Pittsburgh.

The boarding agent scanned the bar-coded image displayed on his iPhone and the device chirped.

"Enjoy your flight, sir," the agent said.

She was a beautiful young woman with a short skirt—the kind stewardesses used to wear back when they were called stewardesses.

Hawk stalked down the jet way, a dinosaur well-adapted to the modern world.

Chapter 47

6:30 a.m. Monday, August 29, 2011, New Cumberland, PA

Rev swooped through frothy white clouds as the earth, lush and green and full of promise, winked at him from below. His perspective changed constantly as he banked, dived, climbed, and rode updrafts—effortlessly, as if he were born to do it. He smelled hot oil and exhaust. His ears rang with engine roar. He felt ebullient, in complete control of his own destiny.

A voice from behind startled him.

"It's the greatest feeling in the world, ain't it?"

He turned and looked over his shoulder.

A solid, sunburned man sat in the rear cockpit. His hair was cropped close and his chiseled jaw stretched wide into an improbable grin.

"Jake?"

"That's right, soldier. Thought it was about time I paid you another call. You've strayed off course, and I'm just the fellow to nudge you closer to the wind. You're closing in on the truth, boy. And the truth will set you free. Time to crawl out of the bottle and get back into the game."

Rev awoke with the feeling that he had just descended thirty floors in a high-speed elevator. When his stomach caught up with him, he dropped his feet over the side of his bed and sat up.

His head pounded to an unrelenting litany. Sophie is dead ... it's my fault ... Sophie is dead. He had consumed a fifth of bourbon the night before. Just like the night before. He'd been living on bourbon and Rice Krispies for three days. His stomach lurched. He made it to the bathroom, just in time.

A long hot shower began the recovery process. Coffee was next. He'd brewed a pot but he was reluctant to sample it. His stomach still flip-flopped with sudden movement. He was sitting in his living room staring into space when he heard a key in his lock. Too hung over to do anything more than stare at his front door, he watched as it swung open to reveal Liv Pearson and Nona.

Liv deferred to Nona, who swept into the room first.

"This room smells like farts and stale whiskey," Nona said.

"I feel like farts and stale whiskey."

Nona laughed. "There may be some hope. He's retained his sense of humor."

Liv took up station on Nona's right shoulder. "You have the look of one afflicted with terminal halitosis."

"Dead wouldn't be a bad thing. You've got a gun. Put me out of my misery, please."

He blinked in the sunlight as Nona made her way about the room, opening the venetian blinds and the windows. "This place certainly is in need of an airing out."

"I'm sorry I gave you a key. You were only supposed to use it in an emergency."

"My favorite grandson is trying to drink himself to death. I'd say that qualifies as an emergency."

"I'm your only grandson."

"And you're an asshole," Liv interjected. "Why wouldn't you return my calls?"

"No fair. You've got me double teamed, and my head hurts."

"Whose fault is that?" Nona asked. "And if you'd bothered to answer your phone, we wouldn't have staged this ... intervention."

"Intervention? That's a fancy word for breaking and entering." Rev pushed himself from his chair, staggering a bit as he gained his feet. "Since you've decided to ... intervene, you might as well come on in to the kitchen. I just put on a pot of coffee and I'm willing to share."

Rev walked a crooked line toward the back of the house with Nona and Liv flying escort at nine and three o'clock, ready to grab an elbow if warranted.

When they got to the kitchen, Nona took charge. "Sit. I'll pour the coffee. You're stumbling about like a blind man."

Rev sat. "Would you like me to roll over, too?"

Liv went to the refrigerator while Nona poured the coffee. Liv examined a bottle of milk, opened it, and sniffed. "This is two days past the sell-by date, but it smells OK. I think we're safe."

"You two are as thick as thieves," Rev observed. "I don't remember introducing you. Remind me of how that happened."

"Hey! His brain is starting to work again," Nona exulted.

"Grayson Collingsworth," Liv explained. "You wouldn't answer your phone. I called the newspaper. Asked Collingsworth if you had any family and he mentioned that you had a grandmother who just might give a rat's ass about you."

"Gray is an asshole," Rev said.

"That's funny. He said the same thing about you," Liv said.

"Guess it takes one to know one. Now, why is it you two are here?"

"I'm here because you haven't given me a full accounting of your trip to San Diego, which I paid for," Nona said.

"And I'm here because I know what's it's like to shoot someone and how easy it is to drown in a jigger of whiskey."

Rev pantomimed clicking a ballpoint. "Where's my notebook? That was a line worth writing down."

"Asshole," Liv said.

"That's my password." His stomach did a barrel roll. "Gang way, girls, I'm coming through!"

Rev pushed his chair back from the table and left the kitchen at a run. He made the first-floor powder room, where he threw open the door, threw up the lid, and upchucked bile and stomach acid, which was all he had left.

He could hear the women tittering and tsk-tsking in the kitchen as he flushed the toilet.

He kept a spare toothbrush and toothpaste in the powder room. He took the time for a thorough teeth cleaning, scrubbing his tongue extra hard to remove a filthy film.

He made his way back to the kitchen, walking like a man on a tightrope. He looked over his shoulder as he sat down to make sure his addled spatial senses were lining up his ass and the chair.

Nona placed a fresh mug of coffee in front of him. "Drink it black. Your stomach can't handle dairy products."

Rev's hand shook as he picked up the mug, emblazoned with the words "Harrisburg Newspaper Guild." He took a sip, winced, and put the mug down.

"Now, about your trip ..." Nona said.

"Well, like I told you on the phone: I met with Chad Tucci at the Grande Colonial where he witnessed Uncle Jake's demise. Said that it was pretty clear to him that the driver meant to run Jake over, but the police never figured out the who or the why ..."

"And?"

"I don't know, Nona. Tucci's a neat, dapper little man and he struck me as a straight shooter, for the most part ..."

"Tell me about the least part."

Rev hung his head. "Give me a break. I'm not at my best here. I'm sick as a dog ... and Sophie is dead."

"Focus. You need to think about something else," Nona said.

"Yeah. Don't obsess. That's how you end up drowning in a jigger," Liv added. "Lord knows I was tempted. Sophie was my friend, too. I've cried. Went to church. Lit a candle for her. It doesn't bring her back, but you have to start the healing process somehow."

"I wish it were that easy," Rev said.

"It isn't," Liv said. "I'm crying on the inside right now." Her voice trembled. "I'll miss Sophie ... for the rest of my life. But the only way I can live with myself is to uncover the responsible son of a bitch or sons of bitches. And I can't do that if I crawl into a bottle."

Rev looked at his grandmother. "She's just as tough as you are."

"Tougher," Nona said, patting Liv's hand. "That's why we're getting along so well."

"At least nobody has said 'rub some dirt on it and get back into the game,'" Rev said.

"That doesn't mean it isn't good advice," Nona said. "Now, back to the game! What makes you think Tucci was ... disingenuous?"

"Tucci knows more about Jake's death than he is telling," Rev said. "He was a political reporter back in the day. I dug some of his old clips out of the microfiche morgue at the San Diego Public Library after I interviewed him. On the same day his story about Jake's death made the paper, Tucci wrote a think piece about the recent republican primary for president, which Ronald Reagan won in a landslide. Nixon wasn't even on the ballot ..."

"The point, Rev. Get to the point."

He glared at her. "I'm not at my best here. What do you expect?"

"The lead at the beginning of the story," Nona said.

"OK. Here it is," he cleared his throat. "Vice Admiral Alan Jenkins, USN retired, is quoted in Tucci's story about Reagan's strategy to wrest the nomination from Nixon. Tucci lied to me. Told me the adviser's name was Fink. But there were no Finks in Tucci's story."

"Sounds like Tucci was the fink," Nona observed. "So, I didn't send you off on a wild goose chase after all. Alan Jenkins keeps popping up like a bad penny."

"Or like a turd in a cesspool, to paraphrase Uncle Jake," Rev replied. "So, Tucci lied, but he also gave me a leg up, suggesting that I visit Uncle Jake's old house. He even gave me the address. Dug it out of an old notebook, or so he said."

"Which is where you found Jake's journal," Nona said. "What does it have to say about Operation Setting Sun?"

"It's easier to let Uncle Jake tell you that story in his own words," he said.

Rev arose on wobbly legs and left the room. He didn't try to muffle his laborious footfalls on the stairs going up and, after a few moments, coming down. Rev returned to the kitchen carrying a black loose-leaf binder. He sat down at the kitchen table, thumbed through the binder, and then turned it around for Nona's inspection.

He jabbed the right hand journal page with his right index finger. "The pertinent section begins here."

Chapter 48

Jake's Journal
Operation Setting Sun

I probably should have committed this to writing long ago when the events of the spring and summer of 1945 were fresher in my mind. Writing 17 years after the fact, the details are obscured by my natural inclination to remember things as they should have been and not necessarily as they were.

Rose-colored glasses were standard issue for Operation Setting Sun. Without them, I could never have landed a captured Japanese float plane in the Sakurada-bori moat around Emperor Hirohito's Palace early on the evening of July 28, 1945. Also on board was my Japanese wife, the highborn Emika, niece to Baron Kijuro Shidehara; and Claude Forsythe, a career diplomat charged with negotiating Japan's immediate and unconditional surrender.

As we over flew the city, the devastation of the recent fire bombing was obscenely evident. General Curtis LeMay's low-flying B-29 bombers had set a 15-square-mile section of Tokyo north and east of the Imperial Palace ablaze, killing more than 80,000 people. Some were burned to death; others suffocated after inhaling blazing hot air, while still others jumped into canals to avoid the fire storm and were boiled alive. These were results that rivaled those of the atomic bombs we dropped on Hiroshima and Nagasaki, although I didn't recognize this until years later when I read up on the firebombing of Tokyo.

The streets to the north and east of the palace were still discernible. They snaked through the burned-out hulks of houses and buildings. Desultory efforts had been made to push the rubble into piles, from which emanated an acidic miasma, affronting the eyes and throat.

It was horribly evident that Japan was losing the war. That they fought on still testified to the grit of the people and the insanity of the military oligarchs who ruled them. We were banking on the pacific tendencies of Emperor Hirohito, who had been overwhelmed by the nationalism of the military ruling class, which had so recklessly taken on a war with the most powerful nation this earth has ever known. And of course the good counsel of Emika's uncle, Baron Kijuro Shidehara, who would become Japan's first post-war prime minister.

In reflecting on the mission in those last hours as the float plane droned east over billowy clouds, buffeted by occasional crosswinds and downdrafts, my eyes were overwhelmed with sunlight and my heart was heavy with dread. I had concluded that we were all going to die, shot down by Japanese fighter planes, or more likely by our own forces because by that time in the war America ruled the skies.

The captain of the USS Gardiners Bay unlimbered the Jake from its stowage on the main deck aft soon after our arrival and slowed our passage eastward for a practice session to renew my acquaintance with the operational quirks of the Jake.

There was considerable danger therein because we occupied an area under the constant presence of our own reconnaissance and attack aircraft, both land and carrier-based. Even though the Jake had been equipped with an IFF radio beacon that would identify it as a friendly aircraft to American forces, the Rising Suns emblazoned on the wings and fuselage made me fair game for hotshot American cowboys inclined to shoot first and ask questions later.

The controls of the Jake were arranged for men much shorter than I. Imagine being six-two and driving a Volkswagen Beetle with the seat shoved all the way forward and you'll get a sense of what it felt like to fly the Jake. I had to be careful not to entangle my feet in the narrow space betwixt the pedals. And I had to cast my head on one shoulder or the other to see through the canopy.

I could open the canopy, of course, and I did for short periods, but aviator's goggles were little comfort in the slip stream of hot Pacific air rushing toward me like the back draft from a raging forest fire.

As we approached unfriendly shores, Claude Forsythe and I drew black cowls over our heads to hide our decidedly non-Asian features from any Japanese planes that might wander close to take a look.

The cowl obstructed my peripheral vision, which turned out to be both a blessing and a curse as I lined up for a landing in the narrow moat rimming the emperor's palace in Tokyo. The Japanese capital city was a virtual ghost town in July of 1945 because the

194

Japanese military had abdicated control over the skies to our Super Fortresses. Absent of the protection of Japan's decimated air forces, both naval and land-based, the civilian population of the large cities had fled to the countryside.

But the AA crews were still in place. Their gun barrels tracked our progress and an occasional black puff blossomed nearby, testimony to the incredulity of the AA crews who couldn't imagine that there might still be a friendly bird aloft in the Japanese sky.

I wasn't particularly concerned about AA fire, because the Japanese were notoriously bad aims. During the battle of Midway, for example, only one American plane was lost to AA fire. The threat lay in the vaunted Zero, but their numbers were so reduced that we drew to within fifty miles of Tokyo before our escort showed up and acknowledged the predetermined radio transmission that identified us and our mission.

As we landed in the moat, I could hear Claude Forsythe cheering from the back seat. The tall, nervous patrician selected by the late FDR to warn the Japanese oligarchy of the horror that awaited its people should they continue to fight, was celebrating our unlikely safe arrival.

Claude, Emika, and I threw back our canopies, unbuckled, and stood, stretching weary muscles. A motor launch pulled alongside. Emika addressed the young Japanese sailor at the tiller of the launch. Her melodious sing song was music in my ears, even though I didn't understand a word of what she was saying. Claude smiled and nodded as if he knew what was going on.

A second sailor aboard the launch inched forward along its narrow deck and tied a line to the starboard float of the Jake, while the man at the tiller edged the boat closer. A third sailor, armed with a submachine gun, was stationed aft.

The helmsman and Emika exchanged a torrent of gibberish while Claude smiled and nodded like a supplicant called before the pope.

Emika and Claude stepped over the edge of the cockpit and onto the wing, then made their way down a ladder to the starboard float.

"You are to stay aboard, husband," my wife called. "Food and drink will be brought to you."

A crewman aboard the launch propped a ramp twixt the float and deck and motioned Claude and Emika to climb aboard. By that time, I had joined them on the float. I bent low to Emika and whispered:

"Goddamn it. I can't let you go off alone. Claude couldn't find his ass with both hands if it comes to a fight."

195

Emika smiled. "You could certainly put up a ruckus, but could you take on the entire palace guard?"

"I'd do it for you," I replied.

"I know you would. But the only thing that would accomplish would be to get us both killed. Stay here. I have a good feeling about the outcome."

And so I stayed.

The drone of an American sortie of B-29s awakened me from a fitful slumber early on the morning of my second day afloat in Sakurada-bori moat. I had slept on the wing of the float plane, wrapped up in a dirty blanket delivered to me by an elderly Japanese man, whom I took to be a member of the emperor's household.

All I ever saw of him was his full moon face, cratered by age and anxiety, and a shock of black hair peppered with gray, as he leaned over the wall of the moat to lower provisions to me in a wicker basket.

I wasn't privy to the bombing strategy of the U.S. command, although I had heard that there was an official reluctance to bomb the emperor's personal abode. But it struck me that a direct hit on the palace, even by mistake, would be something to brag about back home and that the airman who accomplished it would not lose a stripe or a minute of sleep.

I had heard nothing from Emika since she left with Claude Forsythe aboard the motor launch the evening before. All sorts of scenarios played out in my mind. Had she been shot or knifed or strangled or poisoned or thrown in the darkest dungeon because she was a Japanese aristocrat who had consorted with the enemy?

Of Claude Forsythe's fate I cared not one wit. He was an arrogant prick, a patrician of fighting age who had used his pedigree to secure a job with the state department far from harm's way. How ironic and fitting that he was now in the maw of the dragon.

And then the planes were directly overhead and the bombs began to fall. Incendiary bombs they were. They fell beyond the moat wall onto the palace grounds itself. I could feel their hot breath on my cheek and the flames erupted high into the predawn twilight, growling and hissing as if all of the gargoyles of hell had been loosed in this place at this time.

You can imagine my relief when I saw the frightened faces of Emika, Claude, and my little Japanese jailer peering at me over the edge of the wall, backlit by the raging fires behind them.

There was, at that moment, a lull in the bombing. The sounds of the Super Fortresses diminished as they swung out over the city, intent, I prayed, on delivering the balance of their payloads on another target.

"The motor launch has been destroyed, but Yin se says he knows of a rope ladder in an outbuilding not far from here," Claude Forsythe yelled from the top of the wall. "We are going to fetch it."

"Why does it take three of you to fetch a rope ladder?" My scream was to no avail.

As the ether consumed my words, the sound of a single B-29 built in my ears. A dark shadow lumbered along at low altitude on the horizon of that uneasy dawn. Despite the danger, I was visited with a sense of pride of what American ingenuity had wrought. A Super Fortress—what an imposing war bird! Perhaps the bomber had been damaged by AA fire or maybe an engine was just running rough as engines sometimes do, beset by gremlins that even the most experienced aircraft mechanic cannot exorcize.

And then the wooded area that Emika had disappeared into erupted into flames. The solitary bomber had dropped its load. My heart stopped and I implored God to spare Emika. A rope ladder fell from above; the rungs tumbled downward and slapped at my ankles.

Claude Forsythe swung his legs over the wall and kicked about with his feet until they found purchase on the ladder rungs. He moved stiffly with his right arm pressed hard to his side because he was carrying a satchel. "Come on, man. Let's get moving. These Nips are going to be as mad as hell now that we've bombed the palace grounds. We've got to get out of here while we can."

"Not without Emika, we can't."

I shouldered past him and began climbing the rope ladder.

He yelled at me: "Give it up, man. She's dead. A burning tree fell right on top of her. It killed Yin se, too. The best thing you can do for her now is to get us out of here. She accomplished our purpose. I have the Japanese surrender right here."

He waved the satchel triumphantly.

The holster of my service .45 slapped on my thigh as I climbed.

I clambered over the wall and ran into the blazing wood heading toward where Emika must have been. The heat scorched my eyebrows and the hair on the backs of my wrists. Smoke filled my lungs. Red-hot embers churned within the billowing clouds of smoke like a million fireflies chasing each other through hell. And from that firmament burst the burning, screaming figure of a woman.

Emika! It had to be Emika. What small portion of the clothing that had not been consumed by fire resembled the flowered kimono she had been wearing as she peered over the moat wall not five *minutes earlier. She was screaming. I can still hear her screams. She was dying ... horribly ... consumed by the hell fires of unconditional war.*

I yanked my .45 from its holster, and God help me I shot her seven times. Until the clip was empty and the screaming had stopped. She fell back into the conflagration, which in that moment also consumed my heart.

The first thing I did, having descended the rope ladder to the wing of the float plane, was to punch Claude Forsythe in the jaw. I knocked the son of a bitch into the moat.

"She was still alive, you bastard. Why didn't you save her?" I screamed at him as he treaded water in the stinking moat, spitting, gagging, and struggling to keep his precious satchel above the water in outstretched hands.

Relenting, I descended from the wing to the starboard float, relieved him of the satchel, and offered him a hand up.

When we were back on the wing, he asked: "What the hell did you do that for?"

"Because she was still alive and you abandoned her."

"You've lost your grip. I saw a burning tree fall on her. She was dead, man. I'm telling you she was dead."

"She is now. I shot her because she was burning to death. You motherfucker! You highborn shit!"

"I don't know who you shot, but it wasn't Emika. She was pinned underneath the tree. I saw blood streaming from the corner of her mouth. She was dead, damn it! I wanted to spare you the details, but the fucking tree crushed her. She was dead! Dead! Dead!"

Forsythe watched me without comment as I ejected the old clip from my .45, stored it in a pouch on my web belt, and inserted a fresh clip into the handle. I chambered a round and pointed the muzzle at him. Time stood still.

Claude Forsythe didn't utter a word, which probably saved his life ... at least for the moment.

I don't know how long we stood there on the wing of a captured Japanese float plane in the Sakurada-bori moat around Emperor Hitherto's Palace with the sounds of an American B-29 attack rumbling across Tokyo. But I do recall regaining my senses, without shooting Claude.

I holstered the .45. "Let's get going then."

Claude settled into the middle seat as I climbed behind the controls.

Prudence dictated that Claude and I stay put in the Sakurada-bori moat, at least until the B-29 bombing mission had run its course.

Fuck prudence. I never liked that bitch anyway.

I can't tell you much about our escape from Tokyo. I was a man moving within a nightmare. The Jake needed 400 yards for takeoff. We had maybe 425. I barely cleared a bridge over the moat. I juked left to avoid the cable of a barrage balloon and then we were aloft, buffeted by the anti-aircraft burst of the batteries protecting the imperial palace.

An AA round punched a hole through the port wing. The plane bucked. When I glanced over my shoulder to assess the damage, I could see defeat in Forsythe's eyes. He had surrendered to the inevitable. We were going to die.

But we didn't die. The AA round missed the engine by inches and by God's good graces we didn't die. Dying then and there probably would have been better, given the fate that awaited us. But in that moment, I decided that if there was a God He was a cruel son of a bitch. Emika died, but He saved the likes of Claude Forsythe and Jake Addison. What possible profit could there be in that across the wide landscape of His universe?

We droned west with a full tank of fuel, thanks to the Japanese crew of the motor launch that had visited me every hour on the hour the afternoon before while I was marooned there in the moat waiting for Emika's return. The Jake's tanks had been refilled, five gallons at a time. I had a lot to worry about as we made our way west, but running out of gas wasn't on the list.

The .30 caliber machine gun the Japanese had installed in the rear cockpit was of no use to us as we chased the wave tops west, maintaining the lowest profile possible to observers both human and electronic. Forsythe didn't know how to use the machine gun and I couldn't fire it and fly the plane at the same time. So without my guile we were defenseless from behind.

We traveled that way for hours. My ass cheeks were tired of clenching in anticipation of disaster, which could have arrived at any moment. Disaster, after all, was my karma. I had accumulated it by killing Emika and by not killing Forsythe, who knew better than to engage me in conversation. He wore the realization that I had almost murdered him like a cheap raincoat in an icy downpour.

I could live with the fact that I had killed my wife. Ending her life had been merciful. I could not, however, abide the man who had abandoned her to burn to death, no matter his protestation that she already was dead, killed by a falling tree.

My palm itched. The butt of the .45 now reloaded and ready would have scratched it. I longed to alleviate the cramp in my index finger as well. Who would know if I killed him? I could say the Japanese did it as we escaped Tokyo. No one would be the wiser. I could deliver the surrender documents and be the hero who ended the war.

My hand dropped to the butt of the .45 more than once as we fled west. But I resisted the temptation to soil my soul with the indelible mark of a murderer. I attribute my restraint to Emika's influence. She spoke to me from the maelstrom of my madness.

"You do not need to spill his blood in my name," I imagined her saying. "He did not kill me; the bombs did."

In retrospect, I realize that I wasn't hearing Emika in my inner ear. The voice I heard, although I imagined it to be hers, was that of my own conscience which, with Emika's influence, had become a far more formidable foe to rash action than it had been before I met her.

Emika was the reason I quit drinking; she was the reason that I had aspired to a commission; she was the reason I went to college on the GI bill when I finally was mustered out of the navy; and she was the reason I didn't murder Claude Forsythe.

About three hours into the flight, with 600 nautical miles between Tokyo and us, Forsythe finally broke the silence.

"I can't broadcast a radio signal this close to the ocean. I think we're safe enough now. Can you take us up to 10,000 feet so I can let the admiral know we're on our way home?"

I looked at my watch. "I'll start an ascent in another half hour. Even at 10,000 feet I don't think we could send the signal far enough. Not yet anyway."

Forsythe didn't reply, which I took for his consent. Not that I needed it.

I took us up to 10,000 feet gradually. Another hour passed before we were at altitude.

I could hear Forsythe working the controls of the radio they had installed in the middle seat. The crystals were tuned to a specific frequency that would be monitored and exclusively so by Admiral Jenkins' personal radioman.

"Zulu, November, Foxtrot."

Forsythe must have repeated our call sign a thousand times before we finally got a response.

"This is Echo, Bravo, Charlie. Go ahead."

The words of Jenkins' radioman arrived in our headsets as if by magic. They were borne up on a sea of static. Forsythe didn't hear them right away.

"This is Echo, Bravo, Charlie. Go ahead."

"Hey, Claude," I said. *"Get the shit out of your ears. Tell them we're inbound on course 250 at 150 knots. Our latitude is approximately 28 degrees 15 minutes north and our longitude 176 degrees 20 minutes west."*

"What? OK. Sorry."

I could hear Claude broadcast our position, course, and speed. He did this several times until we finally won a confirmation that Jenkins understood, or at least his radioman did.

"Tell Papa Bear: mission accomplished," Forsythe repeated several times before earning an acknowledgment.

The atmospherics suddenly improved and a final message arrived with crystal clarity:

"Zulu, November, Foxtrot. Recommend coming to course 260 and slowing to 130 knots, altitude 7,500 feet, for rendezvous with Mother Hen in approximately two hours and 45 minutes. Repeat course recommendation 260: speed 130 for rendezvous at 1640 hours. Commence broadcasting IFF signal in one hour. We'll let the good guys know you're on your way."

"Roger that, Echo, Bravo, Charlie."

I changed to the recommended course and began my descent.

"Make sure you get on that IFF. I'd start now just to be safe," I told Forsythe, referring to the radio beacon that would identify us as a friendly aircraft despite our markings.

"Got it."

And tedium was restored. The only difference was that now I couldn't kill Claude Forsythe because the good guys knew he was still alive. That, and Emika wouldn't let me do it.

About forty-five minutes later, I caught the glint of sunlight on an object hurtling toward us from the starboard side.

"You sure we're broadcasting an IFF signal?"

"Yes. Why?"

"We've got some company closing on us from three o'clock. Jesus Christ, that guy is fast!"

The air intakes on the nose of the fighter gave it the look of a snarling tiger. The insignia on her wings and fuselage identified her as one of us—an American that is. I didn't recognize the airplane's silhouette at the time because the P-51 Mustang was new to the Pacific theater. Fire spit from the edges of the wings.

"Shit! Sumbitch is shooting at us."

I rammed the nose forward into a steep dive, but I was a dove dueling with a hawk.

Craning my neck over my right shoulder, I could see the Mustang barrel roll to come up on our tail. I dived through a cloud at 5,000 feet with some hope of losing him in the soup, but when I leveled off at 2,000 feet there he was, machine guns flashing.

I rammed the stick forward again and roared toward the wave tops. But bullets stitched the engine cowl and black oil erupted, spattering the windshield. The jig was up. I wasn't dead yet because the Jake was so much slower than the Mustang that the pilot had a window of just a second or two as he flashed by at more than 400 mph.

But I was certain that he'd finish the job on his next pass. I feathered the prop, pulled back on the stick. We stalled and hit the ocean shoving my asshole into my throat. My head cracked against the rim of the cockpit. I saw stars and then I saw nothing.

Water flooding the cockpit revived me. It was up to my thighs before I wrestled free of the unfamiliar pilot restraints. I looked toward the rear cockpit. Claude Forsythe was dead. His head lolled to one side. Blood seeped from bullet wounds in his neck and upper torso. His precious satchel floated away on the rising waters. Water rose to my shoulders. I kicked free of the cockpit and pulled the tabs on my Mae West. The sea was choppy, five-foot swells. I was afloat in a debris field that included the starboard float, which must have been torn off upon impact with the ocean. A 10-foot rope was coiled at my utility belt—to tie airmen together so they didn't become separated from each other having bailed out over water. I used it to tie myself to the float.

The effort exhausted me. I realized that I was bleeding from a scalp wound above my forehead because blood was in my eyes. I worried, vaguely, about sharks, and then I passed out.

And then I didn't worry about anything else for a long, long time.

In May of 1968, the inaugural edition of Winged Warriors of the Pacific arrived in my mailbox. The newsletter, "dedicated to aviators from all branches of the service who vanquished the Japanese in the late great war," included an article by Jules Roberts.

The former Army Air Corps lieutenant recounted flying fighter support for a B-29 sortie that inadvertently bombed the Japanese emperor's palace in Tokyo on July 29, 1945. Boy did that get my juices flowing!

In the article, Roberts mentioned that he would be attending a reunion of pilots who had operated in the Pacific during World War II that July. The reunion would be held in—of all places—San Diego. The newsletter included a registration form, which I filled out and submitted with my check for $25 to Winged Warriors of the Pacific, which was hosting the event.

The newsletter was the first of two portentous messages. (The second arrived from Japan, about a month later, but to say more about that now would be putting the cart ahead of the horse).

When the reunion rolled around that July, I decided to hire a cab to take me to (and from) the San Diego Hilton because I intended to have a couple of drinks. Yes, I was drinking again, but moderately so. I prayed Emika would forgive me.

I arrived in the middle of cocktail hour, wearing my chief's uniform, as per reunion instructions. The uniform fit just fine and thanks for asking.

In a fit of pique, at the end of my last enlistment, I had resigned my commission and reverted to my enlisted rank. The retirement pay wasn't much different and I had always felt more comfortable in the chiefs' mess than the wardroom.

I bumped into Roberts (literally) in the line cueing up behind one of three bars set up in the vestibule outside the ballroom where the rubber chicken was to be served up.

I stumbled into him as thirsty ex-aviators jockeyed for position. He turned and inspected the medals on my chest and the hash marks on my sleeve.

"Damn, Chief," he said. "That's quite a collection of fruit salad. Looks like you're wearing the insignia of an enlisted pilot. I heard about you guys but I never met one."

He was a short fart, short and pudgy, and going to seed in his late 50s. A big diamond pinky ring sparkled on his left hand. Looked like one of those rings they give to high degree masons. I could imagine him wearing one of those pooh bah hats. What do they call them, fezzes?

He was clad in navy blue polyester pants and a pink golf shirt. The essence of alcohol oozed from his pores, although I couldn't determine whether its source was Aqua Velva or Chivas Regal.

I looked him up and down.

"Guess you couldn't fit into your uniform," I said.

He laughed, throwing his whole belly into it.

"Good God, you got that right, Chief. Too much of the good life. Twenty years ago when they mustered me out of the Air Corps I weighed 150 pounds; now I'm pushing 260. I tell my wife there's just more of me to love."

He patted his big belly then extended his hand toward me for a shake.

"Lieutenant Jules Roberts," he said. *"U.S. Army Air Corps, retired. I got sent to the South Pacific in the spring of 1945. Flew 12 combat missions before the Japs called it quits."*

"Son of a bitch," I replied. *"You're the reason I decided to come here. Caught your story in the newsletter and decided I had to meet you."*

"I'm flattered, Chief ..."

"Addison. Jake Addison. And you're right, I was an enlisted pilot. In fact, our paths may have crossed on July 29, 1945."

"How's that?"

I was sworn not to discuss Operation Setting Sun, so I lied. *"I flew seaplane reconnaissance on that mission,"* I told him. *"Heard that a couple of the B-29s unloaded on the emperor and I wanted to get the skinny on that."*

Jules elbowed me and winked. *"Caught a little flak for that. We weren't supposed to target the palace that night but a bunch of the boys bragged about it. I know for a fact that at least two 29s dropped incendiaries on the palace grounds. Burned the gardens to a crisp, I was told."*

"What type of planes did you fly?" I asked.

He puffed out his chest, which offered no competition whatsoever to his belly, protuberance wise.

"I flew the best damn fighting plane the United States ever made, the P-51 Mustang. Got to the South Pacific just in time to pull escort duty on bombing raids over Tokyo."

Jules had moved to the head of the drink line and paused to give the bartender his order.

"I'll have a Chivas Regal on the rocks with a splash of ginger ale."

"I'm surprised you earned the Navy Cross flying seaplanes," Jules said.

That stiffened my spine.

"You'd be surprised at the number of float plane pilots who won Medals of Honor ... for pulling downed pilots out of the drink ... often under enemy fire," I said.

Jules should have been able to tell that I was hot around the collar, but subtly wasn't his forte.

"Is that how you earned the Navy Cross?" he asked.

I shook my head.

"Nope. I got that one for a top-secret mission toward the end of the war. Got shot down, almost drowned."

The words *"top secret"* were gasoline on the fire of his interest.

"What sort of mission?" he asked.

"Can't tell you. As far as I know it's still classified."

To divert his attention I quickly added, "You flew 12 combat missions, did ya? Shoot down any Nips?"

Jules collected his drink from the bartender. "Whatcha drinking, Jake? This round's on me."

"How about a Dewar's on the rocks, with a twist," I said, figuring I might as well take a free drink in compensation for enduring Jules' bullshit.

Jules nodded at the bartender and slapped a ten spot on the bar top. "Keep the change. You know, Jake, by the time I got over there, the war was winding down and the Japs were keeping most of their aircraft in reserve for use as kamikazes. Didn't see more than a half dozen or so Zeros flying support for bombing missions over Japan and they were running for their lives. But I did get one kill to my credit, coincidentally, on July 29 when we were coming back from the raid over the emperor's palace."

He collected my drink from the bartender, handed it to me and said:

"Let's sit down at a table. This has been bugging me for twenty years, so it's high time I told someone."

I followed him to a grouping of tables and chairs set up in the vestibule outside the ballroom so old farts could take a load off their arthritic knees.

When we were settled in chairs facing each other across a small round table, Jules poked an index finger in his drink, stirred it, and popped his finger in his mouth, suckling like a baby pig at the teat. "Nothing beats Chivas Regal. Now, getting back to the Jap plane I shot down. Like I said, something has always bothered me about that encounter."

He paused, took a long drink of whiskey, and smacked his lips. His eyes lost focus.

"What type of plane was it?" I asked.

Jules took another sip. "A Jake ... a single-engine float plane. The kind the Japs used for long-range reconnaissance. I always thought that was odd. It was a solitary plane, heading toward our lines, with no sort of support for at least a thousand miles."

My pulse was pounding so loudly in my ears that I could barely hear him."

"P-51s travel pretty fast. And the Jake, as I recall, didn't have much of a profile. How did you spot it?" I asked.

"I knew where to look."

"How's that."

"Got a radio transmission giving me the coordinates."

"From whom?"

"Squadron headquarters. Radioman said it originated with naval intelligence. The thing that bugs me is that all the time I was shooting at the Jake, I was receiving an IFF signal identifying it as a friendly aircraft. But it was a Japanese plane. No doubt about that. Weird."

My face was pale and Jules noticed. "Hey, Chief. You OK, buddy?"

I took a deep breath. Forced myself to be calm. "I'm hypertensive. Sometimes my blood pressure kicks in and I go pale. Nothing a diuretic won't fix."

Jules guffawed. "Yeah and I'll bet it makes you piss about every ten seconds."

"You're right about that one, Jules. In fact, I could use a piss right now." I arose and shook hands with the man who had murdered Claude Forsythe and consigned me to a week of bobbing about in the Pacific tethered to the starboard float of a Japanese seaplane with only rainwater and my own piss to drink.

I pretended to go to the bathroom, but when I came to the door marked "gents" I just kept on going, out through the double doors where I flagged a cab. At my direction, the cabbie stopped at a liquor store on the way home. I bought a fifth of Dewar's and drank it all that night, trying to forget my encounter with the man who had shot me down almost certainly on the expressed orders of Admiral Alan Jenkins.

Chapter 49

1:30 p.m. Monday, August 29, 2011, New Cumberland, PA

Rev Polk had barely cleared the door of Grayson Collingsworth's office when the burly editor began to shout.

"Goddamn it, Polk! You were in the midst of a gun battle in which my best reporter was killed and you tell the city desk you can't do the story?"

"The state police ordered me not to write about Sophie's murder. Besides, you fired me. Remember?"

"You're unfired. Now write the fucking story. We're journalists. We flout authority. We don't kowtow to it."

Without being asked, Rev sat down in Collingsworth's visitors' chair and crossed his long legs insolently. "Seems like you're the one who's kowtowing ... to U.S. Rep. Sam Jenkins."

"Cheap shot! I'm doing the lawyers' bidding. The family fortune is at stake."

"Yeah, and my freedom is on the line. I've been told there's a cozy little jail cell waiting for me if my byline shows up on a story about Sophie's murder."

"You've been threatened with jail before and it never stopped you."

Rev clenched his jaw and stared at Collingsworth, trying to obscure the truth building behind his eyes. He couldn't write about Sophie's murder because his emotions were jumbled about like tiles at the start of a Scrabble game. He needed time to decompress ... to outline a far bigger story—one he couldn't write if his reputation were sullied by a retraction of his account of Sam Jenkins' Medal of Honor.

He needed Gray to kill the retraction, but his bargaining position was compromised by the loss of the navy's account of Operation Setting Sun. He had made copies from the low-resolution images of the pages he'd taken with his iPhone camera. But when he showed up at Sophie's house that morning to retrieve the originals, he found that her front door had been jimmied.

He'd left the Freedom of Information package where Sophie had put it, on top of her hutch. Whoever had broken in must have known precisely what they were looking for and where to find it because the house was otherwise undisturbed.

Rev would have felt much more secure going into battle with his former editor with the originals still in his possession. Uncle Jake's journal was his trump card. He'd pick his spot and play it.

"The newspaper will stand behind you, Rev," Collingsworth said.

"Just like it has on the Sam Jenkins story?"

"Completely different matter. Your story about the speaker of the House was subject to the interpretation of several witnesses forty years after the fact. In this case ... damn it, you know the difference. You were there for Christ's sake. An eyewitness account by a reporter who used to have some balls. Boy, that would sell some papers."

"You're just going to have to go with whatever the state police decide to tell you. Give the story to Troutman. She'll do a yeoman's job ... as usual. Have her call me. I'll tell her what I can without incriminating myself."

"Fuck Troutman," Collingsworth growled. "You're a newsman ... Sophie was a newsman. She wouldn't put up with a press release. She was a pro; you owe her more than that!"

Rev was surprised by the degree of emotion Gray invested in his words. Undermining his usual floridity, a deep pathos seeped to the surface as the editor tugged a handkerchief from his back pocket and blew his nose. He folded the handkerchief and dabbed at his eyes. To wipe away tears? Rev couldn't be sure, but perhaps there was something to the newsroom rumor. An affair between Gray Collingsworth and Sophie Anderson? Rev shuddered. He didn't want to defile her memory with such thoughts.

"You're right about that, Gray. But my situation is dicey. State police still haven't decided if they're going to charge me with a crime, and I don't want to piss them off."

Collingsworth slapped his desktop. "Christ, Rev. I'm getting calls from other media asking me about Sophie. What kind of woman she was; what kind of reporter she was. We should be making the news, not reacting to it!"

Rev studied Collingsworth's face before saying, "I will promise you this, though—"

"What?"

"When my legal decks are clear, the *Telegraph* gets the whole story ... an exclusive."

"Gee. Thanks."

Rev ignored the sarcasm. "Thank Sophie. She was much more loyal to this rag than I ever was. But I'll warn you ..." He made a pistol of his thumb and forefinger, which he pointed at the editor.

"What?"

"You won't get one word out of me if you publish a retraction of my story on Samuel Jenkins' Medal of Honor."

Collingsworth squinted. "What's that have to do with Sophie's murder?"

Rev paused, considering how much of what he suspected he'd have to reveal to stay the retraction.

"Before she died, she told me that she had been warned by two thugs named Slike and Franklin to back off a story she was working on with me."

"The guys who killed her at the shooting range?"

"That's right."

"There was nothing on her news budget about collaborating with you. She was all wrapped up in Johnston Bradley, the gun shop burglary ... his apparent murder. You weren't working with her on that, were you?"

"Peripherally. But we were working on something else ... off the books. She was helping me investigate a top-secret mission at the end of World War II called Operation Setting Sun. Sophie helped me file a Freedom of Information Act request about the op."

"Wow. Cutting-edge journalism."

"Sarcasm's a low art form. It can't be a coincidence that the package from the navy arrived the same day she was kidnapped. I found it on the top of a hutch in her kitchen and I opened it."

Collingsworth fidgeted with his pen.

Rev could tell that he was losing him, so he picked up the pace.

"According to the documents, Operation Setting Sun was a diplomatic mission launched by the authority of the president of the United States in July of 1945 to negotiate Japan's immediate surrender."

"The mission failed, obviously," Collingsworth interjected. "Japan didn't surrender until September of 1945, after we dropped the bomb."

Rev nodded. "You're due an A-plus, in history, Gray."

Collingsworth brushed the compliment aside. "What's your interest in a sixty-year-old story?"

"My great granduncle, Jacob Addison, was the mission's pilot."

"OK, then I can understand *your* interest, but what does all of this have to do with Sophie's murder? You haven't told me anything that warrants retracting your story about Sam Jenkins' Medal of Honor."

"Care to guess the name of the mission's commanding officer?"

"Nope. Why don't you just tell me?"

"The late Vice Admiral Alan Jenkins, father of Sam Jenkins, the alleged hero of the battle for Hill 875. Gray, I'm pretty sure I can prove that Sam Jenkins was complicit in Sophie's death. That he was worried we'd stumble onto something about that old op that would fuck up his run for the White House. But my whole investigation will be compromised if you retract my story about his Medal of Honor."

"Jesus Christ, Rev. You've got an elephant-sized hard-on for Jenkins. How could he possibly be involved in this? I can't kill the retraction. The legal department has crawled all over this. Your story probably was true and we might prevail in court, but the cost. Good God, the cost. And the risk if we don't win ..."

"It's time to ante up, Gray. This is your defining moment. I've got the story of the decade in my back pocket. It's yours if you have the balls to fight off the lawyers."

"You've got to give me more than that to go on," Collingsworth pleaded.

Rev picked up his computer case, which was propped against the chair leg. He placed it on his lap, unzipped it, and pulled out a manila envelope, which he tossed on Collingsworth's desktop.

"What's this?"

"My great granduncle's account of Operation Setting Sun, and the navy's official report, which I just received under the Freedom of Information Act. Sophie helped me fill out the application and I think that's what got her killed. Read it and then tell me if you still think it's a good idea to retract my story about Sam Jenkins' cowardice."

Chapter 50

6 p.m. Monday, August 29, 2011, Selinsgrove, PA
Liv looked tiny and vulnerable when she opened her door to admit Rev.

She wore jeans and a purple tee. Her feet were bare. Her toenails, red.

Even without makeup she looked beautiful. Rev resisted the impulse to tell her so because he was numb, emotionally. Sensory overload. He'd seen too much death.

Rev followed her to the kitchen. She motioned to one of four chairs pulled up to a Formica-topped table, a throwback from the 50s.

"Have a seat."

Her kitchen chairs were vinyl clad and duct-taped at the cushion corners. Rev sat in one of them while Liv poured two fingers of Jameson into a highball glass.

"Straight up or on the rocks?"

"Rocks," Rev said.

He wasn't a fan of Irish whiskey, but he needed something to take the edge off. He was full of nervous energy, ready to kick down doors and find out what happened to Sophie.

Liv's narrow duplex hugged the Susquehanna River in Selinsgrove, a college town situated about an hour north of Harrisburg. It was hot, and a noisy air-conditioner rattled in the window of the tiny breakfast nook without doing much to dissipate the heat.

Liv poured an equal measure of Jameson into her own glass, crossed the kitchen to the refrigerator, and dropped four ice cubes into each glass. "You're being awfully quiet. I hope you aren't beating yourself up over what could have been."

Rev shrugged. "I'm OK now. Thanks to your ... intervention."

Liv laughed. "I probably shouldn't be tempting you with alcohol, but I think we both need a hair of the dog that bit you. I don't know whether this will make you feel better or worse, but I just got confirmation that you shot Slike and Franklin shot Sophie."

"Who shot Franklin? Not that it matters."

Liv studied her fingernails, which matched her toes, color wise. "Simpson and I both shot him. My bullet did the most damage."

"How is he?"

"No change. Still in a coma. The doctors say he lost four pints of blood and that his heart stopped beating long enough that brain damage is probable. I'll be on administrative leave for a month while the crime scene investigators sort it all out and the psych types get through rooting around in my head."

"Are you OK? Legally, I mean."

Liv nodded. "Johnston Bradley's statement that he had been kidnapped certainly justifies our use of deadly force."

"How about emotionally?"

Liv wiped her nose with a forearm. "I've cried, but I'm coping. How about you?"

Rev stared at her without speaking.

After he had killed those civilians in Fallujah, he had been so full of self-pity that it was difficult to muster the discipline to get out of bed, brush his teeth, put on his clothes. He had taken innocent lives along with the guilty. This time was different. The emotional shock of losing Sophie activated his stress-relief default: booze and lots of it. But ever since Nona and Liv had "intervened," his emotional state was driven by anger far more than by regret. Sophie's innocent blood had been spilled in the service of someone who was not present at the shooting range. Rev was determined to find out who.

Liv mistook his silence for regret at having killed Slike. "It was a righteous kill, Rev, and a hell of a shot. You took the top of his head off without nicking Sophie. You had a target area of about six inches square and you drilled it right in the center."

"Yeah, but while I was killing Slike, Franklin killed Sophie."

"You picked the target that posed the most immediate threat. Colonel Simpson and I are more to blame for her death than you are. If we had come through the door two seconds earlier and started shooting a millisecond sooner, Sophie would be alive. She would have wet her pants at the close call, laughed about the way I looked in Kevlar, and then she would have gotten busy writing her story about what happened at that shooting range."

"You know Sophie and I had been on the outs for a long while," Rev said. "She said that I was emotionally unavailable and she broke things off."

"And then she let you back into her bed."

"You know about that?"

"Yep, and one of the last times I talked to her, she told me that sleeping with you again was a mistake because your relationship wasn't going anywhere. Sophie was damaged by her first marriage, more than she ever let anyone know. She recognized that she couldn't give you the emotional support you need to deal with your guilt. I know what you've been through. I know what it's like to face the decision to kill or be killed."

Tears welled in Rev's eyes. "Why are you telling me this now?"

"So you can live without the regret of what might have been with Sophie. Right or wrong, she was moving on. And now we need to do that, too."

Her words were stark, but Rev took solace in them.

He stood.

She took three steps toward him. He split the difference.

She felt tiny and fragile against him. He could feel her heart beating and smell the lingering essence of the body wash she had used that morning. It had to be body wash because a state police trooper wouldn't use perfume, would she?

The pressure of her breasts and thighs aroused him. He stepped away quickly before amorous thoughts provoked a physical reaction that he did not want to try to explain to Liv, or to himself.

Liv put her hands on her hips and squared her shoulders. There was a challenge in her eyes.

"What now, big guy?" she asked.

Rev stepped forward again and kissed her, delighted that she kissed back.

Chapter 51

6:30 p.m. Monday, August 29, 2011, Selinsgrove, PA
"What just happened?"

Liv's question hung in the air above her bed, dangling dangerous tentacles of regret like a Portuguese Man of War.

Rev risked being stung. "Do you want an anatomical description? Or is your question rhetorical?"

Liv rose up on one elbow and punched him in the arm.

"Ow, but thank you."

"For what?"

"I've always wanted to see what a state police officer looks like naked."

"And now that you have, where do we go from here?"

"Will you marry me?"

She punched him again. "Goddamn it, Rev Polk, don't be glib with me. We've violated a sacred trust here. Never sleep with your best friend's former boyfriend."

She was speaking as if Sophie were still alive. To remind her would have been unkind. Rev stayed with glib. It had gotten him this far, hadn't it?

"We didn't sleep, Liv. At least I wasn't sleeping."

Her eyes were daggers.

Rev sat up, resting the back of his head against the wall. He folded his hands on his chest and stared out into space to avoid the challenge in her eyes.

"Damn it, Liv! I don't want to say anything to cheapen what just happened between us. Glib is how I deflect honesty that's too close to the bone. I don't know where we go from here, but I do know how we got here and for now that's enough."

"What do you mean by that?"

"We've both suffered a loss and we turned to each other for support. I think Sophie would understand that. And we can't let what just happened between us push us apart at the very moment we need each other the most. I am willing to go forward with our friendship and abide by whatever ground rules you want to propose."

"Even if it means no more sex?"

"Even if it means no more sex," Rev agreed.

She grabbed his penis. "You think this guy will sign off on that?"

"Sergeant York works for me."

"No he doesn't," Liv observed as the sergeant came to attention and saluted, ready for a rematch, in which Liv prevailed after four deuces.

She rolled off him. "Shit! That really was the last time, but damn that felt good. Do you have any idea how hard it is for a state police trooper to get laid?"

Rev sat up abruptly and swung his legs over the edge of her bed.

"What's wrong? That was one of my best lines ever and I don't get so much as a snicker?"

Rev shook his head.

"It was a great line, but something just occurred to me. It's important and I want to write it to my hard drive before I lose it."

"What's that?"

"Something wasn't right there inside the shooting range."

Liv swung around and sat beside him. He draped an arm around her and drew her closer.

"Go on," she said.

"When I burst inside, Slike was dragging Sophie toward the door. My eyes were locked on Sophie, but in my peripheral vision I could see Franklin and Brad throwing punches like drunken sailors on liberty."

Liv snuggled closer. The scent of body wash and sex radiated from her. Rev couldn't help himself. He bent down and gave her a lingering kiss on the lips.

Breaking contact, he said:

"Oops. Sorry. I keep forgetting. No more sex."

Liv smiled. "Please keep forgetting."

"What I mean is this: it almost seemed as if they were stage fighting. You know, pretending."

"How could you reach that conclusion? Like you said, you were focused on Sophie."

Rev downshifted. "What kind of shape was Brad in after we rescued him? I didn't see any bruises, did you?"

"What? No. No bruises. But he smelt like piss. He said that they'd tied his hands behind him and he had to pee his pants. He also said that Sophie chewed through his bonds right before we arrived."

"Odd."

"What's odd about that?"

"Two murderers tie up a prisoner, but they don't do him any other damage? And he claims that they were trying to extract information from him?"

Liv nodded. "That's right."

"Don't you think that they would have roughed him up?"

"Maybe they were aiming at a psychological advantage. Question him. Tie him up in the dark; question him again ... that sort of thing."

"That seems awfully subtle for the likes of Furnley Franklin and Jerry Slike," Rev said.

"Maybe they were following the orders of their superiors."

Rev shook his head. "I don't know. But here's the biggest thing..."

"What?" Liv asked.

"Franklin was punching with his left hand."

"So?"

"He was punching with his left hand because he was holding a pistol in his right. Why wouldn't he have just shot Johnston Bradley rather than punching him with his weak hand? We know that he was capable of murder because he killed Sophie."

At that moment, Liv's cell phone chirped from the night stand. She reached across him to collect it. "Hold that thought."

She glanced at the display.

"It's Randy Simpson," she said.

"Randy?"

Liv winked. "We're on a first-name basis now, the good colonel and I."

She answered the phone and listened for a long while.

"I think I can round up Rev Polk fairly quickly," she said. "Give us about an hour and a half and we'll be there. Bye."

She ended the call and looked at Rev without saying anything.

Rev raised his hands, palms ups, and shrugged.

"Colonel Simpson requests the pleasure of our company at the Oliver Hazard Perry Military Academy. It seems that he has uncovered some evidence that he'd like to share with us, but not over the phone."

"It won't take us nearly an hour and half to get there," Rev observed.

"Well there is that thing you keep forgetting," Liv replied.

"What's that thing?"

She giggled. "No more sex."

"I'm not sure Sergeant York is ready for duty."

"The good sergeant works for me," Liv said.

She was right.

Chapter 52

8:30 p.m. Monday, August 29, 2011, Middleburg, PA
"Does the date September 11, 2011 mean anything to you?" Colonel Randolph Simpson asked the question with absolutely no inflection in his voice.

"Duh," Rev Polk replied.

"Yeah, duh," Liv Pearson added.

"That's when they plan to do it. The 10th anniversary of 9/11," Simpson said.

"Do what?" Rev asked.

"I'm not sure."

"And where?" Liv added.

"Same answer."

They were gathered in Simpson's office at the military academy. Simpson sat behind his big desk and Liv and Rev occupied chairs across from him.

Rev rotated his neck. He felt the snap and pop of bone and sinew. "So, we know the when, but not the what, the where, or the why. You can't get a news story to stand up on one leg. We need at least one or two of the others, damn it!"

"Who said anything about a news story?" Simpson asked.

The alarm in his voice told Rev that he'd struck a nerve. The last thing Simpson wanted was a news story.

"I meant that merely as a metaphor," Rev said.

"What's a meta for?" Liv asked.

"A meta is for showing your readers how cultured you are," Rev said.

Simpson's face flushed scarlet. "You and your straight man ought to take this act on the road once this is all over, but for now I'm serious, damn it!"

"I am, too, Colonel. These bastards killed Sophie, and I'd like to figure out why. And figuring out why would seem to hinge on divining their next move," Rev said.

"If they are planning to defile the 10th anniversary of 9/11, three possible venues leap to mind—Washington, D.C., New York City, or Shanksville, PA," Simpson said.

"What makes you so sure of the date?" Rev asked.

"I've intercepted a phone call between Bill Kambic and his father that leads me to believe that some sort of demonstration is scheduled for September 11."

"What sort of demonstration?"

"I wish I knew," Simpson said.

"Why don't you know? Were they speaking in code?" Liv asked.

"No. They were speaking in riddles that only they knew the answers to. I could play the whole damn tape back for you, but you wouldn't find it enlightening. I certainly didn't. The pertinent quote goes like this ..."

Simpson closed his eyes, concentrating so he'd get it right. "Kambic the senior says: 'So our little demonstration is all set?' and Billy Boy replies: 'That's right ... Overlord is on September 11th.'"

Liv raised an eyebrow. "Overlord?"

Simpson said: "George Kambic fancies himself a World War II historian. Overlord was the code name for D-Day."

"Maybe Overlord is code for their next meeting," Liv said.

"It's got to be something more than that," Rev said. "The Blue Mountain Boys just committed murder. They're serious players."

"Or damn dangerous neophytes," Simpson said.

"What about Johnston Bradley?" Liv asked.

"What about him?" Simpson asked.

"I don't know. I always got this vibe from him. Like he wasn't who he said he was."

Simpson sighed. "Brad would be upset to hear you say that. He thought he had you all fooled."

Rev sat up straighter in his chair. "Fooled? Brad's just a kid, right ... a student at the academy."

"Actually, he's much more than that. Brad's 24, a sergeant in Special Forces. And my spy on the inside of the Blue Mountain Boys."

"I knew it!" Liv exulted.

"Brad was supposed to work his way into the inner sanctum," Simpson said. "That's why I signed off on his participating in that stupid gun-shop burglary. Thought it might be a way for him to win his spurs ... to prove he could be trusted."

"So what was up with the mock murder video?" Liv asked.

Simpson sighed. "The idea was sound. We wanted to make the Blue Mountain Boys nervous; edge them into a mistake. And give

Brad a good excuse for not showing up at his preliminary hearing."

"But instead ... they killed Sophie?" Rev's words were bitter. And peevish because Liv had divined Brad's secret and he had not.

"I'm not sure you can trace a cause and effect there. Sophie's involvement was peripheral. I think she posed an unrelated danger to someone at the heart of this conspiracy. Maybe the plan was to put the two of them together and eavesdrop on what they said to each other," Simpson said.

Liv put a hand on Rev's arm. "I tend to agree with the colonel. Sophie stumbled into something dangerous and it killed her."

Simpson cleared his throat. "Anyway, like I said, we were trying to force their hand and thought that if law enforcement began sniffing around; maybe they'd make a mistake. The cover story was that Brad wanted to escape prosecution ... and what better way to avoid a trial than to show up dead?"

"But the Blue Mountain Boys sniffed him out," Rev said.

"That's right. Brad seems to think they broke into his e-mail account and found some incriminating messages to me that revealed him as a spy," Simpson said.

"And you as their enemy," Rev added.

Simpson nodded.

"Where is Brad now?" Liv asked.

"I allowed him to go home to reassure his parents that he's not dead."

"My impression of Bill and Alice Bradley is that they don't need any reassurance," Liv said. "That video is graphic, but when I showed it to them ... I don't know. It was as if they were just pretending to be shocked."

"Maybe Brad told them in advance what he was planning so they wouldn't be worried," Rev said.

"I doubt that," Simpson said. "Sergeant Bradley is gung ho about Special Forces. I told him not to breathe a word."

"Did the Blue Mountain Boys use any enhanced interrogation techniques on Brad?" Rev asked.

Simpson cocked his head. "I asked him that question. He said they punched him hard enough to crack a couple of his ribs. He winces when he inhales too sharply or when he sneezes, but otherwise he seems to be OK. He told me he didn't need to see a doctor."

Rev narrowed his eyes, staring at Simpson. "I've got an idea. Can I use your computer?"

Simpson stood and waved at the laptop computer positioned on the desktop. "Sure. Go ahead have a seat. Computer's already on. You just have to wake it."

Rev sat down behind the colonel's desk. "You're connected to the Internet, right?"

"We've got a wireless network," Simpson said.

Liv moved behind Rev and stood with her hands on his shoulders. "What occurred to you?"

"Google is a reporter's best friend," Rev said.

Rev launched Internet Explorer by single-clicking the icon in the tray on the bottom left of the screen and typed "Flight 93 Sept. 11, 2011," into the space provided for Google searches on the colonel's home screen, which predictably was the website for the military academy.

"Why Flight 93?" Liv asked.

"It's in Pennsylvania; the Blue Mountain Boys are in Pennsylvania. It's easier to project power closer to your home base," Rev explained.

The first item among the results took Rev to the National Park Service's website to a page on which were listed activities commemorating the 10th anniversary of 9/11.

Scrolling through them, Rev noticed that the Tuscarora Unit of the Pennsylvania National Guard would be providing honor guard services for the dedication of the first phase of the permanent Flight 93 Memorial. "The Tuscarora Unit of the Pennsylvania National Guard. Who commands it?"

"The overall commander would be General George Kambic," Simpson replied.

"I think Shanksville is the venue for the Blue Mountain Boys' 'demonstration,'" Rev said. "And get this ..."

He tapped the computer screen with his right index finger. "It says here that the vice president of the United States will be the honored guest at the ceremony marking the 10th anniversary of the crash at Shanksville."

"Son of a bitch," Simpson said. "Do you think they plan to kill the vice president?"

"Who'd want to kill a vice president?" Liv asked. "That would be like shooting the general's horse, wouldn't it?"

Chapter 53

9:30 a.m. Saturday, September 10, 2011, New Cumberland, PA

Rev Polk was feeling curiously ambivalent about his sleepover with Liv Pearson as he climbed the front steps of his duplex on Fourth Street in New Cumberland.

He was excited by the possibility of developing a relationship with the gorgeous state police trooper, but Sophie's ghost haunted his thoughts.

Sophie had yet to be interred, her funeral service delayed by a forensic autopsy, and he had jumped willy nilly into bed with her best friend.

Rev was no prude but he recognized a moral dilemma when he saw one. Should he pass up the opportunity of a relationship with a woman he admired to pay homage to the memory of an ex-lover who had summarily dismissed him from her heart just when he needed her most?

Rev fumbled his keys from his pocket and bent to unlock his front door. Scratches on the brand new brass key plate bristled the hairs on the back of his neck.

He had installed a new lock set and key plate barely three weeks ago after snapping off his key in the old lock as he struggled to open the door with his arms full of groceries. He did the replacement himself after watching a how-to video on YouTube and was proud of the results.

The scratches were a sure sign that someone without a key had tried to open his door. Had they been successful?

Given his recent troubles, he'd taken to carrying his Glock under the waistband of his pants at the small of his back. Liv had expedited its release from the state police evidence locker after her testimony and the forensic evidence proved that he had fired it in self-defense. He thought about drawing the Glock before entering the house but decided that would be too conspicuous. He didn't want to alarm the neighbors.

He sucked his teeth. He could knock on Emily Griswold's door to see if she had seen anything untoward. She occupied the other half of the duplex. Not much escaped her attention. He was pretty sure she had witnessed his homecoming because the curtains on the sidelights of her front door were pulled to one side.

He bounded down the steps from his front porch and ascended the steps to hers. She answered his third knock; flung her front door wide open. "It's about time you got home, Major Polk."

He had told her a hundred times not to refer to him by his military rank. He was a civilian first and a soldier second. The message just never got through.

"And why would that be, Mrs. Griswold?"

"You should have heard the carryings on this morning on your front porch."

His pulse quickened. "What do you mean by that?"

"Well it was about 2 a.m. You know how I like to get a glass of milk and a cookie about then? I'm an insomniac, you know?"

Rev didn't know but he nodded just to keep her story flowing.

"As I was coming down the stairs, I heard heavy footsteps on your front porch. By the time I peeked out all I could see was his backside."

"So there was a man on my front porch at 2 a.m."

"Not just any man. He was huge."

"I thought you could only see his backside."

"That's right. It was a huge backside."

Rev considered. "How old a man was he?"

"I can't rightly say, but he must have had a key because he let himself into your house."

"How do you know that?"

"I could hear him moving around for the better part of 20 minutes. It's tough for a big man to be quiet. He was better than most."

"So you did see the front of him when he came out of my house?" Rev asked, impatiently.

"Course I did."

"And?"

"Like I said, he was a really big man. Taller than you, even, and thick and broad. He looked like a football player wearing shoulder pads, he was so big."

"Did you see his face?"

"Only in profile and just for a second. He sort of ducked his head into his shoulder when he got out there to the sidewalk where the streetlight captured him. He wore a crew cut, dark slacks and a shirt, and he moved like a big cat. Unless I miss my guess he was a military man, or used to be."

"I see. So what did you do?"

"Well I called the police, of course. Right when I first saw him."

"And?"

"They blew me off, just like they always do. I can almost hear the dispatcher grumbling 'crazy old Griswold hearing bumps in the night again.' That's the way they talk about me. I know it is."

"I'm sure the dispatchers hold you in highest regard. The police probably did a drive-by and you missed them."

"Not likely, but possible, I suppose. A girl has to go to the loo from time to time."

"Well, thanks for looking out for things while I've been gone," Rev said.

He turned and walked down her steps, aware that her eyes were boring holes in his back. Disengaging from Mrs. Griswold was almost as difficult as getting out of Iraq.

He pulled his iPhone off his hip and punched the icon for his web browser.

The smart phone recognized his wireless network from out on the porch and he typed New Cumberland Police Department into the Google bar.

The phone number came up as a hot link. He punched it to dial the police department.

He got the 9-1-1 dispatcher instead, which wasn't unusual. The local police's phone rang at county control when no one was on station.

He identified himself to the dispatcher and asked, "Do you know if police made a drive-by of my place at 604 Fourth Street this morning? My neighbor says she reported a prowler at about 2 a.m. I've been out of town and before I go inside I want to make sure everything is OK."

"Wait one moment."

Rev was dispatched to the ocean-in-the-seashell hum of a line on hold.

The dispatcher was back in less than a minute. "New Cumberland Police did a walk-around of your place at about 0230 hours but could find no evidence of a prowler. Would you like me to ask an officer to go through your house with you?"

Rev considered. He wasn't afraid to go inside, but with all the shit that had landed on him recently it might be a good idea to have a witness if he was forced to react to an intruder.

"That won't be necessary," he said. "Things seem to be under control. There's no evidence that anyone broke in. I was just reacting to my nosy neighbor."

That brought a chuckle from the dispatcher.

"You must mean Mrs. Griswold of 602 Fourth Street. All of the dispatchers know her ... and love her."

"I'm sure you do. Good bye."

Rev disconnected and clipped his phone back to his belt. He inserted the key into the lock, turned it, and went inside. A quick walk-through of the three bedrooms upstairs, and the living room, dining room, and kitchen down below demonstrated that someone had indeed wandered through his possessions.

The evidence of the search was subtle. His jewelry box had been moved a half inch to the right, leaving a trail in the dust that had accumulated on his dresser top. Sometimes it was prudent to be a lackadaisical housekeeper. A sticky drawer in the kitchen, which he always pushed on extra hard to close entirely, was open a quarter of an inch. The most telling thing was the empty file folder on his dining room table, which doubled as his work-at-home desk. It had contained his hand-written notes comparing the Freedom of Information report on Operation Setting Sun to what he had gleaned from Jake's diary, which was locked up safe and sound in his car at the moment.

The theft was an annoyance and not a disaster for the story he was compiling about the malfeasance of Samuel Jenkins and his father, the late Admiral Alan Jenkins. Rev already had transcribed his notes and saved them to the hard drive of his laptop. The troubling thing was the other side now knew what he knew ... if they could decipher his handwriting. It would be interesting to see how they would react to that.

Rev decided that the dust trail on his dresser top was a sign that it was time to do some housecleaning. He and Liv had agreed to ride together to Shanksville the next morning to join Colonel Randolph Simpson's unit of soldiers, who would help protect the vice president. She was planning to spend the night, and Rev didn't want her to think that he lived like a pig, although he sometimes did.

He spent the rest of the morning dusting, vacuuming, and wiping the sticky jelly residue from his counter tops in the kitchen. He changed the linens on his double bed upstairs, and the water in the wash bucket was nearly black when he finished scrubbing the kitchen floor on his hands and knees. He knocked off at noon, made himself a ham and cheese sandwich, and ate at his dining room table, which glowed with a fresh application of Pledge.

As he sat there staring out the window at the side of the next duplex over, less than 10 feet away, he heard a heavy step on his front porch. He picked up his Glock, which he had placed on the table close to his right hand, and tiptoed toward the door. The mail slot creaked open and a half dozen letters and assorted direct mail advertising cascaded into his foyer.

Goddamn, he was jumpy.

He put the Glock away and thumbed through the mail, which included a card from the postal service informing him that a registered letter awaited his attention.

He threw open the door, thinking he might flag down the postman and collect his registered mail. Liv Pearson stood on his front porch with an overnight bag clutched in her right hand.

Liv misinterpreted his surprise as dismay. "Relax. I'm not pregnant. But we do need to talk."

He stepped back, beckoning her to enter. "We need to talk? Nothing good has ever come of those words. But, come on inside anyway. And for the record, I did not forget you were sleeping over. We need to be in Shanksville by 9 a.m. tomorrow. I hadn't forgotten that. I was just trying to chase down the mailman. I have a registered letter." Rev relieved Liv of her overnight bag, which he deposited on the landing leading to the second floor. "If we have to talk, we might as well be comfortable. Follow me."

He led her into his small living room, which boasted a floral print couch, two armchairs, a love seat, and a grandfather clock. He sat down on one of the armchairs and motioned to the other.

"Have a seat. What's on your mind?"

Liv perched on the edge of the chair with the demeanor of a sparrow tempted by a bread crumb to forestall the safer course, which is always to fly away.

"I don't know where to start."

"The beginning works."

"And that's the problem. Our beginning. And the sleeping over part. Maybe I should just rent a hotel room nearby."

"Why?"

"Because I think of Sophie every time I look at you and I feel guilty. I've got to get her out of our bedroom. And I don't know how to do it."

Liv paused, waiting for a reaction. Rev's face was inscrutable, chiseled in stone like one of those Easter Island statues.

"Say something, you asshole." Liv's voice was shrill.

Rev took a deep breath, measuring his words so he did not make a bad situation worse. Intimacy with Liv did not make him uncomfortable as it had with other women. Something just seemed right about her, and the rightness defied analysis.

"I don't think I can say anything to diminish guilt," he said, at last. "I have a master's degree in it. I regret not having defined my relationship with Sophie. I don't want to make the same mistake with you."

"What would you have done differently ... with Sophie?" Her voice was tiny; she asked because she had to not because she wanted to.

Rev sighed. "I'd have opened my heart to her. But I was afraid that she ... and now you ... would be revolted by what lies inside."

"What could be that revolting?"

"I'm a murderer, Liv. In Iraq, I killed a man, his wife, and their small child. A terrorist was using them as a shield. He killed two of my men and wounded a third before I shot back. I killed them, Liv. I killed them all, the innocent along with the guilty. Their faces stare at me from my dreams."

Liv settled back in her chair.

"If that's the worst you've got, I can handle it. I've killed, too. It was my first year on the job and I stumbled into an armed robbery at a convenience store. I was carrying a cup of coffee to the register when an armed man burst in and shoved a big revolver into the cashier's face. I dropped the coffee, yanked my weapon from its holster and screamed at him to drop his gun. He whirled around, pointed the gun at me, and I shot him, three times in the middle of the chest."

"Sounds like you had good reason."

"I did, but the gun turned out to be a realistic toy. And the gunman? A 17-year-old kid strung out on heroin."

"So we're both lugging baggage."

"I set those bags down long ago," Liv said.

"You make it sound easy."

"Nope. It was the hardest thing I ever did. It took months of counseling, but I forgave myself ... and the young addict I killed. I returned to work, resolved to be an even better cop than I had been before."

"I haven't arrived there yet," Rev said. "But I do know this."

"What?"

"Making love to you isn't a sin. I admire you, Liv. You are brave and strong ... just like Sophie. It's only natural that you two would be friends."

"And now we're friends, too, aren't we, Rev?"

"That's right. We're friends. And that's a good starting point for any relationship."

"I notice you didn't say that you loved me," Liv said.

"I didn't say it because that would cheapen the experience."

"What experience?"

"The experience of falling in love with you," Rev said. "That's a lot more difficult ... for me anyway. I'm a private person. I like my own company and it's difficult for me to open the door and let others come in."

"Knock. Knock," Liv said.

"Who's there?"

"It's just me and I'd say we've got just enough time."

"For what?"

"To sweat up your bed sheets and take a long nap before we go out for dinner."

Rev stood. "Then I guess we better get started."

Chapter 54

11 a.m. Sunday, September 11, 2011, Shanksville, PA
The trough Flight 93 gouged into the rolling countryside was a healing scar. The site looked nothing like the rough mining scrub patch that had absorbed the impact of the Boeing 747 bearing 40 brave souls to their final resting place ten years earlier.

The earth movers and masons worked overtime to make sure that the first phase of the National Park Service's memorial was completed in time for the 10th anniversary of 9/11. A stone-topped visitor's gateway opened into a memorial plaza rimmed by a stone walkway and a long, low-slung wall at the base of which were installed plaques bearing the names of the men and women who died in defiance of Osama bin Laden's assault on the American way of life. Benches at regular intervals along the walkway offered visitors a chance to sit and contemplate heroism and sacrifice, along with man's infinite ability to do good and evil.

September 11, 2011 was set aside for contemplation, although Rev Polk's thoughts were elsewhere as he stood before the temporary platform erected to accommodate the vice president of the United States, the speaker of the House of Representatives, and a phalanx of lesser dignitaries assembled to put their patriotism on public display.

Rev was thinking darkly that all of the media attention had cheapened the sacrifice the memorial was meant to honor. Many of the visitors, he suspected, were drawn more by the spectacle than by desire to offer homage.

It was a cloudy, humid day with the temperature in the mid-80s. Nothing like the pristine blue hue of exactly 10 years before, which had lent such a crystalline and bizarre juxtaposition of beauty and desolation to the horrific events of that day. Ten years later, the humidity was so high that the gentle breeze deposited tendrils of moisture on Rev's face and neck. It was as if Mother

Nature was weeping in memory of the sacrifice of the passengers and crew of Flight 93.

All Rev could do was sweat in his dress blues and wish he were anywhere but here, prepared to take a bullet for the vice president, or worse for Speaker of the House Samuel Jenkins, the son of a bitch. It occurred to him that two pillars of presidential succession were present on the stage. And he wondered, not for the first time, if he was chasing wild geese while the real threat developed elsewhere.

The right's hatred of the current president exceeded the left's disdain for his predecessor. Rev's years as a journalist had demonstrated that venal behavior was the exclusive property of neither political party; that power corrupted no matter who wielded it; and that a government that tried to do good and failed was far better than one that tried to do nothing at all. He was an independent by registration, as many of his colleagues were for impartiality's sake, but he believed that government did have a responsibility for the welfare and health of the populace.

As he stood, sweating in his dress blues, he wondered about the political persuasion of Liv Pearson. Their relationship was so new that he hadn't had time to assess her politics, which was another reason he had not uttered the L-word.

He felt guilty once again. For being alive. When Sophie and Tex and Mex and so many other nameless martyrs among his brethren in arms were dead, dead, dead. He was alive and able to sweat and to wonder and to contemplate what the new day held for him and for Liv Pearson and for all the people stuffed into the memorial plaza at the Flight 93 site this hot, muggy September day.

Visitors had arrived by the thousands, bussed from the parking areas set up to accommodate them. He could smell their sweat and sense their impatience to mourn ... and then to get on with their lives. Their presence was stifling, almost claustrophobic. God, there must be a million places for an assassin to hide there in the scrub-covered hills surrounding them, he realized. He shivered, imagining what it would feel like to be struck by a bullet.

He had fired many a bullet in anger and had seen the devastating effect of lead upon mortal flesh. People bled. People died. He had long ago shed the schoolboy's fascination with battle. It scared him. It made his bowels loose.

Near Shanksville, Rev and Liv had rendezvoused with Simpson and the special contingent of faux cadets the good colonel had assembled to run interference against whatever mayhem the Blue

Mountain Boys had in store. Simpson had pulled some strings and secured the services of a bus from the Army Reserve Unit in Harrisburg.

The driver dropped them off two hours before the ceremony. The Secret Service had beefed up the usual contingent it dispatched to protect the life of the vice president. But it had allocated even more of its available assets to protect the president.

Rev imagined that the Pennsylvania National Guard's Honor contingent, commanded by Bill Kambic, had received special attention. The Secret Service would make damn sure that the honor guard would be using blanks when it offered a 21-gun salute.

Rev and Liv stood side by side in front of the stage. They, along with the other young Special Forces soldiers Colonel Simpson had assembled under the banner of the Oliver Hazard Perry Military Academy, were arrayed as human shields in predetermined positions chosen to interrupt the field of fire from any number of likely vantage points on the perimeter of the memorial plaza.

They were all wearing Kevlar under the tunics of their dress uniforms. But Kevlar wouldn't stop a bullet to the brain, nor prevent anyone from bleeding out should a well-placed bullet to the thigh sever the femoral artery.

The honorable Samuel Jenkins had kept an association with the Army Reserve and over time had risen to the rank of brigadier general. He wore his dress blues to remind voters of his service and of his sacrifice. The scrambled eggs on his cap visor competed for attention with the Medal of Honor he wore on a purple sash around his neck. Jenkins was in his mid-sixties, but he had kept after it. Rev had to give him credit for that. The tailored uniform accentuated broad shoulders and a narrow waist. How much of it was hard work in the gym and how much of it was the skill of his tailor, Rev couldn't be sure. But U.S. Rep. Samuel Jenkins towered above the vice president, who looked like Richard Nixon sweating in the footlights of public inspection.

Jenkins' face was composed and sweat-free, as if he had concealed an air-conditioner somewhere about his person. The vice president, on the other hand, sweated profusely. Seersucker would have made more sense, but the man a heartbeat away from the presidency had selected a black suit to fit the somber occasion and he was suffering for it.

Rev concentrated on keeping his knees flexed and bent to avoid passing out in the stifling humidity. He looked to his right, where Liv stood also at parade rest. Her features were composed in profile.

Just then, the speaker of the moment, the honorable mayor of Shanksville, introduced the Shanksville-Stony Creek High School glee choir, which would sing "Amazing Grace," over the objections of the ACLU whose lawyers had argued, unsuccessfully, that the ceremony should be bereft of the Christian God in consideration of the atheists and agnostics who had died on Flight 93. Who they were was anyone's guess.

The glee club did an admirable job and went off script to add a rousing rendition of "God Bless America," while their director, a balding middle-aged man, waved a baton as if chasing away bees. When they were done, the director commandeered the microphone and invited the vice president and assembled dignitaries to attend a commemorative service at the high school, which was organized at the last minute to accommodate the local populace who could not secure a spot at the main event.

The vice president strode to the podium and accepted the invitation. Not to be outdone, Jenkins joined him there and leaned over the vice president's shoulder to announce: "I'd be honored to attend as well, and God bless America."

Out of the side of his mouth, Rev observed, "By God. They're going off script aren't they? I'll bet the Secret Service is shitting bricks."

And then ... nothing happened. The ceremony proceeded on script. The National Guard Unit, with Bill Kambic in charge, delivered its 21-gun salute.

The rifle retorts echoed across the plaza. "Taps" was played. People cried. No one died.

Chapter 55

1 p.m. Sunday, September 11, 2011, Shanksville, PA
Rev Polk felt like a fat man was standing on his chest. Oxygen fled the gymnasium, and he gasped in the vacuum. He didn't put much stock in premonition, but he'd just had one. Claws clutched at him from underfoot trying to drag him down to the dark recesses of Hades.

Liv had to sense it, too. She was a perceptive woman, much more dialed in than he. But when he glanced her way, she smiled. Excited by the pomp and circumstance and oblivious of dread's embrace.

They stood before a temporary platform about three feet in height, constructed of two-by-fours and plywood and decorated with bunting. It dominated the east end of the Viking Sports Center at Shanksville-Stony Creek High School.

Rev managed to catch his breath as the milling crowd parted and the inevitable Junior ROTC honor guard marched onto the gym floor. The flag bearers and their attendants stopped behind a wide center aisle between two rows of folding chairs placed atop rubber matting to protect the hardwood from scuffing. The audience rose and turned to face the flag for the presentation of colors.

The lead soprano of the glee club sang the national anthem. Her clear, immature voice bounced about the gymnasium like a ping pong ball in a bingo machine. The sound engineer struggled to keep ahead of the feedback.

Vice President John Hawthorne and Speaker of the House Samuel Jenkins walked to center stage on the invitation of high school principal Emily Patterson, who used the PA system to call Jeremy Wright forward. Wright, she explained, was the president of the class of 2003, which had spearheaded the fund-raising campaign "93 Cents for Flight 93."

Rev shifted his weight from one foot to the other and glanced to his left, where Liv Pearson, Colonel Simpson, and Corporal George Smith were aligned in a neat row. Liv caught his glance, smiled, and winked. Oxygen rushed into his lungs. His affection for her was chocolate on his tongue and the claws clutching at him from underfoot relented.

A four-man squad commanded by Johnston Bradley stood at the other end of the stage facing the audience. When Rev caught his eye, Brad stood even taller and nodded as if to say: "Relax, Major. I've got things clenched tighter than a virgin's drawers."

Rev turned his attention to the audience. Approximately 150 people occupied the folding chairs directly in front of the stage. At least 400 more sat on fold-out bleachers. People fanned themselves in the stifling gymnasium, but Rev shivered with the realization that this was a situation that defied control. Any number of assassins could be hidden among the audience.

Jeremy Wright described to the audience the fund-raising campaign in support of the Flight 93 Memorial, which included current and former students and their siblings, offspring, parents, and grandparents. It was a wonderland of photo ops for dignitaries of all degrees of luminescence who occupied the folding chairs closest to the stage.

Everyone was aglow with bonhomie when the head of the Secret Service detail suddenly screamed: "Gun! Gun! Gun!"

Four sharp retorts followed.

The vice president fell to the stage floor. And a man in the third row of folding chairs dove to the ground and began crawling over people's feet.

An eerie silence was broken after just a few seconds as the gunman made an aisle and began to run toward the back of the gymnasium with four or five Secret Service agents in hot pursuit. Sam Jenkins knocked Jeremy Wright aside in his haste to aid the vice president and was staggered by a bullet that struck him high up on the right shoulder.

Someone else was firing at the stage from the audience, but who?

Staff Sergeant Bradley Johnston reacted even faster than the Secret Service, whose attention was diverted by the fleeing gunman. It was as if he anticipated what was about to happen. He leapt to the stage, tackled Jenkins from behind, knocked him to the ground, and covered him with his own body. Jenkins became the lunch meat in a sprawling sandwich, with Hawthorne on the bottom and Johnston Bradley on top. Bullets cratered the stage bunting. Blood bloomed on Bradley's upper thigh and buttocks.

Rev couldn't tell for sure, but he thought he saw gun flashes from three different spots on the gym floor. Someone tackled the gunman fleeing down the aisle. A cacophony of gunfire and screams assaulted Rev's ears. Liv slapped her thigh as if to draw her service weapon. But there was no weapon to be had. The Secret Service had insisted on being the only armed agents in the hall.

Rev grabbed Liv's hand and tried to drag her away from the mayhem unfolding all around them. His knees weakened with the thought that he might lose her, too.

Liv struggled, pulling away from him as he shouldered his way through the crowd. Rev's eyes darted back and forth, trying to record the positions of friend and foe. A young man in a suit materialized to his right, just as Liv yanked her arm free.

"Goddamn it, Rev, we have to do something. The vice president is shot. I'm a police officer. I've got to do something."

The young man in the suit, obviously a Secret Service agent, aimed his gun into the crowd and panned it back and forth, trying to get a clear shot. Rev dropped to one knee, grabbed Liv by the arm again, and yanked her down to him.

"Stay low!" he screamed.

Rev followed the line of sight of the Secret Service agent's pistol. He saw a gunman in the crowd aiming back. The gunman fired first and the agent's face disappeared in a froth of red. His gun fell from lifeless fingers.

Rev grabbed the agent's gun as it fell. Looking up he noticed with horror that the crowd had parted as people dove out of the way. There was a clear field of fire from him to the gunman.

"I know that guy!" Liv shouted. "That's Colin. I used to shoot with him at the gun range. Colin! Colin! Don't do it. Don't shoot!"

A young woman darted between Rev and Colin. The movement drew Colin's attention. He fired at it. The young woman took a bullet that otherwise would have been aimed at Rev. She crumpled to the floor.

Rev fired. Colin fell and was trampled by the crowd, which was reacting like a herd of wildebeest, surging this way and that to avoid the lions.

A little boy cried for his mother, lost somewhere in the crowd. A fat woman was sprawled on the floor with blood on her breast and a vacant look in her eyes. The American flag toppled from the stage, knocking off the toupee of a tall skinny man, who looked like someone's math teacher.

And then it was over. The gunmen were neutralized and the Secret Service locked the gymnasium down tight. No one was allowed to leave as the sorting out began.

Eight torturous hours later, Rev and Liv were among the last group of people to be dismissed. They left without knowing for certain how many gunmen had been involved. Rev guessed four. They did know, however, that the vice president was dead and that the speaker of the house would survive—thanks to Johnston Bradley's heroism. Jenkins and Bradley were carried out of the gymnasium side by side on stretchers. An enterprising photographer snapped their picture as the two clasped hands and raised their arms, celebrating their victory over death.

Chapter 56

10 a.m. Tuesday, September 20, 2011, Washington, DC
Andy Hawk stooped to clear the door frame on his way into Sam Jenkins' bedroom. Jenkins was propped up in bed with his back resting on an overstuffed TV pillow with pockets, in which were stored pens, a note pad, and the remote for the 36-inch flat screen on his dresser top. The TV was tuned to Fox News. An array of newspapers was scattered across the bedspread: the *New York Times*, *Washington Post*, *Wall Street Journal*, *USA Today*, and the *Washington Times*. Jenkins muted the volume as Hawk pulled a chair up to his bedside.

"How ya doin', boss?" Hawk asked, arranging his long frame on the chair.

Jenkins winced. "I'd forgotten how goddamn much a bullet wound hurts," he said. "It's been what, 44 years since that sniper nailed me in Vietnam?"

Hawk nodded. "Almost 44 years to the day. I joined you in the hospital three days later."

"We've both sacrificed a lot for our country, Andy."

"And now your sacrifice is about to pay off."

"For us ... for the country. We can't lose sight of that."

"That's right, boss. Things are going to be a damn sight better with you in charge."

"So the plan is operational?"

Hawk pulled an envelope from his inside jacket pocket and waved it in the air.

"Your invitation to the White House is right here. I've done some checking and the other names on the guest list are just as we'd expected. The president is grateful for their sacrifice for their country."

"Don't tease me, Andy. Who else is on the list?"

"Emily Patterson, the principal of the high school; Jeremy Smith, the young student on the stage when you were shot; a Pennsylvania state police corporal named Liv Pearson ..."

Jenkins frowned. "Don't know her. Who is she?"

Hawk's smile widened. "Rev Polk's current girlfriend."

Jenkins sat up straighter and winced.

Hawk saw the pain on his face.

"You OK, boss? Taking that bullet wasn't necessary."

Jenkins waved his left hand dismissively.

"It was a calculated risk. I'm the wounded hero again. I don't mind playing that part. I'm quite good at it, actually. Our friend Polk seems to have a fatal attraction to women. Wasn't he fucking that reporter? The one who was shot dead at the militia compound?"

Hawk nodded. "I'd say women have a fatal attraction to him."

"Don't make me laugh, Andy. It pulls my stitches. Who else is on the guest list?"

"Well, let's see. There's Army Staff Sergeant Johnston Bradley and Colonel Randolph Jenkins."

Jenkins exhaled explosively. "Hallelujah! All of the puzzle pieces will be in place. And what of our rabid mole?"

"His enthusiasm for his mission is undiminished," Hawk replied.

"Excellent. Excellent!"

Jenkins made a tent of his fingertips.

"What else could go wrong?" he asked.

The question was rhetorical. Hawk kept his silence.

"You're sure the Chad Tucci situation is ... neutralized?"

"As sure as I can be, boss. I searched his house thoroughly and found the file, which seemed to include all of the documents he used to blackmail you."

"What did you do with them?"

"They're all shredded. No worries there."

"But I can tell something's bothering you."

"When I pulled up to his house, he was leaving with a big manila envelope under his arm. He didn't have that envelope when he came back. And there was a brand new copier in his study."

"You should have followed him."

Hawk shrugged. "Judgment call. His leaving the house presented too tempting an opportunity."

"How so?"

"I cased the neighborhood and was pretty sure his neighbors were all at work. I figured it was an excellent chance to break in ... search his house ... and be waiting for him when he returned."

Jenkins nodded. "I see your point. I'm thinking that we don't have anything to worry about. If that package contained anything dangerous to us, we'd know about it by now."

Hawk nodded.

"OK, let's put that issue out of our minds. The Chad Tucci situation is contained. How about Daniel Shidehara?"

"He doesn't know enough to be dangerous. We paid him off and he signed the document the lawyers prepared, swearing him to silence forevermore and holding you harmless, civilly, in the death of his alleged father."

Jenkins grunted.

"And I provided an added incentive."

"What?"

"Let's just say the cat's got his tongue."

Jenkins stared at Hawk. "So our most pressing problem is what to do about our co-conspirators."

Hawk leaned back in the armchair and crossed his legs.

"State Senator George Kambic was very remorseful about his role in the assassination of the vice president," Hawk said. "He was so remorseful that he killed himself. I know that because I have a copy of his suicide note right here."

Hawk reached inside his lapel pocket and brought out a piece of copy paper folded lengthwise. He handed it to Jenkins, who pulled his reading glasses from the pocket of his recliner pillow.

Jenkins scanned the note and then read it a second time, more carefully.

He grunted. "That should do the trick. Will there be any question of its authenticity?"

"The original was printed out on his own computer. The signature is authentic. George Kambic shot himself in the right temple with his own gun. Tests will confirm gunpowder residue on his right hand and wrist. It will be an open and shut case as far as the police are concerned."

"How did you get him to sign the suicide note? Never mind, I don't want to know. What of his son?"

"Bill Kambic has some unusual sexual preferences. I've laid a honey trap for Billy boy. He'll stumble into it tonight. He and the woman have a history. He won't be able to resist the temptation."

"You're sure?"

"He never has before."

"Bill Kambic is the worst sort of sneak. The kind of guy who'd throw his best friend under the bus and never lose a minute's sleep because he'd convince himself that God told him to do it," Jenkins said.

"I'll take care of Bill Kambic, boss. I promise."

Jenkins nodded. "Your promises are golden. So all I have to do is sit back and wait?"

"And continue to block attempts to seat a new vice president so that you're next in succession," Hawk said.

"That goes without saying. And you'll take care of RSVPing to the president ... in the negative." Jenkins coughed. "I'm much too sick to attend. Wouldn't do to have me present at the assassination of my predecessor."

"But you'll be feeling much better real soon, Mr. President," Hawk said.

Chapter 57

5 p.m. Wednesday, September 21, 2011, New Cumberland, PA
"So you'll go?" Liv Pearson asked.

They had just collected two pieces of registered mail from the post office. The first was an envelope bearing the presidential seal with a return address of Pennsylvania Avenue, Washington D.C. The second was a manila envelope post marked in La Jolla, California.

Liv waved the invitation from the White House in the air like a bidder's paddle at an auction.

"Is that a question or a statement?"

Rev and Liv were sitting at his kitchen table.

He sighed. "Yes. I'll go. I'll put the RSVP in the mail first thing tomorrow."

"What about your package?" she said, pointing at the thick manila envelope on the tabletop."

Rev eyed it suspiciously. "I've never gotten good news from a lawyer," he said.

Liv picked up the package, hefted it, and studied the return address.

"Polanco and Polanco. Attorneys at Law, La Jolla, California," she said. "Think this has anything to do with your great granduncle Jake?"

She dropped the package back on the table.

"I suppose it could be about Jake. But more likely, it's correspondence from Sam Jenkins' lawyer. Now that I'm a former *Telegraph* employee, documents regarding the lawsuit will be mailed to me at home rather than at the office. The U.S. representative from La Jolla is suing me … and the newspaper for libel, you know."

"No, I didn't know. Why don't you tell me about it?"

"Tell you what. Let's get a booth at Nick's. We'll order burgers and beer. I'll open the package and tell you all about my fight with Sam Jenkins, which has a lot to do with why I got fired and why Grayson Collingsworth is such an asshole."

Fifteen minutes later they were settled into a booth at Nick's Bridge Street Café. They sat next to each other on the same side of the table.

Liv laid a hand on his thigh just as their waitress arrived.

"Hi. I'm Jennie. I'll be your server. What can I get for you two love birds?"

Love birds? That startled Rev. Sitting side by side with Liv seemed so natural. He never even considered how others might perceive it.

"Hi, Jennie. I'm Rev and this is Liv. We'll be your customers."

Jennie's laugh was genuine. "I know. I know. That whole I'll be your server thing? It's pretentious as hell. But they make us say it. Can I start you off with drinks?"

"I'll have a Dewar's on the rocks," Rev said.

"And I'll have a Yuengling lager," Liv said.

"OK. I'll be back in a few with your drinks. Give you a chance to study the menu."

Jennie turned, squeaking rubber soles on tile, and walked off toward the waitress station at the bar.

The package from the lawyers had one of those pull tab openers. Rev worked a fingernail under it and grabbed the tab between thumb and forefinger.

"This can't be good news."

"Don't be such a baby. Open it."

Rev ripped the tab, stuck a hand inside the package, and pulled out the contents, which included several pages stapled together in the left hand corner and a second, smaller, but well-stuffed envelope.

The stapled pages were the product of the lawyers. Liv moved even closer so she could read along.

Dear Mr. Polk:

Our client, Mr. Chad Tucci of 1414 Ardmore Circle, San Diego, Calif., has instructed us to deliver the enclosed in the event of his death, which, sadly, occurred on or about August 21 of this year under circumstances that police have concluded indicate a homicide.

Be aware that police may be getting in touch with you to ascertain whether the contents of this package have a bearing on Mr. Tucci's murder.

We make no claims as to the authenticity of the enclosed documents, although we do certify that they were given to us by Mr. Tucci with instructions to send them to you, along with the attached letter in the event of his demise.
Sincerely,
Fulton Polanco, Esq.

Rev started to turn the page and Liv laid a hand on his arm.
"Slow down. You read faster than I do."
"It's my mail. Remember? Addressed to me."
Liv pinched him on the thigh. "As I recall you've been sending your male my way lately. Slow down if you want me to continue accepting it."
"Let me know when you're ready."
Jennie picked that moment to return with their drinks. "Have you decided what you want to eat?"
Rev looked at Liv. "I'm OK with a cheeseburger, no onions, medium well, and can you sub onion rings for the fries?"
"I'll have what he's having, but make my burger medium and I'll take the fries," Liv said.
"What kind of cheese?"
"Swiss," Rev said.
"Cheddar."
"Back in a few." Jennie squeaked off with their order.
"Can I open the smaller envelope?" Rev asked.
"Go ahead."
Rev tore it open and they read:

Dear Mr. Polk,
Ever since you left me, I have been consumed by guilt. There is much more to the story of your great granduncle's death that I did not share with you because U.S. Rep. Samuel Jenkins has paid me over the years to keep my silence.
The truth, they say, will set you free. Well, so will lung cancer. Years ago, I was a heavy smoker and it seems I didn't quit soon enough. The doctors give me three months at the best, or worst, depending on how you look at it. So it's time for an accounting.
It's been forty-four years since Jake Addison came to me with evidence that Admiral Alan Jenkins willfully destroyed an official surrender by the Japanese government negotiated in the summer of 1945 by a career diplomat named Claude Forsythe. Jake insisted that the surrender, had it been ratified by the United States, would have ended the war then and there—well in advance of the atom bombing of Hiroshima and Nagasaki.

A copy of the surrender document is enclosed. It is in both English and Japanese and I'm sure you will study it as assiduously as I have over the years. But, I will spare you at least some of the suspense.

To summarize, the Japanese agreed, upon U.S. acceptance of the terms, to cease hostilities with America and all of its allies on the condition that Japan be allowed to retreat to its pre-1930 borders and to maintain an army, navy, and air force of sufficient size to protect itself from neighbors eager to exact revenge. The agreement also sets a schedule of payments for Japan's wartime reparation.

I told Jake that Harry Truman would have insisted on an unconditional surrender, but Jake was certain that Hiroshima and Nagasaki were unnecessary. In his mind, Alan Jenkins was a mass murderer and he wanted me to bring him to justice. I asked Jake why, after all those years, he was going after Jenkins. And he intimated that recent events in his life had sharpened his resolve to set history straight. What he meant by that became clear after I studied all of the documents Jake gave me, but I'm getting ahead of my story.

I was a young journalist developing a reputation for taking on city hall in the spring of 1968 when your great uncle came to me with the story of his diplomatic mission to Japan in the waning days of World War II. He told me that he had piloted a captured Japanese float plane into Tokyo itself and landed it in a moat surrounding the Imperial Palace. His passengers included Forsythe, and Jake's wife, a woman of highborn Japanese descent who apparently held significant clout at the negotiating table.

I was, of course, skeptical of his story, but Jake was full of piss and vinegar and eager to take on his old nemesis, Admiral Jenkins, who at the time was a senior advisor for military affairs with Governor Ronald Reagan's presidential campaign. Reagan, as you may recall, won the California presidential primary that year but decided to defer to the eventual nominee, Richard Milhous Nixon.

I arranged a meeting with Admiral Jenkins at the Grande Colonial Hotel in La Jolla under the pretense that I intended to write an exposé on Governor Reagan's likely foreign policy. I thought it would be interesting to allow Jake to confront Jenkins and to record the admiral's reaction.

Jenkins' son, Samuel, who had recently returned from Vietnam with a chest full of medals, also was present at the meeting.

Jake arrived with the sworn testimony of the pilot who had shot him down over the Pacific all those years ago. Jake accused Admiral Jenkins of ordering the attack on his float plane as he *returned with Forsythe, who had successfully negotiated Japan's surrender.*

"Goddamn it! Hundreds of thousands of Japanese civilians died because you didn't want the war to end before you had a chance to set off your new toy!" Jake told the admiral.

Alan Jenkins blew a gasket. "You were flying a Japanese float plane for Christ's sake. It's only natural that one of our boys would shoot you down. Your mission was a clusterfuck from day one and if you print anything that says I was involved in its failure I'll sue your ass to Sunday!" Sam Jenkins' reaction was blunter. He pulled a pistol from a holster secured in the small of his back, pointed it at me, and said: "You print any of these outrageous lies and I'll kill you, both of you."

There's been a lot written lately about the toll of unrelenting warfare on then-young men like Sam Jenkins. Forty years after the fact, it's pretty clear that the future speaker of the house was suffering from Post Traumatic Stress Disorder. Back then, I just thought he was fucking crazy.

Alan Jenkins ordered his son to put the gun away. Sam took his sweet time doing it. His eyes were wild, his knuckles were white, and my bowels were loose. When Sam had finally re-holstered his pistol, Alan Jenkins bellowed:

"You sandbagged me, you son of a bitch. If that's indicative of your journalistic ethics you're not going to last long in this business. Now get the fuck out of my room! This interview is over!"

Turning my back on Sam Jenkins was one of the hardest things I've ever done. By the time we made the elevator both Jake and I agreed that we needed a drink. So we retired to the bar where your great granduncle gave me the package of material he had collected proving Alan Jenkins' complicity in thwarting the Japanese surrender of July 28, 1945. Appended to those documents was an installment in a journal he had been keeping. It was in a separate envelope addressed to Annie Mundy of Mechanicsburg, Pennsylvania. It was obvious that he had scooped it up by mistake and included it among the package of information he had prepared for me.

Jake gave me the documents with the understanding that I'd launch an investigation and write a series of stories regarding Jenkins' 'treasonous acts' at the end of World War II. Jake's words, not mine.

I made no promises, but Jake left the bar with a spring in his step because of recent joyous events in his personal life. I'll let him tell you of those events in his own words. The last installment of his journal is appended to this letter. Suffice it to say, I followed

Jake out of the bar and onto the street where I witnessed his murder. There is no other word for it than that.

Samuel Jenkins ran Jake Addison over in the crosswalks in a Hertz rent-a-car leased by the Ronald Reagan campaign for president. I got a good look at him, hunched over the wheel with a maniacal expression on his face. He floored it about 50 yards from the crosswalks. Jake never had a chance.

A crowd gathered around the accident site as the rental car roared away, burning rubber as it went. It turned a corner and disappeared.

It was clear that Jake was dead. The ambulance crew that showed up five minutes later confirmed it. I had a camera with me. I snapped picture after picture of the car as it roared away and of the attendants as they loaded Jake's body onto the ambulance.

A hulking giant appeared at my right elbow.

He grabbed me by the arm, ripped the camera from my hands, removed the film canister, and handed the camera back to me.

He bent low and whispered in my ear.

"Captain Jenkins is an American icon. He saved my life. He saved the lives of hundreds of men in his command in Vietnam. You have kids. They will prosper if you forget what you just saw. If you write about it, those kids will become orphans. It's as simple as that."

The giant shoved an envelope into my hands and stalked away. The envelope contained $5,000 in cash. Fifty crisp new one hundred dollar bills. The first in a series of installments that have sustained a far more elaborate lifestyle than most journalists can afford.

Chad Tucci Jr. is a doctor. My daughter, Sarah, married a lawyer. I have five grandchildren. They are all alive today because I lied. Because I forgot. I have no doubt about that. God forgive me.

If you are reading these words, that means I am dead. And that's OK. I have lived a good life. Was the well-being of my children and grandchildren worth my betrayal of Jake Addison on the occasion of his greatest triumph?

I'll let you be the judge.

Sincerely,

Chad Tucci

Chapter 58

6 p.m. Wednesday, September 21, 2011, New Cumberland, PA
"Wow. What a story!" Liv Pearson exclaimed. "We've got to tell Nona."

She dug her cell phone from her purse, which occupied the bench beside her.

Rev leaned close. "Hold off on that for a minute," he said. "There's more to read here."

"Yeah. Well I'll bet Nona would like to read it with us. She could be here in twenty minutes."

"Nona has waited forty-four years to find out what happened to her uncle Jake. I think she can wait a few minutes more. Besides, here come our burgers. I need to eat. My stomach is digesting itself."

Rev looked up and around as a large man settled into the booth behind him. He caught just a glimpse of the man: tall, heavy, a blondish crew cut. Rev could feel the pressure as the fellow settled into the adjacent booth, with his back pressing against Rev's.

Liv kept talking. "A typical man. Preoccupied with your stomach."

Just then Jennie arrived with their burgers. Rev gathered the contents of the package and stacked them on the side of the table out of the way so their server could set down the food.

"Ketchup and mustard are on the table there. Will there be anything else, folks?"

"That should do it," Rev said.

"Actually, may I have a glass of water, please?" Liv asked.

"Sure. Back in a flash."

"So, to summarize, your great granduncle Jake was run over in the crosswalks forty-four years ago by the speaker of the house of representatives," Liv said. "And you have the proof of it right here."

"Yeah, and there's not much I can do about it because of my history with Sam Jenkins," Rev said, glumly. He felt the big man shift in the booth behind him.

"And what's that history?"

"I wrote a story based on interviews with men he served with in Vietnam that suggested Sam Jenkins didn't deserve the Medal of Honor. One of them in particular, a former grunt named Brett Faust, said that Jenkins hid in his foxhole until the shooting was over. Said that just as the relief column arrived Jenkins emerged to take credit for his unit's heroic defense of the hill."

"So?"

"So, two of Jenkins' men, the ones who had testified in support of his earning the medal, raised holy hell. One of them, a fellow named Andy Hawk, came forward with Brett Faust's service record, which indicated that my informant was a mental patient with a grudge against then-Captain Jenkins. Faust, Hawk said, froze in combat, left his men out to dry. Jenkins busted him from sergeant to corporal. Said he couldn't be trusted to lead a squad of chimpanzees."

"So, Jenkins sued the paper," Liv prompted.

Rev nodded.

"You ever get a chance to confront your accuser?"

"Who, Jenkins?"

"No. Andy Hawk."

"Never clapped eyes on the man, although I understand that he's a member of Jenkins' legislative staff. Cozy, huh? By the time I found out who he was, the lawyers had closed ranks and I was ordered not to have anything to do with Jenkins or any of his staff. They seized all of my notes. Hell, they even locked down my computer hard drive. They imaged it and gave me a copy."

"You don't think you'll be able to sell Grayson Collingsworth on a story about Jenkins' complicity in a murder? There's no statute of limitation on murder, you know."

"True, but this happened forty-four years ago, and the only witness I know of is dead. Even if we can place Jenkins at the wheel of the car that ran over Jake, it would be a stretch to prove intent and motive. There might be enough to support a charge of manslaughter, but ..."

"The statute of limitation ran out a long time ago on manslaughter," Liv finished the sentence for him.

"Yeah. If we go public with the allegations, it sure would put a crimp in his political future. They're talking about his being among the front runners for a republican nomination next fall," Rev said.

They were interrupted as Jennie delivered Liv's glass of water before attending to the booth behind them.

Rev heard her say: "Hi, I'm Jennie. I'll be your server." And he heard her customer's deep-voiced response: "Actually, I've changed my mind. I just got a text message I have to deal with."

Rev could feel the movement as the man arose from the booth behind them.

The booths were high backed and Rev had to rise up to look over his shoulder to watch the man exit. He caught a glimpse of the man's backside. It was a huge backside and Rev flashed back to Emily Griswold's description of the man who had broken into his house.

Rev stood and shouted: "Excuse me, sir. I'd like a word with you."

But the big man didn't turn. He stalked out of the restaurant, and by the time Rev made the parking lot there was no sign of him.

Rev returned to his booth to find Liv deeply engrossed in her cheeseburger and in the package of papers that had arrived from the lawyers.

"What was that all about?" she asked as Rev plopped down beside her.

"I had a break-in about a week ago. That fellow fit the description of the man my neighbor saw on my front porch."

"A break-in? Why didn't you tell me? I'm a police officer, remember?"

"It was right before we left for Shanksville and I just forgot to mention it. Besides, New Cumberland is out of your jurisdiction. Borough police are handling the case."

"Mishandling it, probably," Liv said.

She took another big bite of cheeseburger. "Boy, this is good."

"Best cheeseburger in town," Rev opined.

"I'm not talking about the food, although it is good. I'm talking about your great granduncle's journal. His story is a real tear jerker."

"What do you mean?"

"Read along with me and you'll see."

Rev popped an onion ring in his mouth, took a bite of cheeseburger. He crowded close to Liv, who turned the page back to the first entry in Jake's journal.

Chapter 59

Jake's Journal

Emika is alive!

I heard the phone ring from the back yard as I was returning to the house after having deposited the trash in the big receptacle in the alley. I usually don't run to ringing phones. I hate phones. I prefer talking face to face. But the tone of this ring seemed shriller. There was an urgency to it that made me break into a trot and I haven't trotted for twenty years. Too hard on old knees.

I've talked to my new friend Chad Tucci from time to time about the art of writing and he tells me that a good journalist puts the good stuff in the first paragraph, which he calls the lead.

Well the lead of this story bears repeating:

Emika is alive!

It was her voice on the other end of the line, which stretched thousands of miles from her heart in Japan to mine in San Diego. The reception was crackly. She rose above the fuzz like the lead soprano in a choral solo.

"My God, Emika. Is it really you?"

"Yes, husband. It is I."

I should have felt angry that she hadn't contacted me in the twenty-two years since I'd last seen her. I should have railed at her for abandoning me to loneliness and regret.

But all I felt was ... relief.

"So, I didn't kill you?"

She must have wondered at the wonder in my voice.

"Kill me?" she asked.

"Yes. There in the Imperial Garden. Your kimono was aflame; so was your hair. You were screaming because you were being burned alive. So I shot you. You fell back into the fire and you were gone."

"So that's why you didn't make any attempt to find me," Emika said. "You thought I was dead and I thought you were dead.

Admiral Jenkins' staff sent me your death notice. It said that you'd been shot down and killed. Whoever you killed there in the emperor's garden, you did them a favor. Being burned alive is no way to die. I know because I'm being consumed by the atomic fires."

"Atomic fires?"

"Once I had recovered from my injuries, it was only reasonable that I travel to where nurses were needed the most."

"And where was that?" I asked, dreading the answer.

"Hiroshima. And now, like many of those who responded to that disaster ... I am dying ... of cancer. I don't have long to live, but I would like to see you one more time. Don't weep, husband."

But I was weeping and choking on the rage building from deep within. I had held the salvation of hundreds of thousands of people like Emika in my hands and Alan Jenkins had pissed on it because he wanted to punish the Japanese people for Pearl Harbor and Guadalcanal and the Aleutians and Iwo Jima and a thousand other offenses real and imagined. And he had pissed on me, consigning me to a lifetime without Emika because he couldn't abide one of his men being married to the enemy. The common people caught up in the insane strategies of the warmongers on both sides had not been part in the planning and execution of those battles. They were innocent bystanders. And they deserved better from the likes of Alan Jenkins, men on both sides, who exploited others to fulfill their own sick need to wield the most absolute power of them all: the power of life and death.

Emika must have felt my sorrow and rage. It was a palpable thing and it slithered like a serpent across the phone lines connecting us.

"Be still, husband. I am not guiltless. Grieve me if you must. But condemn me also for not reaching out to you sooner. The ravages of age, disease, and the injuries I received that night in the Imperial Garden disfigure me. I was fearful that you would be sickened by the sight of me and so I didn't seek you out to tell you news that would lighten your heart."

"What news could do that?" I asked her.

"We have a son."

251

Chapter 60

10:30 p.m. Wednesday, September 21, 2011, New Cumberland, PA

"Jake had a son? Holy cow! I think I may know what happened to him."

Liv cleared her throat. "I'm all for pillow talk but could you please tend to the business at hand?"

The business at hand was pleasure. And Rev didn't need much persuading to clam up.

They were naked and entwined in the center of his bed. Rev refocused. Liv groaned and thrust down against him from above. And Rev wondered anew at the differences among women.

Where Sophie had been long and languid in her lovemaking, content to let Rev explore what worked for her and what didn't, Liv was short, compact, and far more direct. She came with a complete set of operating instructions.

Do this, don't do that, can't you read the signs?

Lovemaking with Liv was a competitive sport, with a whole different set of rules. It was a test of wills to see who could do what to whom, compelling the other to be the first to surrender to orgasm's imperative.

This time Rev won. And then he lost. The little ball of fury writhing above him collapsed in a sweaty heap on his chest as he exploded from below.

He spit her hair from his mouth, pulled strands of it off his sweaty neck.

"So, I think I know what happened to Jake's son," Rev said.

"What's that?" she asked.

"Well, I met this guy in California ..."

"No I mean what's that sound?" Liv asked.

"What sound?"

"Shh! There it goes again."

Rev heard it, too. The sound of a heavy man trying to be quiet on the stairs. But the fifth stair up creaked just like always.

Rev shoved Liv to the floor on the side of the bed farthest from the open bedroom door. "Stay down!"

He yanked open the drawer of his night stand. He groped about among the debris littering the bottom of the drawer until his hand encountered the butt of his Glock. He rolled onto the floor beside Liv just as a large shadow burst into the room.

"Nobody move and nobody gets hurt! Give me that package from the lawyers and I'm out of here."

Back lit by the night light Rev kept in a hall socket to illuminate the path to the bathroom, the intruder lurked like a gargoyle. Rev was so adrenalin-charged that he recorded impressions more than certainties: huge, a crew cut, square jaw, porcine nose, an enormous handgun, probably a .357 Magnum, which he panned back and forth across the room, looking for a target. But Rev and Liv were both out of sight behind the bed.

"I'm afraid I can't do that," Rev shouted. "I have a gun and this is going to end badly for you if you don't drop your weapon and back out of the room."

The intruder made a bad decision. He pointed his gun in the direction of Rev's voice. Rev aimed at the center of his body mass and pulled the trigger. The noise bounced off the bedroom walls like the sound of fireworks in the canyons of city streets.

The big man staggered back against the door frame, regained his balance, and fled. They could hear him stumble down the stairs. The front door banged open, and by the time Rev made the front porch there was no sign of him, leaving Rev to consider whether the encounter had been real or a dream.

Liv joined him in the foyer, still naked.

"Better put some clothes on. I have a nosy neighbor. Dollars for doughnuts, she's already called the police," Rev said.

Emily Griswold didn't disappoint.

When Rev dialed 9-1-1, the dispatcher told him that the police were on their way.

They had just enough time to get dressed before the officers arrived.

Chapter 61

2:30 a.m. Thursday, September 22, 2011, Alexandria, VA
A jangling phone awakened Samuel Jenkins from a Vicodin-induced sleep. His shoulder hurt like hell.

"This had better be fucking important," he snarled into the phone.

"Oh it is, Mr. Speaker. It is. In fact, it just might be the most important telephone call of your life."

"Who is this?"

"I think you know."

"No, I don't. How did you get my private number?"

"You gave it to my father, the late George Kambic. And he gave it to me. Before you killed him, of course."

Jenkins' mind was fuzzy with sleep and Vicodin. His mental circuits chugged like an out-of-balance washing machine. *Kachunk. Kachunk. Kachunk.*

"Billy? What's this about your father being dead?" God his shoulder hurt. He sat up, resting his back on the headboard.

"Oh come on, Mr. Speaker. You know Dad is dead. You killed him. Or one of your minions did, which amounts to the same thing. The suicide note was a nice touch. But it was obviously a fake."

Samuel Jenkins forced his mind into high gear. Damn the Vicodin. George Kambic's suicide hadn't broken in the papers. He had to play dumb. "When I talked to your father two days ago, he was fine. Nervous, but fine. Certainly not suicidal. I told him I had his back. He assured me he had mine."

Bill Kambic's laugh was brittle. "If that's the way you want to play it, Mr. Speaker, go right ahead. But the little honey trap you set for me didn't work."

"I don't know what you're talking about."

"That's right, Sam. Stick to the party line. That's what got you this far. But I'm not going to take a fall for you. I need two million dollars, no make that three, wired to a Cayman Island account. I'll be back in touch with you when I've got things set up."

"Wait a minute ..."

Jenkins realized he was talking to a dial tone. He sat up, swung his feet to the floor, and arose gingerly to accommodate his sore shoulder. He needed time to think, but time was at a premium right now. He glanced at the digital clock on his night stand. Three o'clock in the morning. In less than 12 hours, the president would be meeting with the heroes of 9/11 Redux, which was what the national tabloid press was calling the debacle at Shanksville-Stony Creek High School. In less than 12 hours, the president would be dead.

He needed to call Andy Hawk. Andy would know what to do. But first, he needed to pee. He was 66 and his prostate demanded attention. The speaker of the house stumbled off to his bathroom to answer nature's call. On the cusp of his greatest triumph he felt ineffectual and small.

"Goddamn Billy Kambic!" He flushed the toilet and returned to his nightstand, where his cell phone abided among a clutter of wadded up Kleenex, pocket change, and a Dixie cup half full of water.

Andy's number was atop the scroll in his recent calls list. He punched send.

His phone call was immediately routed to Andy's voice mail.

Hawk's rich baritone intoned:

"I can't take your call right now. Leave a message and I'll get right back to you."

After the beep, Sam screamed: "Goddamn it, Andy, pick up. The shit's hit the fan and I need you. Now!"

Clutching his phone in his fist, the speaker of the house stumbled down the stairs to his kitchen to put on some coffee, which he intended to lace with a stiff shot of whiskey. His wife was out of town, visiting their daughter and their new grandson in Kentucky.

He had the whole house to himself. And for the first time in years, Sam Jenkins felt lonely.

Lonely ... and afraid.

Chapter 62

10 a.m. Friday, September 23, 2011, Washington, DC
The armored Lincoln Town Car sneered at Washington, D.C. potholes. Liv Pearson and Rev Polk sat knee to knee in the back seat. They were holding hands like teenagers on their way to the prom. The simile had some legs because they were dressed in their finest. Liv had some legs, too. She had eschewed her state police dress uniform for a black sheath of a dress, short at both ends. The dress accomplished its purpose. She wasn't naked but the stares were, Rev's included.

He could have worn his army dress blues, but opted instead for a simple black tuxedo. Liv had insisted that the tux was the way to go. She'd helped him pick it out and persuaded him to buy rather than rent.

"A man of your station should own his own tuxedo."

"Of my station? I'm unemployed, for Christ's sake."

"By your own choice. Grayson Collingsworth is begging you to come back."

"Gray is an asshole."

"That's funny, he says the same thing about you."

"Haven't we had this conversation before?"

Rev glanced at Liv, alert, attentive, sitting on the edge of the seat, her eyes darting back and forth, capturing the moment and writing it to her own personal hard drive. They occupied the second car in an entourage of three Secret Service-operated limos, which were making their way to the White House. Brigadier General Randolph Simpson and Chief Warrant Officer Johnston Bradley occupied the lead vehicle. Both men had been promoted as a reward for their service at Shanksville.

A Purple Heart and Silver Star gleamed among the medals on Johnston Bradley's chest. The right leg of his uniform pants was slit to mid-thigh to accommodate the heavy plaster that encased his right leg.

Emily Peterson and Jeremy Smith, the principal and her student, rode in the last car in the convoy. Rev imagined they were feeling the same way he was: proud, nervous, and overawed.

The big limo pulled into a driveway off Pennsylvania Avenue. The driver lowered his window and showed his ID to the Marine guard.

The passenger windows whirred down, too, on silent motors. The Marine stuck his head in the car. Looked at Liv. Looked at Rev. The Marine stepped back, saluted the driver. "Go ahead, Jack. They're expecting you."

They pulled along the tree-shaded drive and came to a stop in front of the south portico. An entourage of Secret Service agents carrying scanning wands met them. They had been scanned before, when they were picked up at the hotel, but Rev didn't wonder at the redundancy. When the president's life was at stake it paid to be careful, particularly in the current political climate with the extreme right and extreme left trying to out-crazy each other.

The electronics beeped as Rev was wanded. The magnetic metal clip of his iPhone case must have set it off. The agent, a tall, chiseled young man with razor cut hair, asked him to unclip the phone for inspection.

He returned it to Rev, noting, "You might want to put that on vibrate for the ceremony in the Rose Garden."

To his right and left, the other guests were undergoing similar inspections. The wand beeped furiously when it was passed over Johnston Bradley. He explained that surgeons had implanted a titanium rod in his right thigh to repair the damage done by the assassin's bullet.

As Rev clipped his iPhone to his belt he felt it vibrate, but he ignored it to concentrate on the instructions of the young public affairs officer, a woman in her late 20s who was glowing with the responsibility of being the president's liaison for this official visit of the heroes of 9/11 Redux. She introduced herself as Monica Nissly, second personal assistant to the president.

She had to yell above the clatter of Marine One as it made its approach to its South Lawn landing pad.

"The president is returning from Camp David," she explained. "He will meet us in the Rose Garden in a few minutes. Follow me, please."

She set off toward the West Wing where the Rose Garden was tucked in behind the Oval Office. It was a glorious fall day, cool and humidity free. A slight breeze stirred on the skin like a butterfly kiss.

A Marine unfolded a wheelchair for Johnston Bradley, who sat in it gratefully, propping his plastered leg on the expandable foot rest.

Already assembled in the Rose Garden were several members of the White House press corps and the official presidential photographer. The roar of the helicopter diminished and died. Rev adjusted the collar of his shirt with the index finger of his left hand. Liv held his right hand and gawked at their surroundings.

Monica Nissly led them to the front row of five rows of folding chairs set up in the Rose Garden. They sat in their assigned seats. Rev pulled the creases of his tuxedo tight and Liv straightened the hem of her dress and crossed her ankles primly like a sorority initiate.

A small Marine ensemble played "Hail to the Chief" as the president strode from the back of the garden. Rev's phone buzzed insistently.

As the assemblage rose to greet the president, Rev stole a chance to unholster his iPhone. He punched the button to awaken it and squinted at the display.

He gasped and looked toward the presidential podium, where Johnston Bradley's wheelchair was positioned. Brad tugged at his plastered right leg.

As the last strains of "Hail to the Chief" died, Rev shouted.

"Mr. President! Gun! Gun! Gun!"

Chapter 63

11 a.m. Friday, September 23, 2011, Alexandria, VA

Sam Jenkins felt much better. He received Andy Hawk in the library on the first floor of his row home. The big man was walking stiffly and winced when he sat down.

"What's the matter, Andy?"

"A bulletproof vest doesn't stop the bruising. The round caught me square in the gut. I feel like I've been kicked by a mule."

"So the documents Chad Tucci sent Rev Polk are still in the wind?"

Hawk sighed. "I'm sorry, boss. I blew it. I thought for sure those two would be asleep. That I could get the drop on them, steal the documents, and be gone. How could I know that they'd be wide awake and copulating like a couple of teenagers?"

"You were prepared to kill them?"

"If I had to ... yes, I was going to kill them."

Jenkins shook his head. "What have I done to deserve that type of loyalty?"

"I don't care what Rev Polk's story said about your medal of honor. We hid in that foxhole, sure. But before we made the foxhole, you saved my life. That bullet you took was meant for me. You protected me with your own body. And you didn't dig in until the others were safe ... most of them anyway."

"And those that didn't make it? Shouldn't I have done more to protect them?"

Hawk shrugged. "Fortunes of war. And as far as Jake Addison is concerned ... once you're president you can ride out the storm. No living witness can put you at the scene of his death. It was forty-four years ago for Christ sake. Rev had it right."

"What do you mean by that?"

"I overheard them talking, in the restaurant, Rev and the police officer he's fucking. He knows that after all these years he can't prove that you intended to kill Jake Addison. All that's left is manslaughter."

"And the statute of limitations has run out on manslaughter," Jenkins said.

"That's right, boss. But if Rev were to come forward with this information, it would be devastating to your presidential campaign," Hawk continued.

"But I don't have to run for president. The office will be mine by succession and we can start spinning the story."

"Yeah. Jake Addison was a drunk. He was impaired when he stepped into that crosswalk. You were just home from Vietnam, dealing with the same sort of shit the young guys coming back from Iraq and Afghanistan are dealing with right now. The public will be sympathetic."

"Hell. I might even get elected," Jenkins said.

"Particularly with the republicans in charge of the House," Hawk said.

Jenkins grinned. "Now, what about the Billy Kambic situation?"

"Billy claims to have secured copies of militia documents implicating you in the assassination of the vice president. He says that he got Rev Polk's cell phone number from his former editor and that he'll call him and arrange a drop if we don't cough up the $3 million."

"Goddamn! Polk again. That man is following me so close his nose is up my ass," Jenkins said.

"Boss, it's a calculated risk, but I've transferred the money to Billy's offshore account. A banker sympathetic to our cause will insist that he show up in person to activate the account, and when he does, we'll settle accounts with Billy boy."

"How did we acquire this banker's support?"

"A million dollars buys a lot of cooperation."

"So we have a net loss of one mil. Think the campaign fund can handle that?"

"I prefer to think of it as a net gain. That's two million we didn't give to Billy boy. Besides, you won't be running for election ... at least for a couple of years," Hawk said.

"So, what's next?" Jenkins asked.

"What's next is that we wait for events at the White House this morning to play out. I look forward to their resolution, Mr. President."

"Let's not be premature, Andy."

"I just wish your father had lived to see this," Hawk said.

"My father was a son of a bitch. Said I was weak because I couldn't exorcize the demons I brought home from Vietnam."

"That's why I wish he was here. So we could rub his nose in it. His son rising to the highest office in the land." Hawk stood and looked out the window. "Still think I was being premature, Mr. President?"

Jenkins joined him at the window.

Three black Lincoln Navigators screeched to the curb. Blue lights strobed, casting daggers of light into the library.

The doors of the Navigators burst open. Agents poured out. Six, seven, eight of them, each looking pretty much like the other: young, fit, neatly barbered, and full of self importance.

They banged on Jenkins' front door.

"Well, don't just stand there, Andy. I imagine the Secret Service will want to set up a perimeter until the Chief Justice can make his way here ... to swear me in."

Hawk went to open the door.

Jenkins sat down behind his desk, situated a pile of papers in front of himself, grabbed a pen from its holder, and positioned reading glasses on the end of his nose. He heard a struggle in the hall.

The agents burst into the room.

Their guns were drawn.

This wasn't part of the scenario he had imagined.

"There has been an incident at the White House," the lead agent said. He pointed his gun squarely at the center of Jenkins' chest. "Please stand, Mr. Jenkins."

Jenkins rose to his feet. "What's this about?"

"Sam Jenkins. You are under arrest for the attempted murder of the president of the United States. Billy Kambic survived an assassination attempt in the Caymans. He's pissed and singing like a bird. Raise your hands, you son of a bitch."

Jenkins ignored the order. He yanked open the top drawer of his desk and grabbed the butt of the revolver he kept hidden there.

By that time there were five agents in the room.

Sam Jenkins, the hero of Hill 875, died in a fusillade of gunfire in his own library while his foxhole buddy, Andy Hawk, wept in the foyer.

Chapter 64

11 a.m. Friday, September 30, 2011, somewhere over California
"So, what, precisely, did Billy Kambic say in his text message?" Nona asked.

Rev was sandwiched between Liv and Nona in the middle seat of a Boeing 747 as it made its descent to San Diego.

Rev swallowed to clear his ears before answering. "That's classified."

Liv leaned across the armrest, invading his personal space from her seat next door. "Be nice to your grandmother."

"I am being nice. I'm picking up her airfare, aren't I? Yours, too, for that matter, which is pretty darn considerate given my current employment status."

"Don't give me that sad song. Grayson Collingsworth is begging you to come back. Publishers are lining up for the definitive book on the 9/11 Redux Assassination Conspiracy," Nona said.

"So remind me again why we're going to San Diego?" Liv asked. "Not that I'm ungrateful."

"Because it's sunny and warm?"

Liv stuck out her lower lip, pretending to pout. "No. I mean the real reason."

"It's a surprise."

"For whom?" Nona asked.

"For both of you."

"He's not going to tell us," Liv said.

Nona nodded. "He's stubborn that way. Always has been, ever since he was a little boy."

Rev held up his hand. "Easy, Nona. There will be no grand showing of my baby pictures."

"Too late," Nona said.

"At least he could tell us what Billy Kambic said in his text message," Liv said.

Rev sighed. "You're not going to give up, are you?"

Both women shook their heads.

Rev unclipped his iPhone from his belt. He opened up his text message queue, scrolled down, and handed Nona his phone.

Liv leaned across his lap to read the message at the same time Nona did.

"JB is Jenkins' man. Gun in cast. Will kill prexy so Jenkins can take his place — B. Kambic."

"And on the strength of that, you screamed 'Gun! Gun! Gun!'?" Liv said. "In the presence of the president of the United States? Jesus Christ, Rev, you're lucky the Secret Service didn't shoot you on the spot, particularly when you lunged at Johnston Bradley."

Nona laughed. "That was some sort of performance on the TV news, you tackling a guy in a wheelchair in the Rose Garden."

"Yeah. Way to beat up the cripple," Liv said.

Both women were laughing now. People across the aisle turned to look at them.

"Laugh if you want, but Johnston Bradley was one tough cripple. He punched me in the jaw and I bruised my ribs on the armrest of his wheelchair. And he did have a gun."

"Good thing the Secret Service didn't shoot the both of you," Nona said.

"Yes, that was a good thing," Rev agreed.

"So, how does it feel to be a hero?" Liv asked.

"That's the same stupid question the talking head from ABC asked me."

Liv giggled. "They bleeped your answer. But what you said was pretty obvious."

"Bite me," Rev said.

"I thought it was 'fuck you,'" Liv said.

"That's the way I read it, too," Nona said.

"Like I said, bite me," Rev said.

"Be nice to your girlfriend," Nona said.

"She's not my girlfriend."

"Then what am I?"

"I'll get back to you on that."

"Cop out," Liv said.

"You've got that backward. I'm out ... with a cop."

The pilot rescued him from further inquisition, keying his microphone to announce that the time had come to return seat backs to the upright position and to stow tray tables.

The timbre of the engines dropped as the pilot throttled back and the plane made a sweeping bank to the left. Rev grabbed Liv by the hand. He didn't like landings, particularly at San Diego, where some idiot had constructed a parking garage at the end of the runway.

Despite Rev's certainty that things would end badly, the pilot set the big jet down like he was hauling a cargo of eggs. Rev was grateful to have avoided a crack up.

He collected their carry-ons from the overhead compartment and placed them on his empty seat. He took up his bag and Nona's and started down the aisle toward the exit.

"Sorry, Liv. Out of hands. You'll have to tote your own bag."

Rev had stuffed all of the clothes he needed into his carry-on. He was wearing the only sports jacket he owned. Three pairs of pants and two nice shirts were crammed into the carry-on, along with a swim suit, flip flops, four changes of underwear, four t-shirts, a couple of pairs of walking shorts, and a pair of tennis shoes.

The women had insisted that they needed more room. They went halvsies on one large suitcase and split the extra baggage fee.

Fortune smiled upon them. Their bag was the third one off the carousel, and a Dodge Charger, midnight black with a black leather interior, waited for them in slip A-45, just like the Avis agent said it would. Rev had insisted on a full-size car because he couldn't get his knees under the steering wheel of a compact or midsize.

He stowed their luggage in the trunk while Liv and Nona sorted out who would ride where. They settled on Nona in the front and Liv behind.

Rev climbed behind the wheel. "Just what I need, a state police officer for a back seat driver."

Liv cinched her shoulder belt. "I'm a very good back seat driver, so you'd better mind your driving. I'm out of my jurisdiction, but I can still make a citizen's arrest."

Rev activated the Garman GPS unit he'd brought from home and put it on the console between the front seats. He'd already programmed the address.

Nona picked up the GPS and studied it. "Acquiring satellite signal. What does that mean?"

"The unit is a receiver. It calculates data from satellites overhead to determine our position and plot a way to a destination of our choice," Liv explained, leaning forward between the seats to study the GPS.

"4606 Altadena Avenue. What's at that address?" Liv asked.

"Let's go find out," Rev said.

He started the car, engaged the transmission, and pulled out of the parking space.

They drove for about 15 minutes. Rev hushed the women so he could hear the instructions from the GPS, which was programmed to speak in a woman's voice.

"Destination is ahead on the left," the GPS intoned.

Rev pulled the car over to the curb. He turned off the car and alit, pocketing the car keys. After he got out, he opened the doors for the women and said, "Follow me." Rev led them to the front door, rang the bell, and whistled tunelessly, ignoring the glares of the women.

The front door swung open.

An Asian man in his mid-sixties stood just inside the threshold. He squinted at them through thick bifocals.

"Oh. Hello, Mr. Polk," he said. "It's nice to see you again."

Rev turned toward Nona.

"Well, don't just stand there, Annie," he said, startling her with the use of her Christian name. "Say hello to Daniel Shidehara, Jake Addison's only son and your long lost first cousin."

Chapter 65

1 p.m. Friday, September 30, 2011, San Diego, CA
"My mother was dishonored by the failure of the peace treaty she helped negotiate," Daniel Shidehara said.

His voice was soft, with just a whisper of the Asian singsong lilt stereotyped by Hollywood.

Nona, Rev, and Liv leaned close from the edges of their comfortable armchairs arranged in a conversation semicircle in Shidehara's living room. The Oriental rug at their feet looked authentic, and somewhere off in the distance the central air-conditioning provided an electric baseline for the gentle sound of chimes and soft strings oozing from speakers hidden on shelves overhead.

The music reminded Rev of the sort of thing massage therapists played to take your mind off the fact that only a thin sheet separated your nakedness from inspection by a complete stranger.

Rev cocked an ear toward the speaker and Daniel smiled. "You like the music? It's called *Oriental Spring*. It clears the mind."

Rev thought the music sounded like Yani on Prozac, but he smiled and nodded. "You were saying ... about your mother?"

"Oh, yes. It brought her great dishonor when the Americans did not accept the peace treaty she and Claude Forsythe had negotiated with emperor Hitherto. Even though she had been burned terribly on the neck and right shoulder in the firebombing, she insisted on rushing to Hiroshima in the week following the dropping of the atomic bomb ... to use her nurse's training ... to help the people suffering there."

Daniel's eyes misted over and Nona, who was sitting in the chair closest to his, leaned forward and touched his arm. "That was very brave of her. She must have been pregnant with you at the time."

Daniel nodded. "I was born seven months later. And by the grace of God was not afflicted by the cancers that decimated so many people who were there at Hiroshima when the bomb dropped and immediately after. I have thought about it often and concluded that mother protected me ... with her own body. That she absorbed all of the radiation and bled it away before it could harm me. It certainly harmed her, although not at once—that's the insidious thing about it."

Daniel stood, tugged a handkerchief from his back pocket, took off his glasses, and polished the lenses. He placed the glasses back on his nose; he wiped his brow, shoved the handkerchief back in his pocket, and sat down with a plop, rather harder than he had anticipated given the surprised look on his face.

"Immediately after the war, my mother petitioned the U.S. authorities for information about her husband. She was told that he had been killed in action in July of 1945, shot down while flying a reconnaissance mission over the Pacific. Her request was answered under the endorsement of Vice Admiral Alan Jenkins, deputy commander of the U.S. occupation force."

Rev bolted forward in his chair: "Goddamn Alan Jenkins ... a true bastard to the end. How did your mother figure out that Jake was still alive?"

"Mother liked to read American newspapers. In December of 1967, when she was wracked with the final stages of the blood cancer that would take her life, she encountered a story AP picked up from the *San Diego Union-Tribune*. It was written by Chad Tucci to commemorate the anniversary of the attack on Pearl Harbor and included quotes attributed to Aviation Chief Machinist Mate Jacob Addison, retired."

Rev smacked his right fist into the palm of his left hand. "Son of a bitch! Another thing Tucci lied about ... or at least glossed over." He looked at Shidehara. "Sorry. I shouldn't have interrupted."

Shidehara shrugged and squinted. "Mother agonized over whether she should try to get in touch with Jake because he hadn't looked for her over all those years. She didn't know that he thought that she was dead. Finally, she decided to call him ... just to tell him that he had a son. Jake was on a plane to Tokyo within 10 days. I met him at the airport. Took him to see Mom."

Nona asked a question around her tears. "What were your first impressions ... of your father?"

Shidehara shifted uncomfortably in his chair. "I hated him because, like my mother, I thought that he had abandoned us. I do remember being impressed with how tall he was; how substantial. And even though I tried not to, I could see myself in him. It was like staring at my own reflection in one of those fun house mirrors."

Nona stood and walked closer to her first cousin. She studied his face and said: "Welcome to the family. I am sure that Jake was proud of his son."

Shidehara arose and they embraced, awkwardly at the onset and then genuinely.

They broke the embrace after about 30 seconds and returned to their chairs.

"Jake was a whirling dervish," Shidehara said. "He arrived with all of the documents he needed to substantiate his marriage to my mother, and within a month had cleared up issues of citizenship and paternity. He was devastated by my mother's disease, blamed himself for failing to ensure that Japan's surrender had ended up in the right hands."

Rev interjected: "Actually, there is some doubt that the Truman administration would have accepted the terms of the surrender Claude Forsythe negotiated with the emperor. It allowed Japan to keep certain remnants of its military ... to protect itself from neighbors eager to exact revenge ... a far cry from the surrender aboard the USS *Missouri* three months later."

"That sort of nuance was lost on Jake," Shidehara replied. "He blamed Admiral Jenkins. When he learned that Jenkins had conjured Jake's killed-in-action notice, well, he went ballistic. My mother didn't tell him that until several weeks after he had brought us home ... to this house. A week or so later he read Chad Tucci's story about how Alan Jenkins was convening a council of war at the Grande Colonial Hotel to strategize on how Ronald Reagan could steal the nomination from Richard Nixon.

"He called Tucci, who agreed to set up a meeting with Jenkins. Mother begged him not to go, but he told her that he owed it to her and to all of the innocent people who had died at Hiroshima and Nagasaki to set the record straight. To reveal to the world that Vice Admiral Alan Jenkins had deliberately destroyed a peace accord that would have made dropping the atomic bombs unnecessary."

"How could he have possibly proved that?" Nona asked.

"Mom kept a copy of the surrender. She brought it with her from Japan and gave it to Jake as a souvenir of what might have been," Shidehara said.

Rev cracked his knuckles and leaned forward. "So what happened after Jake was killed?"

"Mother died a week later. I was overwhelmed with grief and by the lawyers. Jake had changed his will, made me and Mother his only heirs. I was twenty-two years old. I didn't speak English, at least not very well. Luckily, I found a lawyer who could speak Japanese. Otherwise, I would have lost this house, which, apart from a twenty-five thousand dollar military life insurance policy, was all Jake left us."

"How did you meet Andy Hawk?" Rev asked.

Shidehara sighed. "Through Chad Tucci. He had an attack of conscience about ten years after Jake's death. By that time I had learned the language, found a job ... teaching Asian studies at San Diego State. He explained what had happened to Jake. Sam Jenkins by that time was a California state representative. Andy Hawk was his aide. Mr. Hawk is an imposing man. He made it clear that if I kept quiet no harm would come to me ... or my wife and children. He offered me $25,000 in hush money, provided I sign a document releasing Jenkins of any responsibility in Jake's death."

Shidehara hung his head. "And to my discredit I took it."

Rev snapped his fingers. "And the late PussPuss?"

"A reminder."

"That silence is golden." Rev said. "Now there is no need for silence. Sam Jenkins is dead. And Andy Hawk is in prison."

"And we are a family once again," Nona said.

Epilogue

1 a.m., Saturday, September 30, 2011, San Diego, California

The hotel's air-conditioning kept a hot San Diego twilight at bay as Liv slumbered next to him, curled in an open parenthesis to his left in the big, king-sized bed. He rolled onto his side and inched closer, trying not to awaken her. She sensed the movement and backed up, completing the spoon.

"Go back to sleep, tiger," Rev said. "I've had enough for one night."

Liv didn't respond, other than with a slight snore.

Rev set aside the events of the day and settled into a deep slumber.

He ran along a narrow street under a brilliant sun with the smell of carrion all about him. This wasn't Iraq. It was far too humid. The rifle he carried at port arms had a bolt action; an antique nothing like the M-16. The clip couldn't have contained more than four or five rounds.

The awful stench of burning flesh emanated from a pile of smoking debris. Mingled with the fuel oil used as an accelerant, the stench overwhelmed him. He realized that the debris pile consisted of bodies, human bodies, empty eye sockets and limbs entangled in an obscene group hug. Buzzards circled overhead crying in outrage over the waste of food.

Someone ran at him at a crossroads. Bullets spattered a wall behind him. Shit! Rev dove right, rolled on his right shoulder, and chambered around as he rose to one knee. A figure careened toward him. He pulled the trigger, worked the bolt, and fired again. His attacker collapsed before him and Rev stared into the eyes of a dead teenager, a mere boy with a gun who had been trying to kill him. But why?

Veracruz. It was 1914 and he was in Veracruz.

That epiphany startled him to consciousness. He must have cried out because Liv stirred beside him, mumbled something, and curled into an even tighter ball.

Rev rolled onto his back. He shivered as the faint breeze from the air-conditioning evaporated the sheen of sweat on his naked chest and arms. He pulled the sheet to his chin, kicked around to make room for his feet, and forced himself to take deep breaths. Slow in. Slow out. Slow in ... sleep recaptured him.

He stood before a hospital bed set up in the master bedroom of an ordinary house. The walls were lavender. A family portrait hung on the back wall directly above the bed. Rev realized that the picture had been taken right here in this room. He stepped closer to examine it.

A woman was propped up in the bed. Her features were Asian. Her face was gaunt, her cheeks hollow, her hair a thin grayish halo arranged on the pillow about her head. Emika? It had to be Emika. A young Daniel Shidehara, no more than 20 or so, knelt on one knee next to his mother.

Rev's eyes traveled to the man kneeling on the other side of the bed. Good God that couldn't be! He was staring at himself, his features PhotoShopped over Jake's. The camera captured joy radiating from his face. He had never felt that joyful. Not in this life. Emika was dying. Why should he feel happy about that?

Jake whispered in his ear: "Because it proves that we have second chances. We've had them in Veracruz and Iraq. And now we have them right here and right now. Emika slumbers next to you. Nothing can be better than that."

Rev reached out for Liv in his sleep. His fingers crawled over acres of cheap hotel room linen until they encountered a silky thigh.

He rose up on one elbow, dragged himself closer to the warmth. He wrapped his arms about her as if he were drowning at sea, grasping for a lifeline. He drew her near and whispered in her ear: "Is it really you?"

Rev wondered about that as he fell into a deep sleep, at peace ... at last.

Afterword

Now that you've read my fictional account of the World War II exploits of Chief Jacob Addison, I'd like to introduce you to the real Jake, my granduncle, Jacob Wissler Utley (1894-1962). *Rising Sun Descending* is a fictionalized account of his wartime experiences, underpinned by my recollections of 50-year-old conversations with my maternal grandfather, the late Robert Wade Utley, for whom I am named.

Robert Utley graduated from Elon College in 1925 with a bachelor of philosophy degree, cum laude. He went to work in public education, which he served faithfully for more than 40 years, first as principal of Nathanael Greene School and later as assistant superintendent for buildings and grounds for the Guilford County School System, headquartered in Greensboro, N.C.

Robert Utley served in the U.S. Navy during World War I. He was apprenticed to the tailor on the navy base at Norfolk, and could recall years later the precise number of spools of number-two thread he sewed into the brim of a sailor's white hat to give it the requisite jaunty air.

He was swept up in the great influenza epidemic of 1918 and nearly died in the service of his country. When he spoke of his own naval service, the conversation, inevitably, turned to his older brother, Jake, a chief petty officer, who served aboard the USS *Enterprise*, the most decorated ship of World War II.

The real Jake was something of a black sheep of the family. He joined the navy as a teenager in 1910 and followed his naval career around the world to San Diego, where he disappeared into the mists of family folklore. Who was this old salt?

My mother, Beverly Utley Fowler-Conner, recalled that her Uncle Jake had been married twice. That he had a daughter by his first marriage and an adoptive daughter by his second. The last time she recalled seeing Jake was April 12, 1945, when he stopped by a baseball game her father was coaching. She remembers the date specifically because later that evening they learned that Franklin Delano Roosevelt had died at Warm Springs, Georgia.

Several years ago, with nothing more pressing to do, I typed the words "Jake Utley'" and "USS Enterprise" into the Google search bar and was directed to a World War II reminiscence by Ron Graetz, a radioman/rear gunner who served VT-6, the squadron of Devastator torpedo bombers stationed aboard the USS *Enterprise* at the beginning of World War II.

Graetz described his experiences aboard the *Enterprise* as it steamed back from Wake Island on the morning of December 7, 1941 and into the teeth of the Japanese sneak attack on Pearl Harbor. VT-6 spent most of that day at station on the flight deck, awaiting orders to take off in pursuit of the retreating Japanese.

After hours of fruitless waiting, by Graetz's account, Chief Jake Utley wandered by and suggested that Graetz and another crewman go below to grab some lunch on the chow line. The ship's PA system didn't broadcast on the mess deck and Graetz missed the order for VT-6 to take off. He arrived on the flight deck just as his plane catapulted into the air. He was expecting a court marshal. No charges were brought because Chief Jake Utley intervened.

Graetz was still grateful, more than 70 years later, when I reached him by phone in his apartment in San Diego. He remembered Jake as a slow-talking southerner, a Texan, he thought, but couldn't conjure up any more stories as specific as the one he recounted in his memoir.

Ron suggested that I contact John Eberle, another veteran of VT-6 living in the wine country of California. I wrote Eberle a letter and he replied promptly. The only specific thing he could remember about Granduncle Jake was that he was an unfair supervisor, having assigned Eberle to consecutive stints as a compartment cleaner.

Meanwhile, I had launched a more pervasive online search for Robert Utley's brother. I found records of his graduation from flight school in Pensacola, Florida, in October of 1920; of his arrival in the Port of New Orleans from Coco Solo in the Panama Canal Zone aboard a banana boat called the SS *Sixaola* in 1935; and of his death in May of 1962, and subsequent burial in the Fort Rosecrans National Cemetery near San Diego.

The San Diego Public Library, for a modest fee, sent me a copy of his obituary, recorded in the local daily newspaper, the *Union-Tribune*. Listed among his survivors was his daughter, my second cousin, Jeannie Woodstrup, whom I was able to track down to northern California.

Jeannie, Jake's adoptive daughter, graciously provided me with his record of continuous service and other documents relative to his 30-year career in the U.S. Navy. My mother's recollection of the last time she saw Uncle Jake jibes, incidentally, with his service record, which shows that he was transferred from San Diego to Headquarters Squadron 5-2, Norfolk, Va. in March of 1945, before returning to San Diego, where he was retired from service in September of that year.

The real Jake led a life almost as interesting as that of the pretend Jake in *Rising Sun Descending*. A chief aviation machinist mate, Jake Utley was among a relatively few enlisted men the navy trained to be pilots. They were called Naval Aviation Pilots; NAP for short.

His record of continuous service shows that he was stationed variously at South Island, San Diego; Pensacola, Florida; Hampton Roads, Virginia; and Coco Solo in the Panama Canal Zone, where his seaplane squadron likely fell under the authority of the base commander, John S. McCain Jr., father of the senator from Arizona.

Researching the history of naval aviation, I was surprised at how soon after the Wright brothers' first flight at Kitty Hawk sailors began trying to figure out how to fly planes off of ships. They put ramps and catapults on the turrets of battleships and flung rattletrap biplanes into the air with the abandon of little boys let loose in a toy store. And damned if it didn't work. The USS *Enterprise*, CV-6, and other similarly modeled aircraft carriers were America's salvation in the early and dismal days of World War II.

Among the Jake memorabilia Jeannie mailed to me were two pictures of him in naval attire. One of them was taken, I think, aboard a seaplane tender somewhere off Alaska. It is paired with a second photograph showing Jake in foul weather gear.

Jake was stationed with VP-7, a patrol plane squadron based in San Diego from 1930-1934. During that time the squadron participated in an aerial photographic survey of Alaska.

In 1937, Jake Utley was ordered east from San Diego to join the commissioning crew of the USS *Enterprise* in Virginia. He told Jeannie that he rode the *Enterprise* down the rails on the day it was launched. He was the leading chief petty officer for VT-6, the squadron of Douglas Devastator torpedo bombers that was decimated at the Battle of Midway.

Jake served with VT-6 until just before the famous Doolittle raid on Tokyo. He was stationed at Barbers Point, Hawaii, at the time of the epic battle of Midway.

Jeannie says that he left the *Enterprise* because of a bout with appendicitis. And he finished the war as an inspector at the Consolidated Aircraft Company in San Diego, where the famous Catalina float planes, so instrumental in the victory in the Pacific, were mass produced.

When Jake died in May of 1962, I was an 11-year-old boy, infatuated by my grandfather's stories of his mysterious brother, leading chief of the USS *Enterprise*.

My sincere appreciation goes to Ron Graetz, John Eberle, and Jeannie Woodstrup for introducing me to the real Uncle Jake and for investing a make-believe character and his wartime exploits with flesh and blood.

Wade Fowler
New Cumberland, PA

Want to hear more from Revere Polk and Liv Pearson? As a bonus to readers of *Rising Sun Descending*, the first five chapters of their continuing exploits follow. *The Honey Trap* will be published in 2015 by Sunbury Press.

Chapter 1

11:30 p.m. Friday, January 6, 2012, Harrisburg, PA

The exotic dancer known as Crystal Cleavage bumped and ground her way toward his table through a miasma of cigarette smoke, cheap perfume, and testosterone, having just finished her set at the Pink Pony. Up onstage, a shopworn prostitute named Galaxy strutted to Queen's "Fat Bottomed Girls" for the benefit of a bachelor party's rowdy guests. The song choice was apropos, but the groom-to-be and his drunken entourage didn't seem to mind that Galaxy's stuff was better left un-strutted.

He had selected this spot, set far back from the stage, specifically to avoid intimate contact with the dancers. He had no dollar bills to dispense and no desire for a lap dance. Crystal had summoned him here. He acquiesced because they had a history rife with repetition despite his best efforts to forestall it.

"Do you really enjoy doing that?"

"Doing what?" Her feigned innocence belied her outfit. A G-string, pasties, and a thin dressing gown did little to obscure her assets both fore and aft as she pulled out a chair and sat down across the table from him. Young, tall, honey blonde, green-eyed, and buxom, Crystal outclassed the other dancers by several city blocks.

Her legs, in the vernacular of the bawdy house bard, extended all the way to her ass.

"Parading naked for the amusement of men."

"You love a parade, or at least you used to." She winked and licked her lips.

He recoiled, raising his arms and waving them like an evangelist beckoning the sinners to the altar. "We're related for Christ's sake. I want better for you than this!"

"I'm your stepsister. We are not related by blood ... other than the blood I shed the first time we—"

"Enough!"

She laughed. "Don't be such a prude, bro. You didn't do anything I didn't want you to do. I seduced you all those years ago because virginity was such a drag."

"Yours or mine?" he asked, his bitterness palpable.

"It was your first time, too?"

"Nah. Steph Baker. In the tenth grade. In the basement when Mom and Dad were at one of your peewee soccer games."

She cocked her head to one side, activating her bullshit sensors.

"Liar."

"Slut."

She stuck out her tongue. "Stuffed shirt!"

That was his stepsister all over. It was as if two people resided within her skin: a temptress in one breath, a silly school girl in the next.

"So why did you ask me to meet you here, other than to humiliate the both of us?"

"I'm not humiliated," she retorted. "I'm empowered. The men in here? They belong to me, the poor bastards. They think they own me. But it's the other way round. I don't please. I tease ... at two bills an hour, on average."

"There are better ways to earn money," he said.

"Such as being a high-and-mighty lawyer? That, by the way, is why I asked you to stop by."

"You need legal advice?"

"No. You do."

"How so?"

"Your boss. He's doin' the dirty with some of the dancers here."

He put his finger to his lips. "No so loud. We might be overheard."

She smiled. "So, Counselor, you concede that sexual impropriety on the part of your employer does not lie beyond the realm of possibility?"

He shrugged. "He's a man's man, and his wife ..."

"Is a conniving bitch." Crystal finished the sentence for him.

"I didn't say that."

"Your boss did. He's a regular here, an adrenaline junkie. Doesn't shy from a quickie in the alley if the price is right and the girl is willing. Says ever since his second tour in Afghanistan, nothing gets him off like danger. There's a big payday here for the both of us, but I need your help springing a honey trap."

"I'm not interested in selling out my boss," he said.

"You're already selling him out. If he knew who you were in bed with, he'd throw you under the bus quicker than you can say scat."

"How do you know with whom I am in bed?"

"There's no shortage of loose women and loose talk in a titty bar."

He leaned forward. "Come on, sis. Cut me a break, I've got my own game going here."

"Yeah, and if you don't let me play, too, I'm going to tell him what you've been up to. And don't play coy with me. You know what I mean."

"He'd never believe it. You have no credibility. You're just ..."

"A slut? Maybe so. But these give me all the credibility I need." She grabbed her breasts jiggled them, enjoying his discomfort. "Come on, bro. Let me play, too."

"What do you have in mind?"

Onstage, Galaxy bent over and shook her ass in the face of a bachelor party reveler. The jukebox blared, providing musical accompaniment for a crime against good taste.

Crystal Cleavage leaned forward, centering her stepbrother in the crosshairs of her 38s and committed a felony of her own.

"Here's what we need to do," she said.

Chapter 2

11:30 a.m. Tuesday, January 24, 2012, Harrisburg, PA

The floor beneath Rev Polk's feet trembled as the presses hit third gear down in the basement, churning out copies of the metro edition of the *Daily Telegraph*. Rev looked up from his computer screen and let his eyes wander. Sunshine streamed through banks of windows on the east side, bathing the newsroom in a warm glow on a cold winter morning.

The shutter of Rev's internal camera clicked, capturing the moment like a still from a motion picture. In that image written forevermore to Rev's metaphysical hard drive, Roxy Burton, the lifestyle editor chatted with George Berk, the slot man on the copy desk. Her fingers floated in the space between them like butterflies. Roxy couldn't talk without moving her hands.

Back in the sports department, a collection of desks grouped to Rev's right, Sammy Smith, the sports editor, muttered around the end of an unlit cigar, his eyes moving back and forth across hard copy. Sammy didn't truck with computers. He did his editing on paper and gave the changes back to the reporter to input on the computer. It was an anachronism that management tolerated because Sammy could pump up a mediocre sports story with just a couple slashes of his red pen.

The big door leading to the southern stairwell banged open and a copy boy, a high school kid who for some strange reason aspired to be a print journalist in the electronic age, backed into the newsroom carrying a big stack of newspapers hot off the presses. He plopped the pile down on the nearest desk and began distributing the newspapers among the various departments.

The *Daily Telegraph* still offered its readers an afternoon paper, the metro edition they called it, designed for commuters to read on the bus on their way home from work. But the editor, Grayson Collingsworth, had become increasingly strident in the last two months. The p.m. product was dying. Circulation and profits were down, down, down, corresponding with Collingsworth's mood: foul, foul, foul.

Rev thought of these things as he crossed the newsroom to pick up a newspaper, unwilling to wait for the copy boy to arrive at his work station. Rev had hurried back from a 9 a.m. press conference at which the governor had dropped a bombshell. Nothing got his adrenaline pumping like deadline writing. His synapses sizzled still in the afterglow.

Collecting his prize, he made his way back to his desk, sat down, and snapped the paper open, grunting in satisfaction when he saw his story in the hard news spot: front page upper right, with a three-deck headline over two columns.

Governor reverses field
Opts to support lottery
Privatization plan

I didn't matter to Rev that a six-graph synopsis had been up for 40 minutes on the website. He snapped the paper a second time for emphasis. This was journalism. The newspaper's website was no better than TV and radio, in Rev's humble opinion. Synopses are for sissies.

His enmity for the electronic media was unchanged by management's recent embrace of it. This was the real thing. It had substance, weight, and it would endure much longer than the newspaper's current system software, which was incompatible with the six or seven versions that had preceded it.

A hundred years from now no one would be able to read the stories stored in bits and bytes, the programs that created them moribund. But newsprint? Rev mused: it's immutable, baby.

Rev took solace in that thought as he reread his story to make sure the copy desk hadn't messed it up.

By Revere Polk
Daily Telegraph Staff Writer

HARRISBURG, PA, Tuesday, January 24, 2012 – In a dramatic reversal of position, Pennsylvania Gov. Casey Lawrence indicated today that he will entertain legislation now hung up in the State House Finance Committee to privatize the state lottery.

The plan, the brainchild of state Rep. Shelby Winters, R-Bellefonte, would put the management of the lottery, which generates $530 million annually, in support of the Office of Aging, up for competitive bids.

"I think that there is an opportunity here to infuse the budget with a substantial amount of revenue without raising taxes, while at the same time ensuring that senior citizen programs continue to be funded at their current pace for the foreseeable future," the governor said before a stunned press corps in the briefing room at the state capitol.

"I know that this announcement will not be welcomed by many of my Democratic brethren, but the time has come in the state budget process to think creatively and to reach out across the aisle when the other side comes up with a viable alternative to a dismal status quo."

The privatization plan was based on a model developed by Jonathan Kelley Associates LLC, which would be among the top contenders to manage the lottery. Kelley, who lived most of the year in London, was a notorious recluse, and, reputedly, a front man for oil money flowing out of Russia.

Winters was delighted by the governor's change of heart, saying: "The privatization plan will generate nearly a billion dollars up front by the most conservative of estimates, and guarantees annual revenues equaling or exceeding what is now being generated under state operation. There are certain things the private sector does better than the public. And one of them is making money."

The governor's announcement at his regular Tuesday morning press briefing drew immediate and sharp criticism from his Democratic base.

"Winters' bill would give the new managers license to open up all sorts of new games not envisioned under the original legislation empowering the lottery," said Roosevelt Franklin, D-Philadelphia, the ranking Democrat on the House Finance Committee. "The availability of even more lottery games will prey on the very poorest among us, and while it will infuse the state budget with a one-time lump sum, a steady stream of revenue over the years is by no means assured.

"Typical of most Republican plans, this one balances the budget on the backs of the working man. To generate the kind of revenues Winters' plan promises would require the furlough of hundreds of state employees now making a decent living wage, replacing them with underpaid, overworked employees willing to accept positions beneath their station due to the horrible state of the commonwealth's economy."

Anticipating that criticism, the governor, in his press conference, said that one of the modifications he will insist upon will be the gradual furlough over several years of state workers now employed by the lottery, a generous severance package, and employment counseling and placement services, all at the expense of the new managers of the lottery.

281

Those words of assurance fell on deaf ears at the Harrisburg Chapter of the Pennsylvania Association of State Workers, an affiliate of the AFSME.

"Governor Lawrence is a traitor," said chapter president Sylvester Adkins. "He won the governor's house with the help of union workers and he will lose the governor's house in the next election cycle due to his treachery."

Chapter 3

2 p.m. Wednesday, January 25, 2012, Harrisburg, PA
Sprewell Madison and Russell Thompson sat knee to knee in a tiny anteroom on the third floor of the glass-fronted Locust Street Building in Harrisburg.

They had been escorted to the room by two buzz-topped rent-a-cops half their size, Sprewell from the basement mail room and Russell from a first-floor ladies room, which he was cleaning at the time.

The two men, one white and the other black, respectively, both were enormous, almost 13 feet and 500 pounds between them. Neither of the rent-a-cops had the authority or the physical attributes to compel Madison and Thompson to do anything they weren't willing to do. They would stay until they decided to leave.

Sprewell and Russell knew each other well, but they couldn't show it because there was no way to tell whether they were being watched. They were undercover cops, state police troopers to be more precise, attuned to the risk of indiscretion.

It had taken them three months to land their jobs with Jonathan Kelley Associates LLC, Russell as a janitor and Sprewell as a courier. It took two more months of grueling, mind-numbing work for them to secure passwords to the firm's Cloud accounts—lots of searching under mouse pads, desk blotters, and paper clip trays when no one was looking. But the forensic guys couldn't follow the supposed electronic trail from the Russian mafia to a Native American casino to an offshore account in the Caymans.

There had to be another level of security, another layer of intrigue to peel away. But how?

Being called together into the same room was ominous. They took pains to ignore each other when their paths crossed at work. So why had they been summoned to this tiny airless anteroom?

Their chairs faced a desk, back dropped by a bank of windows. Locust Street, one way east, lay three floors below. Behind the desk directly in front of the windows two large Klieg lights affixed to tripods lurked like props in an inquisition chamber. The lights were pointed squarely at their chairs.

Sprewell was the first to risk speech.

"Wonder what's up with the lights."

"Dunno, man."

A circuit closed with an electronic *kachunk*. The Klieg lights flashed on and built from a startling intensity to a blinding one. It was like staring into the sun. Both men shaded their eyes with their hands.

A door opened to the right of the desk and someone entered the room, moving like an animated stick man, a skeleton skinned by the intense light. A chair scraped, and Stick Man sat down behind the desk. "I'd close my eyes if I were you," he said.

"Turn out the light, asshole," Russell said. "I can't see a fucking thing."

"That's more or less the point," Stick Man said. His voice was high-pitched but smoky. Contralto. "You two are quite the pair. Sneaky as silent farts in a sewer plant."

Stick Man sniffed. "But I have a bloodhound's nose. I had you pegged on day one."

"Whatchu talking 'bout?" Russell said, staying in character.

"What law enforcement agency are the two of you working for? Feds, local, or state?"

"You so smart, you tell us," Sprewell said.

He had a tiny voice for such a big man.

"OK, Mr. Knox. I will. You seemed surprised. I know your real names. Know who you work for, too. Ted Knox and Tayshaun Russell. Neat trick using your last name as your first, Tayshaun. Probably made it easier to remember who you are supposed to be."

Stick Man had a nasty laugh.

"I've done some checking up on the two of you. Haven't had exactly sterling careers with the state police, have you? Well, I suppose sometimes you have to cross the line when you're a good guy pretending to be a bad guy. Skimming cash from a drug bust? Tsk, tsk, Mr. Russell. Sleeping with prostitutes? Bringing the clap home to your wife, Mr. Knox? Not cool. Not cool at all."

Knox lurched forward in his chair, rising to a half crouch.

"I wouldn't come any closer if I were you," Stick Man said. "You'll never see the bullet that kills you in this light."

Knox closed his eyes tight and settled back into his chair, clenching ham-like fists.

"That's more like it," Stick Man said. "You two farts have fallen into a cesspool, but do as I say and you'll come out smelling like roses. I want you to keep in contact with your handlers, but you'll be giving them stuff that I feed you."

"Why would we want to do that?" Knox asked.

"Because I'm paying you so well."

"Huh?" Russell said.

"For the past month you both have had active offshore accounts in the Caymans. Bank balances of seventy thousand each. Do as I say, and I'll add ten thousand a week for as long as you are in my employ. But if you refuse my offer, or if you accept it and betray me, your superior, Lieutenant Frank DePalma, will get a tip about your offshore accounts."

"So we're guilty even if we're innocent," Knox said.

"Won't work. DePalma's a smart guy. He'd catch on real quick," Russell added.

"Oh, it won't be false info. It will be golden. It will lead you to some real bad guys. Some of whom just might happen to be my ... adversaries."

"Aren't you the clever one?" Knox said. "That doesn't seem like much for ten large a week. What's the catch?"

"Well there is another little matter than needs the attention of men with your training and experience," Stick Man said.

"What's that?"

"A newspaper reporter has stumbled too close to a project that I cannot afford to have compromised. He possesses some dangerous information that he needs to be relieved of and persuaded to pursue no further."

"Persuaded ... or killed?" Russell asked.

"May the record show that you broached that topic? I will leave that option to your discretion in the event that other methods of persuasion fail. And should you be forced to effect such an extreme solution, well then your Cayman accounts will get fatter still."

"How fat?" Knox asked.

"Imagine a five with four zeroes following."

"Each?" Russell asked.

"Each," Stick Man agreed.

"So who is this reporter?" Russell asked.

"I'm going to leave an envelope on the desk. The details will be inside, along with your account numbers and current balances. I think it will make for interesting reading."

"How will we get in touch with you?" Knox asked.

"I'll call you."

"I suppose you'll want our cell phone numbers," Russell said.

Stick Man laughed. Fumbled with something on his desk. Both Knox and Russell's cell phones rang. "I already have your phone numbers," he said. "Now, I'm going to leave the room. The lights will go out in two minutes. When they do, get up and go about your business like nothing happened. Because nothing has."

A chair scraped. A door opened. And two minutes later the lights went out. Just like Stick Man said they would.

Chapter 4

6 a.m. Thursday, January 26, 2012, New Cumberland, PA
"So, when are you going to tell her?"
"Tell her what?"
"That you're pregnant."
"Smart ass."
"Reincarnation isn't something you discuss on a first date," Rev Polk said.
"You're not on a first date. You've been living with her for two months now. You need to tell Olivia her that she used to be my second wife," said Jacob Addison.
"Second wife? You never told me about the first."
"That's a story for another day."
Rev stared at his reflection in the medicine cabinet mirror. Jake Addison stared back at him and Rev sighed, exhausted, suddenly, by the prospects of another day defined by an intermittent yet ongoing inner dialogue with his great granduncle, a World War II naval aviator who was murdered in 1968, three years before Rev was born.
"Tell Liv that your love for her transcends time. I like the sound of that, don't you? Wouldn't that be romantic?"
"Romantic? Romantic is not the right word for it at all. Try insane! Liv would be within her rights to have me fitted for a straightjacket."
"They don't make straightjackets in 46 extra long."
"Shut up, Jake! You're driving me crazy."
"You arrived at crazy long before I showed up."
Was he crazy? Rev had pondered that question for some time and had concluded that his symptoms did not meet any textbook notions of mental illness.
He wasn't schizophrenic. Jake's voice inside his head wasn't telling him to do anything dangerous or dastardly.

Multiple personality disorder also could be dropped from consideration. He had not experienced lost time, which would occur if another distinct personality took possession of him.

Rev wasn't manic, clinically depressed, or any combination of the two.

That left but one thing—one thing that made sense to Rev, anyway. Rev was Jake reincarnate. However, Jake thought it so, too, which was reason enough to dismiss it. But, in all fairness, reincarnation was the only explanation that made any sense, even though Rev couldn't find any case studies in which a patient had such direct contact with his or her persona from a previous lifetime.

Rev decided that his "conversations" with Jake Addison were a psychological artifice of his own creation. They allowed him to integrate two distinct strands of memories, which often converged and sometimes collided as they—he and Jake—confronted events in their "current" lifetime.

He had considered consulting a psychologist to confirm that. But now wasn't the time to show up crazy. He'd just survived a harsh round of furloughs, having salvaged his journalistic career on the strength of his reporting about the recent conspiracy to install the speaker of the House of Representatives in the Oval Office by assassinating both the president and vice president of the United States.

Vice President John Hawthorn had been shot to death during a commemorative service at Shanksville on the 10th Anniversary of Flight 93's heroic conflagration, but Rev had tackled a gunman in the Rose Garden at the White House just in time to save President Derek Satchel from a similar fate several days later.

Rev's reporting on the coup attempt revealed the complicity of the late speaker of the House, U.S. Rep. Sam Jenkins, R-La Jolla, Calif., who died by his own hand when confronted with the evidence implicating him in the plot to kill Hawthorn and Satchel.

Jake had helped Rev unravel the conspiracy by visiting him in his dreams, laying down bread crumbs that led to evidence of Jenkins' guilt. But now the lines of communication with his former self were more direct. Jake often spoke to him at odd moments when his brain was idling in neutral—such as while he waited for the tap water to heat to a proper shaving temperature.

"And here's another thing. You've got to tell Liv you've been called to duty in Afghanistan."

Liv Pearson was Rev's brand new live-in girlfriend. A former state police trooper, she had recently accepted a job as chief of police for the Borough of New Cumberland, which stared out across the Susquehanna River at Harrisburg, the capital of Pennsylvania.

New Cumberland was Rev's hometown, and Liv had followed him there because he had asked her to. Each morning he awoke beside Liv Pearson was a testament that hope—and love—really does spring eternal.

Rev had ample reason for despair. He was a citizen soldier, a major in the Pennsylvania National Guard. He had killed men ... and innocent civilians in combat. Those memories had haunted him for five years. But, now in his 43rd year, he had finally achieved a small measure of peace.

But peace was a fragile bubble forever threatened by a pinprick from his past. Rev had survived two tours in Iraq, for the most part physically unscathed, but he bore the emotional scars of having to choose between life and death ... for his men, for himself, for the enemy, and for all of the innocent civilians who occupied that infernal and eternal war zone.

His alter ego, Jake Addison, had faced similarly tough decisions during World Wars I and II. Jake's wartime memories were jumbled with Rev's recollections of Iraq. They created a malodorous stew that reeked of man's inhumanity to man and awakened Rev screaming and sweaty even when the mercury dipped into single digits in Central Pennsylvania's deep January freeze.

The wrong choices of two lifetimes wove gossamer strands of regret into the fabric of Rev's karma. But even more damaging was the realization that, sometimes, there are no right choices. Heads you lose. Tails you lose. Those were the most insidious memories of all because they proved that if there is a God, He falls far short of infallibility ... or maybe He really just doesn't give a shit.

And now with America's involvement in Iraq at long last ended, citizen soldier Rev Polk was once again being summoned from the relative safety of his civilian job to the turmoil of the ongoing war on terror.

The letter told him to be ready to deploy on 27 February 2013 for a month of training before reporting to Kandahar Province, Afghanistan. How would he ever tell Liv?

Jake opined: "Not telling her is not an option."

"Isn't that a double negative?"

Liv's voice startled him from beyond the bathroom door: "Who ya talking to in there, big fella?"

"Myself. I'm a terrific conversationalist," Rev said. "Goddamn it, Jake. I've got to get you out of my head. She's going to think we're crazy!"

"What?" Liv shouted.

"I said that I'm talking to myself!" Rev shouted back.

Jake said: "You got that right, sailor."

Rev studied his reflection in the mirror and rubbed the ball of his right thumb over the perpetual shaving nick on his Adams apple.

"How am I ever going to tell Liv?" he whispered.

Chapter 5

10 a.m. Thursday, January 26, 2012, Lemoyne, PA
"So, when are you going to tell him?" asked Dr. Jed Armstrong.

"Tell who?" Liv Pearson asked.

"The father," Armstrong said.

"As soon as I work up the nerve," Liv replied.

"I take it that your pregnancy is an accident?"

"That's my story and I'm sticking to it."

"Now there's a dangerous game. Are you married ... to the father?"

"How is that any of your goddamn business?"

Armstrong should have been insulted. That was her intent. She wanted to shut him up. But it didn't work.

"I treat the whole patient. Problem-free pregnancies are no accident; they often are a product of solid relationships."

"Yeah, yeah. And it takes a community to raise a child." Her voice oozed sarcasm.

"Even better are two people who love each other," Armstrong replied, refusing to take offense.

Liv realized she couldn't insult him into silence.

"I'm not married to Rev, but we're living together. Happily. It's just that I'm thirty-six. My biological alarm is ringing off the hook. I won't say I got pregnant on purpose, but I will admit to being something less than meticulous in the handling of a condom."

"So now you have a relationship problem?"

"More than that. I have a professional problem. Nothing is more inconvenient than a pregnant cop ... who just took a job as chief of police for the Borough of New Cumberland. In the back of my mind I wanted this to happen sometime ... I just didn't think it'd happen now, when I owe my employers my undivided attention—and now my loyalties lie elsewhere."

She patted her stomach.

"That's a challenge that has faced professional women for decades: balancing motherhood and career," Armstrong replied. "I may not be able to help you in your specific situation, but I can listen."

"I wish Rev had listened more carefully when I told him it was time to have a baby."

"Wouldn't marriage have been a good prerequisite? Or were you hoping that your pregnancy would solidify ... a commitment of a more concrete nature?"

"It's a different world out there, Doc. By the time my mother was my age she had three children and a husband who had died of a heart attack."

"Society's different for your generation than it was for mine. I get that," Dr. Armstrong said. "It takes two incomes to provide a roof, clothing, and three squares a day for two people, making it all the more difficult to support three or more. It's just that the most successful pregnancies are ones where there are two people willing to share in the responsibility of child rearing—emotionally and economically."

Liv nodded. "Rev's a good man. He'll come around. I just need to be diplomatic when I tell him he's going to be a father."

"So abortion is off the table?" Armstrong asked.

"It is as far as I'm concerned," Liv replied.

"Good," Armstrong said. "I think you're going to make a great mom. You're in terrific shape. Take your vitamins. Keep on exercising moderately and eating right and I predict an uneventful pregnancy. See the receptionist on the way out and she'll schedule your next appointment."

"OK."

"And Ms. Pearson?"

"Yes?"

"Perhaps the father will accompany you to the next appointment? Do him good to listen to the baby's heartbeat."

"He'll come along if he knows what's good for him," Liv said.

Dr. Armstrong nodded, turned, and left the room.

As she was getting dressed, Liv stared at her reflection in the mirror over the sink in the examining room.

"How am I going to tell Rev?" she asked herself.

40128761R00167

Made in the USA
Charleston, SC
24 March 2015